The Hunt for Wolf_Eyes

Vigilante Hacker Extraordinaire

A Novel

Ty Strange

Beach Life Books   Santa Rosa, CA

Published by Beach Life Books
Santa Rosa, CA.
www.tystrange.com

This is a work of fiction. Names, characters, places, and incidents either are the product of the author's imagination or are used fictitiously. Any resemblance to actual persons, living or dead, events, or locales, is entirely coincidental.

Cover design by Peter O'Conner
Formatting and layout provided by Polgarus Studio

ISBN 978-0-9905392-0-9
Library of Congress Control Number: 2014914293

For my parents—my dad, who instilled in me the necessary discipline and work ethic to succeed in life; and my mom, who imparted a creative streak that allowed my imagination to soar.

Prologue
Noble Endings—New York

A lifetime of honorable deeds subverted by one Wall Street sociopath's confession. The man affectionately known throughout the investment world as JP shook his head, disbelief imprinted across his face. His office suite showed little life, save for the urgent buzz of his cell phone and muted cacophony of the city rising up from the streets eighteen stories below. Seated at the French antique writing desk, posture upright and noble, he resumed meticulously entering the day's financial transactions into the oversized leather-bound ledger; a daily ritual that merited him a vaunted position of trust, bestowing upon him immense respect and admiration from those acquainted with him, professionally or otherwise.

The day's work complete, he returned the early twentieth-century Parker pen, a treasured gift from a longtime friend and investor, back to its holder before closing the ledger, neatly positioning it in the upper corner of the desk. JP's bookkeeping etiquette personified an antiquated tradition. He preferred the indelible indentation of ink to the ones and zeros that computers use for recording transactions in the modern world. For him the written form held meaning, had a discernible weight to it, reflecting someone's soul much like a handwritten signature, exuding a textural quality one could see as well as touch. Computers lacked such physicality, in his humble opinion.

Stowing the chair under the desk, he walked over to the rustic cherry liquor cabinet for his nightly libation of cognac, a bottle twenty-five years in the making. Snifter in hand, he closed his eyes, relishing a sip that warmed his body and soul while the ceiling fan lazily pushed the muggy New York City air around in circles above him. This time of the evening marked the only moment during the day, any day, that JP truly called his own: a moment where he could reflect on matters large or small, personal or impersonal, in solitude. He'd let the office staff go home early on this particular Friday, devoting more time than usual to ponder the burden of his current situation.

Outside, the full moon rose in a cloudless sky, casting a long, shimmering band of light across the East River and surrounding buildings, landing on the balcony where he stood, his genteel but weary portrait moist from the warm spring-evening air. From his perch, JP gazed out over the city as it steadily simmered down from the surreal revelations that shook the financial sector that morning. Revelations so inconceivable, JP found them hard to fathom, as did the world.

His cell phone buzzed again back at his desk; it had been that way all day. He ignored it, shaking his head once again. *What's done is done, and cannot be undone.*

He glanced down at the vintage timepiece wrapped around his steady wrist; his wife would be expecting him soon.

JP took one last sip of the cognac, savoring the peppery, cinnamony spices, then stepped off the balcony, disappearing into the darkness: an abyss of eventual shrieks, mourning, and questions. It was the only way home.

SPILT MILK

Alex Smyth froze in her tracks. A woman's distant scream pierced the wool cap warming Alex's ears, and her breath drifted lazily in the walk-in freezer as she stared blankly at rows of neatly stacked ice-cream containers. *Who was that?* Cold silence lingered.

She burst through the thick vinyl strips that hung across the doorway, left flapping in her wake. Unsure where the commotion emanated from she ran toward the dairy department, where her mother had last been, restocking the milk. Alex sprinted down the natural-cracker aisle, hung a sharp left, and promptly knocked over half the organic-bath-soap display she'd spent an hour setting up earlier. *Crap!*

She recovered her momentum as bars of soap scattered across the floor, continuing down the aisle that eventually intersected with the back of the store. Screeching to a halt, slightly out of breath, she broke into laughter; her mother, Maggie, stood in what resembled a shallow ocean of milk. Maggie looked at Alex with an incredulous expression but couldn't help but laugh too.

"Got milk?" Alex sputtered out between fits of laughter and endearing snorts. "Hold still, I'll grab a box of cookies to mop up with," she said, barely able to finish her sentence, her mom's laughter growing by the moment.

"What happened?" Alex's father, Phil, shouted, having arrived to the scene. A broad smile filled his face. "Well, the cows aren't going to be happy," he said, adding a hearty chuckle to complete the Smyths' family circle.

Phil grabbed a mop as their laughter and teasing subsided, passing it to Maggie, who tiptoed from the vast spread of dairy product to begin the task of cleaning it up.

"Hey, Alex, watch the register for a bit, will you?" her father asked, taking off his apron, a green canvas rife with poultry stains, dried flour streaks, and smeared produce bits, tossing it to her. "I need to run over to Trent's."

"Why can't Mom do it?" Alex protested despite the obvious answer, fixing her hands on her narrow hips. A childlike pout spread across a face left rosy from the walk-in freezer and subsequent dash.

"Your mom looks like a milkmaid without the hair braids."

"Hey," Maggie shot back, stifling another round of laughter.

"But a sexy one at that." He flashed a wink her way. "It's just until we close up. Another half hour … OK, Doodle Bug?" He turned to walk away. "It's Sunday night, nobody's here anyway."

"But—"

"You'll be OK," his fading voice offered.

Alex didn't get a chance to form a rebuttal. It would've been useless, anyway. He was right; Maggie's shoes squished with every step as she pushed the mop around.

"Honey, grab the mop bucket for me before you head up," Maggie said. "You'll be fine."

Twenty-two-year-old Alex sighed, retrieved the bucket for her mom, then shuffled up to the front of the store, head hung down, kicking a gum wrapper several feet along the freshly waxed floor. She bent over and picked it up, thrusting it deep into her apron's soiled pocket.

"Hey, Alex," Kara said, restocking shelves when Alex walked by.

Alex glanced up, but quickly averted her eyes from Kara's, reflexively closing them for a brief moment. Alex shuddered. The "wolf eyes" chants echoed again in her head, flooding her with painful images of kids on the playground throwing their heads back, howling into the sky when she passed them by. "Hey ..."

Those eyes, their rare color, attracted more attention than she cared for growing up. Their amber hue, a mixture of yellow and hints of copper, evoked images for adults of a beautiful sunset enjoyed through twin oval windows. For children, however, the unique trait she shared with wolves conjured up imaginative lone-wolf stories. *Window to the soul? More like window to my nightmare.*

Alex settled in behind the checkout counter, focused on the store's closing tasks, and repressed the hurtful taunts from childhood.

The small bell jingled as the front door pushed open a few minutes before the store was scheduled to close. Alex groaned under her breath, "Great." By the time she finished arranging a stack of twenties—faceup and in the same direction—and looked up, the customer had passed by, headed toward the produce department. Alex glanced at the clock, shaking her head. She wanted to wrap things up, go home, and disappear in the virtual world of the Internet.

"I'll see you at home, honey," her mom said, walking by. "Your dad's going to be late so I'm not making anything for dinner. Grab something from the deli for yourself. Oh, and there's a woman in the back picking up some items. She asked about the angel-food-cake special. Give her half off on it, OK?"

Eighteen, nineteen, twenty, "OK, Mom," *twenty-one, twenty-two, twenty-three ...* Alex responded in the midst of counting coupons, her resolute focus a by-product from years of self-absorbed activities.

Alex tallied the totals for the day on the computer, her nimble fingers dancing over the keyboard. She had designed and developed the point-of-sale and bookkeeping software systems for the store while in high school, saving her parents valuable time and money for a business whose financials often showed more red than black before the software's existence. Later, during her first year in college, she implemented her pride and joy: custom software managing the store's inventory and order-processing tasks—an accomplishment that landed her on the cover of the local business magazine for its innovation. For someone who shunned attention, Alex's personal achievements often cast an uncomfortable spotlight on her.

The last-minute shopper arrived at the counter a few minutes later, plopping her hand basket down on the conveyor belt that started moving toward the price scanner. Head down, Alex began unloading the items, politely asking, "Did you find everything you needed tonight?" The scanner beeped as each item passed over the infrared beam.

"I did. Thanks for asking, Alex."

Alex's eyes darted up. *What? Do I know you?* She didn't recognize the tall, casually dressed woman with the charming smile and soothing voice who appeared to have a couple years on Alex. *How does she know my name?*

"Your name tag," the woman said, pointing toward Alex's tag clipped to her green long-sleeve T-shirt that bore the store's name and motto, "Maggie's Organic Market, serving Palo Alto since Woodstock."

Alex glanced at her shirt and shook her head. "Oh, right. Doy."

"You're a *doy* girl, are you?"

Alex eyeballed the woman, this time bewildered.

"Don't worry, I've had the name-tag trick pulled on me many times." The woman paused a moment, taking a long, curious look into Alex's eyes. "You know … you have the most beautiful eyes I have ever seen."

Tongue-tied, Alex cracked a reserved smile for a couple of quiet moments before muttering, "Thanks," then promptly dropped the quart of milk she'd been holding to the floor; it split open on impact. "Arggggggggggh."

Alex's cheeks flushed instantly, the woman's laughter prompting Alex to speak in her usual rushed cadence—it often lacked periods or pauses—and move a mile a minute. "I'm so sorry. Here, I'll total you out and grab another quart," she said, her hands tapping the keyboard as fast as she spoke and expertly bagging the groceries in short order. "Swipe your card and sign the signature pad and I'll be right back."

"That's really not necessary, Alex."

"It's no trouble," she replied, dashing off toward the dairy aisle for the second time that night.

Alex returned panting with the quart in hand, but the woman had disappeared. Alex walked out the front door, scanning the sidewalk in both directions. There was no trace, just darkness. Sigh.

Alex went back into the store, locked the door, and retrieved the mop bucket; again.

Phil Smyth sat lifeless, digesting the news, his expression a million silent questions, his stare fixed on Trent Hudson.

"What do you mean it's underperformed?" Phil asked.

"Phil," Trent started, clasping his weathered hands together, as if searching for a palatable way to tell his friend the bad news again, "GIM announced the Vegas Land Grab Fund has not been the boon they had hoped for. It's lost most of its value."

"But what about the yearly dividends we're supposed to get? Are they going to continue? We haven't seen anything since the first year."

"I'm afraid not. They have placed a hold on—"

"Dammit," Phil said, collapsing back in the cushy chair in front of Trent's desk, the furrows deepening along his forehead. "Can't we simply pull out what's left?"

"I'm afraid not. It has to be a group decision, all-or-nothing vote. The group wants to let it ride. They feel it will bounce back in time."

"I've already paid Alex's tuition for this semester. You said we'd be able to cover the amount. Christ, Trent, I'm leveraged up the yin-yang. I've already tapped our savings and taken out a second mortgage on the house to cover the last three years. We were supposed to have cashed out by now." He gazed out the oversized window to the street. "What am I going to tell Alex?" Phil closed his eyes.

"Phil, I'm not going to bullshit you. We've known each other too long for that. I have a stake in this too. I'm getting ulcers from it. I was going to retire at the end of the year. Now—"

"I want a meeting with the guy, the one who was out here pitching this thing five years ago. What was his name?"

"Frank Gordon, but—"

"Yeah, Frank. I want to hear what went wrong on this deal. The market had already bottomed out when we jumped in. They purchased the toxic home loans for pennies on the dollar. This was a 'no brainer,' his quote. I want some rational explanation for this."

"I'll see what he says, but from what I understand he only works with those who brokered the investment, like me."

A palpable silence followed between the two friends who'd cavorted around the Berkeley campus during the days when the university stirred the nation with its protests and beatnik lifestyle. Graduate students owning nothing more than old Peugeot bikes, Birkenstocks, and dog-eared copies of *The Electric Kool-Aid Acid*

Test, they reveled in the freedom that sprung from minimalism. Their motto, to quote their favorite author, John Steinbeck: "It is better to have traveled hopefully than to arrive."

"Trent, I trust you like a brother. I know your neck is on the line with the entire WCOF community. If you say there's nothing we can do, then there's nothing we can do," Phil said, rising, offering a handshake.

Trent brushed Phil's hand aside, embracing him. "Give Maggie and Alex my best. We'll get through this together, my friend. Somehow. We've simply hit a few bumps in the road on our journey."

Hungry and finally home, Alex slumped her tired, five-and-a-half-foot frame into the chair at her desk, opened the laptop, and booted it up. Sundance, her Labrador retriever, ran into the small bedroom, smothering her lightly freckled face with kisses. "Who's the good boy?" she cooed, giving his black coat several strokes.

She popped the lid off the pasta-salad carton she'd brought home, scooping out a healthy portion; then chased it with a chug of milk straight from the quart she'd retrieved for the woman at the store. *Soy milk! Who drinks soy milk?* She shook off the unexpected aftertaste.

She logged into the university's student dashboard, checking on the status of her waitlisted "Fine Arts 101" course. *Ah, crap.* Two weeks into the last quarter of the school year and she was still waitlisted. Her plan had been to complete the remaining elective during the current quarter in order to load her final year with core political-science courses, her declared major. Her ambitious schedule wouldn't allow for electives then.

Impatient, Alex closed the website, pushed her bedroom door closed, and opened up a terminal window on the laptop, where she began trolling through a list of known IP addresses—a computer's unique identifier to the Internet—near the campus. She found one that looked promising and pinged it with a reverse lookup. *Yep, that'll work.* She shoveled another helping of pasta salad into her mouth, and as she chewed began typing commands into the open black window.

Login prompts appeared for the handful of commands she rapidly entered until the university registrar's website appeared. She launched a self-made utility program designed to sniff through thousands of names, finding the one she needed, capturing their encrypted password. *Don't they know five-character passwords aren't secure?* Another program running on her desktop unscrambled it, and in less time than it took to swallow the food in her mouth she'd hacked into Stanford University's master scheduling system.

Poring over the waitlist she found her name, seventy-eighth. *I'll never get in that far down.* Alex leaned back in her chair, nibbling on some carrots, running a hand through her dark, ash-blond hair that draped a few inches over her shoulders, picturing her next play. A few moments later she executed several direct database transactions, bypassing audit trails that would normally leave behind her digital footprint and arouse suspicion. *Well, Miss Alexandra Murphy Smyth, we're pleased to inform you that you've been added to Dr. Pierre's Fine Arts 101 class. Sometimes in life, you just have to nudge things along.*

Alex stretched her legs out, petted Sundance's snout, and logged into the widely popular website "Virtual Presence—Tammaré." She polished off the rest of the soy milk, shrugging her shoulders. *It's not that bad-tasting.*

Phil trudged into the kitchen of his family's modest home in suburban Palo Alto, where Maggie hummed a quiet tune while slicing a mango. They were an affable couple who met and married as teens, his long now-graying hair pulled back in a ponytail and her flowery secondhand dresses remnants of the era. Tonight he would test their basic philosophical view: the glass is always half full.

"Hi, sweetie." Her soft voice greeted him like they hadn't seen each other for days.

Phil walked up behind her and held her tight, resting his cheek on her warm neck.

Maggie paused from slicing the mango. "What's wrong?"

"Is Alex home?"

"She's in her room."

Phil stood quiet a few moments listening to the muffled sounds coming from Alex's bedroom. "Trent says ..."—a tear was forming in his eye—"that the Vegas Land Grab Fund tanked."

Maggie didn't say a word. She wrapped her arms around him, holding him with the same consoling passion he'd come to know during the ups and downs of their forty-four-year marriage.

"When should we tell Alex?" Maggie said, breaking the long contemplative silence.

"Well, this quarter is all paid for. When does she register for next year?"

"I'm not sure. Probably early summer."

Phil sighed. He did not look forward to telling his little girl they couldn't afford her last year at Stanford. "OK."

"You know she'll understand. We raised her to believe things are never as bad as they seem."

"I know. She just deserves so much more."

"Life is full of risks, dear. That investment guy made it sound like it was a sure thing, but there are no *sure* things." Maggie paused until Phil looked her in the eye. "We've made it this far when it didn't seem like we'd even be able to send her to a state college. We'll figure things out."

Maggie handed him a mango slice. The sweet tropical taste gave him a moment of respite from the mental anguish he harbored, though his expression remained afflicted.

"I'll tell her next week," he said.

"*We'll* tell her together."

HACKER 101

Alec Gordon peered over his computer monitor to the sound of his name echoing throughout the small, windowless office, whose heating system did little to ward off the early Monday-morning chill. "That was the college. They had another breach," Thomas's robust voice said.

"Registrar's office?" Alec asked, his breath visible as the question left his mouth.

"Yeah. Last night."

"Great." Alec jumped up, grabbing the college's file. "Did they have the trace going this time?"

"Yeah … '172, 343, 238, 101,'" Thomas read from the pad he'd jotted it on. "They'll e-mail you the server log entries later today."

"172, 343, 238 …" Alec muttered, comparing them to the list in front of him.

"101."

"Yep, that's the same one," Alec said, logging the IP address into the evidence sheet. "OK, call Judge Walters. Get a warrant for the address 1725 Palo Alto Street ..." He stopped short to pick up the ringing phone on his desk.

"Got it," Thomas said, writing the rest of the address down from the file labeled HACKER 101, the codename for Alec's first bona-fide cybercrime case as lead investigator. Six months on the task force, and juggling a full load of classes at the local college, Alec had previously handled the back-office work for the veterans of the small task force, CCEA—CyberCrime Enforcement Agency.

Alec hung up the phone. "Let's plan a visit for ... six tonight," he continued, retrieving the file and scanning the surveillance sheet. "Have local law enforcement meet us there."

"How many?" Thomas asked, taking notes.

"Two uniforms will suffice."

"Only two?"

"Yes. It's a college computer wiz living at home. Hackers are only tough when they have a keyboard in front of them. Take that away and they're scared as mice. Two uniforms will be more than enough intimidation." Alec turned a page in the folder. "The mother should be home by then too."

"Roger that, boss."

Like every first day of class since grade school, Alex entered Dr. Pierre's Fine Arts 101 classroom early, headed toward the last row, and sat at an aisle desk where she would hide in anonymity. Though college aroused less emotional trauma than the mean-spirited span from K through twelve, the habit eased her social anxiety, especially during the first week of a new class when kids tended to exploit the social and physical differences that existed among classmates, until it got old, cliques formed, and school life settled down. Sitting in back during roll-call as a child allowed Alex to anticipate the call of her name, raise her hand quickly, signaling her presence, then lower it before the rest of the class had a chance to connect the dots and toss a snide remark or look her way. It was simply a matter of self-preservation.

Alex thumbed through the course book she'd bought on her way to the Monday-morning class, reviewing the chapters previously assigned from the syllabus as students trickled in, pushing aside her uneasiness over bumping herself off the waitlist.

"Pssst, Alex," came a low whisper that caught her attention over the din of the classroom waiting for the professor's arrival.

Alex recognized the voice from the previous night; it was the soy-milk woman. Alex smiled shyly, whispering, "Hi."

"Is this seat taken?" the woman asked, motioning to the empty desk next to Alex, who had reflexively placed her jacket over it in hopes of discouraging anyone from sitting next to her.

"No." Alex swiftly removed the jacket, wrapping it over the back of her chair.

"Thanks." The woman took a seat, tossing her oversized handbag onto the desk. "I'm Nathalie. I was in a bit of a hurry the other night."

"No worries. I'm Alex." She shook her head as soon as the words left her mouth.

"Doy?"

Alex's cheeks turned red. *What is wrong with me?* "Yes, doy."

Nathalie playfully pushed Alex's shoulder as the professor entered the classroom, launching into the lecture before he'd set his briefcase down.

Dr. Pierre concluded his lecture on Florence, Italy's turn toward "craft guilds"—a type of formal apprenticeship system—in the early fifteenth century as the catalyst that gave rise to the greatest abundance of artistic achievements the world has ever known. All Alex had to show for class notes, however, were the handful of goofy doodles she and Nathalie drew on each other's notebooks.

The only thing she learned during the fifty-five-minute lecture was Nathalie had a silly sense of humor, a mischievous smile, and her strawberry-blond hair smelled of citrus and mango, Alex picking up whiffs of it whenever Nathalie leaned over to write on her notebook.

Alex didn't mind missing the content of the day's lecture, the course only moderately more difficult than the one she attended in high school. Its easy nature offset the tougher courses she was enrolled in.

"What are you up to now?" Nathalie asked as the women strolled outside the Arts Center Building into the bright midmorning sun.

"Poly-Sci 236, Ethics and American Business," Alex replied, snatching the sunglasses, or "sunnies," as she referred to them, off her head to cover her eyes.

"Ah, with Dr. Sneezer."

"Who? No, Dr. Milner, portly guy who never takes his coat off."

"Sneezer is the name everybody calls him."

"You're right, he does sneeze a lot. What's with that?"

"I hear," Nathalie said, lowering her voice, "that he's allergic to some sulfate found in most shampoos and the students in front always make sure to use it in the morning before class."

"Ah. I thought the chalk dust caused it. He's always waving one of those erasers around like a baton." Alex said, becoming animated as she continued. "It's entertaining to watch when he sneezes, like watching a walrus barking; it comes in waves and his mouth opens wide—" Nathalie's amused expression froze Alex midsentence. *Stop babbling.*

"You're adorable," Nathalie said. "Well, I'm heading this way." Nathalie dipped a shoulder in her intended direction. "I'm glad I ran into you again, without the milk bath."

Alex appeared to blush, though with her fair complexion the warm sun made it hard to tell. "Me too."

"Wanna get together for dinner some night?"

"Ah, yeah. I work most nights except Fridays."

"Great, it's a date. See you then," Nathalie said, turning away.

A date? Like date, *date?* Alex's social skills were challenged enough, but the word "date" confused her even more. Before she could put her distraction on pause to ask how they planned to meet up, Nathalie had walked away, her sundress swaying gently with each graceful stride.

"Pardon me, miss," Dr. Pierre's animated voice called out as he approached Alex, his focus on the piece of paper he held. "Could you please tell me your name? I noticed you in class today, but I don't recall your prior presence."

"Ah … Alex Smyth," she said, tightening her grip on her backpack. "I had been waitlisted."

"Oh, I see. Smyth …" he muttered, scanning the list. "I don't see—"

"I received an e-mail late last night. It'll probably be on your next update."

"Right, right. I'm sure it will. Now, your friend, the one with the exquisite smile, what is her name?"

"Ah … Nathalie," Alex answered, a bit confused. "I don't know her last name. I just met her today, in class."

The professor searched for Nathalie's name, coming up blank.

"She mentioned she was auditing the course," Alex added, though the topic never came up, unless one of Nathalie's doodles contained a hidden message about it.

"Ah, that would explain it," Dr. Pierre exclaimed, as if he'd found a newly discovered Michelangelo painting. "She still needs to declare that with me personally. Let her know, thanks." And he was off.

"Sure," Alex muttered to no one. She glanced back the way Nathalie had walked off, but she was gone. *She certainly has a way of disappearing. Well, off to Dr. Sneezer's class.*

Alec killed the lights to the black SUV as he turned the corner onto Palo Alto Street, lined with old-growth Norway maples in front of silhouetted, single-family homes as dusk fell on the neighborhood. He parked a couple houses down from the hacker's address to ensure the element of surprise. The last thing he or Thomas wanted was for the hardware they planned on confiscating to be quickly wiped. Alec doubted they were dealing with someone that sophisticated, but he wasn't taking any chances, not on his first case.

"Excited?" Thomas asked.

"Yes."

"Yes … that's it?"

"I'm focused."

"Of course you are. You've certainly made some of the other investigators look very good. I overheard Henry on the phone the other day going on about you, how you *deduce* the identity of cyberthieves from so little information. He actually used the word 'deduce.' It's about time you got your shot."

"Thanks, Thomas."

A few minutes later local police pulled in behind Alec. One of the uniformed men stepped up to the driver's window. "You Alec Gordon?" the aging officer asked bluntly.

"Yes," Alec replied, showing his task-force credentials.

The officer gave it a cursory glance, eyed Alec, and roamed to Thomas, then back. "How old are you, son?"

"Twenty-two."

The officer shook his head. "Christ, they're getting younger every day. So what's the plan?"

"Did you read the case summary I sent over?"

"Yeah, college punk with a computer causing trouble. Dumb smart kid."

"I'll do the talking to see if I can get them to admit hacking into the college last night. I also want to learn of any accomplices. I suspect there are. If they balk during the interrogation I'll tap my nose. That's your cue to pull out your handcuffs."

"Tap my nose … like from the movie *The Sting* with Redford and what's-his-name?"

"Newman, yes."

"I love that movie." The officer sported a wide grin. "One of the best con movies of all time."

"I agree, great classic."

"OK, so we'll make the kid nervous. It's your show, Gondorff."

Alec smiled at the character reference, tucking the warrant inside his long black trench coat as he and Thomas exited the vehicle. The four men moved briskly up the uneven concrete path that led to the front door of the house, each scanning the surroundings for anything that might pose a threat.

Alec opened the rickety screen door, took a deep breath in, then exhaled, controlling the rush of adrenaline welling up in him before ringing the doorbell. The door opened. A short, older woman with hair pinned back peered up at him, her face expressionless.

"My name is Alec Gordon. I'm with the CCEA," he said, flashing his badge. "Does Yuri Aleksandrov live here?"

A few moments passed as the woman's eyes inspected each of the four men before answering, "*Sushhestvuet ne odna zdes', no mne. Pozhalujsta, uhodi.*"

Thomas flashed a confused look at Alec, then back at the officers, who shrugged their shoulders.

"*Menja zovut Alek, i ja s CCHW. Yuri li zdes' zhit'? U nas est' order na ego arest,*" Alec returned undaunted, pulling out the search-and-seizure warrant, presenting it to the woman. "Miss Aleksandrov, your son is in trouble."

The woman's grip on the doorknob tightened, her face rigid and pale. She stared at the official document for several seconds before looking back at Alec. "OK, you come in," she said. "Yuri! Company here."

"What, Ma, who is it?" The boy's voice sounded annoyed as he rounded the corner from the kitchen. He froze at the sight of the four strange men standing in the living room, his mother sitting on the couch lighting a cigarette.

"Yuri Aleksandrov?" Alec asked in a measured tone, studying the tall, lanky eighteen-year-old's body language. Alec had prepared for this moment over and over in his head, how to handle the approach, the interrogation, every detail. What he hadn't counted on, though, was the kid making a break for it. "Yuri!" Alec shouted, but Yuri was out the back door in a flash, his mother shaking her head, shouting in Russian again.

"Want me to chase him?" the younger officer asked.

"No. I'll get him," Alec replied, flipping his trench coat off and tossing it over to Thomas. "Confiscate all the computer equipment in his room and load it in the SUV." He took off through the front door.

Alec stopped out at the sidewalk, scanning the street in each direction before he spotted the boy sprinting down the middle of the road, deeper into the quiet neighborhood's maze. He took off after him but at a slower pace. *All I have to do is keep him in sight for a couple minutes, then he'll hit the wall.* Alec knew that unless the boy was an Olympic miler he'd be gassed in five or six hundred yards at that pace, probably less. *Just let him wind himself, then haul him back home.*

Yuri's escape plan appeared erratic; he turned left on one street, right two streets later, then another sudden left, stumbling on speed bumps while frequently checking over his shoulder, his face more strained each time. Unlike the fleeing hacker, Alec cruised through the Hollis, Queens, neighborhood effortlessly, breathing under control, his stocky five-foot-eight-inch frame taking the same quick, efficient strides that once propelled him down the sidelines on the football field and the tartan-track straightaways during high school. He glanced at his watch: *Ninety seconds down.* He looked back up, waiting for the inevitable to happen to his target, Yuri's form deteriorating with every passing second.

A few blocks later the boy slowed, as if he now carried a piano on his back. Alec sidled up alongside. "Where are you going, Yuri?"

"I ... didn't ... do ... anything," the kid sputtered out between deep inhalations.

"Then why are you running?" Alec could see the kid was tying up, unable to respond. "You live at home, don't have a car, your cell phone and computer are back at the house ... What's your endgame here?"

The boy stopped, hunched over, and placed trembling hands on wobbly knees, gasping for as much oxygen as he could suck in.

"This isn't some virtual game. You can't just log off and disappear," Alec continued, patiently standing over him. "Let's go back to the house and talk it over."

"Are you ... going to ... cuff me?"

"Do you want me to cuff—?"

"No!"

"Then I won't," Alec said, peering around the area where the chase ended, straightening his short, dark-blond hair with a hand swipe through it. *Good, I don't carry handcuffs anyway.* He peered up at the night sky. "That's quite a full moon tonight."

Yuri looked at Alec, then the sky. "I hadn't ... noticed."

"You should. It's like a big spotlight ... sees and knows everything going on down here."

Again the boy glanced at Alec, a worried expression spreading across his face, as they walked back to the house.

Back at the Aleksandrov residence, Alec poured the young hacker a glass of water. "Here, have a drink. It'll take the burn out of your throat."

Yuri sipped from the glass, watching the officers haul his prized computer equipment out the front door. "Will I get it back?"

"That depends," Alec replied, initiating the interrogation he'd long been anticipating.

"On what?"

"On how much you cooperate with me, and how truthfully you answer my questions."

The boy shot a furtive glance at his mom, who remained impassive, taking short drags on her cigarette.

Alec cleared his throat, the fresh outdoor air long expelled from his lungs, replaced with toxins that didn't agree with him. "Why do you think we're here?"

"I dunno," Yuri replied, his feet shifting under the couch where he sat alongside his mother.

"You're a pretty talented programmer, aren't you?"

"Guess so."

"Guess so? It says here," Alec said, reading the file he'd brought along, "that you aced your final exam in Advanced Programming Logic 101, 201, and 301 without attending a single class."

The kid repetitiously rubbed his hands up and down his pant legs, eyes darting around the room.

"Are you familiar with IP addresses?"

"Yeah, it's the ID for a computer when you're online."

"That's correct. Do you know what your IP address is?"

The boy fidgeted for a few moments until his mom smacked him up alongside the head uttering, "*Skazhi emu.*"

"172343238101."

Alec handed him a piece a paper from the previous night's server logs at the local New York City college where the kid was also enrolled. "Do you see the IP address I highlighted?"

The boy's face froze with wide-open eyes and mouth agape, staring at the log report.

"Now do you know why we're here?"

The boy nodded.

Young Yuri confessed to hacking into the Registrar's Office computer the previous night, as well as many other times during the previous three weeks. Over the course of the next hour he conveyed the story of how he pledged for a small hacker fraternity on campus called Black Hat Society. His online name was RushOn, and the Registrar breach was the initiation rite.

The boy hadn't done any serious hacking until recently. Transplanted to the area, his mom harped on him to make new friends, to get involved. He met a few like-minded students interested in computer programming, who invited him into their circle; the college hacks seemed like harmless pranks. The group never met in person, rather online in a special chat room moderated by the fraternity president, who went by the code name ByteMe. Real names were never used, though some were known because they had computer-science classes together; invariably the topic would come up.

"I'll make you a deal," Alec said, satisfied with the wealth of information he'd obtained. "Give me a name and we won't take you down to the station to book you." In reality, he had no intention of taking him in. *The mother would be punishment enough.*

The boy's head drooped, staring into his lap, sitting silent. Alec ran his index finger across his nose. On cue, the older officer slowly opened his jacket, tugged the handcuffs off his belt, and let them jingle in his hand.

The mother immediately started in on her son in her native tongue.

"Neal," the boy blurted out.

"Neal what?"

"Watson," the boy looked back up at Alec. "He's the one that invited me to pledge."

"Thank you, Yuri," Alec said, rising to his feet.

"I told you everything," the boy said as the men moved toward the front door. "When can I have my stuff back?"

"We'll need some time to run forensics on your hard drive to ensure there's no stolen data on it."

"But I need my computer for school. My assignments and homework are on it."

"I'll tell you what," Alec said, anticipating the boy's response, motioning to Thomas. "I'll loan you this laptop for the next week while we have yours." Alec passed the laptop to the boy. "What folder is your school information in?" he continued, pulling out his notepad. "I'll e-mail you the contents of the folder … if it's clean."

"A folder called CJCNY."

"OK, I'll get it to you tomorrow."

Back at the cars the younger officer asked Alec, "You gave him a laptop? Isn't that like giving the guy the keys to the car parked next to the one they just got busted for stealing?"

"It has software installed on it that will track his e-mails and other activities," Alec replied, settling into the SUV. "My guess … right now he's sending an e-mail out to his friends about what just happened. By the time I get home I'll have the e-mail addresses for the entire BHS fraternity."

The officer grinned, his partner chortling, "Nice work, Gondorff."

Crossing the Fifty-Ninth Street Bridge over the East River, Alec took in the splendor of the full moon arcing high above the city. His mind often wandered when the sky was clear enough to view it. Its magnificent, pockmarked face spoke to him on some level he didn't fully understand. He would stare at it, hypnotized, wondering if some nugget of his subconscious might come forth. His grandmother once told him, after she saw him sitting by his bedroom window mesmerized by it as a young boy, that perhaps he was searching for something, and the moon held an important clue. He still didn't know what it was.

Traffic was light getting home to his Tribeca loft in lower Manhattan. Cassidy, his mixed bulldog terrier, would be excited to see him. The city wasn't the most practical place to own a pet, as his parents constantly informed him during his youth, but he loved dogs and made it work once he moved out on his own.

Settling into some Chinese takeout he'd picked up on his way home, and ESPN airing in the background, Alec eagerly fired up his laptop to see what the college hacker, RushOn, had done since the bust while Cassidy detected unfamiliar scents on Alec's pant legs and hard-soled shoes. He logged into the administrative "StealthWare" website that managed the spyware the task force subscribed to. The tool he found on the Web allowed him to install a hidden program on any computer; then monitor the person's activities—e-mails, chats, website visits, search queries—via the website that picked up the secretly transmitted information.

Alec didn't consider himself above the law when it came to tracking hackers. On the contrary. He took citizens' rights, honest or otherwise, seriously. The task force employed the software when they had a warrant for its use, or if the laptop belonged to the CCEA, as was the case with the college boy this evening—an old but effective trick.

Bingo. Yuri had sent out nineteen e-mails via a distribution list entitled "bhs." Alec recorded the new e-mails in the Hacker 101 file. *Like putting the fox in the hen house.* He resolved to explore them further in the morning, and set up surveillance on the other accounts.

Cassidy barked. He needed to go out. "OK, big dog," Alec said, playfully roughhousing his excitable friend, grabbing the leash on their way out the door.

003 A Guild by Any Other Name

Members of the Worshipful Company of Organic Food—WCOF—trickled into the engineering classroom on Stanford University's campus, something they did every fifth Sunday evening throughout the year; except tonight was Friday. A special meeting had been called, practically mandated, to address the messy rumors surrounding the VLGF—Vegas Land Grab Fund—brokered by Trent Hudson, the guild's current president. Nearly all the members had assembled, including Phil Smyth, lapping up the free drink and food supplied by fellow members.

Inspired by the Worshipful Company of Grocers, founded as a guild in fourteenth-century England to maintain purity standards of spices, local Silicon Valley natural-food grocers and growers banded together in the same spirit to ensure accurate food labeling standards: natural or organic advertisement meant just that, pure organic food, not subject to genetically modified organisms. Many food items are often labeled as "natural" or "all natural" when their origins are anything but. Transparency was their ultimate goal.

Trent began quieting the group down. "Fellow members, please, let's take our seats so that we may begin." The good-natured crowd simmered more quickly than usual this warm spring evening. "Thank you all for attending this special WCOF meeting. We are now in session." He deferred to Phil Smyth, who acted as the guild's secretary, for the reading of the meeting minutes from the last session, which were subsequently approved, before proceeding directly to the single item on the agenda. "We have Larry Henderson here from New York City on behalf of Gordon Investment Management to discuss the current state of the VLGF."

A few members clapped, but a smattering of sighs were more prevalent, among them from Phil, who wanted Frank Gordon, the investment firm's president to address the crowd. *Looks like this guy's dressed for senior prom in that zoot suit.*

"Thank you. Actually, I'm from Los Angeles," Larry started off, his energy-drink-infused cadence gathering momentum. "I handle West Coast operations for GIM on a contract basis."

Phil rolled his eyes.

"Could we dim the lights and turn on the overhead?" Larry continued, gesturing to the equipment he'd brought along. "Thanks. So, tonight I'm going to go over the Vegas deal from inception to present, and show you where it is with regards to performance. I'll follow that up with the challenges of the present-day economy so you're all on the same page."

The first PowerPoint slide appeared. Phil didn't bother reading the content. Rather, he glared at the flamboyant border and lavish background that stole focus from the overall presentation, its ostentatious GIM logo dripping with conceit and pretentiousness.

"As you can see, back in 2008 when GIM offered the deal to this group the housing market was pretty bad off," Larry said, highlighting the trough on the market-value graph with his laser pointer. "The Vegas area was hit particularly hard, specifically the Shady Willow township, the worst in the nation, which is why they felt it was ripe for the biggest rebound, and thus the best bet for huge returns."

"How many houses were purchased?" one of the members up front asked.

"I don't have an exact number with me, but I can tell you they purchased several bundled lots, which covered two-thirds of the area in distress. They wanted more, but at the time that was all the banking industry would allow. I think to prevent a monopoly."

Another member chimed in, "What was the value of the bundled sale purchase?"

"Again, I don't have those numbers with me, but the dollar amount isn't important. The relative change is what we're interested in. Next slide … here you can see that things were stagnant during 2009, then ticked up a bit in 2010, stayed flat in 2011, and dropped slightly in—"

"So what is the relative gain to this point?" Phil asked, impatient with the Wall Street dog-and-pony show.

"Loss," Larry corrected him. "You mean what is the relative drop since the investment's inception."

The crowd looked at one another, mumbling.

"OK, what's the loss, then?"

"93.85 percent."

The group fell quiet. Phil's stomach did a somersault, and his face drained of life, staring at Larry as if he'd made a life-threatening statement.

"What GIM hadn't counted on was another drop after they purchased the toxic loans in 2008. It was 67.15 percent, to be exact. So they tried to rent them out through various rental-management groups, and the cost of doing so nicked another 12.65 percent from the investment capital."

"What about the last 14.05 percent?" a young woman's voice called out from the back of the room. Everybody turned to see who had posed the question.

Phil didn't have to turn around to know it was Alex. Though she had not attended a meeting since she'd tagged along with him as a kid, Phil reckoned his less-than-jovial demeanor over recent weeks had caught Alex's attention on more than one occasion at home and the store, despite his best attempts at concealing their financial concerns in her presence. *She must've overheard me talking about the special meeting and wandered over after her last class.*

"Excuse me?" Larry said, his eyes straining through the projector's beam of light

"There's 14.05 percent missing in your relative-drop figure of 93.85 percent," Alex rattled back, leaning against the wall near the entrance in a pair of old jeans she'd worn constantly since high school, arms folded tightly across her chest.

"Ah, of course, that's the firm's administrative fees in handling the investment."

Everybody started talking amongst themselves.

"What is left for us if we pull out now?" someone in the middle of the room inquired.

"GIM has incurred a significant loss in maintaining the land, property taxes, et cetera. There's nothing to pull back at this time, or anytime soon—"

"How did this happen?" Trent asked, though the noise level in the room left his question unanswered.

Phil had heard enough. He shook his head in disbelief, now out personally $350,000, and a second mortgage on his home, to boot. By the time he turned back toward Alex, she'd left. This was not how he wanted her to find out. He knew she often internalized family matters, and would assuredly take on the burden of blame for the investment in the first place.

004   Alex Andra the Badass

The pothole-riddled street in the run-down section of town lay in darkness, the witching hour upon it. Alex Andra stood patiently, peering down the street, searching for Cideral and Pelitine. She'd been hot on their trail since the mysterious explosion at the Shaolin Buddhist Monastery hours earlier. Newalks' high-order law officials saw nothing other than an accident, but Andra knew better; her intuition screamed cover-up: Skikoku's ancient scrolls went missing, not tragically burned in the fire that destroyed the monastery. They were in the hands of a couple of very bad men who planned on exploiting a hidden tribe that preferred the world knew nothing of their existence.

She pulled out her infrared-sensor binoculars in hopes of picking up their heat signature. *Nothing.* She glanced down at her gyro map, trying to figure out where they may have eluded her. It didn't seem possible the duo had evaded her completely. They had to be nearby, perhaps cloaked in the background farther down the street.

A thunderous crack overhead jolted Andra from her thoughts. The earth began to rumble beneath her boots, causing her to drop the gyro map. Instinctively, she grabbed her camouflage gun and fired off a round of brilliant light flares as she dove behind a stack of empty steel containers, popping her head over the top, searching for the root of the trouble. *It has to be them ... seismic disturbance is straight from their playbook.*

The building behind her started to break apart, bricks and mortar raining down. She didn't want to risk running out into the open away from the crumbling building just yet; it would expose her to the tag team of miscreants. Instead, she grabbed the virtual clonator off her utility belt, twisted the bevel like a safecracker, then pointed it in the opposite direction she intended on escaping. *Ready.* The clonator made a few clicking sounds as it conjured up the virtual image of Andra before releasing it. Her likeness sprinted out from behind the steel containers.

A large chunk of the building's facade broke off with a loud snap. Andra reacted, sliding back against the building before it crashed down on the containers, flattening them instantly. Laser bolts and spiked grenades immediately started chasing her virtual presence, serpentining its way back up the street. This was the break Alex Andra had hoped for. She covered her eyes with night goggles, pulling both brain-scramble guns from their holsters. *Time to get nasty, boys.*

The building behind her began to implode, crashing to the ground as she leaped out into the street, the dust providing cover while her virtual presence drew the bad guys' attention. She quickly homed in on the location of Cideral and Pelitine through the haze of laser lights, grenade blasts, and flying building debris. She holstered one of the weapons, replaced it with a distraction bomb, yanked the pin from its dense mass with her teeth, then lobbed it high into the sky. The bomb lofted benignly for a few moments before engaging its onboard motor, jettisoning forward at blinding speed until it reached the first sign of body heat. The motor cut out, the trajectory back to earth several yards behind the trigger-happy duo. As soon as it touched down a loud whistle filled the air and a brilliant flash backlit Cideral and Pelitine, rendering their cloaking efforts ineffective.

Startled, the duo turned around, shooting indiscriminately in the direction of the luminous, multicolored plume. The bomb slowly fizzled out, and the men ceased their fire, looking confused. Cideral switched off the seismic modulator, settling the earth down. The night was still again except for the gentle grinding of metal rolling over asphalt. The men stared at each other as the ominous sound grew louder; it was coming up behind them.

Cideral and Pelitine spun around to find Alex Andra standing a stone's throw away, two full-barreled Pentar brain scramblers whose scopes were locked on their foreheads, her ponytail draped over a bare shoulder and goggles atop her head. Even if the scroll thieves fired off a round before she did, her hand weapons would finish the job; their guidance system would ensure it. The duo did a double-take, yet despite their dreadful situation raised their weapons.

"I wouldn't do that if I were you, boys," Alex Andra warned, fixing her eyes on the two softball-sized metallic spheres she'd rolled toward them.

Cideral and Pelitine cast their eyes downward, puzzled at the rolling objects. They stepped back, but as each ball came into contact with their steel-toed boots the homemade shackle devices sprung open like bear traps, enveloped their ankles, and locked tight around them. Stunned, they tried to fire their weapons at Andra, but before their fingers reached the triggers the ankle shackles zapped each of them with ten thousand volts of electricity. The weapons fell to the ground with a thud, the men shaking uncontrollably for several seconds before collapsing.

Alex Andra holstered her weapons and walked over to the men, brushing dirt and dust off her face. She secured their hands while they lay writhing in pain, then pulled Skikoku's ancient scrolls out from Pelitine's backpack, unfurling the indoctrination cover. In a world where information was no longer written but rather entered, the yellowed parchment scribed in an eloquent, Old World typeface looked all that much more impressive; from a time before tech time. She knew she was privileged in viewing the scrolls, one of only a handful of people throughout history to do so.

She rolled the document up, carefully placed it inside a secure sky-mail tube, and entered the recipient's address on the digital keypad—1B3TY Ministry of Honshu Affairs; they would be relieved to see the scrolls' return.

The chirp of sirens could be heard in the distance heading her way. *No doubt someone called in the firefight.* Alex Andra locked the cap on the tube, pressed the Activate button, and tossed it up in the air as she started running. Her mission was complete: vigilante justice served up what the bureaucrats were too inept to do or care about. As soon as the sky-mail tube detected downward movement it absorbed the chroma of the night, turned invisible to the naked eye or any surveillance equipment, and sped off at the speed of light.

Running down the street away from the legal system on wheels, Alex Andra glanced at the GPS patch adhered to her forearm that was beeping for attention; her virtual brother-in-arms had signaled for help again. She'd told him not to go out on his own. He was always getting into trouble with his insightful hunches. *Too smart for his own good, he is.*

Sundance leaped up from his slumber alongside Alex, launching into a throaty bark, racing from the bedroom. His sudden departure startled Alex's empowered state, sitting in her oversized beanbag, headphones on, game controller in hand.

"What's up, Sundance?" Alex muttered, removing the headphones. Between barks she heard the doorbell ring. She glanced at her Tammaré wristwatch; it displayed a little past eight, the house silent and dark, Sundance's barks casting an ominous pall throughout. *Dad probably went back to the store after the WCOF meeting, and Mom is closing up shop tonight.*

Alex scampered up from the beanbag, undoing her ponytail as she headed to the front door. She peered through the living room's large windowpane. *Nathalie!* With the impact of the WCOF meeting weighing on Alex she'd dove straight into the virtual world of Tammaré to quell her anxiety, forgetting all about the "date" with her new friend.

Alex flipped on the porch light, opening the door.

"Hey," Nathalie greeted her with a twinkle in her eye. "You ready?"

"Ah, yeah … I mean no. Come in. I wasn't sure what time we were … Sundance," Alex said, pulling the excitable, sixty-pound lunging Lab back from the door.

"No worries."

"How'd you find me?"

"Your mom."

Alex wrestled Sundance into the living room. "My mom?"

"I stopped by the store. She said you were here," Nathalie replied, taking in the room while she appeased Sundance's need for attention. "Nice place. It has a warm feel to it."

"Definitely a throwback look. That '70s wood paneling really needs to go."

"I like it … it says 'home.'"

Alex went around the front part of the house turning on more lights, exposing modest but well-kept furniture from the decade following the wood paneling. "Sundance, let's go, boy," she said, steering him away from Nathalie, sending him to the backyard. "I just need to change clothes real quick."

"OK, but you look fine as you are."

Alex reached her bedroom when she heard Sundance burst through the back door, which hadn't been shut all the way. He dashed through the retro living room, headed toward Alex's bedroom. Nathalie grabbed his collar as he went by and ended up getting pulled along for a ride.

"Sundance!" Alex shouted, but her best bud jumped onto the bed, sitting there with a panting grin. "He's a little protective of me … sorry about that."

"Ah, that's sweet. Your very own watchdog," Nathalie teased, examining Alex's small room, whose light-blue walls were decorated with art posters and framed sketches she'd drawn during childhood, with various pieces of expensive computer equipment neatly stacked throughout, their connecting wires and cables discreetly bundled and tucked away from sight; it had an orderly appearance to it. And despite the obvious tech presence it lacked the traditional "geek" vibe with one exception.

"Is that you?" Nathalie asked, pointing to the high-definition still image of Alex Andra on the thirty-two-inch monitor. "Very sexy."

Alex whipped around from the chest of drawers she was rummaging through, stumbling on Sundance's rawhide bone. Paused after the last Tammaré quest stood her avatar, sporting a form-fitting beige tank top with dirt marks splashed over it like an abstract painting; it overlapped camouflage cargo shorts with a weapons belt wrapped around her hips. Her face, painted with smudge marks, and her long, braided ponytail draped over a bare shoulder projected a tough yet feminine demeanor.

"Argggggg," Alex blurted out, lunging for the controller.

"No, you look great," Nathalie said, striking a Wonder Woman pose, complete with hands on hips. "Very tough, sexy superhero."

Alex didn't know what to say, unsure if Nathalie was making fun of her or not. She slowly wound the cord around the controller before stowing it away. "It's just an online game I play."

"Did you get the bad guys?"

Alex gazed at Nathalie, standing there looking lovely in the middle of the bedroom, sensing that moment of truth when someone is about to reveal a side of themselves they normally keep private. "Yes."

"Well then, I feel safe enough to go out tonight."

A slow smile formed as Alex exhaled her held breath.

"Hurry up, get ready," Nathalie said, rubbing Sundance's snout.

"What are we going to do?"

Nathalie winked. "It's a surprise."

Surprise? I don't like surprises.

LEAN ON ME

Alec's cell phone chirped, waking him from a late-evening nap on the couch at the loft. The day had begun early, when he and Thomas caught up with the suspected Black Hat Society ringleader in the campus parking lot.

"Hello," Alec answered without checking the caller ID.

"Where are you? Tell me you're on your way," the caller said in a familiar, hearty voice.

Alec had to separate the phone from his ear. "Thomas, we talked about this. You don't need to shout into the phone. I can hear you." Thomas was still adjusting to cell-phone usage while out in public.

"Sorry, boss. So, are you on your way or what?"

"Thomas, I'm not your boss. And yes, I'll be on my way in a few minutes. But let's meet at Café Java Server & Apps instead."

"Café what? That doesn't sound like a bar, chief."

"Chief? No, not chief, either." Alec shook his head. Thomas gave everybody nicknames. He preferred them over real names for some strange reason. "They have beer. Meet me in fifteen. It's on the corner of West Thirty-Ninth and Ninth, across from Tulips Nightclub."

"Roger that, Gondorff."

"Stop it."

Café Java Server & Apps was bustling with business on this particular Friday night. Self-anointed New York hipsters proclaimed it the best java in the city on a popular social review website. With free Wi-Fi, unique baked goods, beer, wine, coffee, an information technology motif, and plenty of seating it was *the* place to hang out before or after a Broadway show or concert event. The nightclub across the street always provided a lively crowd of women in the early morning hours. For Alec, the atmosphere showcased New York's shoddy attempt at capturing the Silicon Valley vibe of Northern California. What it lacked in authenticity, though, it made up for in opportunities to "hacker watch."

Thomas walked in, spotted Alec sitting in the corner of the café, and trundled over. "Busy place."

"Yes it is. I ordered you a Guinness."

"Thanks." Thomas settled into the wooden booth, surveying the room. Thomas was thirty, perpetually single, and always on the prowl, though his obtrusive yet unintentional manner of leering offset his above-average Italian good looks. "Some nice women here."

Alec took notice, but his interest lay elsewhere. "A toast," he said, raising his large stein of locally brewed root beer, "to bringing down our first case, Hacker 101."

"Hear, hear. Ain't no use hacking when we're tracking."
Clink!

"When do you leave for San Francisco?" Thomas asked with a newly formed foam mustache.

"In the morning. I'll be back on Thursday."

"Thursday?"

"Yes, I added an extra day after the conference so I can drive down to San Jose to meet with the new task force they've opened."

"Always the networker, eh?"

Alec nodded, peering around the room, taking stock of certain individuals who sat by themselves.

"How'd you know about this place? I never heard of it before."

"I come by from time to time."

"Really? Why? Doesn't look like your type of crowd."

"Free Wi-Fi."

Thomas raised an eyebrow. "Free … Wi-Fi?"

"Yes, this place doesn't just have one Wi-Fi hot spot, they have eight. That's a large number of Wi-Fi connections for a place that has at most, according to the fire marshal's maximum occupancy sign, 122 patrons," Alec explained, pointing to the sign above the doorway. "Large hotels have two or three times that many guests, yet offer only one connection. So I ask myself, Why so many hot spots? Then I look around and I see a handful of people sitting alone, with laptops and small peripherals attached. Your average café customer has at most a smart phone or tablet. Some might have a laptop, but nothing connected to it. Why do you think that is, Thomas?"

Thomas paused midway through a sip of his beer. "Ah, gee, I don't know."

"The best way to go undetected in the cyber world is to do your hacking from a location that would be tough to track down, one that wouldn't lead the authorities directly to your home."

"Riiiight. And because it's busy no one is paying attention to them. Except you, of course."

"I come here from time to time, take note of those that fit the profile, snap a quick picture, then compare it with past visits. Over time you come up with a short list of people who call this place their online home. If we ever get a case where the trail leads us here, we have some possible suspects."

"Nice work, Sherlock."

Alec grinned. *That one's not bad.*

Alec's cell phone lit up, displaying a picture of his father mugging with the mayor of New York City at a recent charity auction. Alec let it go to voice mail.

"Old man still giving you grief about your career?" Thomas asked. "He must know how good you are."

"Not sure if he does ... or cares," Alec said, staring into his half-empty stein, the celebratory nature of the evening quickly dissipating.

"Back in junior high school, I'd spent weeks working on this project for the computer-science fair. I created this program that could identify the author of a book by analyzing several pages of its text. Basically, identify their *voice*. My teacher thought it was a great idea, said I'd have a shot at winning and going to the national competition in California." Thomas took a gulp of his beer. "I thought it'd be cool because my dad's a writer and all. I used chapters from different books he had in his library, including stuff he wrote. When I showed him the results he got furious. He started yelling at me, saying, 'You can't quantify creativity, Tom-Tom! Literature is art, not an equation!'" Tom-Tom shrugged and finished off the rest of his beer. "Anyway, he wouldn't let me enter it, so I had to withdraw from the fair."

Both men took in the café's ambience, an eclectic mixture of conversations dotted with raucous cackles, grappling with the weight of their respective father-son challenges.

"Yeah ... that about sums it up," Alec replied as a twentysomething blonde strolled by the table, flashing him a smile.

"Dude, forget your old man," Thomas whispered after the woman had passed.

"Not my type," Alec said, finishing off his drink. "I prefer redheads."

Alex stared at the helmet Nathalie handed her as if it were a prop from a science-fiction movie; its chiseled black casing, battle-ready archangel decal, and dark tinted, Plexiglas shield evoked images of military attire for deep space.

"Let's take my car," Alex said, returning the helmet while eyeing Nathalie's mode of transportation—a sleek black Ducati motorbike, equally sci-fi-looking under the dim streetlight.

"Oh, come on. Be adventurous," Nathalie said as she dropped a helmet over her head. "What would Alex Andra do if she needed to make a quick getaway?" Her voice sounded muffled through the vents.

"She'd take the car that's in the driveway."

"Really … Andra would escape in a dirty old Toyota Corolla?"

"It's got a metal shield to protect you from road rash."

Nathalie handed the extra helmet back to Alex then straddled the Ducati, firing it up as she tilted her head toward the saddle behind her.

Alex reluctantly put the helmet on, an effort that felt like sticking her head into a bowling ball, then clumsily climbed onto the back of the two-wheeled rocket. She'd barely settled when the engine roared, lurching them forward. Alex wrapped her arms around Nathalie fast, holding on for dear life.

They sped down the wide suburban streets, hardly slowing around the sharp corners, the engine's piercing whine sending shivers down Alex's spine. Her heart and mind raced trying to anticipate the next turn, fearing they'd tip over from the deep leans Nathalie put the bike into, offsetting the sensation by leaning the other way.

"Lean with me on the turns, hon," Nathalie's voice said clear as day from inside the helmet. "If you go the other way, we'll crash."

"OK!" Alex shouted, Nathalie's laugh echoing in her ears.

They eventually roared onto the freeway, accelerating to twice the posted speed limit, rushing by and weaving through the Friday-night traffic as if it were at a standstill. Alex clenched every muscle in her body, tightening her hold around Nathalie's waist. Her heart pounded so fast that each beat overlapped with the next. She wanted to close her eyes, the blur of potential death too real, yet the fear of missing something overshadowed flying off the back into nothingness.

Alex winced, sensing a near out-of-body experience when Nathalie suddenly leaned to the right, veering the Ducati from the fast lane to the off-ramp five lanes away; the blur of red taillights streaked across Alex's retinas, disrupting her equilibrium, while the rapid deceleration as they dropped below the freeway and onto the surface streets surged her forward into Nathalie. For all Alex knew, they'd arrived in downtown Los Angeles before pulling into a large parking lot whose towering sign overhead read AROUND THE WORLD MINIATURE GOLF. Nathalie killed the engine, tapping Alex to loosen her death grip.

"Sorry!" Alex unwrapped her shaky arms before awkwardly dismounting the bike.

"Hon, there's a mike and speaker inside the helmet. You don't need to shout."

Alex struggled to extract her head from the bowling ball, her trembling leg muscles making it that much harder. Nathalie helped lift it off, setting it down on the back of the bike.

"Ready for some fun?" Nathalie asked, flipping her hair back and forth until it appeared to fall magically into place.

Alex's legs wobbled as if still moving despite standing on asphalt, her stomach situated somewhere near her throat. "What state are we in?"

Nathalie grinned, handing Alex a hairbrush. "Loser buys dinner."

"Yay!" Nathalie cheered on the par-four course when her bright-yellow golf ball disappeared into the hole after traversing several feet of open tubing depicting the Seine River and dropping out onto the artificial grass for a hole in one.

Alex lost track of the ball as soon as it entered the scaled-down Eiffel Tower. Instead, she watched Nathalie apply body English to the ball as it made its journey around the treasured landmark. Alex didn't know why she liked Nathalie. So far every minute with her since the spilt-milk incident had been a mixture of awkwardness, giddiness, embarrassment, sheer terror, and zany fun; a roller-coaster experience sans the seat belt and protective cage.

"Sweet shot," Alex said, averting her eyes from Nathalie's tight jeans that hugged her shapely derrière and long, slender legs.

"You'd better get your game on or dinner's going to be on you," Nathalie said, gloating over her current lead.

"What, are you a putt-putt pro?" Alex responded, deflecting the playful taunt while she lined up her ball on the faux Champs-Élysées fairway.

"By night, yes. By day I tell people how to spend their money."

Alex steadied herself, reviewing the three options of where to send the ball.

"The crowd has gone quiet here at the Gai Paree Mini Open," Nathalie said in hushed tones, pantomiming with the end of her club that acted as a microphone. "Alex needs a solid tee shot in order to keep pace with Nathalie, the chick from nowhere, a Cinderella story in the making."

Alex smirked at Nathalie, waggling her hips as if playing to the mock audience. *Cinderella she's not.* Alex lined up her shot. She was going for the hole-in-one option.

Smack!

Alex had been hitting the ball tentatively up till that point in the game and added extra oomph to this swing.

Tink! Crack!

"Look out!" Alex shouted as her faded orange ball ricocheted off the tower post, hit the side of the wooden Parisian café facade, and wound its way back toward her, ultimately landing in a jumbo cup filled with soda.

Plunk.

Nathalie dropped to her knees laughing hysterically. The mother and father of the family waiting their turn looked on in stunned silence while their three kids laughed uncontrollably until tears formed. Alex turned beet-red, momentarily mortified until she realized the ball had landed in the cup on one swing. "That counts," she said with nervous laughter. "That's a hole in one … certainly more impressive than your shot."

Nathalie, still laughing, moved on toward the next hole, shaking her head. Alex retrieved her wet ball and sheepishly passed by the parents, offering her apologies, while their kids gave her high-fives.

"What do you mean you tell people how to spend their money?" Alex asked after she ten-putted down Wall Street into the New York Stock Exchange hole.

"Financial consultant. I advise clients on how to manage their money," Nathalie replied, penciling in their final scores for the night.

"Hopefully you don't advise them like you ride your bike."

"Everything has risk. You don't get anywhere in life without taking them," Nathalie said, her voice striking a serious tone. "The trick is to understand the risk and manage it as best you can."

All I know about risk is that if you lose, you end up with nothing. "I suppose."

Nathalie's focus narrowed on Alex. "Haven't you ever wanted something in life so bad it was worth risking everything … even if it meant ending up with nothing?"

Alex stood motionless, captivated by Nathalie's sultry voice, soul-searching gaze, and thin moist lips.

"You prepare yourself for success and harbor no regrets if it doesn't pan out," Nathalie added, flashing what appeared to be a self-assured smile. "Let's go. I'm hungry, and you're buying."

"Hot-dog stand?" Alex said as they rolled up to Honest Frank's Hotdog Stand a few miles down the road from the miniature golf course. "This is what you want your winning dinner to be: hot dog, pretzel, and soda?"

"Best in the city, I'm telling you."

"Do you *know* what's in hot-dog meat?" Alex, with her steady organic diet since before she could remember, conveyed a hint of disgust. Sure, she had the occasional craving for junk food or less-healthy choices, but that generally meant gluten-free, homemade cookies. Hot dogs never made it to her palate.

"They have a tofu dog if you're a vegetarian," Nathalie said, getting in line.

"I'm not a tofu eater," Alex said, defending herself like she had so many times as a teenager. "We eat meat, but hot dogs aren't meat. Fish, chicken—"

"Suit yourself, but you don't know what you're missing. Everything in moderation, I say."

Alex stood there taking in the small crowd seated on street-side tables and benches, enjoying Frank's dogs, munching on large, warm, salted pretzels, and sipping various beverages. She had to admit, the smell was intoxicating. Once a month at her parents' store they offered polish sausage links, handmade by her dad in the morning, grilling them up on the garden terrace out back. The smoke would waft throughout the store, tempting her senses, but she had always associated meat in a bun with junk food.

"I'll have one sausage link loaded," Nathalie requested from the unusually tall vendor, whose hands extended well beyond his jacket sleeves, "a pretzel with hot mustard, and a peach tea."

"Make that two, but a root beer instead," Alex added. *When in Rome … ah, the Coliseum. Probably my best score tonight: a seven.*

The two women found an empty spot near the local park's pond, where retired men navigated radio-controlled vessels of varying shapes and sizes around an obstacle course of buoys; some better than others. Alex ate slowly, testing the waters of her first hot dog, while Nathalie savored each bite, chasing it down with cold tea.

"What do you think?" Nathalie asked, tearing apart her pretzel before dipping it into the spicy mustard.

Alex, mid-bite, gave a thumbs-up. *I hope the grease doesn't make me sick on the ride home. I doubt you can throw up at a 130 miles per hour and not have it go right back down.*

"You seem quiet. Everything OK?"

Alex took a sip of her drink. "Yeah, I'm fine."

The Tammaré quest, motorbike ride, and golf game had sufficiently distracted her from the bad news revealed at the special WCOF meeting, but now its harsh reality crept back into her mind.

"It's just that … my parents have worked so hard," Alex blurted out, "and tried really hard to send me to Stanford, but they made this investment, and I guess it didn't work out, and now they are in debt. They lost a lot of money, and it's all my fault. I told them Stanford had a great program, so they made it happen, and now they're broke." She stopped to dry a tear running down her cheek, replacing it with a streak of yellow mustard.

Nathalie leaned over, dabbed her wetted finger on Alex's cheek, and wiped it clean, then gave her a hug. "It's not your fault. I'm sure they don't blame you. Parents always want to give their kids everything they can, even if it's risky."

Helpless and disconsolate on a matter she couldn't control, Alex gazed up, oddly comforted by Nathalie's presence; it had a certain familiarity to it. She normally sought solace from her dad, especially during childhood when there were many such moments.

"Let's head over to my place and chill out. You can tell me about it," Nathalie offered, peering into Alex's puffy eyes.

Alex nodded, trying to un-stuff her nose as a text message arrived on her cell phone. "It's my dad wondering where I am," she said, composing herself. "I forgot to leave a note." She quickly typed her reply: "I'm fine. Out with a friend. Be home late. See you at the store in the morning. Love ya."

Nathalie's two-bedroom condo exhibited a distinct European flavor to its décor—silk flora sprouted from colorful ceramic vases, sturdy, Old World furniture placed for optimal sociability, and an oversized, ornate area rug covering most of the dark wood floor. Alex strolled around the living room with its muted faux-texture painted yellow walls that created an airy atrium atmosphere, taking in the hanging canvas paintings and scenic tapestries, as well as the table-sized sculptures. One sculpture in the corner depicting two naked figures intertwined caught her eye. In the dim light she couldn't tell whether it was a man and a woman, or two women. *Interesting.* She wandered over to the large picture window, where she could see on this clear night all the way down to San Jose, the freeway a quiet portrait of red and white streaks snaking their way there and back.

"Here," Nathalie said, handing Alex a glass of wine.

"Thanks." She took a seat on the leather couch, her view the night sky through the window, sampling the 2008 French Pinot Noir that warmed her throat and chest. "It's good."

"*Merci.*" Nathalie sat down at the end of the couch, pulling her feet up. "After the shameful scandal in France a few years ago, Americans have been slow to come back to it."

"Scandal?"

"You didn't hear?"

Alex shook her head, instantly intrigued.

"Your store probably didn't carry the falsely labeled brands. Pinot was selling big here in the States, but they didn't have enough of the proper grapes to meet demand. So a dozen winemakers in the Languedoc-Roussillon region of France started using cheaper grapes but passing them off as Pinot, which has very strict guidelines." Nathalie paused to take a sip. "Fraud on a grand scale. They were convicted and sent to jail."

"The grapes of wrath."

Nathalie smiled. "So what happened with the investment?"

Alex explained what she understood, which wasn't much, about the investment opportunity her parents and many others from the WCOF had taken part in several years ago, shortly after the country's housing meltdown.

It had all started sophomore year in high school, when her honors political-science class took a trip to Washington, DC. By the time she returned home, jazzed by the experience, she was ready to pursue poly-sci in college. Raised by socially conscious parents, who encouraged her to get involved and not accept life at face value simply out of convenience, it fulfilled that aspiration in her.

Alex knew Stanford had a respected but expensive program. She tugged on the heart strings of her close father-daughter bond, and Phil couldn't say no to his only daughter. Later that year she overheard her parents discussing an investment opportunity the WCOF had been pitched, involving bundled underwater home loans in the Las Vegas area. Her father was pretty excited about it, but Maggie had expressed concern about taking out a second mortgage on the house and borrowing from savings to fund the investment.

Nathalie sighed. "I've seen this before, people borrowing from their nest egg, attempting to parlay it in the securities market. It's not a path I advise my clients to take. And real estate of all things." She shook her head.

"I don't think they consulted with any money advisers. The WCOF group as a whole seemed pretty comfortable with it, like a safety-in-numbers deal."

"Do you know which investment group it was?"

"GI ... M, I think. I stopped by the meeting today and some guy was giving an update to the group. He looked like a suit who didn't know anything other than to say there were unexpected challenges that resulted in massive losses."

"Are they local, GIM?"

"No, New York."

"Gordon Investment Management?" Nathalie asked, getting up. She walked over to her antique rolltop desk.

"Yeah, I think that was what the logo said on the slides. Why?"

Nathalie picked up a copy of *Insiders Business Review*, flipping to an article from a couple months back. She sat down alongside Alex, handing her the magazine.

"'Too Bulky? Gordon Investments Rise to the Top,'" Alex read out loud the article's title. On the page was a picture of Frank Gordon, who headed the private investment firm.

"Basically," Nathalie jumped in as Alex began reading, "the reporter, George Orkan, suggests that the returns from GIM's general holding accounts are beyond what one would consider realistic for the current market. And the reported dividends aren't in keeping with other investment firms competing in the same asset class. In essence, it sounds too good to be true. He also questions the amount of securities held in relation to investor money coming in for the Vegas Land Grab Fund. I believe he's quoted somewhere in there as saying 'Frank's returns are an illusion.'"

"When was this written?" Alex asked, turning to the cover. "Did anybody investigate?"

"The matter went largely unnoticed. I watched a follow-up blurb on a news show that reported the SEC had looked into the allegations, but the firm checked out."

"My Business Ethics class discussed Madoff this week, talking about how his influence and stature in the community aided in his ability to hide his Ponzi scheme for so many years."

"Yeah, the SEC took a beating over that. All the red flags were there for years. I don't think they take anything lightly these days. They said GIM had all their paperwork in order, proper securities were filed, so they dropped the investigation."

Alex read a few more paragraphs, but somewhere between the author's explanation of hedge funds, derivatives, toxic loan buyouts, and an empty glass of fraud-free Pinot, she nodded off.

"Alex, sweetie," Nathalie said, brushing aside the few strands of hair covering Alex's cheek. "Let's get you home before Sundance starts looking for you."

Alex opened her eyes, stirred by the soft touch of Nathalie's hand. Through her sleepy haze she gazed at Nathalie, taken in by the angelic face smiling back, nodding. "OK."

Cyber Con San Francisco

Alec leafed through the conference program, searching for the room number to the day's first lecture, "Classification of Crimes Related to the IT Cloud." The DES-sponsored cybercrime conference had been on the verge of cancellation a few weeks earlier due to budget cuts until some last-minute corporate funding kept it alive. *Such is the state of cyber protection in this country: they all want it, but no one wants to pay for it.* Because of the conference's go/no-go upheaval, many logistics were left up in the air when it was given the green light: conference rooms were switched, schedules changed, guest speakers swapped, all poorly reflected in the program's agenda. Alec nearly canceled his trip, but with his expanding job role he wanted to visit the new cybercrime task force in San Jose. *At least the Las Vegas conference in a couple weeks promises better organization.*

He walked into the BayView Room, the smallest of all the conference rooms the facility offered once the portable partitions had been configured. There were two rows of ten chairs, mostly empty. Alec observed the few attendees already seated, playing the what's-their-story game he often engaged in. *That guy, in the wrinkled white shirt and tie, probably from a midsized company given the cheap briefcase and oversized laptop next to him; middle management in IT no doubt. Her, now, she's tougher. Pantsuit, smart blazer neatly placed over the adjoining chair, electronic tablet, Bluetooth earpiece …* While Alec attempted to pigeonhole the woman, who sat engrossed in something on the tablet device, legs crossed, gently dangling a foot, he couldn't help but notice the delicate anklet jostling with the foot's every move.

"Excuse me, is this seat taken?" Alec asked the woman, whose long auburn hair, cascading down her back, shined under the artificial lighting.

The woman glanced up, then around the room. "Sure." She didn't bother removing her jacket from the chair Alec had inquired about.

Alec took a seat while the woman went back to reading. "Would you like something from the table?" he asked, getting back up, gesturing toward the table with complimentary beverages and pastries spread across it.

"No, thanks."

Alec perused the drink choices, grabbed an orange juice, then selected a croissant that tasted a day or two old.

"See that guy over there," Alec said, settling into the chair again, "in the neatly pressed suit and perfectly matched tie, with the terrible comb-over, reading the latest issue of *Insurance Risk Management*?" He paused, peering out his peripheral to see if the woman had taken the bait. She hadn't. "Probably bored to death, but his manager said this information is important, and if you want that promotion then you'll go. He probably thinks the Cloud is a computer that predicts the weather."

Nothing. The woman's attention remained devoted to her tablet.

"But you. You are a bit of a mystery. Hair let down, nicely dressed, no laptop—"

"I'm an enigma, all right."

"You're reading something about …" Alec continued, leaning over to see what held her attention, catching a hint of her hair's fruity fragrance, "insurance riders. No one here seems to be the right representation for their company's best IT-related needs. Might just as well have phoned into the conference. But then, I suppose it is a free trip on the company's dime."

"See the guy sitting next to me?" the woman chimed in, taking a break from her article. "Keen observer, dressed like he works undercover as a white-collar crime-fighter. Nice, but not obvious. Doesn't carry a briefcase so he's not here to sell anything. No laptop with him, so he stays in the moment, listening to what people have to say, as much with their words as with their body language. But the most important thing about him is that he's lost," she finished with a satisfied smile, returning to her read.

"Excuse me?"

"While your astute observations of the crowd not portraying what you'd expect for the typical cyber topic are correct, what you failed to observe is that you're in the wrong conference room," she said, glancing down at the open program page on his lap. "This is 'Cybercrime and Insurance Risk Analysis.'"

Alec sipped from the juice bottle, examining the woman's delicate features and assured smile. "Who's to say I'm in the wrong room?" he said, setting the nearly empty bottle down and rising to his feet.

"Aren't you?"

"How else could I strike up a conversation with you, Nat?" he replied, reading the "I am …" name tag affixed to her silk blouse.

"If you say so, Alec Gordon."

"What can I say?" Alec said as he strolled from the room. "I'm a sucker for ankle bracelets." He caught the grin on her face in a framed inspirational poster's reflection by the door—a free-climber hanging precariously from a sheer cliff by his hands with the caption "No Challenge Worth Doing Is Easy."

Alec stood outside a late-afternoon lecture that had wrapped up, talking with his counterpart from a cybercrime task force out of Houston, Texas, when he noticed Nat smiling in his direction from across the hallway.

"Pleasure to meet you, Jason," Alec said, exchanging business cards. "I'll see you in Las Vegas."

"You forgot your orange juice," Nat said, finishing the last sip before handing the bottle back as he approached.

"I saved you the pulp. I read it's quite nutritious."

"Considerate of you. But a girl doesn't live by pulp alone."

"Done assessing the risk of cybercrime for all your clients?"

"I head up the underwriting team for REM Insurance. We're writing policy on what constitutes loss for claims in cyberattacks. It's easy for companies to claim attacks since they occur all the time and companies often place exorbitant price tags on their losses."

"Yes, yet another way to cover company losses and generate higher premiums for the insurance industry, though I have to admit, hacking is a far greater threat than, say, art theft or space junk falling from the sky."

"New York man?"

"Yes, as you undoubtedly surmised from my direct manner of thought."

"No, the jacket … it's an Odin, right?" she said, reaching behind the collar. "Only really available in New York City."

"You're just full of surprises, aren't you," he said, enjoying the way she gracefully tugged at his jacket.

Nat winked. "First time to the Bay Area?"

"Yes."

"Tell you what, Alec Gordon," she said, slipping her arm inside his as they strolled towards the exit, "I'll take you on a tour of the city, and then dinner is on you."

"Deal."

Sitting comfortably in the sanctuary of her bedroom with Sundance sleeping alongside, Alex methodically hacked into American Bank's mainframe computers located in West Virginia. She'd spent the past month exploring their networks and domain addresses, trolling for unattended or mismanaged proxy ports that would give her deeper access to databases that housed mortgage information on millions of homes across the country. Tonight she slipped in the backdoor that gave her the keys to restitution.

Alex knew the banking industry would take a decade or more to sort out the mess, the great housing meltdown of '07, fueled by robot loans, shaky credit checks, and greedy brokers; all of which conspired to set the housing industry back fifty years, and possibly destroyed the American allure of owning a home. Though her parents were spared such hardship, Alex's intolerance for the rampant bureaucracy affecting families caught in the crosshairs of foreclosure threats, unemployment, and apathetic banks unwilling to work with consumers bubbled over; she hated to see their dreams fade away.

Sweet. Alex began the laborious task of understanding and mapping out the hundreds of tables the mortgage database held. *This is going to take some time.* She took a gulp of chocolate soy milk straight from the container and dove right in. *OK, let's fire up DB Snooper and point it to their main database file. Browse to their database server STHOME56$, then ... the D drive. Backups, backups, there. Better to use backups than live ones for this session. Companies rarely secure their backups like they do current data. OK, last week's version works. Done, now let 'er rip.*

Alex's homespun DB Snooper began interrogating the database; every index, field, table, view, and stored procedure began displaying on her dashboard. As relationships between the different objects were detected, arrows joined them, visually displaying a data diagram worthy of a professional technical writer. It was rare that such a visual document existed even for the company that built the database. *I could probably make a fortune with this utility.*

Alex had never taken a computer course. In fact, the thought of it bored her. Her insistence on staying indoors during her formative years worried Phil and Maggie, who feared she wouldn't be exposed to the forces that formed and governed the world. Enter the computer. Her dad brought home a used one that a guild member could spare when Alex was six years old. Its operating system was a few years old for the time, but that didn't matter. From the moment she fired it up and connected to the Internet, she was captivated; and when Phil showed her the QBASIC program embedded on the system, coding a simple little program he'd learn to write in college that displayed hello world, her eyes lit up with visions of a world within a world; she was hooked. Within a week, she'd already figured out how to bypass all the built-in security measures, as well as create a spreadsheet for her parents, showing them where they were wasting money at the store; a computer aficionado was born.

Once the DB Snooper finished, she initiated her "SaveMyHome" script to ferret out hardship cases. While it ran in the background, Alex reached for the game controller to dive into another Tammaré adventure when she noticed sitting underneath it a copy of *Insiders Business Review*. *Nathalie must've left it for me.* She turned to the article on Frank Gordon and read it again, muddling through the parts on hedge funds, derivatives, and bundled underwater home-loan packages, but she got the gist of the journalist's angle. *He doesn't think the firm is legit.* The article appeared to be well written, laying out the basic facts. *Then why did the SEC not find anything? Nathalie mentioned they passed the investigation, so why would someone go to the trouble to out them publicly. Where there's smoke, there's fire? Something's missing. Cooking the books? I may not understand investing, but I understand business.*

The San Francisco Bay shimmered under the dull blue, late-afternoon sky, resplendent in all its activities and sights. Small sailboats tacked back and forth across the wide Golden Gate strait, kayakers worked the strong currents headed out to the Pacific Ocean, and seals basked lazily under the sun on marine docks yielded by boaters long ago. Alec and Nat stood on the charter boat's upper deck, the brisk, salty air rushing across their faces, as they ventured out to one of the city's most notorious landmarks: Alcatraz Island.

"Insurance?" Alec said, holding the collar of the trench coat tightly around his neck, a modest attempt to limit the amount of cold air pelting his chest.

"Yeah, Dad's influence," she replied, hands fixed on the railing, eyes closed, body leaning forward with her head tilted up. "He always told me that all people really want in life is to feel safe and secure. Insurance was the way to give them that." She glanced at Alec. "You look cold. Let's go down below."

"It's invigorating."

"Your face is turning white."

"Probably best, then. I don't want to be mistaken for the ghost of a past inmate out on the island."

The two descended below the top deck, where the wind retreated and heat lamps warmed the surroundings.

"I figured you New Yorkers would be use to the bitter cold," she teased.

"Sure, when it's not coming at you at thirty knots," Alec said, stepping up to the boat's concession stand. "Two large hot chocolates, sir." He grinned at Nat. "You want anything?"

"So, cybercriminology … you go around stalking the bedrooms of twentysomething loners living at home?"

"See that gentleman sitting over there away from everybody?" Alec said as they sat down to a cozy view of the receding city.

"Not this again. You got my attention already."

"True, but still, see how he's intently focused on his laptop, oblivious to everything outside his monitor, urgently typing as if his life depended on it?"

"Yeah, so? Maybe he's e-mailing his sweetie, or blogging about the sexy guy in the trench coat with the crazy beautiful eyes."

Alec turned to Nat, momentarily derailed from his line of thought. "Perhaps, though, he'd more likely be sharing with the world the redhead with the crazy long legs," he said, sipping the hot cocoa, warming his hands around the cup. "That is, if he were aware of his surroundings. He hasn't looked up once since we came downstairs. Based on the thumb drive plugged in, and the small, range-extending antenna, it's more likely that he's using the free onboard Wi-Fi to stay anonymous and hack into some company's network. Why else would you go on a short fifteen-, twenty-minute boat ride to a tourist attraction and bring your laptop? My guess, he'll stay on the boat when we get to Alcatraz and return immediately back to the pier."

"Really? I like the blogging story better."

Tourists from around the world chattered in a variety of languages as they disembarked the charter boat onto the infamous prison grounds. Alec took in the lifeless, rectangular windows evenly spaced along the brick buildings, and the imposing barbed wire strung tight above the steel fences that surrounded them, imagining himself as a prisoner sentenced to hard time there on "The Rock," as it was often referred to.

"You're right, the guy stayed on the boat," Nat said excitedly. "And it's getting ready to head back." She was tugging at Alec's coat. "Aren't you going to arrest him?"

"It was just a hunch. He might be blogging," he replied with a wry smile. "It's out of my jurisdiction for the most part, unless he's hacking into some network of computers located in New York City. And even then, there's proper protocol to follow in tracking his activity. You can't just walk up to him as if you've witnessed him breaking into a car or safe. It's a tough crime to track down, harder than physical crime, and even tougher to enforce. It's like the wild, Wild West for hackers in cyberspace."

"How'd you end up doing this type of work? Why not Daddy's investment firm?"

"I don't recall telling you about my father," Alec replied, staring at the mysteriously intriguing woman whose soft, European-inspired features and sparkle in her eyes seduced his senses.

"You didn't. I read your last name back at the conference. Since you're from New York I figured you were Frank Gordon's son," she said, turning her head away. "From the press photos I've seen, you look like him."

"Actually, we don't look alike at all. Some say I have a few of my mother's features, but even that's a stretch if you ask me," Alec responded, staring at an empty prison cell not much bigger than a large walk-in closet. "But yes, Frank Gordon is my father, and CEO of Gordon Investment Management, which you obviously knew...."

Alec sullenly wandered off, rejoining the tour group. Nat followed but remained silent. They listened to the tour guide tell the story of the only successful escape off the Rock in its twenty-nine-year history. The three escapees created dummy heads that fooled the guards during their rounds one night, which gave the prisoners plenty of time to make their break. No trace of them was ever found, and the case file on their escape remains open to this day.

Alex jumped onto the Internet, researching Frank Gordon—fifty-two years old, living in New York, married, with one son; gives generously to a variety of cultural art charities throughout New York state; the firm he runs has been passed down through three generations dating back to 1946; on the board of three Fortune 100 companies; has received several honors including the key to the city; owns a New York Yankees Delta Skybox suite. *Ugh, I already don't like him … and look at those nose hairs … scary.*

"What do you think, Sundance, do you like this guy?" Alex said, contorting her face.

Sundance let out a couple of disapproving barks.

"Me neither," she said, pleased with Sundance's allegiance, bringing up GIM's website, scouring for information that would be helpful in hacking into the company's network so she could do a little digging of her own. *Let's see … yep, that's the same ugly logo I saw at the meeting the other night. Boy, he sure doesn't spend his money on Web design. You could do better, Sundance.* She tossed him a fresh carrot chunk. *Offices are in downtown Manhattan … that's a large number of IP addresses to search. Let's try to alter the URL and see if I can view the root directory of their web server. Bingo. They sure haven't secured their site very well. OK, let's open their back pages up and check out the source code. Nothing, nothing … really, seriously? That shouldn't be in here. I doubt I'm the first to break into this site. Their system administrator should be fired for that.*

Alex used some basic recon to figure out key bits of information that allowed her to easily hack into GIM's network. Much like their external website, their internal network was rife with poorly set-up configurations that wouldn't stop most "script kiddies," those wannabes who download hacker kits from the Internet, running them without doing any real work themselves. *Like buying a model car kit already built, then claiming you're an enthusiast.*

Over the next hour, she snooped around various computers that were connected to the network, getting the lay of the land, taking notes on their naming conventions. She found folders with financial-sounding titles in various directories, downloading any file that appeared worth reading through.

"This is quite novel," Alec said, spooning out a helping of New England–style clam chowder steaming from a large hollowed-out sourdough bread bowl while joggers, cyclists, speed walkers, and Rollerbladers moved in perpetual motion around them. The Golden Gate Bridge loomed spectacularly in the background.

"You like?" Nat asked.

Only small talk had taken place between them on the return trip from Alcatraz.

"Fashion the spoon out of a celery stick and you have a complete meal that leaves no trace of garbage behind," he replied, amused by the concept.

Nat laughed. "Are you always this easily entertained?"

"Man seems to go to great lengths to package everything. This is both eloquent in taste and ecology," he said, tearing a piece of bread off. "And if you're too full to finish the bowl, the pigeons hovering around us will most kindly digest the remainder."

Nat giggled some more. "Well, I'm glad you like it," she said, playfully bumping his shoulder with hers. "Sorry about back there, on the tour, bringing your father up."

"It was a knee-jerk reaction. It's not your fault," he said, relieved he hadn't turned her off with his mood shift. "I get that often. 'Why aren't you working for the family business, helping the old man out?'" He chewed on a moistened piece of bread as the sun dropped behind the Marin Headlands Open Space Preserve that towered over the Golden Gate Bridge from behind, silhouetting the bridge whose lights had come on, outlining the sweeping suspension girders and majestic twin columns.

"Finance, business, investing … didn't interest me," Alec continued. "I watched my dad pitch his investment packages to prospective clients when I was in grade school, and he always came across like a used-car salesman. After the group would leave, whether they invested or not, he'd have some sarcastic comment to say about them; like he had somehow pulled the wool over their eyes."

Alec tossed shredded pieces of his bread bowl to a grateful swarm of pigeons that enthusiastically pecked at the treats.

"I don't remember my grandfather having that type of relationship or rapport with clients. He used to treat them like family, just as his father had when he founded the firm. Anyway, I wasn't interested in managing the business, because I figured if that's the way the investment world worked, then it wasn't for me."

Leaned up against Alec, Nat sipped her soda as he expressed his desire to do more for humanity than add extra commas to their bottom line. He drew Nat in closer, his arm wrapped around her shoulder. "In high school, I watched this MSNBC special on TV about some middle-class families who'd had their life savings stolen by hackers. The police couldn't do anything about it, and the bank wouldn't do anything to help them. It made me mad that somebody could sit in the cozy confines of their bedroom behind a computer in total anonymity and ruin someone's life so easily and quickly. Later I found an article on cybercriminology, and I knew that's what I wanted to pursue."

Alec surprised himself by how much he was opening up to her concerning the challenged relationship he had with his dad, and his career choice and aspirations. He enjoyed the way she leaned against him, her eyes never leaving his, there on the water's edge of the Bay, at sunset.

So this is what they mean by leaving your heart in San Francisco.

A ding sounded on Alex's laptop; the "SaveMyHome" script had completed. She pored over the list of 321 homeowners whose mortgages were upside down, but because they were working and paying their mortgage, the bank refused to modify their loan to ease the pressure of the balloon payments that had begun or were about to. *Why help someone who is already paying them?* The homeowners all shared the same traits: minimal qualifications, set up with a risky mortgage, but now they were paying for it through the nose.

Alex took the list, transferred the unique identifiers for each account to a spreadsheet, and linked it to a script whose algorithm would set up new mortgage terms, resetting them with the bank's latest prime lending rate. Once complete, 321 homeowners would breathe a sigh of relief without making a single phone call.

Alex groaned when she remembered she hadn't logged off from GIM's network during her American Bank escapade. *Not good to leave a connection open like that. At least it's the middle of the night in New York.* She located and noted the last update time on the log files that tracked user activity, set the system clock to a minute earlier, opened the files, and deleted the lines of text that had recorded her presence. She then reset the clock back to the current time. *I was never here.*

Alex's cell phone chimed a couple of times; a text message came in from Nathalie. She blushed when she read the message: "Are your hands busy?"

"What do you think, Sundance … should I reply to Nathalie?" Alex asked, blowing kisses his way. Sundance perked his head up, sporting a big grin and panting.

"Good answer," she said, typing her reply as she giggled, "Very. They're moving a mile a minute."

"Slow down there quick-key."

"What you need a helmet?"

"Touché. Thanks for the hot dog last night."

"No problem. You know your way around a putt-putt course."

"Not my first time."

"It was for me."

"I know. That's why I took it easy on you."

"Want to do it again."

"Of course."

"I have a question about GIM too."

"Busy hands indeed. I'll call you when I get back into town. Night."

"OK."

Alex reread the text-message conversation. *Hmmmmm, interesting.*

Nat tenderly traced the outline of the long, jagged scar on Alec's left shoulder that extended several inches down onto his arm as they lay intertwined, naked on the couch in his hotel room, drifting in and out of sleep. "How'd you get this?"

After their day on the Bay, Nat had taken him back to his hotel, but when they arrived, he didn't want the evening to end. He had thoroughly enjoyed her company throughout the afternoon and evening, persuading her to stay for a drink and a dip in the Jacuzzi. "Car accident, when I was a baby. My parents were driving home one night and were sideswiped by a drunk driver, so they tell me. I was too young to remember it."

Alec's cell phone burst into rings, startling their blissful state. *It's well past his bedtime.* "What's wrong, Father? Is everything all right?"

"Where are you?" Frank's voice sounded panicky. "I need you to come by the office."

Alec sighed. "I'm in San Francisco. I told you the other day I would be out of town for a few days at—"

"I don't recall that."

"You asked me if I could drop by the house, and I said … never mind," he replied, taking a deep breath in through his nostrils. "Why are you calling?"

"I just received a call from Sam down at the office. He was working late updating the software on the—"

"It's about time. I've been harping on you for the last six months to get that patch in place. Your network is—"

"Alec, half of what you talk about I don't understand."

Alec shook his head as he watched Nat get up and slip on a robe.

"Just listen. Sam said while he was on one of the computers he saw someone erasing information from a log file, whatever that means, and then they changed the time on the computer."

Alec perked up. *Someone took the time to erase log file data and change the system clock so it wouldn't be detected? That's pretty slick. Most hackers, even the stealthiest, don't bother going that far. They have other ways to minimize their presence, but even their digital footprints are left in log files. Clever.*

"Did Sam run diagnostics on the network to see if any virus or Trojan was left behind or launched?" Alec asked, grinning at Nat as she picked up the box of Trojan condoms they'd purchased at the hotel gift shop, shaking it for effect. *Damn, she's looks great in that robe. Certainly too sexy to call her by her nickname.*

"Yes. He said nothing came up. It's clean."

"Then I wouldn't worry about it," Alec said, no longer interested in his dad's benign problem. "Systems are constantly being probed by hackers searching for old versions of software they can exploit. They obviously found GIM's and dropped in to snoop around. If they didn't sabotage or leave anything behind then I wouldn't—"

"I want you to stop by when you get back into town and investigate. That is what you do, right?"

Alec picked up on the condescending tone. "I investigate cybercrime, Father, and one innocuous breach on an antiquated system chock-full of holes doesn't constitute grounds for opening a case. Patch up the system and you'll be fine," Alec said with more grit in his words than he normally directed at his dad. "Besides, I'm not the head of the CCEA, and Henry isn't going to allocate resources based on so little—"

"When do you get back?"

"Thursday."

"Stop by the office around noon."

Alec surrendered. "Fine," he said, simply wishing to get off the phone and back to Nat, seductively posed on the bed, the robe exposing her long legs and molded tightly over her breasts.

Alec hung up the phone and ambled over to her, planting a sensual kiss on her lips. "Don't move a muscle, Nathalie," he said, preferring to use her full name, which rolled off his tongue more smoothly than "Nat." "I'll be right back."

When Alec left the room Nathalie picked up her cell phone and sent out a text message: "Are your hands busy?"

CLOSE ENCOUNTERS

Alec squinted through the gift-shop sunglasses he'd purchased on his way to Alcatraz the day before, attempting to read the freeway sign that hung from the overpass, but neither the sunglasses nor rental-car windshield did anything to cut the glare of the sun pouring through. He made matters worse by accidentally turning on the wipers, smearing seagull droppings across it. *Dammit, I'm already lost. The man at the concierge desk made it seem so easy: get on the 101 freeway southbound; it'll take you straight into San Jose. But Nathalie said to take the 280, less traffic into downtown....*

Alec had decided to take the 280, but upon leaving the city he found himself swallowed up by the midmorning commute, shunted to the wrong lane that placed him southbound on the 101. *Driving the freeways out here is crazy. No wonder Nathalie prefers her motorcycle over cars.* Alec didn't get outside New York City proper much, at least not by car. Navigating the West Coast freeways in a rental he wasn't comfortable with made matters worse. The car's GPS unit he'd upgraded to would save him, so he hoped, but instead squawked out confusing directions amid exasperated "rerouting now" commands.

Despite resigning himself to trust the concierge's directions, he could see signs ahead indicating 280 loomed again as an option. *Do I stay on the 101? Do both freeways end up there?* After the fiasco in the city he wasn't sure what lane to pick, and the sun played havoc with his vision, confusing him about the upcoming freeway split.

Frustrated, he tossed the hotel's abstract map into the backseat, taking the next off-ramp. Removed from the freeway, no longer required to make quick decisions at sixty-five miles per hour while cars rushed by even faster, Alec glanced around for a place to stop, collect his thoughts, and eat something—anything. He spotted a New York City–themed deli on the other side of the street, but unless he could cut across three lanes in less than fifty yards that wasn't going to happen. Instead, he made the right-hand turn local traffic engineers strongly encouraged him to make. *This is nuts!*

He pulled into the first parking lot he came to, pleasantly surprised to find a charming grocery market. Outside the rental car he stood arching his back, releasing the tension in his neck and shoulders, staring up at the signage over the entrance: MAGGIE'S ORGANIC MARKET. *Hopefully, they sell more than wheatgrass and tofu.*

Alec wandered in, greeted immediately by an older woman working the checkout stand. "Hi there, stranger." Her effervescent mood jarred his senses, so soon after his chaotic freeway experience.

"Hi," he said, cautiously entering, peering around, half expecting the smell of burning incense and Janis Joplin playing in the background.

"Beautiful morning out, isn't it?"

"If you're not behind the wheel attempting to go somewhere, I suppose it is," he replied, approaching the woman, whose name tag read Maggie, optimistic about his prospects of finding food and directions to San Jose. "Do you have a deli department? I'm starving and would like a sandwich, preferably with something that had parents at some point in its life cycle."

Maggie chuckled at Alec's apprehensive wit. "Honey, organic doesn't mean vegetarians grazing on roots and sprouts." She chuckled some more. "It means the food comes from organic farming methods, grown without the use of chemicals. You must be from out of town."

"New York. I haven't been exposed to the organic-food movement."

"Well, you're in for a treat today," Maggie began, pride in her delivery. "Once a month, my husband hand makes a batch of sausages, stuffing them with a special family seasoning recipe, and then we grill them up for you out back. Toss in some chips or pasta salad, something to drink, and for eight dollars it's the best-tasting deal in town. My daughter is out back right now firing up the grill."

"Say no more. I'll take two links."

As Maggie rang up the sale she answered the store phone, "Hello, Maggie's Market. How can I make your day better?" and handed Alec his change and receipt, whispering to him how to find the grill.

I think I can handle those directions. Just follow the aroma.

Alec stepped out back into a fragrant cloud of smoke wafting up from the grill, where plump, seasoned links sizzled. *Maggie was right; they sure smell good.* He shook an all-natural, mango smoothie carton, popping the top to quench his thirst. Through the thin haze that filled the enclosed garden patio he could see a young woman busily organizing stacks of crates.

"Are you the daughter?" he asked, not sure she was. Based on his surmised age of the mom, the daughter would be ten or more years older than she appeared.

"Yeah. You here for lunch?" she replied with her back to him.

"Yes. I ordered two links."

"It'll be a few more minutes."

"No rush. I'm lost anyway."

"Aren't we all," she said, straightening up, rolling over the dozen links on the grill with one efficient swipe of the tongs.

"Impressive," Alec said, watching each link settle into an adjoining slat.

"Do you have your ticket?"

"Yes." He handed it through the smoky barrier. "Do your sunglasses help with the bright sun?"

"My sunnies, yeah. Can't live without them."

"Mine don't seem to help at all. I'm more blinded with them on than without." He fiddled with the pair in the intense sunlight flickering through the surrounding trees while dodging the aromatic plume from the grill that shadowed his every move.

"They're probably cheap, don't have good tint or UV," she said, opening up a bag of soft sourdough rolls.

"I picked them up on the Wharf in San Francisco."

"That'd explain it … tourist glasses."

"You attend Stanford?" Alec asked, noticing the Stanford Cardinals shirt she had on, surprised she was wearing long sleeves on such a warm day, especially working alongside the grill.

"Yeah. For now, anyway. Third year."

"What are you studying?"

"Poly-sci."

"Bold choice. Thoughts on what you'll do with it?"

"Maybe something in business, or in nonprofit," Alex explained, shooting furtive glances his way. "What do you do … school, job?"

"Like you, both. I'm studying cybercriminology at John Jay College—"

Crash!

"Arggggggggggh," Alex groaned as she jumped away from the falling crate of sausages she'd lost her grip on, fixing an alarmed glare on Alec.

"Are you OK?"

"No, yeah, I'm fine," she said, picking up the crate, storing it out of the way. "At least it wasn't milk."

Alex quickly scooped a couple links off the grill, tucked them neatly into the roll slits, and handed them to Alec on a compostable plate. "All the fixings are over on the stand, and there are some picnic tables around the corner," she said, retreating inside the store.

Alec grinned. *Something I said?*

Content with a happy belly, Alec tossed his trash away, ready to take on California's road system again. "Thanks for the lunch," he said to Alex, still tending the grill. "Tell your father the links were great."

"OK."

"My name is Alec, by the way." He extended a hand across the smoky grill.

"Alex."

As their hands met, her delicate grasp caused his head and neck to tingle, disorienting him briefly with a moment of déja vu, their perplexed stares reflected in the other's sunglasses, the handclasp lasting longer than one would expect for a casual introduction. Alec released first, while Alex lowered her head, shuffling the links around.

That was weird. A few moments passed before Alec spoke as a couple customers appeared on the patio, ready to collect their lunch. "Do you know the way to San Jose?"

"Ha-ha, funny."

"Funny? No, seriously, do you?"

"Ah, yeah, but my mom can help you out. She's up front at the checkout stand."

"Thanks," he said, exiting the patio. "Be careful of those wild crates."

"Buy better sunnies next time."

He smiled and nodded. *Cute.*

"Maggie, the lunch was great," Alec said, approaching the checkout stand and rubbing his belly. "Thank you."

"Well, I'm glad you enjoyed it. Tell all your New York friends about us."

"Your daughter seemed nervous around me. She dropped a crate."

"Oh, Alex, she's pretty shy around most people," Maggie said in a hushed voice. "And she's a bit of a klutz. Just the other day she dropped a quart of milk right here where I'm standing. She takes after me, though … I do the same thing. She prefers working in the stockroom and avoiding crowds."

"Understandable," Alec replied, passing off the subtext he'd observed as nothing more than a hazard of his job, similar to when someone announces they're an English professor and soon those nearby channel Shakespearean prose or clam up entirely. "Could you point me in the right direction to San Jose from here? I've gotten turned around between the 101 and 280."

"Why sure, hon," she said, pulling out a scrap piece of paper. "Where in San Jose?"

Alex handed the customers their lunch, then checked the door where the man whom she'd shook hands with disappeared. *That was weird.* She didn't know what to make of Alec when he mentioned his college major in cybercriminology; she wasn't even aware of such a degree. That she'd even spoken to him long enough to find out was surprising. She rarely took conversations beyond the point of *Did you find everything you needed?* while working. With him she lacked the self-conscious, often awkward dialogue she generally displayed with those she didn't know. Casual banter was not her strong suit. His chattiness, while annoying at first, didn't bother her all that much, though she wasn't sure why. It seemed familiar in some strange way.

Then there was the handshake, a fuzzy moment of confusion, her mind blanked as if she'd forgotten something. Dropping the food crate at the discovery of his career track quickly ended any further inquiry about him, where he lived or attended school, and the smoky exterior of the patio partially obscured a clear view of him. For all she knew, they may have shaken hands before at some function. Her parents knew many people, and her dad was always introducing Alex to eligible men despite her protests against such meddling.

Still, she wondered.

Alec stood in the naturally lit foyer of San Jose Technology Task Force's headquarters, perusing their wall exhibits of early forerunners to today's hackers. The first framed display featured Kevin Poulsen, aka Dark Dante, who back in the '80s had hacked into the FBI's database—five-year prison sentence and now tracks down cyberstalkers. Next to him John Draper, king of "phone phreaking," who in the '70s used a toy whistle from a Cap'n Crunch cereal box to make free long-distance phone calls—four months in prison and now a computer security specialist.

On the other wall hung Adrian Lamo, aka the homeless hacker, who from abandoned buildings hacked the likes of Microsoft, Yahoo!, MCI WorldCom and the *New York Times*, the last of which pressed charges that ultimately put Adrian on the fugitive list for six days before he turned himself in—six months' house arrest, two years' probation, and now a tech journalist. Adjacent to him, Kevin Mitnick, the most wanted hacker in the country back in the '90s, who stole proprietary software from Digital Equipment Corporation, hit cell-phone giants Nokia and Motorola, and even hacked a fellow hacker, who turned the tables on Kevin by teaming up with the FBI to track him down—served five years in prison and now writes books on his exploits and offers computer-security consulting services.

Not a bad career path if you don't mind a few years in prison. Earn your stripes hacking at an early age, get famous, get busted, serve your time, then get out and work on the other side of the fence from where you pilfered in your irresponsible, carefree youth. Something oddly poetic about it. Not many criminals come out with such job opportunities. Hard to keep a good hacker down, I would imagine.

"Alec," said Robert Tongner, whose energetic voice pitched above the incoming calls at the receptionist's command center as he approached, "it's a pleasure to meet you." He enthusiastically shook Alec's hand. "Your boss, Henry, speaks highly of you."

"Nice to meet you, as well," Alec replied, shifting gears mentally to match Robert's energy. "I like your place here. Much nicer than our office, which is more along the lines of cyber-gumshoe sleuths by comparison. And we're in Manhattan."

"When you're headquartered at the epicenter of computer technology, you'd better look the part or no one will take you seriously."

"Understandable," Alec said, turning his attention back to the exhibits. "Ever notice that all the well-known hackers of yesteryear and today are male?"

"You know, I hadn't," Robert said, scanning the posters as if long since blurred in his mind. "I wonder why that is."

"My theory is women are less prone to daring acts of bravado at the age when hackers get their starts. I think that will change as young women embrace technology. And they will bring to the table a different approach to hacking, one that is perceptually shrewd. They may even hack for good rather than evil."

"Interesting … My fourteen-year-old daughter only uses the computer to order items off Amazon and update her Facebook status. Hacking is not even a blip on her radar. Well, let's go inside and have a look around," Robert said, retreating to the security door he'd come through into the foyer. "We have a meeting with Karen Mickles at fourteen thirty hours sharp."

Alec lurched into motion, hanging a Visitor security badge around his neck as he caught up to Robert.

"And this is the War Room," Robert announced thirty minutes later as his handprint scanned on the large electronic pad that beeped its approval, the deep metallic click of the lock releasing, "or, as we like to call it, the 'Joshua' room after—"

"The movie *War Games* back in '83. I had a big crush on Ally Sheedy," Alec said.

"Who didn't?"

Robert showed Alec around, introducing him to colleagues focused on one particular task or another. Alec marveled at the advancements of cybercriminology on display before him, and the rapid growth of cybercrime task forces in general, having spawned from the need to bridge the gap between what the FBI preferred to pursue—cases that netted big payouts, often in the millions of dollars, or threats to national security—and local law enforcement, who were often ill suited and undermanned to handle such criminal cases.

The War Room played host to a handful of men and women all dressed like they might be selling life insurance over the phone rather than tediously tracking criminals who lived and breathed on the Internet, leaving subtle and not-so-subtle footprints in the form of data. They toiled at sterile workstations, operating specialized equipment and software to recover data from confiscated hard drives that had been purposely destroyed or wiped clean. Others posed as cyberthieves in known chat rooms frequented by hackers to sniff out information. Alec stood with awestruck eyes absorbing the highly specialized nature of the task force and the immense amount of resources at their disposal, inspired that one day he, too, would move up to the world-class level of cybercriminology.

At fourteen thirty hours sharp Alec was glancing over the list of hacker names and their known aliases that Karen had handed him. Karen Mickles had been tasked with the high-profile job of protecting Silicon Valley's most prized assets against cyber threats near and far. Her background and qualifications were impressive in Alec's opinion, but the undertones he'd picked up around the building during Robert's tour told him others were not as impressed.

"See any familiar names on the list?" Karen asked, spreading out a stack of folders she'd brought in for the meeting. Robert had informed him she was a no-nonsense person who got straight to the point in any conversation. Her conservative attire, pulled-back hair, and tattoo of a coiled sidewinder with a dagger instead of a rattle on her right forearm from her days in Army intelligence suggested as much.

"Yes … these three," Alec replied, circling them before returning the sheet. "The last one recently hit our radar on an ever-expanding college fraternity of hackers." He passed her the Hacker 101 file.

Karen slid over the three files Alec had identified as well as punching them up onto the wall-sized plasma monitor at the front of the small private conference room off the War Room. "We think these two are working together but we're not a hundred percent sure," she said, drilling into the details of their exploits, most of which had touched computers in New York and

California, making it necessary to collaborate with other task forces specialized in interstate cyberespionage.

"My hunch, based on the grievous nature of the attacks, is that they are. Hackers used to work alone," Alec explained, distilling the profiling research he'd done for a paper, "The Hacker Mindset, Then and Now." "These days they work in groups. They are much more organized and dangerous that way."

"I agree. Since Samborg Corp. has their servers in New York as well as out here, we need to set up communications with your team so we can take the investigation to the next level."

"Agreed. I'll let Henry know," Alec replied. "As for the hacker fraternity, it's pretty much just for kicks with them at this point, but with its ever-expanding circle, including Stanford and Berkeley, it might be considered a feeder system into a larger entity. I'm working that angle at the moment."

"Interesting," Karen mused, viewing the data on the monitor. "It's inconsequential as far as technology theft is concerned, but you're right; if it's a feeder system, then having them on our radar out here makes sense. Keep us posted."

"Will do," Alec said, convinced she was the right person for the job over the other senior staff he'd met earlier. "I noticed an alias on the list that didn't have a real name associated to it," he continued as Karen reached the door to leave. "Wolf Eyes."

All eyes in the room turned to Karen as she paused with her hand on the door latch.

"Ever heard the code name before?" Her voice had an impatient ring to it.

"No."

"Then don't worry about it."

"I also noticed that it has a red threat_level associated with it, and known attacks in the greater New York metropolitan area. Sounds like something I'd be interested in."

Karen returned to the oval table and punched the profile up on the monitor, sliding the file over. The room collectively expired its held breath despite Karen's pursed lips and rigid stance.

Alec quickly gleaned the highlights. "Why hasn't this been brought to our attention before? Twenty-six attacks in New York City alone over the past two years. Dozens of others all over the country. Has anybody been notified?"

Karen stood over the table in the now-silent room, both hands placed firmly on the table, palms down, a thumb tapping out a regimented beat.

"We shared it with Henry last year, as a courtesy, but he felt, as did we, that it was not a priority," Karen said in a measured tone. "We also reached out to a half dozen other task forces and agencies throughout the US."

"And?"

"They all said the same thing as your boss: not a significant threat. And quite frankly I don't blame them."

Alec stared at Karen, contemplating how one hacker who'd been linked to hundreds of cyberattacks on small and large corporations across the country could *not* be considered a priority or threat. *Are they insane?!* "Why the hell not?"

"There's been no measurable monetary loss."

Alec started to respond, then paused; his words lacked comprehension to continue. "What?"

"The companies who reported the breaches have not found anything stolen, copied, sabotaged, et cetera. Nothing. One claimed some type of vigilante justice because money had been moved from one account to another, but the net loss totaled zero so it could've been a simple accounting error. Only one report suggested they traced the hacker's IP address to a block of addresses assigned to northern California. As far as I'm concerned it's a myth. Wolf_Eyes doesn't exist."

Alec digested the intrigue that was Wolf_Eyes, figuring Karen had finished discussing the subject, only to hear her continue on with the theory.

"I believe these companies, since there is no connection or pattern among them, and no obvious motive, are simply making up the attacks, then filing insurance claims for compensation or to cover up their inept network administration."

Alec's disbelief morphed into a smile as Karen concluded her insurance-scam theory. *Sure wouldn't be the first time insurance fraud took place. It's simply reinvented itself, keeping step in the twenty-first century. I'll have to ask Nathalie more about the insurance process with cybercrime.*

"All the same," he said, "I'd like to take this file with me. I noticed some interesting comments in a couple of the report summaries."

"Suit yourself," she said, gathering her stuff and clearing the monitor. "But I wouldn't spend much time on it," she continued as she opened the door to leave. "You'll be chasing a figment of your imagination."

 # Read Between the Lines

"Hey, Mom," Alex said, bouncing through the kitchen door at home with Nathalie in tow, "you remember Nathalie?"

"Well, hi, Nathalie." Her mom's greeting was congenial as always. "Nice to see you again."

"You too. I love your home."

"Thanks. It's simple … just the way we like life."

"Mom, Nathalie is going to catch me up on the Fine Arts class notes I missed out on."

"Of course, honey," Maggie replied. "I'm baking some fresh cookies. They're in the oven right now."

"Yum," Nathalie and Alex chimed in unison. "Jinx," they echoed, still at a stalemate.

"Jinx!" Alex quickly added, winning the battle.

"You two are like twins." Maggie laughed. "Go be students and I'll bring in the cookies and milk when they're ready."

"Are you sure you want to have milk around this one?" Nathalie asked Maggie, rolling her eyes toward Alex.

"Hey," Alex groaned in protest, her cheeks turning red, pushing Nathalie by the shoulder. Maggie chuckled even though Alex hadn't told her mom how she came to drop the milk at the checkout counter, just that she had.

Sundance heard the sound of Alex's voice, and pounced to greet her. "Who's the good boy?" She smothered his snout with kisses, scratching his floppy ears. "Let's go."

Maggie watched the women run off behind Sundance like two teenagers on summer break.

Nathalie took up residence in the oversized bean bag that dominated what floor space was left after the bed, dresser, and desk had staked their claims. "Let's play a game," she said, grinning as she grabbed the controller off the desk, "of *Alex Andra.*"

Alex shot her an annoyed look. "It's not called *Alex Andra.* That's my avatar's name. The online game is called Tamm—" She shook her head after hearing it out loud.

"Whatever, I want to see her in that outfit again. Sexy, tough, ready to kick some ass."

Alex blushed, snatching the controller from Nathalie. "I'll sic Sundance on you."

"I thought Andra fought her own battles."

Alex threw a legal pad at her. "Zip it or you don't get any cookies."

Nathalie sealed her lips with a pretend key, tossing it into the air.

"So ... I did some digging around on the Internet and found GIM's investment strategies, but I don't know how to interpret them," Alex said, settling down next to Nathalie, spreading printouts across her lap of the files she downloaded from their servers. "I thought you could take a look at them to see if there are any red flags."

Nathalie glanced at a few of the documents, which presented nothing more than one might find on a stock search engine for balance sheets and profit-and-loss statements. Digging deeper into the pile she came across financial information not readily available unless a person subscribed to expensive financial services—usually reserved for big firms—or they had direct access to them through the company itself.

"These are client statements showing the flow of money in and out of GIM over the past several years," Nathalie weighed in. "Where did you get these, Alex? This type of info doesn't come in their annual report to shareholders. This here," she said, pointing to a thick, bound stack of documents, "is their client list, with position and investment allocations." Nathalie dropped the stack, her eyes focused sharply on Alex. "Well?"

Alex stayed quiet as a knot formed in the pit of her stomach, contemplating how she should explain the GIM hack without admitting anything.

"Alex, this is privileged info. You must know someone on the inside to have—"

"Not exactly," Alex said, realizing she hadn't given any thought on what to say to Nathalie if the question came up. "There are ways you can go online and—"

"You're a hacker!" Nathalie blurted out, folding her arms across her chest.

Alex sat motionless, her eyes darting back and forth between Nathalie's piercing stare and Sundance's slumber-induced eye flutter, the knot in her stomach tightening. She feared she'd put a damper on their budding friendship by exposing herself as a hacker.

"Cookie time," Alex's mom announced, breaking the silent tension when she popped into the room bearing a plate of freshly baked chocolate-chip cookies. Sundance barked his approval.

"Looks good, Mom," Alex said softly, clearing some room on the table next to where the women were sitting. "Thanks."

"Well, you girls look busy, so I'll let you be. Enjoy."

Alex quickly took a cookie and dunked it in the glass of milk she'd grabbed from the serving tray.

"Makes sense," Nathalie started back in, unfolding her arms, waving them around Alex's room. "You have some pretty sophisticated computer equipment in here. I read the article at the store about your innovative software. You're a computer wiz, shy, don't get out much, and somehow come up with sensitive financial documents. Makes sense that you're a—"

"Yes," Alex confessed, like a kid admitting they'd broke the lamp in the living room after days of trying to cover it up. She offered a cookie to Nathalie. "I got into GIM's network and did a little poking—"

"What's your hacker name?"

No person on the planet had ever put a face to her code name. She didn't know what Nathalie would do with the knowledge. Alex slowly nibbled on her cookie, deciding on what she should say, slowly forming the name in her mind. "CyberOwl," she said softly, her wolf eyes frozen on Nathalie's reaction.

Nathalie accepted the cookie, dunking it into the milk for a few moments, her eyes staring into the glass. "Well," she said, pulling the cookie out, "aren't you Little Miss Cyber-Mysterious." She bit into the moistened cookie. "This isn't soy milk," she added, laughing, moistened crumbs tumbling down her fitted shirt.

Alex nervously laughed along. "Now who's the messy one?"

"You should've seen the look on your face," Nathalie said, cracking a huge grin that turned into a hearty laugh.

Alex's face lit up. "Not funny!" She flicked milk at Nathalie, the stomach knot replaced with fits of playful laughter, though her mind reeled from the corner she had nearly painted herself into as well as the improvised hacker name she now needed to keep track of.

"Gentlemen, this is the opportunity of your lifetime," Frank Gordon pledged to a small group of potential investors comprised of self-employed carpenters who'd made the long drive down from New Hampshire for the Thursday-evening meeting. "There's a saying on Wall Street: 'When there's blood in the streets, buy property.' And believe you me the streets are flowing crimson. This really is a no-brainer."

Frank Gordon stood six feet tall with thick black wavy hair, though the way he postured in his dark, immaculately pressed suit he appeared taller. His barrel chest, confident swagger, and gift of gab made him a formidable salesman when it came to convincing everyday investors to part with large sums of their hard-earned money. He'd taken over the family owned investment firm when his father, Jack, began experiencing health issues a few years back. Now the third man in the family to run granddaddy's business, Frank was bringing the firm into the twenty-first century, capitalizing on the innovative financial products and opportunities available in the marketplace; he was ambitious that way.

Donald Gordon, Frank's grandfather, opened the Gordon Investment Management firm in 1946, shortly after the conclusion of World War II. He envisioned an opportunity for soldiers returning home, to help them invest in the new economy and profit from the rebuilding taking place in the United States. His simple mission statement—help those who helped our country—appealed to a wide audience. Donald had studied finance in college, exhibiting a knack for investing for the long haul in the simple finance world that existed in the 1940s. Donald, and his son, Jack, thereafter, didn't promise investors vast riches; simply a better way to let their money grow beyond savings accounts and bonds. For Frank, the time had come to move the firm in a new direction for his current clients, and to attract new ones. His immediate success made him the latest darling on Wall Street, and the favorite of wealthy investors who formerly eschewed the more moderate gains the firm historically boasted. Frank had a fresh model and investors were buying into it.

"Are there any questions?" Frank asked the group, who murmured among themselves, taking in GIM's snazzy brochure, VLGF prospectus, and the small, simple room projecting Frank's giving nature through his charitable activities: pictures of him cutting ceremonial ribbons to break ground on new projects benefiting local artists, shaking hands with heads of various cultural art groups, and with local dignitaries who championed more art and music programs in New York schools.

There were no questions. "OK, then let me know by seven p.m. tonight how much you'd like to invest as a group. Remember, the window for this is small as we negotiate with the banks to purchase the toxic home loans in bulk. There are many other firms bidding on them, so we need to seize the moment or other investors will win out over you," he concluded, driving home the final point: Get in now or lose out to someone else.

The group of middle-aged carpenters who aspired to improve their lifestyle, or send kids off to college, or ensure a prosperous retirement shook Frank's hand before filing out from the room past Alec, who watched his dad make the type of pitch he'd come to despise. *I wonder what type of snide remark he'll make about this group.*

"Alec," Frank said, motioning him over, "we had another attack last night."

"Nice to see you too, Father," Alec said, smirking over Frank's blunt greeting. "When did you get into the bulk home-buying business?"

"Back in '08, when the banks were a mess. Remember the trip we took to Vegas? It's brilliant. They write off their bad debt and we make money off the likes of those who whittle wood for a living."

And there it is. "Father, they are more than that. They work hard at their craft—"

"Sure, sure," Frank said mindlessly, searching his desk for the log report. "Sam said it came in around one a.m."

Alec glanced at the report handed him without much focus. "Was there anything taken or otherwise disturbed?"

"Wouldn't it be in that report?"

"No. This merely shows when the hacker would've dropped in, and I don't even see—"

"Go talk to Sam. He can tell you what he saw."

"Saw?"

"Yeah, I told him to watch the system all night in case they came back."

Alec sighed, shaking his head. His dad's lack of basic technology knowledge exhausted him. "You don't need someone watching a computer twenty-four-seven." He started rubbing his forehead. "That's what the tracking software is—"

"Just talk to Sam. Get it sorted out. I'm trying to run an eight-hundred-million-dollar firm here. I can't have lazy computer nerds snooping around whenever the hell they feel like it."

Alec retreated from his father's moody presence, heading for the door. "Are we on for dinner with Mother tonight?" he asked. "Johnny's at eight?"

"We'll be there," Frank replied, reaching for the phone. "Don't be late."

Alec left the office, walking past the office admin, who gave him a consoling look, his gait the tired expression of striving for a closer connection with his father. *I never am, Dad.*

As best as Nathalie could discern, after poring over the assortment of documents Alex had randomly pilfered from GIM's servers, something seemed amiss; it just didn't jump out at her. She was able to corroborate George Orkan's findings as reported in *Insiders Business Review* several months earlier: investment returns and dividends appeared exceedingly higher than one might expect. She also observed that only certain accounts reaped the benefits of the high-dividend yields despite many more accounts holding similar positions.

Another oddity that stood out was an account called CharDons. It lacked the same structure and information as other client accounts and showed a high level of activity, filling up, then emptying out quickly. She couldn't tell what funded the account or where the money went once disbursed.

Then there was the VLGF, the fund Alex's parents had invested in with other WCOF members as a group a few years back; its lack of transparency muddled Nathalie's ability to delve into the inner workings to explain why so much money flowed in but little flowed out.

"Like some sort of Ponzi scheme?" Alex said, attempting to sum up Nathalie's review.

"Probably not, since there are real investments being made and securities on the books. Might incorporate an affinity scheme in some way, though, where groups are brought in like with the WCOF community. Could even be something where he shares profits with preferred clients and the rest are told the investment didn't pan out, like a pyramid scheme. I'm not sure."

"What other info do we need?" Alex asked, moving from the beanbag over to the desk chair, opening her laptop.

"We'll need to get a hold of the files that have information on the VLGF, for starters. We need to see how it's structured, its holdings … what are you doing?"

"Watch and learn," Alex said, shifting into overdrive, her grin mischievous and her wolf eyes conveying a thousand creative ideas.

"Yuri Aleksandrov?" Alec said with a curious tone when he walked into the small storage room that acted as all things information technology at GIM.

The kid spun around on the swivel chair. "Yes, sir!"

"How, or should I say, *what* are you doing?" Alec smiled, recognizing the Russian student he busted during the Hacker 101 case. "Do you remember me?"

"Oh, hey," Yuri replied, his eyes as wide and distraught-looking as they had appeared during their first encounter. "Did I do something wrong?"

"That depends," Alec toyed with him, "did you?"

"No, no, I haven't—"

"Relax. I'm just busting your chops." Alec grinned as the kid's face slackened. "What are you doing here, though?"

"Mr. Gordon applied to the college to bring interns in for experience on company networks. I'm interning."

Of course he did. Dad doesn't spend a nickel unless it's dressed in a top hat. "Where's Sam? I need to talk to him."

"About the hacker?"

"Yes."

"Sam went home. He was up all night watching the servers."

"Did he tell you anything?"

"Yeah, just that he saw someone log on, scan for other users, then check the services that were running. He said it was quiet for a while, then he watched them change the system clock, clean up some log files, then reset the clock. That was it."

Same person as the other night. Interesting. Someone is actively checking out GIM. "Did Sam get the patches applied?"

"Yeah, but the hacker came in through the open port on the old web server."

Alec sighed. He knew Sam was not qualified for the role of system administrator. "What did the tracer file show?"

"Disabled."

"What?"

"Yeah, Sam said he enabled it, but when he went to look at the tracer file, it didn't show any activity. He looked at the service, but it was turned off. Very weird, since he didn't see the dude disable it."

Alec stood quiet a few moments, his thumb and index finger massaging his temples as he ran through the scenario. *How could someone disable a service undetected with the screen being watched? Perhaps Sam stepped away for a moment. Either way, we have nothing useful to review.* He took in a deep breath, then exhaled. "I'll touch base with Sam later," he said, turning to leave.

"OK."

Alec paused when he reached the doorway. "Ever heard of a hacker named Wolf_Eyes?"

"Sure," Yuri answered nonchalantly. "Pretty legendary. Most think his hacks are myths, since they're never reported in the newspapers, but some say they're for real. He pops on the HCR once in a while."

"Really? The Hacker Chat Room?" Alec was surprised in light of the conversation he recalled with Karen in San Jose. "Why do you think Wolf_Eyes has received so much credit if the hacks are never publicized?"

"Easy. Process of elimination. There are only so many hackers good enough to pull off what's been done and all but Wolf_Eyes have denied doing them. Hackers want recognition for their work."

"Have you chatted with him?"

"No. He chats mostly with another hacker called limeStone."

"Thanks," Alec said, keenly interested. "Stay out of trouble."

Alex's slender frame sat nearly motionless at the desk, her hands the exception, feverishly tapping the black custom keyboard as if desperately swatting an annoying gnat, oblivious to Nathalie, a bundle of nerves pacing back and forth behind her. Her favorite musical group, Black Betty and the Bad Habits, filled the room with Janis Joplin–esque, soul-inspired lyrics fused with alternative rhythms, camouflaging the clickety-clack of the keyboard. The current track playing, "Vigilante," was no coincidence.

The monitor's brightness cast an eerie glow upon the otherwise dark bedroom as night fell. Alex's intensely focused face appeared ghostly. Her amber-colored wolf eyes meticulously scanned lines of stealth programming code rapidly filling the black command window open on the laptop. She paused a moment to dunk the last of the homemade cookies, turned toward Nathalie, who fretted and chewed on her fingernails, and offered her one last chance for a warm, milked soaked cookie; Nathalie waved off the offering. Alex grinned, shrugged, and downed it, giving Nathalie a clownish come-hither look. Nathalie stopped pacing long enough to laugh, shaking her head at Alex's impish gesture.

Alex resumed typing, her body wiggling in rhythm with the music. Nathalie tenderly rubbed Alex's shoulders through the sweatshirt she wore, watching her compile and bundle up the code that would spy on GIM's computer servers in New York City. The only thing left to do … give the Trojan Horse a name. Her hands held still, poised over the keys, pondering the possibilities. A devious smile formed as she tapped out *Scarab*.

Johnny's Steak House, whose doors opened in 1963 in midtown Manhattan, exuded fine dining for the movers and shakers of the investing world. Anybody searching for new investment opportunities could easily score a business card or two for the cost of a reservation or buying someone a drink at the lavish bar. Alec didn't care much for the starchy atmosphere with its white table linens and neatly pressed and creased white tented napkins, but that's where his father enjoyed going for their once-a-month "family" dinner.

Frank's rise in the financial world was discernible in the subtle pecking order where one dined in the restaurant. The heavy hitters took up residence against or near the immense 180-degree window overlooking Central Park. Farther removed, lesser-known yet still-sought-out names ate, while those seated on the fringe near the entrance, where the view consisted of bustling waitstaff and coat-check lines, indicated someone had either stepped in off the street without a reservation or had no clout in the industry whose rally flag bled green ink.

Frank's forefathers once held the admiration of Wall Street when they enjoyed an un-obstructive panoramic view of the park. Though still highly respected, their dining experience had slowly ebbed over the years as the tides of high-risk returns trumped reason and sound advice, especially during the dot-com era; GIM was risk-averse by design. Their dinners were rarely interrupted as the hedge-fund industry percolated and derivatives stepped into the picture, financial products the elder Gordons steered clear of, criticizing them as too complicated for the commoner to understand and therefore subject to abuse and misuse by those who oversaw them. Frank changed all that, boldly diving into the sea of complexity, his table reservation flowing closer and closer to the coveted horizon, proof of his intention.

"Hi, dear," Alec's mother, June, said, embracing him. "You look good. Must be that California air."

"Hi, Mother. How are you doing?"

"Oh, I'm doing fine. Busy as usual. Between your father's philanthropy efforts and preparing for Gordon Galleries' grand opening, I don't have a moment to myself," she said as Alec took her coat off. "Things should settle down after PAG next week."

"PAG?"

"Philanthropy Awards Gala. Your father has been nominated again. We have an extra ticket for you." She lowered her voice. "How was California, dear? Meet anyone special? I heard you stayed an extra day."

Alec glanced around the seating area to locate his father, without success. "No. I stayed the extra day to meet with the new task force in San Jose."

"Oh … well, that sounds nice too."

"Where's Father?"

June took the table napkin and placed it across her lap, making a few adjustments to it; a satisfied smile followed. "He ran into Jerry in the lounge," she said unemotionally.

Alec settled into his chair, shifted around for a more comfortable spot, and tugged at his shirt collar a couple of times, gazing glassy-eyed around the room full of Wall Street titans, their lack of austerity suffocating his disciplined perspective on life. He knew it made no sense, raised in a family of means yet didn't want to be swaddled in it. His mom told him he had a different, more nurturing soul; his dad told him he was simply rebelling and would one day embrace it, something Alec doubted.

"Alec, what did you find out about the situation at the office?" Frank asked as he stepped up to the table.

"Father, long time no see. My official report," Alec started off, playing along with Frank's straight-to-the-point tone, "is your network has more holes in it than a colander. An infant could crawl in there." He eventually got eye contact with his dad, zeroing in on the bottom line. "You need to hire an experienced system administrator. Sam is not capable part-time at twenty dollars an hour, and bringing interns in isn't the answer either."

Frank stared a few moments. His eyes appeared to search for something other than critical analysis. "OK, we'll talk about it later. Is everybody ready to order?"

Alec smirked. He knew what that meant: *Fix my problem for me.*

Alec sat quietly while his dad left the table every ten minutes to work the room like a politician stumping for reelection. *He is good at what he does ... I do admire that.* At one point during dinner, Alec brought up the Hacker 101 case he spearheaded, cracking it wide open, even uncovering a West Coast connection. It made the local paper's Technology section.

"Oh yeah," his father said, chewing through an overpriced porterhouse steak. "Glad to see you're keeping crime off the streets. Oh wait, they're already off the streets." He finished his usual glib remark with a chuckle.

"Now, Frank." June shook her head, pursing her lips. She placed a hand on Alec's forearm. "That sounds wonderful, Alec. We think you're doing a marvelous—"

"You should put that talent to good use and find out who's stealing from us," Frank interrupted, wiping Worcester sauce off his bold chin.

"There was a break-in at the office?" June asked, alarmed at the news.

"No, Mother—"

"Yeah, and Alec would rather go off chasing college students playing pranks instead of finding a real criminal."

Alec knew the politics his father was playing. "No one broke into the office, Mother, just the network, and no harm came of it," he said, but it was too late; Frank had rushed over to greet an Asian man dressed like he could be a diplomat.

Alec's mom put her hand on his arm again. "Dear, your father is proud of you. He just doesn't know how to show it. He wants the same thing you do…."

"I know, but he belittles my work and studies, like they're some flight of fancy. Just once, I'd like to hear him say, 'Good job, son' without it coming off as some left-handed compliment," Alec said, watching his dad shake the dignitary's hand. "Even a handshake would suffice."

Alec fidgeted with his wineglass, staring at it blankly, after his mother excused herself to join Frank doing what they did best: kibitzing with other patrons. His cell phone vibrated on the table when a text message from an unfamiliar number arrived. *Area code 408?*

"When am I going to see you again?" the message read.

"Not sure who this is."

"Forgotten about me already have you?"

Nathalie. "Hardly. I wanted to call but I didn't have your number."

"Nice save. Good trip to SJ?"

"Yes though the freeways were interesting."

"Such a subway boy. I'll be in NY soon. See ya then?"

"Yes."

"Night. XOXO."

Alec smiled, adding the new number to his contacts list, assigning to it the romantic cell-phone photo he'd taken of them at sunset, the Golden Gate Bridge in the background. He swirled the remnants of the Pinot wine in the glass like she had showed him back at the hotel lounge in San Francisco, wondering why he felt smitten: *her beautiful blue eyes, flowing auburn hair, witty banter, sexy smile, smart as a whip, the way she looked in the hotel's white fluffy robe, the ankle bracelet* ... He couldn't decide.

"Scar ... ab?" Nathalie said phonetically while fiddling with her cell phone. "What the heck is that?"

"Ancient Egyptian dung beetle," Alex replied flatly.

"O-kaaay."

"It's a signature of sorts, a calling card."

"Won't they be able to trace it back to you then?"

"Please ... their server security is so lame. It took me all of fifteen minutes to get inside the first time. Even if they did try to track me, they'd be chasing their tails for years. Besides, if they're running some sort of investment scam, they aren't exactly going to run to the authorities."

"True," Nathalie said as she started pacing again, her cuticles enduring further damage.

"Relax." Alex opened up a homespun browser window on her laptop. "You ready?"

Nathalie stopped midstride. "You're going to do it *now*?"

"Yeah. What's gotten into you?" Alex said, quickly hacking into GIM's main server. *I'm surprised she's so tentative.*

"I'm not sure anymore. What if we're wrong and they're legit?"

"Trust me, no one in the financial sector is without some skeletons in their coffers."

"Nice one."

Alex grinned, opened up a couple DOS-based windows, and typed in several commands, prompting each window to flutter with scrolling rows of unintelligible code.

"Z-sharp?" Nathalie asked.

"You mean C-sharp?" She liked Nathalie's efforts to understand her cyber world. "No."

"Oh."

"It's HPL."

"HPL?"

"Hieroglyphic Programming Language."

"Now you're making stuff up."

"It's the *original* programming language, lost and forgotten. See my special keyboard?" She paused, showing Nathalie the keyboard with its unique layout, the letter keys emblazoned with hieroglyphics instead. "You know that trip I took to DC with the poly-sci class? I stayed behind a couple days and drove down to New York—"

"By yourself?"

"I went with a friend from high school, Billy Nordall. Besides, no one makes eye contact with you there. I felt like a stranger in a city of strangers. Anyway, I spent an afternoon going through the Met and they had this *huge* Egyptian exhibit. It was so cool. I wandered around the maze of walls that were covered from floor to ceiling with hieroglyphics."

"I love it when you talk geek," Nathalie said with a sultry whisper, opening a bottle of wine.

Alex pressed Enter on the keyboard, deploying Scarab.

The Morning After

Alec entered the CCEA offices early Friday morning as spring arrived in the New York region. Henry, CCEA's middle-aged director, sat at his desk staring at the monitor, watching a live cybercrime lecture, ears covered with antiquated headphones.

"Morning, Henry," Alec said, sensing Henry wasn't participating in the call. Alec admired Henry, not simply because he gave him the chance to work ahead of other more experienced applicants, but because Henry gave him a certain latitude, for a rookie, on hunches and theories that others scoffed at.

"There he is," Henry said, removing the headphones from his balding head to greet his star protégé. "Nice work on the Hacker 101 case. That one really opened up a hornets' nest and brought us some publicity. We've had an uptick of intruder attempts on our network since it appeared in the press."

"Thanks, Henry. They've even tried hacking mine at home. Guess it struck a nerve."

"It's like a game with them."

"I agree. You'll love this … my father brought in an intern, the guy I initially interrogated."

"That sounds about right," Henry said, shaking his head. Alec knew Henry didn't like his father much. The disdain partly contributed to him getting hired at CCEA—Frank's attitude toward Alec's career path was no secret to Henry. The rest of the disenchantment stemmed from Henry's past law-enforcement experience, the gut feeling he often developed regarding certain financiers on Wall Street. "How was the trip?"

"The conference was sparsely attended due to the funding issue. The lectures suffered as well, but there was one good topic I enjoyed. Vegas should be better."

"I would hope so. Damn DES can't seem to get their act together. Stunts like that really undermine the work we're trying to do. What'd you think of the task force in San Jose?"

"They sure have a lavish budget, and all the latest toys to show for it. I think their foyer alone is our yearly budget."

Henry laughed. "Yeah, they certainly are the apple of everyone's eye out there."

Alec restrained his grin. *Apple?* Henry was pun-challenged.

"What'd you think of Karen?"

"Commanding presence. No nonsense."

"She's tough as nails, all right."

"I touched a nerve when I inquired about one of the files … Wolf_Eyes."

Henry chuckled. "I thought it might. When I spoke with her before your visit, I told her to read you in. She wasn't too thrilled."

"Yes, I got that impression as well," Alec said, recounting the interaction for Henry, along with his surprise that Henry had renounced the prolific hacker as a threat.

Henry had been in law enforcement for many years before suffering a gunshot wound that rendered his left leg unfit for continued patrol work. The resultant desk assignment bored him to no end, motivating him to pursue cybercriminology, appeasing the detective in him, offering a more compelling career than shuffling papers and enduring the ambulatory precinct jokes that came his way.

Henry explained to Alec his initial alarm at the large number of Wolf_Eyes's hacks, but upon further investigation they failed to pan out. It seemed futile chasing someone who left little or no trace, claimed no responsibility, and as best as anyone could tell failed to profit from the breaches. As far as Henry was concerned, there had been a watershed moment, the first hack, that set into motion a convenient way for companies to blame a phantom every time they suffered network issues or benign hacks; they would simply blame it on the one person whom nobody knew, who would not come forward and say, "Yes, I, Wolf_Eyes, am responsible." Over time the myth simply grew, as did the reports.

"Karen thinks the companies cash in on insurance claims despite no monetary loss," Alec said.

"That wouldn't surprise me," Henry replied, putting the headphones back on. "I wouldn't spend much time looking into it. Like I said, I think Wolf_Eyes is a myth. But if there is anyone who can prove or disprove their existence, it's you."

"Thanks, Henry."

"Hey, before I jump back onto this call, what's this expense on your report for 'StealthWare,' annual subscription $999 a year?" Henry asked, settling back into his chair.

"The tracking software we've been searching for that wouldn't break the bank. I used it with great success on Hacker 101. Already paid for itself."

"Did you vet the vendor?"

"Yes, they checked out with the Better Business Bureau. Other small agencies have deployed it as well."

"Great. Be careful on how you use it, though. As evidence in the courtroom, things can get sticky."

"Way ahead of you."

"You always are."

The early morning sun filtered across the bed, where Alex stirred from the previous night's Trojan Horse launch and wine-induced slumber, something brushing against her face. She opened her eyes to find Sundance circling nearby, toting a wadded-up item in his mouth, the ingrained habit of Labrador retrievers. She sat up and swung her feet onto the floor, attempting to convince Sundance to stop being so coy with his gift. *He usually brings me my socks or one of his squeaky toys.* Alex rescued the now slobbery item; it was Nathalie's yellow shirt.

Alex jumped up, turning toward the bed; there lay Nathalie, topless, her back to Alex, the sheets draped over the lower portion of her body. At first Alex stared, recalling the events of the night before, how Nathalie came to be in the bed, sans top and wearing a pair of Alex's shorts; then she simply gazed at Nathalie's smooth naked back as it curved down to the shorts that clung to the outlines of her derrière before her legs disappeared under the sheets.

Sundance let out a hearty bark, startling Alex and waking Nathalie, who slowly rolled over, stretching her arms and legs. "Morning, sunshine." Nathalie yawned and turned on her side, not bothering to cover herself.

Alex tried unsuccessfully to avert her eyes, fascinated by Nathalie's uninhibited nature and supple breasts. Forever hampered by shyness and modesty, Alex's sexual curiosity had generally remained in check. There had been an awkward kiss during high school with her close friend Billy Nordall, and an amusing encounter with a foreign exchange student, whom she dared to show her *his* in the walk-in cooler at the store one summer evening. He complied in hopes of seeing *hers*, but Alex's giggling put a quick end to that. Though her laughter was nervous in nature, she ultimately found the imagery ascetically unappealing. Nathalie's semi-bare form, on the other hand, roused her curiosity.

"Did we ... um ..." Alex slowly stuttered, "experiment?"

Though Nathalie grinned, she shook her head.

 STONE SOUP NIGHT

Woodstock, where Phil and Maggie met during a mind altering mud fight, was just one of their many adventures together. They soaked in the natural movement of the day, including one summer before they opened Maggie's Market, when they stayed at a commune in Oregon and embraced living off the land as much as possible, keeping life simple while shunning possessions superfluous in nature. During Phil's Spartan college years—when he and Maggie shared a large home in constant need of repair in the hills overlooking Berkeley with a transient crowd of roommate vagabonds—Maggie would sell fresh produce they'd grown on the hillside in the backyard out of Phil's old VW bus on the side-streets near campus.

Inspired by the book *Stone Soup* by Marcia Brown, which Maggie had read as a kid, she would invite like-minded friends and friends of friends to their place during those meager years with the provision that guests bring something to toss into the oversized soup kettle. In keeping with the tradition for bringing others together to cooperate and live on the cheap, the kettle would fill as attendees arrived until it brimmed with an eclectic mixture of vegetables, spices, and other assorted wares of nature.

These days the tradition lives on at Phil and Maggie's home—one that could use a few repairs as well—though the contributions to the soup are less hallucinogenic than back in the day. The once-a-month affair generally attracted anywhere from ten to thirty hearty, fun-loving friends ranging from married couples and their children to those fortunate souls Maggie befriended at the store that day, giving them a small bag of vegetables to bring over.

Alex methodically worked her way around the large living room, setting out folding chairs while Sundance followed, giving each one a quick sniff. *What are you doing, boy?* "Will fifteen chairs be enough, Mom?" Alex asked, glancing at her wristwatch for the sixth time since she'd started helping out, unsure who or how many would be attending. She mostly tolerated these nights once the crowd arrived and settled into the festivities; until then she battled the apprehension by counting each chair as she unfolded it, the running tally less stressful to her as a number.

"Yeah, hon. I think it's going to be small tonight," her mom replied, placing the old rock she'd used for the first Stone Soup Night forty years ago into the large kettle, filling it with water. "Is your friend Nathalie going to come by? She seems nice."

"I don't know." Alex had forgotten to mention it the other morning, after they woke up together. "I'll send her a text."

"OK, hon." Maggie smiled, watching her daughter eagerly type out the text message. "I'm glad you found a new friend."

Alex knocked over a serving tray when she caught sight of her mom's smile. She righted the fallen item, then hastily completed her remaining set up duties, unsure if Maggie knew Nathalie had spent the night or not. Overnight guests weren't frowned-upon in the Smyth abode. Alex had been encouraged throughout childhood to have sleepovers. Unlike most kids, however, Alex never took advantage of it. During grade school, she once attended a sleepover at a schoolmate's house, but ended up coming home in the middle of the night after playing Truth or Dare. On a rare dare, she was to kiss Amy Fetters, a shy, bespectacled girl who smelled like toast all the time. Rather than go through with it, and suffer more ridicule at school, Alex walked home, clutching her pillow to her chest, crying most of the way.

Music and lively conversation filled the living room as the eclectic group of longtime friends caught up on the latest gossip in the community, fretted over the soured WCOF investment, debated the current state of politics in the country, and slowly drained by the spoonful the soup of the day.

"Hey, Doodle Bug," Alex's father said, hugging Alex as she rinsed her plate off in the sink. She grinned and appeared satisfied that she'd fulfilled her social obligations for the evening and could retreat to her bedroom.

"Doodle Bug," the pet name Phil had bestowed upon her at the age of five, came about one summer day when he entered her room as she lay on the bed. She'd discovered her mom's old art pads from the time when Maggie would sell sketches at weekend events on the square in Sonoma. Phil asked little Alex if she'd rather be outside playing. She expressed no such desire while doodling scenes of her and an imaginary brother, who beat up bullies for her on the playground at school. Phil noticed the numerous sketches neatly organized around the room and dubbed her his little Doodle Bug, which made her smile.

"Hey, Dad."

"We haven't had a chance to talk since the WCOF meeting," Phil said, grabbing a handful of grapes. "Your mom and I wanted to tell you together. We're very sorry."

"I know, Dad," Alex said, drying her hands. "Please don't apologize. It's not your fault, it's mine. I'm the one that begged to go to Stanford. It wasn't fair …"—a tear welled up—"for me to be such a …" Her words were no longer audible.

Phil reached out and hugged her close, his willingness to risk their financial security already a testament to how much he loved his daughter. "Don't cry, my little Doodle Bug," he said, stroking her hair buried in his shirt. "Don't think that way. We'll be all right. Remember"—he paused, leaning back so she could see his face—"what do we say about the glass?"

Alec wiped tears from her face. "It's always half full."

"And?"

She let out a snort of a laugh. "Things are never as bad as they seem."

"That's right," he said, squeezing her tight. "Now, go dry those eyes before we start playing Charades. Besides, Billy just arrived and he's been asking about you." He finished with a wink.

"Oh, Dad," Alex groaned, rolling her eyes.

Maggie walked into the kitchen carrying a serving tray full of dirty dishes and glasses. Alex gave her mom a peck on the cheek. "Love you, Mom."

"What did you promise her," Maggie asked Phil, who stood watching Alex make a beeline for her bedroom.

"Nothing," he replied wistfully. "She's so grown-up."

Maggie set the tray down, wrapped her arms around Phil and gave him a kiss. "She may not be our real daughter, but we raised her like our own. She'll always be your little girl."

The years since Woodstock passed by quickly for Phil and Maggie. Children had never been part of the plan until they both approached their fortieth birthdays, when their sentiment changed. Worried about pregnancy at Maggie's advanced maternal age, they spent the Christmas holidays soul-searching, agreeing that adoption would be the way to go, befitting their philosophy of helping others. When Alex came along they knew they'd made the right choice. She was a special gift, and her unique eye color made them feel blessed. They decided not to tell her about the adoption simply because they didn't want her to think she'd been left behind.

"Hey, Alex," Billy said, knocking on the partially open door to her bedroom.

"Oh hey, Billy," she replied, hurriedly closing screens and windows on her laptop. She'd been checking Scarab's progress on GIM's servers.

"Whatcha doing?"

"Ah … just reviewing the Trojan War for my Art History class."

"I heard about your senior year being up in the air."

"Yeah, we'll figure something out," she said, preferring to switch topics. "How are your studies going?"

"Good, good. I'm concentrating on computer science," he said, admiring Alex's computer equipment, "and I have a part-time job at Front Line Software Solutions, doing mostly database stuff, but occasionally they give me code development work."

"That's cool," Alex said, gazing at him and his tousled, curly blond hair sincerely for the first time since the night of their awkward kiss three years ago. Billy Nordall had lived down the street during grade school when they became buds, in part because he, too, was an introverted kid who once ate iceplant straight from the neighbor's yard, mistaking it for grapes, and in part because she made him promise never to mention anything about her eyes. He readily agreed—to avoid being punched by a girl and to have a friend—and they hung out during the long summers, messing around with old computers and playing virtual online games.

High school senior year, their platonic friendship took a turn when they each began to look at each other more curiously. One night at Billy's house, while his parents were out of town, Alex was showing him an algorithm she'd put together that compared all the students' grade-point averages at their high school with those from a rival school. As Billy leaned in closer to view her work their hands overlapped on the mouse, followed by a long moment while their eyes locked on each other. Alex leaned in to kiss him; their foreheads knocked, spawning laughter as they rubbed their aches. Sexual curiosity undaunted, they each took turns undressing, Billy going first at Alex's insistence. As he stood there tall and skinny like a beaker in his white briefs, she slipped off her shorts and long-sleeve shirt, then fumbled with her bra before it fell to the ground.

Alex trembled, butterflies fluttering in her stomach, standing semi-naked in front of someone other than her reflection in a mirror. She watched Billy's eyes take her in as probably the first time in his life that he'd seen breasts. Striking a taller pose, a confident grin emerged across Alex's curious face as the cool room air caressed her skin.

The moment didn't last long, however, when Billy's gaze drifted to the long, serrated scar on her right shoulder that spread wider as it cascaded onto her arm just above the elbow. Alex tensed, her eyes following his to her shoulder, holding her breath. It didn't matter that he'd seen it before, that he'd never teased her about it, she grabbed her shirt and shorts and ran from his bedroom, tormented by something she had no memory of occurring, tears starting to flow. Her mom had explained that it came about before she was old enough to remember, and to simply view it as a unique birthmark. Alex never adopted the notion, opting to wear long-sleeve tops year-round to conceal it, even during the hot summer days of Northern California when other kids sported tank tops and swimsuits.

"You should think about software development." Billy was still talking. "You're the best I've ever seen. I could get you a job down at the company I work for."

"Thanks, but I'm working full-time at the store."

"Wanna ... go out sometime?" he asked as Alex's cell phone chirped the arrival of a text message from Nathalie.

The message read, "Thanks, sweetie, but can't make soup night. Talk to you soon about our experiment…I mean project. XOXO."

Alex smiled to herself, stood up, and gave Billy a hug. "I have a lot on my plate right now, but thanks," she said, leaving the room to rejoin the festivities.

Dreams Are Made of These

Alec's body jerked violently from the sudden jolt that sent him spinning endlessly around and around like a top … a bright-orange light illuminated his face with a hot flash … he could see a young girl gazing at him with big eyes through broken glass; he reached for her but she faded from sight.

"Ahhhhhhh," Alec yelped, awakening in a cold sweat, steadying himself from the recurring dream that reminded him of the accident he'd been told he was in as a young child but couldn't consciously remember. Cassidy jumped up on the bed. "It's OK, boy," he said, patting the dog. Wide-awake a few hours before he would normally rise, Alec slipped on a sweatshirt and socks, and headed for the living room while Cassidy plunked his head on the bed, content to go on dreaming.

In addition to the dream stirring his subconscious, there was Nathalie, creeping into his mind like no other woman before. Checking his cell phone, he found a text message she'd sent during the night. The three-hour time difference put it in after he'd dozed off. "Thinking of you. Sweet Dreams. XOXO.

Staring at the cell-phone photo of them in San Francisco, Alec thought back to their pillow-talk the morning after they met, the back of her naked body molded serenely against his chest, enveloped in his arms. *Perhaps she's right. I should take a serious look into the hacks on GIM. For my dad. Maybe then he'll see what I do is worthwhile and not a computer fantasy game.*

To that end Alec ruminated on why someone was poking around GIM's network and servers. Yuri the intern had discovered a Trojan Horse labeled "Scarab," which marked a more deliberate attempt to gather information. Alec was well versed in the modern-day tech version of the Trojan Horse story from ancient Greek lore, designed to invade computers and lay in wait, surreptitiously gathering intel on an unsuspecting population entering login IDs and passwords, as well as for-your-eyes-only internal documents while they are read, written, and disseminated. Unlike a virus, whose aim is to destroy and wreak havoc on computer systems and networks, the Trojan quietly sits like a fly on the internal walls of the system, collecting and transmitting electronic thoughts and ideas.

It still didn't have enough teeth in it to open an official investigation, not that Henry would allow it in any case; Alec knew Henry's reservations about Frank, but more important the case lacked a credible threat, at least for the time being. Reverse-engineering the Trojan, he hoped, might give him some clues as to the nature of the hacker's intent.

Then, percolating in the recesses of his mind was Wolf_Eyes, the mysterious hacker extraordinaire who hacked for the pure pleasure of hacking, eschewing financial gain, at least for themselves. Some of the reports Alec read through suggested the attacks altered financial records, though after further investigation it was determined these same companies lacked adequate record-keeping systems and processes, making it hard to prove mischief.

Something happened, but they couldn't prove it. Like the log files at work. Is there a connection?

"Let's go," Nathalie said, striding through the door into Alex's bedroom just before noon.

Alex's arm twitched, knocking an open textbook off her desk.

"Pack an overnight bag. Time for some fun."

"What? No, I have one more class this afternoon and I need to finish this paper," Alex replied as Sundance stirred on the bed with the sudden change of energy in the room.

"OK, finish your paper. I'll pack for you," she said, finding a duffel bag in the closet. "E-mail your paper in and skip the class," she continued while searching through the vanity dresser. "Where's your swimsuit?"

"No, I need to go to class," Alex said, irritated with the way Nathalie directed her. "And I don't have a swimsuit." She refocused her attention on the paper.

"No suit! How do you show off that cute bod of yours at the beach?"

Alex snorted. "The beach ... no," she said as her fingers tapped out verbiage comparing and contrasting the causes, effects, and recovery strategies between the 1930s Great Depression and 2007's great economic implosion. "I don't do the beach."

"Not even with me?" Nathalie purred, leaning over Alex's shoulder.

Alex paused a moment, peering up at Nathalie, into her mesmerizing blue eyes, momentarily lost in them.

"Tell you what: attend your class and we'll go to Santa Cruz afterwards," Nathalie suggested, caressing Alex's covered shoulders. "You can buy a cool surfer-chick suit when we get there."

Alex didn't need to think about it; she wanted to go away with Nathalie. Her hesitation revolved around going to the beach and buying the swimsuit, something she always wanted, but with her shoulder scar avoided.

"OK, but I'm picking out the suit and you better not make fun of me or I'll have to hurt you," Alex said, shrugging off Nathalie's hands before resuming her keyboard dance.

"Deal."

Cassidy sauntered into the living room, midmorning light streaming into the airy loft decorated with assorted framed pictures of Alec's father and mother and himself on vacation when he was younger, and football and running action pictures from high school. The space had that Spartan college look, an assortment of furniture that didn't match—a well-worn leather couch without pillows; an oddly heavy coffee table made of dense wood; a three-tiered entertainment center comprised of cinder blocks supporting unvarnished shelving; and an oversized restaurant tabletop originally designed to seat seven or eight customers now repurposed as a desk placed atop two medium-sized bookshelves, which themselves played home to his array of networked computers, servers, and printers—yet was arranged in orderly fashion without appearing out of place, with the possible exception of the spin bike. It had a functional quality to it.

Alec was putting in the last few minutes on the bike, a textbook open on the handlebars; his days always started better with physical activity in them, stimulating his mental acuity for all manner of thought. On the whiteboard propped up on the small garage-sale-bought dining-room table, he'd spent the morning diagramming out bits and pieces of relevant information from the hundreds of case reports on Wolf_Eyes, gleaning any clues that would give him a glimpse into this person's psyche. So far nothing coalesced.

The intercom buzzed, interrupting Cassidy's futile morning ritual of sniffing around the kitchen floor searching for food bits. "Hello," Alec said, pressing the Talk button.

"It's Yuri, sir."

Alec buzzed him in. He knew he'd made the right decision in not prosecuting the college kid. He could tell that night during the interrogation that Yuri was scared, unwittingly sucked into something where he really didn't belong. The case netted far more malicious individuals, uncovering a wider network of fraternity hackers than previously imagined. The kid was obviously talented and could prove to be a valid ally. *He just needs to be put on the right path*

"Hi, sir," Yuri said, entering the loft, letting Cassidy give him a once-over sniff before the dog moved on to something more interesting.

"You don't need to call me sir. I'm not your father. Just call me Alec."

"OK."

"How are your studies coming along?" Alec asked, offering Yuri a glass of juice and a cream cheese covered bagel.

"Oh, thanks," Yuri replied, taking the breakfast. "They're going all right, I guess."

"I have something I want you to look over." Alec opened a screenshot of the code he had attempted to reverse-engineer from the Scarab Trojan. "Does this look familiar to you? It's the executable you found the other day."

The kid examined the strange code. "No. What is it?"

"I was hoping you could tell me. I decompiled it this morning. I don't recognize the language."

"Sure is wicked-looking. Does it work?"

"Yes. I loaded it on a test machine and it runs fine."

"Wow, pretty sick stuff. Imagine having a language no one knows about," Yuri said, smiling enviously until he caught Alec's reaction, then stiffening. "I mean … if …"

"No, you're right," Alec said, imagining the larger implication. "If you hear anything about this on the HCR, let me know, will you? I'll see if I can get you some side work with the task force if you're up for it."

"That'd be kewl, sir."

The Ducati serpentined its way across the Santa Cruz Mountains, the warm, arid air of the San Jose Basin giving way to the cooler breezes of the Pacific Ocean. Alex snuggled up tight against Nathalie, more relaxed than her first experience on the motorcycle, taking in the sights as they blurred by. Despite her initial trepidation of going to the beach, she now embraced it, the freedom and excitation, something she hadn't experienced in a long time. She couldn't put a finger on it, but she knew it had something to do with Nathalie.

Phil and Maggie had brought Alex to Santa Cruz many times when she was little, as most families in the Silicon Valley inevitably did during the beach-going summer months. Alex enjoyed those early trips, the freedom of running around in minimal clothing, letting the sand filter between her toes, splashing in the surf that flirted with and chased her along the shoreline, her laugh infectious, smile pure, Phil and Maggie vicariously living their younger, carefree days through Alex's eyes.

Then came the "awareness" years, as Phil and Maggie often referred to them in private conversation with close friends: when she noticed boys and boys noticed her. Adults fawned over young Alex, pointing out her beauty, but what she heard, the jeers about her eyes, her boyish name, her sizable scar, conveyed something else: different, outcast, undesirable. The beach became a torment to her; she balked whenever her parents suggested future trips. Alex hadn't been back since.

Nathalie swung the bike into the first surf shop she spotted once they reached the coastal highway on the outskirts of town. Alex's legs wobbled some after the hour-long ride, but she managed to remove her helmet without fanfare, her ears lightly buzzing.

"You were more comfortable this time," Nathalie commented.

"Yeah, that was fun," Alex replied, staring at the SURF SHACK sign tacked to the small weathered structure with dark, overlapping wood shingles that looked like it had been designed by Dr. Seuss, or by someone who was really high on life at the time. "Do we have to do this now?"

"That's the deal we made," Nathalie said, grabbing her purse. "Let's get you undressed for the beach."

Alex reluctantly followed Nathalie. *Time for green eggs and ham I am ... not.*

"How about this one?" Nathalie asked, lifting a hanger with a white two-piece bikini draped from it.

Alex stared at the frilly fringe that ruffled along the straps and across the cups. "Nooooo. Too Disney *Pocahontas*," she replied, less concerned about the fringe than the lack of coverage for her shoulders.

"You're right. You're too pale to pull off white," she said, putting it back and then thumbing through other choices.

Alex peered around the rows and rows of hanging taunts, searching for something, anything, that would suffice as beach wear, conceal the scar Nathalie knew nothing about, and end the uncomfortable shopping experience. Then, out of the corner of her eye she found the answer on a poster: some female surfing legend, her athletic body clad in a skin-tight, long-sleeved surf shirt with matching bikini bottoms. The top had a zipper that plunged down below her breasts. "For those longs days out in the salty water it is the perfect way to avoid board rash while paddling," read the caption underneath the sporty blonde.

"I want that one," Alex proclaimed, pointing to the poster, hopping up and down in place.

"Honey, that's not a swim—"

"Yes it is. You said I could buy a cool surfer-chick suit, and look," Alex continued, returning her attention to the poster, "cool surfer chick … she's ripping and curling and wearing it."

Nathalie stood shaking her head, staring at the poster, then at Alex, who looked exuberantly relieved. "Fine, but let's find another print."

Alex bounded off, searching for the rack with the answer to her physical insecurity.

"Ah, shibby choice, Little Grommet," the sandy-haired twentysomething rattled off in his Aussie accent as Alex laid her purchase on the counter. "This will keep you from getting nipped. You gonna hit the swells at glass-off? Should be hiddie."

Alex stared at the shirtless Surf Shack employee, clueless as to what he had uttered, admiring his bronze-colored muscular chest; it was a far cry from Billy Nordall's pasty-white scrawny torso.

"Ah … yeah, maybe," Alex replied.

"Bitchin'," he said, ringing up the sale. "If you're not noodled afterwards, head to the bonfire at the Point for some tasty lybations and grub. Queebs, trolls, and landsharks uninvited."

Alex signed the credit-card slip, working on something cool to say. "Aces." *Crap. Aces?* She admired the animated surfer, completely comfortable in only board shorts and speaking the way he did.

"Take a puck of Sex Wax for your stick," he said, handing Alex a pink, hockey-puck-shaped product. "It'll make your ride rad."

Alex took the cellophane-wrapped item and dropped it into her bag, unsure what to make of it.

"How 'bout you, Stretch?" he said, checking Nathalie out. "Your board need waxing?"

"I'm good, brah," Nathalie replied, smiling at the surfer as the two women left.

The quaint Victorian-styled bed-and-breakfast room Nathalie had reserved overlooked the Santa Cruz boardwalk and pier, where tourists and beachcombers meandered and seagulls dive-bombed scraps of food left behind. The room was small, just enough space to walk around the queen-sized bed piled high with variously sized pillows, which had matching nightstands, a small writing table lit by an antique fringed-covered lamp, and a gas fireplace with a gnarled log made of granite.

Alex had never stayed at a B&B, just the infrequent two- and three-star hotels her parents booked on trips, and the one field trip she took to DC during high school. The room appeared nice—a place newlyweds might stay on their honeymoon. A faint smile formed as she stared at the only bed in the room.

As Alex watched Nathalie slip out of her clothes without inhibition, despite the open drapes, and put on her idea of a swimsuit—a yellow two-piece whose bottom connected the front and back with colorful, laced beading that exposed the flesh of her hips—she wondered how someone became so comfortable with who they were, to the point of working without a shirt and talking in a foreign (albeit English) language like the guy at the surf place; or Nathalie, stripping naked in front of someone she'd only recently met. Alex never changed clothes in front of anyone, including gym class, where she would simply play in what she wore to school, skipping the showers afterward.

"What do you think?" Nathalie asked, tugging, pulling, and arranging various parts of the two-piece over her toned body.

"I like it," Alex replied, admiring the perfect color of yellow against Nathalie's olive skin, which appeared tan without her spending days worshipping the sun. "Someone's going want to wax your board, Stretch." Alex's face turned red immediately.

Nathalie laughed, placed her hands on her hips, and swayed them back and forth. "Why thank you, my Little Grommet."

Alex burst out laughing. "What the hell did that mean, anyway? I haven't heard so many words in one sentence I didn't understand since this Indian guy at school asked me a question after class one time." She continued laughing. "I'm like, buddy, I have no idea what you are saying … I think I heard the word 'cafeteria' somewhere in there but with his singsong voice I wasn't sure."

Laughing hard, Nathalie asked, "What'd you do?"

"I just smiled and pointed toward the exit of the building and got the hell out of there."

Both women lit up laughing.

"I'm hungry," Alex said, walking up the steps from the beach to the pier with Nathalie, slipping their sandals on.

"Me too. Let's grab something out there," Nathalie replied, gesturing toward the end of the pier. "You look good in your surfer outfit."

"Thanks. I like it, but it feels like the bottom is always creeping up my butt." Alex giggled, avoiding the temptation to tug at it in public.

"Naw, it's just showing off your cute butt curves."

Alex blushed, quickly making the necessary adjustments to it.

For a spring Friday, the pier was sparsely populated, except for the handful of fishermen with their poles leaned up against the tall railings, the lines taut down to the ocean's surface below. A few seagulls drifted lazily in the breeze overhead while others took up residence on railing tops, stalking little kids with ice-cream cones on the brink of toppling to the wooden planks.

Nathalie treated Alex to fresh fish and chips and a milk shake; more junk food in Alex's mind, but the tartar sauce and shake were tasty enough. As they soaked in the sun, they chatted about school, Alex's parents, and a little about the new information Alex had come by from Scarab. Mostly they people-watched and tossed crunchy bits of french fries to grateful pigeons lurking about while seals basked atop one another below the pier planks, their barks echoing up through open vents.

"How'd you end up doing financial planning?" Alex asked, biting into a fish chunk laden with sauce.

"Have a little fish with that tartar sauce," Nathalie said, grinning at the excess sauce perched on Alex's lip. "My dad was a financier." She wiped Alex's lip clean with a finger, then licked the same finger clean. "When I was little, he used to bring me into his office on Sundays when he did his week-ending bookwork. After I vacuumed, cleaned the break room, and took out the trash, he'd show me these big, thick ledgers with columns of financial transactions in them."

Nathalie paused a moment, subtly drawing in a breath of salty air through her nostrils.

"He'd tell me how important they were, that people trusted him with what he recorded in them. It fascinated me and I started helping him balance the columns. I liked how at the end of the day everything evened out. It was like you could rest easy at night because there was order in the world. So when it came time to go to college, I studied finance and accounting. It made sense to me."

"Is he still doing that?"

Nathalie took a deep drag on her straw. "No, he's retired."

Alex removed her sunnies as the sun dipped behind the fish-and-chips shack. "When did you graduate?" she asked, realizing that Nathalie already had her degree.

"Three years ago."

Alex nursed her milkshake, opting not to inquire about the Fine Arts class where they formally met; she preferred the mystery of Nathalie.

"I'm close to my dad too," Alex said, reflecting on the special bond. "He always told me I could be anything I wanted. He took me to some political rallies on the Berkeley campus when I was a kid. I used to ask him what the crowds were doing with all their shouting, slogans, and colorful posters, and he'd say they were questioning the status quo. 'You should always question and understand what's going on around you. You never know when it could save you,' he'd tell me."

"Amen to that," Nathalie said, standing up, tossing her leftovers into the trash bin. "Hey, let's grab a couple beach cruisers and bike down to Natural Bridges for the sunset. Then we can hit the bonfire."

"Aren't we going to look over the GIM data?" Alex asked, not interested in socializing with strange surfers who spoke a private language.

"There'll be plenty of time for that later," Nathalie said, giving Alex a pat on her bikini-clad bottom. "Tonight we're going to have fun."

"Thanks for the wedgie, Stretch."

PAG

New York's treasured landmark, the Prince George Ballroom, with its restored Neo-Renaissance ceilings elevated high over a palatial oak hardwood floor by heavy columns ornately steeped in gold cartouches and angels, was rivaled only by the vast crowd of dignitaries, celebrities, local politicians, and contributing donors for New York's Philanthropy Awards Gala held every spring to pay tribute to the previous year's biggest donors. One of the more hotly contested categories by some of New York's biggest names in the world of giving back was "Philanthropist of the Year," the award Frank Gordon cherished the most and had been nominated for.

The Gordons—patriarch Jack; Frank; his wife, June; and son, Alec—filed in with the hundreds of other well-dressed guests, Frank and June performing their usual networking as the service attendant escorted them to a reserved table near the presenting stage, where contending award nominees were corralled. Word on the street favored Frank as the frontrunner for Philanthropist of the Year honors. The previous year, for the first time, he'd been nominated, but like the handful of other nominees lost to Kenneth Perkins, who'd been a venerable juggernaut in recent years for his energy, personal commitment, and general love for giving; a tough act to outshine, but Frank had taken up the challenge.

Frank's rise in the philanthropy world had been meteoric, to which he has credited his winning strategy at GIM; the wealth and generosity of his client list; and his wife, June. "For without them this wouldn't be possible," he was often quoted as saying. During the past year, Frank's personal generosity and fund-raising efforts had topped many of the local charities' targets, a feat that did not go unnoticed by this year's committee. Even Kenneth Perkins had quipped, "He's a man who puts his money where his mouth is, and deserves serious attention for his community involvement."

"Hi, Grandfather. How are you feeling?" Alec asked, hugging Jack as they lingered around the table they'd be sharing with two local celebs, one who was currently starring in the hit Broadway show *Money for Nothing, and Checks for Free*, and the other who had won a reality-TV singing competition.

"I'm doing fine, Alec, thanks for asking. And you?"

"No complaints. Busy with work and school."

"Congrats on your first cyber case. I read the article," Jack said, giving him a hearty pat on the shoulder. "That's great."

"Thanks. I enjoy the challenge. It doesn't pay much right now, but—"

"Money's not everything, kid," Jack jumped in, startling the others around the table. "Don't let Frank skew your perspective of what's important in life. This," he continued, waving his bony arm draped in a suit ten years past its prime, "is just for show—vanity, nothing more than strutting in front of the world. He's doing what he's always done: covering up his insecurities with showmanship and passing it off as leadership. All it demonstrates is someone trying to get everybody to like him, to feel important. He doesn't care about these people or the investors at GIM, for that matter. They're just a means to an end for him."

Jack ordered a whiskey neat from the server who'd caught the last part of the diatribe.

"And you, sir?" the server asked Alec.

"What kind of root beer do you serve?"

"Pardon?"

"Root beer. What brand do you carry?"

"I'll have to check."

"Thanks."

"I like your style, kid," Jack said, chuckling. "Don't succumb to the pressures of Frank. And for chrissakes stop seeking his approval. You're never going to get it. You have more smarts, chops, and character than he'll ever have. You sure didn't get that from him and he knows it." He finished with a wink as Alec's mom joined them.

"Are you telling tales again, Jack?" June said with her usual jovial attempt at sounding stern.

"Nothing the kid shouldn't know," Jack replied, taking a stiff belt of the whiskey straight from the server's hand. "Better keep them coming, my good man."

The speeches rolled on for an hour or more as the night wore on, honoring one entity, group, or individual, with the occasional charity recipient telling a story about how a contribution to one program or another affected their life. The personal stories interested Alec more than the praise lavished on the honorees, whose thinly veiled modesty blended together into one long litany of *I just want to make the world a better place....*

Alec held nothing against the people and organizations that helped make the world go around a little smoother; he simply tired of the posturing that came with their gracious charity. He idealized the anonymous donor who, for whatever personal reason, chose to stay behind the scenes in making life better in some regard. The world needed more Secret Santas, in his view.

Alec keep himself entertained when the speeches exceeded their allotted due respect by exchanging text messages with Nathalie, placing his cell phone on his lap, avoiding the ire of his mother and father. "Tell me more about cyberinsurance. What does the company have to show to make a claim?"

"Monetary loss," came Nathalie's reply, "either actual or aggregated from time lost for recovery, downtime, and a host of other incidental soft costs. Some companies who claim proprietary loss try to build in future costs. Are you dressed like a penguin?"

"Yes."

"I'll bet you look sexy. I'd want to rip your clothes off."

"It's a rental."

"Deposit … gone!"

"What are you wearing?"

"Yellow bikini."

"I wish I could see that."

"Soon."

"Need to go. Dad just won Philanthropist of the Year."

"Congrats. I'm sure he deserves it."

The crowd rose, applauding when Frank Gordon's name crackled through the speakers for the award Alec knew his dad desperately wanted. Frank hugged and kissed his wife, squeezed Alec's shoulder, and patted Jack on the back before strolling up to the front to accept the award. He paused periodically to soak in the jubilation; he beamed with pride.

Alec watched the room celebrate his dad's achievement, laugh at his jokes during the lengthy acceptance speech, and marvel at the man who put his money where his mouth was, encouraging others to step up their efforts. "After all," Frank said, concluding his speech, "there's always more where that came from."

Despite grandfather Jack's cautionary words, Alec filled with pride for the man who was making a name for himself, not only on Wall Street but, as of tonight, the philanthropy world as well. *Perhaps Dad is trying too hard to get his father's respect, replacing it with adulation from others. At the end of the day, the charities win out, and that's what's important.* At that moment, Alec decided to devote his full efforts to investigating the GIM hacker. *I owe it to him.*

013   Under the Boardwalk

Atop old squeaky beach cruisers, Nathalie and Alex wound their way through families with strollers, oblivious camera-toting tourists, and joggers playing chicken with slower-moving pedestrians toward Natural Bridges State Park, a popular destination at sunset on a clear evening. Seagulls dotted the sky as the day's blue hues faded and brilliant yellow, orange, and amber ones took their place. A handful of surfers holding out for one last wave bobbed up and down on slow swells headed for shore.

Sitting parked on their cruisers overlooking rock formations beaten for centuries by a relentless stream of waves, Nathalie and Alex shared a view that quieted the mind, relinquishing modern-day matters to nothing more than trivial asides. The hushed voices around them commenting on the beauty did little to distract them. Nathalie leaned her bare shoulder against Alex's thinly covered scarred one as the sun dipped below the horizon; the electric charge of the touch, the warmth of Nathalie's skin, and the green flash on the horizon from the settled sunset sent a shiver down Alex's spine.

"Pretty sweet, huh?" Nathalie said, gazing at Alex.

"Yeah," Alex replied, momentarily forgetting her name or where she was.

The women retraced their path back to the B&B, cleaned up, remounted their bikes, and headed toward the Point. Alex didn't look forward to hanging out with a bunch of locals, anticipating she would simply hide in the dark, out of view, and people-watch until Nathalie got bored, then they could leave.

The bonfire vibrated with life as they strolled across the cool sand, the tips of the flames reaching eight feet high, taller than the surf that evening. Two volleyball nets surrounded by jagged, foot-drawn lines divided athletic bodies in various modes of dress, dimly lit by the fire and the streetlamps along the boardwalk. Someone with a guitar joined by a circle of carefree locals swayed in unison to the string's rhythm near the fire pit.

"Stretch and Little Grommet!" The lively voice from the Surf Shack greeted Nathalie and Alex as they approached the festivities, handing them each a large plastic cup of beer. "Welcome to the bon bon omondo." His name was Doob, which, as he explained it, was short for Dubious because he was always saying how things were dubious. Alex glanced at Nathalie, a different interpretation in mind. Doob amused Alex, his torso still shirtless in the chilly air, putting a smile on her face instantly. *He's like a cartoon character.*

Doob ushered the women around, introducing them to oddly named individuals who either nodded in acknowledgment or gave them a variety of handshakes, the women giggling with each successively more bizarre one. Doob gathered the grub he had promised earlier in the day, and Nathalie and Alex chowed down on barbecued skewers of various marinated meats.

Nathalie divided her time between text-messaging and an intense conversation about financial reform with some girl sporting a shaved head covered in tattoos, while Doob dragged Alex off to the sandy volleyball courts. Alex played like she'd never played before, which was the case, but Doob kept her laughing; the teams weren't exactly playing to win, as no one bothered to keep score.

When the game began to break up, the crowd headed for the fire pit while Alex hung back, laughing and giggling like a teenager, chasing Doob around the volleyball nets every time he playfully tossed the ball at her when her attention drifted to the crashing surf. The night brought back memories from the time when she enjoyed the beach with her parents, before insecurity covered up her body and life, steering her toward a virtual-world existence.

Nestled between Doob and Nathalie, seated around the flickering fire, laughing, socializing, tossing marshmallows at random revelers Doob goaded her into, Alex glimpsed the happy-go-lucky girl from yesteryear, with strangers who paid her snort of a laugh and unusual eye color no attention. The mixture of fun, quirky people, strong libations, and wafts of homegrown nature put Alex in a state of bliss, something she hadn't experienced in many years.

Late into the night, her pitch a bit off-key, Alex sang and swayed along with the carefree circle as the guitarist with dreadlocks strummed a Joni Mitchell song in accompaniment. She felt a gentle tap on her shoulder and glanced over, reading the question in Nathalie's eyes: *Time to leave?* Alex shook her head, smiling, not missing a beat of Joni's lyrics about clouds, love, and life's illusions.

IN THE EYE OF THE BEHOLDER

Alec stepped in from the detail-oriented streets of New York City to the abstract world of art and artifacts at Gordon Galleries in Midtown, where his mother curated. He'd been loosely aware of his parents' attempt to open a gallery in the family name as a legacy of sorts, showcasing local artists, but hadn't known to what extent. Since the summer before his collegiate sophomore year, when he moved out on his own, a gulf had developed between him and his parents on the particulars of their daily lives. He often played phone tag with his mother, and the conversations with his father were generally limited to their monthly family dinners at Johnny's Steak House.

He strolled around the spacious room, taking in the works currently on display that hung along freshly painted white walls towering over the open space mostly devoid of sound with certain exceptions: the occasional scuff of dress shoes on the hardwood floor, muffled conversations between well-dressed patrons, and the repetitive rat-a-tat-tat of a keyboard off to the side at a desk where his mother sat, apparently flustered.

"Morning, Mother," Alec said, stepping in behind her, instantly recognizing what frustrated her.

"Oh, Alec dear," she said, "do you know—?"

"Just click the little red button here and the window will close," he said, pointing to a persistent window advertising the latest software upgrade.

"Really? That's all? I've been trying everything all morning," she replied, exasperated. "You were always good with technical things."

"That's because you and Dad bought me a computer instead of the puppy I wanted when I was six. I could just as easily have become a veterinarian." Alec smirked as he gave her a hug. "The gallery looks great. I'm impressed."

"Thanks," she said. "We're still short on pieces, but there are more coming tomorrow, before the official grand opening in a few days." She showed him around the room, pausing in front of the handpicked piece she seemed to admire most, depicting a local avant-garde artist's recent vision.

Viewing the dramatic oil on canvas piece entitled *Altocumulus, the Calm Before the Thunderstorm*, Alec found his focus fragmented, left wanting in the abstraction of the talented artist's theme. He couldn't readily discern its meaning; it lacked the finer points he preferred to fully understand the reason for its *what* and *why*.

"I have a very good feeling about Boulier," June said of the young artist. "He really exposes his inner self. Of course, you'd have to meet him to fully appreciate that. What do you think?"

Alec continued staring at the cloudy theme that portended a calamity on the canvas' horizon. "It's aesthetically pleasing in a peacefully ominous way."

June turned her head toward Alec, her smile on her generally cheery face expressed fascination. "I wish your father could appreciate you for who you are."

"It's not his fault. He was never good at sports. I was. He likes finance. I don't. Different interests, that's all," Alec responded, as if rehearsed many times before, his eyes still fixed on Boulier's horizon. "I know he has a hard time relating."

His mother stood there listening, her average build and height poised gracefully in the prim and proper attire she constantly wore, hands clasped in front, eyes conveying perhaps a different explanation. "You know, when your father and I brought you home from the hospital he was so proud. He just didn't know how to be a caring parent. He didn't have very good role models."

"I know. He loves me the best way he knows how." Alec knew his mother understood; heck, even Gina the office admin at GIM understood; it was just Frank's way. But even his mother's love appeared more reactive than proactive, only there when he needed something. In the end, Alec's emotional connection with his parents reflected abstract art: ambiguous in nature; it could be felt, but not in the form he could understand or would be satisfied with, unless he knew what to look for, and even then in view-only fashion.

June rubbed his shoulder. "What brings you to Midtown?"

"I wanted to see the gallery and find out if Father has discussed anything about the VLGF with you or Jack," he said, swapping out the gallery's broad strokes for finer ones.

"VLGF?"

"Vegas Land Grab Fund," Alec replied, the answer already apparent.

"Not really. Frank doesn't bring it up much, especially if Jack's around. It was a contentious topic between them. Still is. Why?"

"I'm attempting to figure out what a hacker might be delving into GIM for."

"I'm glad you're helping out. He appreciates it."

"It seems like a good place to start, since it's mostly responsible for the increase in the firm's asset base. I'll devote more time to it when I get back from the conference in Vegas."

"Sorry, dear. He doesn't discuss business much with me. He and I talk quite a bit about what charities to fund, and more recently this gallery. He wants to be known for more than his investment success, to get out from the shadows of his father. He wants to give back to the community. You know he's never been about the money."

"I know. Money is simply a means to an end for him. A toy to play with. Makes him the cool kid on the block," Alec said, his commentary more bitter when voiced than it had been in his head. "Sorry, I meant—"

"I know, dear. He comes off as if he's trying to impress, but he also knows how important it is to me, and he loves me. When we first met, he immediately went out and bought me a painting after our first date. It was hideous. He didn't know a thing about art. I educated him, showed him a world very different from the one he grew up in. He's embraced it, though he still doesn't completely understand it." Her smile bordered on a faint laugh.

Alec chastised himself for dispensing his private thoughts on the matter. His parents had given him most things—bikes, football camps and gear, computers, college tuition—and more recently helping out with rent on his loft. It just wasn't always what he wanted.

Through Alex's sleepy morning haze she could feel the touch of a hand tenderly caressing her shoulder like that of an artist sketching out a nature scene with charcoal. She stirred to the warmth of a body close to her bare skin, opening her eyes to find herself focused directly on Nathalie, whose eyes followed the pattern her fingers were tracing along the long jagged scar on Alex's shoulder.

Alex's mind came around quickly, fully aware she'd slept topless for the first time ever, and that Nathalie could see her scar.

"Is this why you didn't want a two-piece?" Nathalie asked softly.

Alex closed her eyes, in part to calm her anxiety, and in part to embrace the bliss of Nathalie's gentle touch. "Yeah," she whispered.

"It's beautiful."

Her eyes opened again, this time absorbing every movement of Nathalie's expressive beauty. Not even Maggie, who tried in vain to get Alex to embrace the scar, had made such a comment.

"Imperfections, flaws, vulnerabilities ... life is beautiful no matter what it took to get to this point. In the end you're a survivor, stronger because of your past, and this is merely a symbol of that."

Alex smiled. Nathalie's assuaging words couldn't erase all the unwelcome stares, comments, and questions that accompanied her childhood, but they did comfort her; especially in the way Nathalie admired it, touched it without wincing, and leaned over, giving it a tender kiss.

"Wolf_Eyes," Alex said, her eyes locked on Nathalie's. "My *real* hacker name is Wolf_Eyes ... spelled with an underscore between each word." The nerdiness of the name seemed less disconcerting than revealing her alter ego for the first time.

Nathalie smiled. "Suits you better than 'Cyber Owl.'"

"You're not upset?"

"You were being cautious, protecting yourself. I understand that."

Alex nodded, her trusting wolf eyes showing relief from the lie they had concealed.

"You hungry?" Nathalie asked.

"Yeah. I think I got a contact high last night."

"Let's hit the breakfast downstairs. We can go over the GIM information too," she said, getting out of bed, rummaging through her duffel bag. "Here." She tossed a clean tank top to Alex. "Wear this to breakfast."

Alex glanced at it. "Nope. It's one thing to show it in private with you, but not out in public," she replied, flipping it back.

"You need to own it, not let it own you," Nathalie countered, slipping on a pair of shorts. She put the tank top back in her bag, stepped into the bathroom, and turned the water on to rinse her face.

Alex rolled out of bed, self-conscious in just panties, staring at the revealing garment in Nathalie's bag. *Nope, not yet. I'll own it another time.* She slipped on some shorts and donned her new favorite top she'd bought at the Surf Shack. She smiled when she caught a whiff of Doob's lingering scent from when he gave her a hug and peck on the lips as she left the bon bon omondo.

Nathalie sipped coffee, reading through GIM's financials while Alex sampled everything from the gourmet spread put out by the owners of the B&B. Alex enjoyed her mom's breakfasts when she had time to prepare them, but the scrumptious feast now before her looked better than any Maggie or any restaurant she'd ever frequented had ever served.

"You know," Nathalie said, hunched over the small café-style table, her hands wrapped around the coffee mug, "it appears he's taking money in from the group of investors associated with the VLGF, then paying out to a few investors who are invested in his other financial products or holding accounts." She sounded astonished.

"And that's wrong because …?"

"Because the VLGF investors are only getting a token ten-percent dividend after one year." She paused, peering closer at one of the documents. "Then those accounts look like they go dormant, never receiving another dime. It's a consistent pattern over several years.

"OK," Alex said, less focused on Nathalie's observations than the flaky croissant melting in her mouth.

"Also, his holdings don't look right. His assets seem pretty lean compared to the volume of money coming in on the VLGF. I seriously doubt there are enough homes in the Vegas area to support all those investors, even if he were buying more every so often."

"So he's cooking the books?"

"Sort of, yeah. Pretty clever, too. Keep recycling the same security he bought years ago, bringing in new money to use for—"

"Philanthropy!"

"Yeah, that might be how he's making all those huge contributions … probably through the CharDons account."

Alex's hearty appetite precluded her from fully appreciating or caring about what Frank appeared to be doing with his books, opting for a another helping of blueberry blintz and seasoned scrambled eggs instead, missing the more telltale signs of fraud Nathalie presented: GIM's preference since Frank took control to use different banks each year to perform their annual audits, and his notable disinterest of investing personal money in the VLGF, which purported better returns than the savings account and conservative investment funds he did manage his money in.

Alex stepped in behind a little boy who impatiently waited for his younger sister to decide which Danish pastry to get. After much deliberation, the little girl chose the last jelly-filled one on the platter.

"Hey, I want that one," the boy shouted, snatching it from her plate.

"Hey, that's mine … Mom, Tommy took my food," the girl said, on the verge of tears.

"Hold up there, partner," Alex said when the boy spun around, ready to abscond with his newly acquired pastry. Alex plucked the Danish from his plate. "How would you like it if someone bigger than you took your food?"

"Mom—"

"That's right, you'd cry for help," Alex replied, placing the pastry back onto the girl's plate, who stood there in her Sunday-school-styled dress beaming at Alex. "You need to look after your little sister so big bullies don't steal things from her. Your mom isn't always going to be around to help. Understand?"

The boy stood bewildered, staring at Alex, then over at the table where his parents were sitting, the mom watching the scene without a concern on her face. "Yes, ma'am."

"We're cool." Alex tousled his hair. "Look, there's a chocolate one with your name on it."

"Well, aren't you the little superhero," Nathalie said when Alex returned.

Alex was too busy digging into her replenished plate to respond.

"So … you're going to think this is weird … but we should go to Vegas."

Alex stopped chewing as her eyes popped wide open.

"I know: you, Vegas, bad idea, but hear me out," she said, continuing to build her case by setting down a document in front of Alex. "It's hard to tell how much suburban property is out there from his financials. The banks aren't going to tell us because they've already offloaded it. We need to see the area for ourselves, then we could tell if this make sense."

Alex resumed chewing, ignoring the document, not letting Nathalie ruin the morning's culinary bliss.

"Well … what do you think?" Nathalie asked, chasing a grape with a fork around her fruit bowl.

Alex cleansed her palate with some fresh orange juice. "I think you're still on a contact high." *Me, Sin City, yeah right.*

Nathalie continued picking at the variety of chunked fruit.

"Besides, I have school and work."

"OK … you're right," Nathalie said. "I'm just not sure how we can prove he's doing anything wrong without going—"

"I can hack back into his—" Alex started to say, her reluctance to go raising her guilt level, when the little girl in the Sunday-school dress walked up to their table.

"Here," the little girl said, removing a shell necklace from her neck, handing it to Alex. "You can have this." She gave Alex a big hug before skipping back to her mom, who smiled at her daughter's gesture.

Alex was taken aback, shyly smiling at the girl and mother. She stared at the necklace, its delicate seashells linked loosely together around colorful string. She put it on, casting an eye toward Nathalie. "OK … Vegas it is."

"So said the superhero."

015   Vegas Baby

Alex peered out the small airplane window at the mitosis of lightbulbs forming against the twilight of the surrounding desert. Las Vegas, Nevada, at once defied logic and lauded man's ingenuity, supporting life in excess in one of the more unlikely spots on Earth, giving rise to a pot of gold at the end of the neon rainbow as well as convincing tourists to hand over their hard-earned cash for nothing more than free drinks, gaudy shows, blinking lights, and fancy gambling tables marginally more legit than the makeshift table tended by the hooded man on a big-city street corner inviting tourists over to play the shell game.

Alex fiddled with the ring of shells around her neck the little girl in Santa Cruz had gifted her, already sensing the energy of the city mixing with her anxiousness, unconvinced the trip would net them anything more than she could obtain from hacking. She wasn't even certain GIM had done anything wrong. *The SEC had done their due diligence. They certainly wouldn't let another Madoff-type scam fester in their backyard. Besides, Nathalie said their books showed they owned property in Nevada. Real estate is speculative at best these days, so who's to say if the investment didn't tank. The firm has been around since practically the Stone Age.*

She sighed.

Let's just get through the next couple of days without freaking out, then you can get back home.

Her bigger concern was the promise she had made to Nathalie, wearing the strapless evening top she'd bought on the way to the airport at least one night in Vegas. *Why did I promise that?* Alex looked over at Nathalie, whose face appeared intensely focused on an article about card counting the MIT way, before gazing back out at the desert. *Maybe I could get those tattoo sleeves.*

"So the basic idea is cards 2 through 6 are assigned a value of 1; 7 through 9 a 0; and all the rest minus 1?" Nathalie said, summarizing the article Alex gave her to read on the flight while they waited for the rental-car agent to process their reservation.

"Yeah," Alex quietly answered, taking furtive glances at those within earshot.

"And the higher the count means it's ripe for the picking to win," Nathalie exclaimed as the agent handed her the paperwork with probably the same smile he gave all would-be card-counting tourists ready to bring down the house. "Simple enough."

"It's not, Rain Woman," Alex said, relieved to be clear of the eavesdroppers. "It's very hard—"

"And it's not illegal?"

"What, counting or winning?"

"Counting."

"No. You have to *count* cards or they'll laugh you off the table," she said. "There are no signs; they can't control what you do with your mind."

"Well, that's a relief." Nathalie grinned as they piled into the mid-sized sedan.

The women made the short drive from the airport toward the pulse of Las Vegas, cruising the Strip, searching for their hotel among the dozens of high-rises whose well-illuminated signature motifs screamed for attention. Alex peered around with the wide-eyed wonderment of a child visiting Disneyland for the first time. *Wow.*

They found the place, checked in, and upon entering the luxurious suite, Alex's jaw dropped, awestruck, slowly taking in the room. *It's bigger than our house.* In reality it wasn't, but its spacious nature, in-room Jacuzzi, wet bar, and view of the city quiet behind the twenty-first-floor's sealed windows made it seem as much.

"We're only staying a couple nights, right?" Alex asked, checking out all the amenities.

"Yeah, the company … I mean, I can write it off, so why not go big?" Nathalie replied. "It's Vegas, baby."

Nathalie's brief stutter fell on deaf ears as Alex stood by the large window engrossed in the view of the city lit up like an electric parade.

"So here's the plan, hon," Nathalie continued, checking her cell phone. "Let's grab some dinner, then hit the casinos. I want to try your card-counting trick. Tomorrow we'll drive to Shady Willow to check out the suburbs and see if GIM's holdings make sense."

Nathalie's card-counting comment caught Alex's attention and spun her around. "No, we haven't practiced it as a team. It's really not that easy, Nathalie. If it looks like we're doing something, they'll rough us up."

"Really?"

"No, but they'll ask us to leave," Alex said, preferring to avoid any confrontation.

"It'll be OK. We'll try it for a little bit and have some fun."

"We can't gamble that way in our own hotel—" Alex continued to protest, but Nathalie sat on the bed preoccupied with her phone, looking concerned, typing quickly. Alex turned back to the city view and sighed. *It won't be that bad because we won't win anything anyway, so it's all good. Except for the strapless top I have to wear.*

She rolled up the sleeve of her shirt.
Damn this scar.

Alec stood curbside at McCarran International Airport, engaged in a text-message conversation with Nathalie while waiting for the shuttle to his hotel on the Las Vegas Strip. The dry heat, even after sunset, quickly reminded him of the last time he was in Vegas with his father a few years back.

"By the way, I'm in Vegas for a couple days attending another cyber conference," Alec wrote, unsure if he'd mentioned it in San Francisco. A long pause followed in what had been quick, witty banter. "Still there?"

"Yeah, got distracted. Where are you staying?"

"The Palms."

"Better stock up on singles."

"Only if you're the entertainment."

Alec glanced up when he heard someone shout his name from a car slowing down. "Jason, how are you?" he said, recognizing him from the Bay Area conference.

"Hop in. I'll take you down to the Strip. You staying at the conference hotel?"

"Yes, thanks." Alec settled into the rental car, glancing at the last text message from Nathalie: "Oh là là."

"Girl back home?" Jason asked, obviously catching Alec's grin.

"No. Met her at the San Francisco conference."

"The hot redhead I saw you leave with on the back of the Ducati?"

"Yes, that's the one."

"Damn, son, you're the man. What's she do?"

"Cyberinsurance."

Jason chuckled. "Watch out … insurance women come with a high deductible."

Alec and Jason discussed the pertinent details of their lives on the drive to the Strip and later during dinner at the trendy restaurant in the hotel. Jason, a short, portly gentleman, who at the age of fifty-six had a full head of hair and a jovial laugh that could make someone laugh all by itself, was originally from New York before moving with his wife, who, like him, happened to work in the insurance industry, and teenage son and daughter to Houston. He was on his second career with cybercriminology.

Jason spent quite a bit of time in hacker chat rooms, including the HCR, explaining to Alec what to look for in communication between hackers. After a few years, Jason had become an expert on the art of drawing out hackers suspected of selling classified information they'd pilfered, earning him the right to run a separate division. He appeared a natural-born leader to Alec, someone he could instantly respect and learn from.

After dinner and brief stroll along the Strip, Alec returned to his room and flipped on the oversized TV, catching up on the sports scores for the day as he opened a textbook he'd brought along to stay current with his classwork, but not before rereading the previous text-message exchange he'd had with Nathalie, smiling and wishing she were there in Vegas.

"Natural twenty-one, player wins," the dealer announced. The large crowd lurking around the table erupted in celebration as the mounds of neatly stacked chips in front of Alex topped $70,000. Though strained, she smiled at the players alongside her, their congratulatory gestures making her nervous and excited at once. Casino employees dressed in suits swarmed her, comping dinner, shows, anything she needed, while pit bosses hovered behind the dealer, having silent conversations with the eye in the sky.

Alex had gone over the basic team strategy with Nathalie back at the room concerning how to tell if a table was hot or cold by the count, positive or negative; to bet erratically so it appeared like Nathalie didn't know what she was doing; and to pretend they didn't know each other. Nathalie seemed confident in her grasp of the concept, sitting in on a few tables before she gave the subtle signal, twirling the end of her hair, to let Alex know it was hot. It made more sense for Alex to scout the tables because of her better grasp of the complex card-counting math and the intense yet nonchalant focus it required, but Nathalie insisted on playing the part of the counter, telling Alex she was good with numbers too.

Alex settled into her first real-life blackjack game, knocking over her orderly arrangement of chips twice before the first cards were dealt. She caught herself placing a hand over her scar, fully exposed in the black strapless top that tied neatly around her waist. But once the dealer tossed out the cards, Alex's ability to focus on numbers and strategy kicked in, diverting her attention away from her appearance and insecurities.

Betting big when the odds are in the player's favor is the way to win the most money; it is also the way to lose the most should Lady Luck turn her back on the player. Nathalie staked their gambit $10,000. Alex cringed at the amount, but Nathalie held firm, saying it would be fun and not to worry about losing. It was Vegas, after all.

Alex tossed down her first chip, $5,000, the table's limit, drawing a few curious glances from the others already anted. Even Nathalie showed surprise. "Why prolong the suffering?" Alex said to the young, neatly dressed couple seated beside her. The cards were dealt and the best hand in blackjack landed in front of her; it only got better after that.

Nathalie sat in on a few hands to maintain the ruse before parting, not straying far from the table. Alex's winning streak attracted a large group of onlookers, as winning often does. She peered around at the excited gaggle, young couples dressed to the nines, older couples dressed as if they'd missed their cruise ship to the Bahamas, all who united, sharing a common bond around a half table of plastic chips, playing cards, and patterned felt.

Overwhelmed by the attention, intoxicated by Lady Luck's energy rush, Alex floated in a state of confused bliss, recognizing a mirage when she stumbled upon one, a Tammaré quest with a happy, but illusory ending. In the morning she'd wake up the same person who balked at going to Vegas in the first place, though perhaps with enough money to pay for her senior year at Stanford, assuming she kept it. She pondered how such artificial attention heaped upon someone could change how they perceived it; the need for more feeds upon itself until they can't tell the difference between genuine adulation and "What have you done for me lately?" *Is Frank Gordon caught in that trap, seeking admiration no matter how artificial it may be? Would he go to any ends to get it? Does he even know it? Money makes you popular, that's for sure.*

Alec walked a few blocks down the Strip from his hotel, venturing into a casino where a fabled hacker story had taken place. As he strolled through the onslaught of glitz, he watched gamblers of all shapes, sizes, and ethnicities cavorting around gambling tables, listening to coins drop down slot machines deposited by bored retirees, the bells of which tolled the fortunes of winners or elicited loud moans from disconsolate losers; all which showcased man's hopes, dreams, and despair across seven thousand lavish square feet.

Staring at a bank of noisy slot machines, he recalled the story told during a lecture he had attended about two creative hackers who bought the same model of machine for personal use, pulled the computer chip out, reverse-engineered the programming logic, found flaws in it, figured out how often the payouts would come, and then exploited the casino with their knowledge without getting caught. *They scored big.*

Bored of reviewing hacker profiles, case studies, and study questions, Alec took to wandering amidst the excitement and energy that Vegas offered. His only other trip had been sophomore year in high school with his dad, who scouted out bulk real-estate-purchase opportunities for GIM in a little bedroom community called Shady Willow. Alec spent his only night in the hotel room, doing homework.

Alec heard the distinct roar of a crowd celebrating someone winning big in the blackjack area and decided to check it out. He approached the table that was the center of attention, but the tightly packed crowd blocked further progress, and even at his height he didn't have much of a vantage point so many rows removed. He wandered over behind the dealer area, where pit bosses roamed like hippos, their sublime exterior watching over millions of dollars quickly changing hands in the form of plastic chips, yet underneath a voracious will should it appear that someone was cheating the house.

From his new vantage point, Alec could see right away who the big winner was, a young attractive woman wearing a fetching top with hair similar in color to his that draped over her exposed shoulders. Her smile appeared shy, almost embarrassed, not altogether in keeping with the rich towers of chips stacked neatly in front of her. Something else caught Alec's eye. Leaning forward in an attempt to get a better look he caught sight of a sizable scar on the woman's shoulder. *That's odd. Looks like mine, only on the opposite shoulder.*

Alec did a double-take once the woman's face came into view. *Is that the sunnies girl from the market in California?* From across the room, he wasn't sure. He'd never gotten a clear look at her that day as she tended the grill; the smoke that hovered in the small patio area always provided a distorted partition between them. *Could that be her? What are the odds … in Vegas, of all places?*

Alec moved toward her to gain a better view. *What was her name again … Alex?* As he worked his way through the crowd a hand grabbed his arm, jerking him around. *Hey!*

"Nathalie?" Alec said, shocked but pleasantly so. "What are you doing here?"

"Meeting with some clients tonight," Nathalie replied, planting a deep kiss on him that nearly took his breath away. "How about you, sweetie?"

Alec let the tingle down his spine subside before answering. "Another conference … I mentioned it—"

"That's right. Sorry. Been an hectic day," she said as a portion of her lower lip curled underneath the upper one, eyes dancing from his to over his shoulder and back. "Hey, let's get out of here." Nathalie tugged Alec's arm, pulling him out from the growing crowd. "I'm hungry. Want to get something to eat?"

"Yes, but—" he started before bumping into a couple who acted like they'd recently gotten off a spinning amusement-park ride. Alec glanced back toward the blackjack table to catch one last glimpse of the sunnies girl, but she was insulated in a different world as another roar erupted.

Alex looked away from the blackjack table, catching a peek of Nathalie talking to a vaguely familiar man on the fringe of the crowd surrounding the table at which she held court. She squinted, attempting to make out his profile. *Is that the guy with the cheap sunglasses, Alec, the cybercriminologist?*

"Ma'am, your play," the dealer said.

She waved the two cards fanned in her hand toward herself, beckoning another. Alex glanced back at Nathalie, watching her leave with the guy. The dealer tossed her the eight of spades. Without looking, Alex laid her cards down, the ten and three of hearts.

"Player has twenty-one," the dealer announced, the crowd erupting in another chorus of celebration for the night's hottest streak.

"Can I rub your lucky scar," the older gentleman next to her asked, rubbing his hands together.

What? Lucky? "Ah, no," Alex said, abruptly standing.

"Would you like to color-up, ma'am?" the dealer asked, handing her a chip tray amid the boisterous crowd slowly disbursing.

She nodded, took the tray, and loaded her converted chips quickly, tossing each player and the dealer a $500 chip; a chorus of thanks followed in her wake.

Alex had two immediate concerns on her mind. The first, what to do with nearly $80,000 worth of chips; she had no intention of cashing them in. The second, the one that scared her the most: what if the guy *was* Alec and turned out to be friends with Nathalie? She trusted Nathalie regarding her hacking exploits, but a friend that connected, with what he did for a living, made her uncomfortable nonetheless.

She sat down at a table on the perimeter of a nearby cocktail lounge, gathering herself, averting her eyes from the petite hostess who asked if she wanted something to drink. The plan called for her and Nathalie to meet back at the hotel around nine, never speaking until then, just to be safe.

Alex jumped, nearly spilling her tray of chips when a professionally dressed man stopped by the table. He inquired if she needed anything, citing he was with casino security and wanted to ensure she was all right since she'd left the blackjack table in a hurry. He wished her congratulations and moved on after she assured him she was fine, feigning fatigue.

Her eyes darted around the boisterous casino, her hands fidgeting with the chip tray whenever anyone glanced her way or pointed in her direction. The ubiquitous black orbs dotted along the ceiling conjured up childhood memories of kids on the playground teasing her; those eyes, that scar. *I need Nathalie.*

"You OK, hon?" said the cocktail waitress with the Southern accent, interrupting Alex's childhood flashback. "You look frightened."

Alex stared at the woman in her early thirties, a cheery demeanor upon a tired face, whose large breasts behind a sheer blouse rode high on her chest with the help of a tight black bra that bunched them together like the cantaloupe on display at the market back home. A black leather skirt hugged her flared hips, and faded fishnet leggings disappeared down into tall, dark boots.

"My kids get that look every time those thunder bumpers crack overhead; vicious they are," the cocktail waitress continued.

"No, I'm fine," Alex replied. "Just tired."

"That's a lovely top you're wearing. I sure wish I had your shoulders. I couldn't pull that look off."

"Thanks."

"Hey, tits on a stick! Get your ass over here. We're thirsty," hollered a man from across the lounge. Both women looked over at the man waving his hand as if hailing a cab.

"Actually, I prefer Charlotte," the woman said, smiling at Alex. "I do it for my kids." She turned to leave, waving good-bye. "You take care, hon. Get some rest."

As Alex gave a faint wave good-bye she took note of Charlotte's bare ring finger, which gave her an idea.

Alec and Nathalie strolled down the Strip watching folks from all around the world take in the artificial sights set up in the middle of the desert. If there were ever a birthplace for "If You Build It, They Will Come," this was it. Cars chugged by slowly with windows rolled down, low bass tones thumped from their interiors, while front- and backseat passengers hooted and hollered like sailors on leave.

"When'd you get in?" Alec asked while overhearing a hooded man convince a family the Cirque du Soleil tickets he held were for the front row at half price—if they didn't mind going in through the back entrance.

"Just a few hours ago," she answered, gazing up at him, her arm interlocked with his. "It was a last-minute trip for a company meeting. Hey, congrats on your dad's award. That must have been some night for you and the family."

"Yes, it was. He sure is the toast of New York right now. I'm amazed at his ambition."

"You're pretty ambitious yourself, mister," she said, squeezing his forearm. "Getting a four-year degree in three, working full-time, making a big splash at the task force …"

"And learning Russian."

"Really?"

"Ty vygljadish' prekrasno."

"Wow," Nathalie said, her mouth agape. "What'd you say? Better not be 'How much for the night, babe?'"

"'You look beautiful.'"

Nathalie smiled. "Why Russian?"

"I read *Doctor Zhivago* in junior high and developed a crush on Lara. It made me want to learn the language."

Nathalie leaned her head against him as they continued their stroll down the Strip until they reached a festive line of people that disappeared inside a brightly lit gelato shop. Once they ordered and collected two cones of Italy's finest flavored creams, they took a seat outside on the cobblestone patio, where Nathalie kept glancing at her cell phone.

"Expecting a call?" Alec asked, annoyed at Nathalie's lack of attention to his question about cybercrime and insurance. Meeting with the San Jose Task Force director, Karen, had piqued his curiosity on the use of insurance as a means to cover up a company's poor system administration on their networks. *How does it work?*

"Sorry, Alex," she said, putting her phone on the table. "I'm waiting for a text from the client I'm supposed to meet."

Alec grinned. "So how do the claims work?" he repeated, unconcerned that she'd referred to him as Alex; it often happened back home.

Nathalie explained that PII—personal identification information—was the most frequently stolen entity, followed by PHI—personal health information. Topping the list of the most frequently breached industries were financial services and health care, whose average cost per breach came in at $2 million, mostly spent on legal services. But hacker attacks weren't the only claim a company could file. Most cyber-liability insurance policies allowed customers to atone for a wide variety of Internet problems that affected their business: denial of service attacks, widespread Internet issues associated with viruses, or Internet service provider problems.

Alec licked his gelato cone, absorbing the magnitude of the process. *Quite the big business, and, with so much wiggle room and gray area, ripe for fraud.* "You mentioned in San Francisco that you were writing policy on what constitutes loss for claims in cyberattacks."

Nathalie smiled. "Someone was listening." Her eyes were back on the cell phone, catching the arrival of a new text message.

"I would imagine you had to analyze hundreds of reported security breaches in order to arrive at an appropriate policy."

"Of course," she replied, drawing her phone closer.

"Ever come across the hacker name 'Wolf_Eyes'?"

Splat!

Nathalie's gelato cone hit the cobblestone patio.

Alex sent a text message to Nathalie, "Where are you? I'm back at the room. Meet up soon." She tossed the phone across the bed and flopped back, relaxing in the luxurious hotel robe. The in-room Jacuzzi did wonders for her nerves, massaging away the blackjack adrenaline rush. *Between riding on Nathalie's Ducati and tonight, I feel like I'm living on the edge. Who am I, Lara Croft?* She giggled.

After offloading the tens of thousands of dollars in chips, less the ten grand Nathalie staked her and the grand that Alex estimated Nathalie had probably dropped in scouting the early tables before the hot one, Alex could stop worrying about what to do with the plastic fortune. She had purchased a small satchel from the casino gift store and filled it with the winnings after she watched Charlotte endure the lounge customer's demeaning behavior. She added a note that read, "Find a better way to love your kids. Hugs, no longer frightened."

Sure, it could've paid for her next year at Stanford, completing her degree, or replenish part of her parents' lost savings, but the efforts at testing the boundaries of her acquired skills and talents were a cerebral exercise, or to benefit others, not for personal consumption. Her natural curiosity and desire to question the status quo drove her hacking exploits, and even card counting with Nathalie, but to profit from it at the expense of others was not something she could accept.

Her cell phone chirped: "Ran into a client who is worried about his money. See ya soon. XOXO."

That's a relief. I could see it now, if they were friends, talking on the phone: "By the way, do you know any hackers?"

Giddy with delight, Alex pressed Play on her phone's music library. The heavy-handed guitar solo ignited the room, a hard-hitting drummer delivered the thumping backbeat, and throaty female vocals unleashed a torrent of cathartic lyrics. She thrashed around on her back atop the thick down comforter, performed her best air guitar solo, and flung pillows off the bed like guitar picks into the crowd. She had survived the crowded elevator ride, the walk and dinner on the Strip, and beat the house, all in her shoulder-baring sequin top. The night had been liberating, though exhausting. She was ready to go home, but the Vegas suburbs beckoned. *Maybe we'll find a ghost town. That'd be cool.*

She grabbed the complimentary national newspaper, amused they still printed the news, along with a snack from the large basket of chocolate and fruits. She mindlessly flipped through the sections to kill time and spotted a picture of Frank Gordon accepting New York's Philanthropist of the Year award. Alex didn't like his smug smile. *Are you robbing Peter to pay Paul, Mr. Gordon?* She learned nothing more than she already knew after scanning the article, except for his desire to find the next big challenge in giving, something that would really make a difference. *Read between the lines: "I need more money from my investors." Hmmm.*

Nathalie sat laughing, face red from embarrassment. Pedestrians filtering by shared a knowing grin at her clumsiness: her gelato cone sat upside-down on the ground, resembling a top hat on a clown's painted face. Alec joined in with a rare outburst of laughter.

"That's what I get for trying to do two things at once," she said, wiping cream off her pantsuit.

"Yes, you, your phone, and gelato don't play nice. Alexander Graham Bell and Bernardo Buontalenti will be most disappointed," Alec quipped, retreating to the café for more napkins.

As soon as Alec disappeared Nathalie zipped off a quick text message: "Ran into a client who is worried about his money. See ya soon. XOXO."

Despite jet lag and a long day ahead of him—the conference and red-eye back to New York—Alec wanted Nathalie to come back to his hotel room, but she needed to meet with her client right away; it was urgent. They embraced in a long, passionate kiss in front of choreographed water follies showcasing one of Vegas' signature hotel casinos, the Bellagio, then parted ways, promising to meet again in New York. It couldn't happen soon enough for him.

Before heading back to his hotel, Alec took a stroll through the fabled hacker casino, glancing around the blackjack area for the woman whom he might've recognized. The tables lacked the excitement he'd witnessed earlier, replaced instead with the solemn faces of hopeful souls.

She was gone.

 # Shady Willow

Nathalie let out a chuckle as she and Alex hit the end of the Strip, heading north in the rental car, the air conditioning already in high gear at ten in the morning.

"What?" Alex asked, rubbing copious amounts of sunblock on her face, neck, arms, and shoulders.

"I can't believe you gave away all your winnings," Nathalie said. "You should've seen yourself last night. You were on fire. That was the most incredible thing I've ever seen."

"It was insane," Alex replied, relieved Nathalie wasn't upset over giving the windfall to the beleaguered cocktail waitress. "And it was too much to deal with."

"Why'd you let it climb so high, then?"

"Does anybody stop when they're winning … at anything?"

Nathalie shrugged her shoulders. "True."

"I don't know … I was beating the system and nobody tried to stop me," Alex admitted, no longer defending herself. "I got carried away." She peered out the windshield, Las Vegas suburbia looming in the desolation.

"So on your"—Nathalie paused, glancing at Alex—"let's call them late-night cyberquests, is that what you do, just mess around?"

"Tammaré?"

Nathalie gave Alex a doubtful look.

"Oh, that," Alex replied, hoping she could share with someone her love of the virtual world. "Yeah, sometimes. I'll hear chatter about an unbreakable network and I take it on as a challenge. Other times I check out systems of companies that are suspected of doing something wrong but nobody can prove it; like, this one bank had customers send their credit-card payments to one address in the Midwest, then the bank would forward it to another processing center on the East Coast, but the company didn't give them credit for the payment's arrival until the second center. Since people generally send in their payments near the end of the grace period, they'd get dinged a late fee. So I hacked the second center's system and added a few scripts to their batch-processing job that backdated the received date by five days."

"Really? What happened?"

"Well, eventually someone in Accounting noticed a sharp drop in late-fee revenues. It took a few days but they figured out what was going on. They reported the breach, which got the FDIC involved, and after some investigating they reported the scam. Class-action suits galore."

"Landover Limited? You were behind that, Alex?"

"Actually … Wolf_Eyes," she said, attempting to take a bow until the seat belt's safety restraint locked her halfway into it. *Oof.*

"Smooth," Nathalie said, laughing. "Oh, I think this is our exit."

Just a short drive north from the Las Vegas Strip lay the most foreclosed zip code in the country, Shady Willow, NV. A decade earlier it had been the fastest-growing metropolitan area in the country. Much like one's luck on the Strip can change in a heartbeat, so too did the fortunes of those swept up by creative financing. One moment they're all-in, the next gone. Alex and Nathalie drove around the desolate neighborhoods, reading signs posted in front yards whose messages didn't support one politician or another in an upcoming election but rather invited someone to "buy me" or "rent me." Tens of thousands of homes built on a grand-master plan scale dotted the hundred square miles like the classic virtual game Sim City, the echoes of *blip, blip, blip* for whole blocks going up at once still resonated. *How can a dream billed as so affordable become a financial nightmare?*

Alex peered around as they drove through the distressed area of small lots with unmaintained landscaping that surrounded poorly constructed homes cooled by immense A/C units; where playground equipment slowly rusted, weeds poked their way up between slabs in the sidewalk, and stray fast-food bags drifted through the streets in the hot desert breeze. *It is like a ghost town.* She wondered if any of her past mortgage-readjustment hacks had affected anybody in Shady Willow. *Perhaps that house with the fresh paint job and clean windows and green grass in the front yard….*

"What are we looking for?" Alex asked after an hour of driving around, getting bored and depressed as well as irritated by the cold air spewing out from the A/C unit. "And why are you wearing a jacket?"

"I get cold easily."

"Then why do we have the A/C on?"

"The inside of the car gets hot."

Alex let out a low groan and rolled her eyes.

"Hey, I have an idea," Nathalie said, swerving the car into a gravel parking lot with a dingy double-wide atop cinder blocks at the back. The wooden sign above it read SHADY WILL__ REAL ESTATE, the "ow" long gone.

Alex snorted. "This looks promising," she said, though happy she could get out, stretch her legs, and soak in the sun's warmth on her skin.

"Howdy, ladies," said the spry elderly man with a gracious smile and manner about him as he opened the front door to the trailer. "Get in here out of that blasted heat."

Arggggh, more A/C.

"The name is Earl, but most folks around here call me Old Earl on account of my age." He chuckled, giving the chairs in front of his desk a quick dusting. "Have a seat."

Alex didn't respond, but rather stood staring, taking in Old Earl, whose bolo tie and broad, sweeping smile that took up most of his gaunt face made her grin. The cowboy tan that caused his white hair to appear even whiter amused her as well, though his formal attire delighted her the most: the pink flannel shirt tucked into his Levi's, and the black-and-white checkered jacket he wore fully buttoned, as if ready to sit in the back of a marshal's car at a local parade to honor a high school team's victory.

"Earl, my name is Nathalie," she said, giving Alex a stern glance while extending her hand, "and this is Alex."

"Pleasure to meet you two lovely ladies. What can I do you for today?"

Nathalie explained her position as a personal finance advisor, attempting to get a handle on the bulk-home-buying deals that were commonly used to lighten a bank's distressed loan assets. She wanted to advise clients on whether it was a good investment or not. The investment handlers back home made it seem like easy money. Alex listened to Nathalie, wondering whether Earl would know anything and, if he did, whether he would reveal it.

"I've been in the real estate business for fifty years. My first sale was to this group of guys who wanted a little place to go to party in private off the Strip. They were so famous that when the motels on the Strip filled up, the fans would sleep in their cars just to see them. They were a big thing back in the day when Vegas was the real Vegas, not this Disney-themed horse puckey they got going on now. Pardon my language, ladies."

Alex chuckled at the effervescent gentleman who spoke about a group she didn't know and a time long before she was born.

"You mean your first sale was to the Rat Pack?" Nathalie said.

Alex swiveled her head toward Nathalie. *Who?*

"You betcha. They invited me to several of their parties, and," Earl dropped his voice, "the stories I could tell …" he said, shaking his head. "But I swore to Dean and the bunch I'd take them to the grave, and I'm nothing if not a man of my word."

Earl had plenty to say, so much so that Nathalie started taking notes, pulling a piece of scratch paper from her jacket pocket. He explained that the banks and land developers wanted to offload large chunks of homes and undeveloped lots in the area to investment groups, and they could be bought at pennies on the dollar. They had a big investment auction where firms came to bid on them. It was quite the big deal. Since the government backed the distressed banks, it was a win for everybody—except for the homeowners, that is. No one would modify their existing loans, causing a mass exodus. The investment groups started renting them out, failing to put any additional money into them. Modern-day housing slum lords, as Earl referred to them.

"Ever heard of the firm GIM, Gordon Investment Management?" Nathalie asked.

"Frank? Oh sure," Old Earl said, walking over to retrieve some fresh-squeezed lemonade for his guests. "Big blowhard. He talked and talked and talked. I've been in this business a long time. I know bull when I hear it. Con artist if you ask me."

Alex perked up. "Why do you say that?"

"I knew his grandfather, Donald. We attended high school together. He started that firm for the vets coming back from the Big One. Frank is all about the money for those that already have money. I don't know why he was even out here. He bought one measly bulk lot, the minimum buy-in."

Alex and Nathalie looked at each other with the same astonished expression.

Earl waved good-bye to the women from the steps as they pulled out from the parking lot. He gave the impression of a contented soul despite living in such a forsaken place as Shady Willow.

Alex mindlessly tugged and twisted her necklace while recounting what she already knew about GIM, adding in what Old Earl had shared. "So … what do you think?" she asked on their way back to the hotel.

"Well, it's obvious GIM doesn't have enough housing assets on the books to support the number of investor groups he's bringing in through the VLGF," she replied. "And he must be telling them to not spread the word, because even if Frank was continually buying more bulk lots there are only so many of them. Eventually someone would question why others are getting in on a limited resource."

"Yeah …" Alex muttered, pondering the full reality of the situation, the images of thousands of distressed and empty homes blurring together in her mind.

"I'd say that's why the SEC didn't find anything after George's article came out. Frank can show he has securities on the books, paperwork of actual investment transactions, and none of the investors are filing complaints. Sad to say, but it's pretty slick and airtight."

"Uh-huh."

Back at the hotel room, sprawled across the bed, Alex monitored the HCR from her laptop. On the drive from Shady Willow, she worked on a plan that would expose GIM for the crooked investment deal it was peddling. She was fairly certain after all she'd hacked, read, and heard that her parents, and the whole

WCOF community, had been swindled and didn't even know it. The *Insiders Business Review* article had brought many irregularities to light on Frank's investment firm but had fallen on deaf ears. *If no one can prove you're cheating, then what's to stop you from continuing?*

Nathalie suggested to Alex that she simply hack back into GIM and set up some wire transfers that would replenish Phil and Maggie's savings account, as well as those of the other WCOF members. Alex knew that might work, but it would be risky since large sums of transferred money would trigger red flags at banks, which would then need to report it. As soon as GIM figured out what was going on, things could get ugly for the wire-transfer recipients.

No, Alex knew it would take something creative to get her parents' money back, something that wouldn't be considered stealing, which the wire transfers would ultimately be considered if performed outside normal business activity. That's why she was logged onto the HCR, shopping for the special equipment she'd need to pull it off.

"What are you doing?" Nathalie asked.

"I've got a plan," Alex said excitedly.

"Do tell."

Alex explained why rogue wire transfers wouldn't work: too risky, legally messy, and ultimately Frank would continue duping more and more investors. He needed to be taken down. The best way to expose Mr. Gordon was to appeal to his ego, give him what he wanted, the big charity he craved to endow him with immense recognition. She'd already profiled his preference for supporting the cultural arts, which narrowed down the potential hooks considerably.

"Let's set up a fake up-and-coming charity that would put him on the map," Alex said proudly. "We set up a con, get him to bite, track him moving money through his firm, then leak to the press about a bogus charity. They'll start investigating and uncover the fact the charity is set up to funnel the money right back to his own account."

Nathalie sat on the edge of the bed, captivated by Alex's thoroughly devious plan. "And how do we go about doing that?"

"Well, Miss Herringbone, we're going to New York," Alex announced, christening Nathalie with the genteel name for the occasion. "You're going to pose as an investor."

Alex continued to watch the interminable chatter on the HCR, one of the more serious chat rooms hackers flocked to, sharing secrets, selling information, bragging about their exploits, learning the trade, and picking up work. It was also a place, thanks to its anonymity, where law enforcement and cybercrime task forces lurked.

For Alex's elaborate plan she needed some special equipment not readily available at local computer stores. In fact, what she needed wasn't even out on the open market yet. In a pinch, she hoped to find someone locally who could sell her one. It would be expensive but in New York the cost could easily triple.

"limeStone, need vCloud with intern rout and fire, 1 tera, & C2C fast, 89-blc-100," Alex typed in an open chat window to a hacker friend she knew. *He should know someone in Vegas with it.*

"Wolf_Eyes, sick request. Taking down a big one? zNiNo can hook you up @8p. Not cheap, bring $$$$+. autyrncwphmwovr - qwertytenhzapme."

"Thanks. Stay vigilant."

Nathalie watched over Alex's shoulder with an astonished expression. "Wow, you guys are so cryptic."

"The careful ones are," Alex said as she converted the alpha string of random letters into GPS coordinates for the location where she would meet the hacker named zNiNo to buy the equipment.

"Hey, Wolf_Eyes …" Another chat window popped open with a name Alex didn't recognize, DocZhiv.

Alex ignored the chat request, instead loading the unscrambled coordinates into her phone and locating the address. She had just about logged out from the chat room when another message appeared from DocZhiv: "Someone topped your Fingle hack last night. You're not alone."

Alex stared at the message, amused. Her hacking exploits, especially Fingle, were not about the competition, other than with herself. She never bragged or boasted about her hacks. The legendary status she'd obtained without once promoting herself amazed her—the online community constantly churned the rumor mill. What bothered Alex was the hacker name, one she'd only seen a couple times over the last few months, but never interacted with.

"Go phish," she returned with a smirk on her face, logging out from the chat room.

"Go phish." *Clever.*

Between afternoon conference lectures, Alec grabbed a bite for lunch, sitting out by the hotel pool with his laptop, jumping onto the HCR. He was eager to explore the chat room deeper after his conversation with Jason the day before, ready to apply the new deciphering techniques he'd learned. Alec had previously dabbled on the HCR with the code name DocZhiv, but simply to observe.

Alec watched the often-incoherent conversations scroll down his screen when he spotted the code name Wolf_Eyes enter. His heart skipped a beat. *The great mysterious Wolf_Eyes.* He waited to see if they'd join in or simply sit around, lurking. It didn't take long before he witnessed a cryptic message exchange between Wolf_Eyes and another hacker named limeStone. Alec leaned back in the chaise longue, amazed at the brevity of the dialogue yet the amount of information communicated between the two. *They really do have a special language. At least these two do.*

Alec copied and saved the exchange, reviewing it in more detail. *vCloud must be some special system that is self-contained. 1 terabyte is quite a bit of storage capacity. C2C ... I'm not sure what that refers to.* And limeStone's reply was a bit harder to decipher for Alec. He'd read case studies about the hacker zNiNo, wanted all over the world for stealing personal identity information on a grand scale. *Wow, Wolf_Eyes and zNiNo meeting tonight. That's like setting up a rendezvous with Al Capone and John Gotti.*

Alec took a crack at figuring out where the meet would take place, but *autyrncwphmwovr - qwertytenhzapme* meant nothing to him. He focused his attention on *89-blc-100*, something Jason had taught him to do. *Let's see, if you strip out the hyphen and "blc" you get a generalized zip code.* Alec searched zip codes starting with 89100, shocked to see they were assigned to the Las Vegas area. *They're going to meet here in Vegas?*

He glanced at his watch; twenty minutes until the next lecture. He revisited the longer string *autyrncwphmwovr - qwertytenhzapme.* *It has to be the exact location. Scrambled GPS coordinates? Jason said they were nearly impossible to decrypt.* Alec calculated what time it was in New York. He might be able to catch the intern at GIM.

"Yuri, it's Alec."

"Oh, hi sir."

"Quick question," Alec said, quite excited. "On HRC, what's the commonly used cypher key for GPS coordinates?"

"Ah ... don't know right off but I can find out. Hold on."

While waiting for the intern, Alec decided to call Wolf_Eyes out in the chat room since the name continued to display after the interaction with limeStone had concluded. Alec knew he wasn't well versed in hanker lingo, opting not to pretend like he was, but rather to portray himself as a novice. He recalled the company Fingle from the previous night's review of Wolf_Eyes reports. After saying good night to Nathalie, he'd returned to his hotel room but had difficulty falling asleep with Nathalie's sweet scent overwhelming his senses. Instead, he pored over his notes on Wolf_Eyes from the files Karen had given him, correlating them with the newfound knowledge Nathalie had discussed with him, on how companies use insurance claims in cyberattacks. One high-profile case involved a company named Fingle that claimed Wolf_Eyes had hacked into their network.

Yuri returned with the cypher code, which allowed Alec to quickly decipher the coordinates. He checked the time again. He had two more lectures and a final Q&A session with the FBI before heading to the airport. Now that he'd figured out where Wolf_Eyes and zNiNo were meeting, he needed to rent a car, find his way there, hopefully get a clear view without intruding, and snap off a picture, then hightail it to the airport for his red-eye back to New York.

It sounded good on paper.

017   Brother in Arms

Darkness descended heavily upon the seedy outskirts of downtown Vegas in sharp contrast to the bright lights of the Strip, where night receded to a vague background color in the sky. Alex and Nathalie sat in the rental car across from the meet point, a few blocks down from a couple of strip clubs and an all-night dive diner whose flickering neon lighting cast an eerie glow around it. Alex counted off the hundred-dollar bills in her hand, organizing them like she always did before stuffing the stack neatly into a blank envelope; $7,000. She tucked an additional four grand in another envelope in the event zNiNo played hardball as limeStone warned with the *$$$$+* portion of his chat-room response.

"I don't know why you didn't use the leftover cash from last night," Nathalie said, twirling her hair and sipping a chilled coffee drink.

"I have my own monies," Alex replied, stretching a rubber band around each envelope. *I can't believe the amount of cash I've been handling the last two nights. I feel like a gangster.*

"OK, but that brings up another question," Nathalie said, watching Alex prepare as if going undercover for a sting operation.

"How do you have so much money saved up with school and all the computer equipment you own? The store can't pay that well even if you are living at home."

"Shoot, I forgot a jacket," Alex mumbled, searching for something with bigger pockets than what her jeans offered.

"Here, use mine."

"I developed some cool software called StealthWare that allows people to spy on other computers," she explained as she slipped the jacket on, stuffed the pockets with the envelopes, and pulled her hair up, tucking it into the baseball cap she'd bought at the convenience store on the way. "I sell it on the Web and it brings in a little extra cash."

"Really? And it's legal?"

"Of course. I have a business license and everything. Check out the website I built for it sometime."

The irony was not lost on Alex: people paying her for the ability to spy on others. In need of some faster, but expensive, computer processors and high rpm hard drives a few years back, she had packaged a scaled-down version of a unique Trojan—forgoing the malicious and illegal backdoors they often contained—making it available online. The endeavor thrilled her parents, though Alex never said specifically what it did, only that it helped people stay "informed" on important matters. *Just a little white lie, no biggie.*

"That's probably him," Alex said, spotting a lone figure leaned up against the building, the caper's reality setting in as she zipped up the jacket and put her sunnies on.

Nathalie appeared to marvel at Alex's transformation into the type of person one might expect to find hanging outside a sporting venue scalping tickets, ready to flee at the first sign of trouble. "You sure you want to do this, hon?" Nathalie asked, taking hold of Alex's arm when she opened the passenger door. "You don't have to—"

"Don't worry," Alex replied. "Hackers are just paranoid. This isn't illegal. It's just a quick business deal, in the dark, outside of town, with nobody in sight." She snickered, leaning over to kiss Nathalie on the cheek. "Keep the car running just in case," she said, winking as she exited.

Alex strode briskly across the deserted parking lot, her hands digging deeper into each jacket pocket as she neared the hooded man, who stood under a dim light that hung high off the warehouse's steel beams, its crusted bulb splashing a dingy yellowish glow over the ground. She glanced around, but with few streetlights, those curious enough could easily lurk in the shadows.

"z Ni No?" Alex asked, stopping several yards away in case he wasn't.

"It's z *NiN* o," the man said slowly. His partially concealed pockmarked face made it hard for Alex to see what his eyes were fixed on.

"Sorry. Got the equipment?"

"Interesting," he returned, taking a drag on his cigarette. "Wolf_Eyes is a woman…. I'm impressed." zNiNo stood there attempting to blow smoke rings that formed poorly and collapsed too quickly. "Got the green?"

Alex tossed him the larger of the two envelopes, causing him to drop his cigarette in order to catch the bundle. Alex winced. "Sorry," she said, then held her breath a moment. She'd heard of this guy before, roamed the world so the authorities could never track him down. He was good, often employed social-engineering skills to gain access into highly secured firms. Alex felt he was sloppy, though, often exercising brute-force tactics rather than less conspicuous, more elegant methods. *Probably wouldn't have to move all the time if he'd leave less collateral damage in his wake.*

"Feels light," zNiNo said, juggling the envelope while stamping out the lit butt on the ground.

Alex stood quiet, staring at him, calculating her options until raucous laughter momentarily diverted her attention. She glanced twice toward a group of men exiting the nearby strip club. Her hand squeezed the last envelope tucked deep in the jacket's pocket. "Let's see the drive."

zNiNo smirked, pocketed the money, and pulled out the sleek black vCloud drive. "It's all ready to go. You must have something special planned to require this beauty," he said, gazing at it for several seconds before stepping forward, handing her the device.

Alex tried to remain calm, but her pulse accelerated when zNiNo's tall, shadowy figure loomed over her. With a shaky hand she took the drive and stepped back to examine it, ensuring it had all the necessary ports.

"It's all there," zNiNo said, lighting another cigarette.

"Where are the coms?" she asked, placing the drive in her pocket.

"Like I said," he replied, exhaling smoke in Alex's direction, "light."

Alex fanned zNiNo's carcinogenic breath away from her face, letting out a cough. As she reached for the last envelope the clank of an empty can echoed from across the parking lot. They both shot glares in its direction. With her sunnies on, Alex couldn't make out much beyond her own shadow. She glanced over to the rental car, Nathalie's silhouette still inside. An unsettling hush filled the night.

"Tell you what," zNiNo said, handing Alex another bag, "I'll spot you the coms if you show me your face, so I can see who the *great* Wolf_Eyes is." His bony, nicotine-stained fingers squeezed her arm tightly.

Alex recoiled, jerking her arm back several times, each time more forceful, until she freed herself from his grasp, falling backward. The ground abruptly shot shockwaves through her body. Stunned, she scooted backwards on her butt, scooped up the other packet of money, and tossed it at him. "Just take the cash. That's all you're going to see tonight," she shouted, fear vibrating in her voice.

Alex scrambled up as fast as she could with the equipment, turning to run, but zNiNo grabbed the back of her jacket, pulling her against his stocky body. "Let ... go ..." she yelled, panic now driving her into a terrorized state, unable to complete the sentence out loud. *Of me ... help!*

"Come on, I need to know. Are you bangin' hot, look like a troll? I need something fresh for the spank bank," he implored, wrestling with Alex, pawing at her hat.

Alex twisted and flailed, attempting to free herself from his tight grip, the rough groping, the attempt to expose the person only Nathalie knew as Wolf_Eyes. Nothing worked until a spine-numbing shrill from the rental car distracted zNiNo briefly when the ignition turned over on an already idling engine.

Alex seized the moment and immediately freed one arm, taking swipes at zNiNo's face, clawing with a hand meant for a keyboard, but she couldn't shake herself loose. Just as she felt the hat lift from her head, her sunnies tumble to the ground, and her anonymity fade, the dull thud of heavy footsteps swiftly approached. A strong, throaty voice commanded, "Let go of her!"

Alex tumbled hard to the ground when the dark flash of a man landed a right hook across zNiNo's unsuspecting cheek that sent him stumbling backward, crashing hard against the building. The man grabbed zNiNo before he could retaliate, turned him around, and pushed him headlong into the aluminum siding, the loud pop and dented panel signaling the end of the scuffle. zNiNo groaned and crumpled to the ground.

Alex rapidly crawled over to the two bags of equipment that had scattered across the gravelly pavement, scooping them up, along with her hat. She sprang up, catching a sideways glance of the mysterious man in the trench coat standing over zNiNo. She froze, shocked by the sight. *Cheap-sunglasses guy?* Quickly she turned and tossed her hat back on before he could get a glimpse of her face, then sprinted toward the car Nathalie had ready to go on the street. The passenger door already open, Alex dove in as

Nathalie hit the accelerator. The door slammed closed. The engine revved, tires squealed, both at a fever pitch before fading into the night.

Alec stood over zNiNo, who mumbled about the injustice just served him, watching Wolf_Eyes dive into the car waiting out on the street before it quickly disappeared around the corner. He'd come so close to putting a face with the name. *At least I know it's a woman now. How interesting.* He'd hoped to capture a picture, but inadequate lighting for his cell phone camera forced him to creep up closer to the interaction for a visual, kicking a stray soda can in the process. He feared he'd blown his cover.

"Here, get up," Alec said, offering zNiNo a hand, surprised at his impulse to jump into a fracas that had nothing to do with him. He'd normally reserved such physical aggression for the football field during his playing days.

"Man, what was that for?" zNiNo grumbled, using the wall instead to right himself. "That's police brutality." He rubbed his jaw and shook his sweatshirt clean. "Look ... you crushed my ciggies. Man!"

"I'm not a cop," Alec replied, picking up a thick envelope from the ground.

"What? Hey, that's my ... envelope."

Alec tossed it to him. "What'd she buy?"

"Man, if you're not a cop then I have nothing to say to you. I'm out of here," zNiNo said, turning away.

"I investigate cybercrime z *NiN* o, or should I say Julius? ... What'd she buy?"

Julius stopped in his tracks, his back to Alec. "A hard drive and some com devices."

"That's it? Did she say what she's planning?"

"What do you think, *man*?"

Alec stood quiet a few moments, the dry Nevada air cooling the perspiration on his forehead, flexing knuckles that tingled. "Don't hit women, *man*," Alec warned with a protective instinct that startled him.

Julius took off running across the parking lot. *What is it with hackers running?* He shook his head. Alec wasn't interested in zNiNo. The feds and Interpol were tasked with finding him. He would put a call in to report zNiNo's last known whereabouts, though with his reputation he'd be gone before daybreak. *What are the odds ... first the sunnies girl, then Nathalie, then Wolf_Eyes and zNiNo together in one spot? Only in Vegas can you ride a hot streak like that.*

Alec started back toward the rental car parked around the corner when he caught sight of a piece of paper on the ground next to a pair of dark sunglasses. He picked them up where Wolf_Eyes had fallen. *Nice sunglasses.* He unfolded the paper, squinting to read it in the poorly lit parking lot. All he could make out were the initials "GIM" and some notes about Frank Gordon. Alec's head jerked up, and he stared off in the direction where Wolf_Eyes had escaped, holding his breath as he cell phone rang.

Wolf_Eyes is going after GIM?

"Are you OK?" Nathalie asked again, her hands trembling on the steering wheel, taking corners recklessly until they were well away from the meet-up spot with zNiNo. "The creep—"

Speechless, Alex stared out the windshield, face frozen like a trauma victim, Nathalie's verbal stream of panic falling on deaf ears. She wasn't even thinking about zNiNo's clumsy attempt to expose her, though the knee ache where her jeans tore open and the bloodstains on her hand were reminder enough. *How could Cybercop be there at that exact moment? Perhaps it was a coincidence last night, but no way tonight. He KNEW I would be there.*

Alex slowly turned her head, eyes filled with fury, narrowing and then fixing them on Nathalie, searching for answers. It had been Nathalie's idea to come to Vegas, to drive around the desert looking at empty houses. *Lame! She supposedly runs into this guy, the "client," in the casino last night, then the next thing I know he's fighting off zNiNo in a dark parking lot. Is she trying to get me arrested? Maybe the two of them are working together.* Alex's mind spun through the possibilities.

"Alex! Answer me, are you OK?"

"Yeah, I'm fine," Alex said flatly, her heart still racing, assessing the damage to her jeans, Nathalie's jacket, and the palms of her hands. "My right knee is scraped up and a little tender, that's all."

"I thought someone was going to get killed. Did he have a gun?" Nathalie said, her voice still frenzied. "Who was that other guy?"

"You tell me!"

"I don't know! He came out of nowhere. That hacker guy attacked you and I tried to start the car, but it made this awful screeching sound, then the other guy—"

Alex wasn't buying Nathalie's innocent expression of surprise about the events that went down. *She might not have known zNiNo would grab me, but there's no way Cybercop was there on his own.*

Alex spotted the convenience store they'd stopped at on the way to the rendezvous point. "Pull in here," she ordered. "I need some ice for my knee."

"Sure, anything, hon," Nathalie said, squealing the tires into the parking lot. The car abruptly shook to a stop after it bumped the curb near the storefront. Nathalie jumped out, racing into the store.

Alex grabbed Nathalie's cell phone and rapidly thumbed through her contacts, searching for Cybercop's name. She found a reference to Alec. She dialed the number, letting it ring a few times before someone answered, "Can we talk later?" Alex disconnected instantly. *That's his voice, all right.* She glanced up, checking on

Nathalie's whereabouts while searching the phone for any calls, voice mails, text messages or e-mails to or from him, finding an outgoing call to him at 7:45 p.m., just fifteen minutes before the meeting with zNiNo. *That's when I was in this very store buying the hat and envelopes.*

Nathalie returned with some ice from the soda fountain in a takeout bag. Alex shoved the phone into her jacket pocket next to the vCloud drive, applying the makeshift ice pack to her tender knee as they drove back to the hotel, Nathalie chattering on incessantly. Alex simply tuned her out.

Back at the hotel, Alex hurriedly exited the rental car and slammed the door shut while Nathalie briefly searched the car for her cell phone then gave up. Nathalie couldn't bridge the gap to Alex, who strode steadfastly and with singular focus from the parking garage through the lobby toward the bank of elevators, catching an open door that departed before Nathalie arrived.

In the room, Alex gathered up her belongings, tossed what clothes weren't already packed into her duffel bag, and stuffed the computer equipment, including the vCloud that cost her eleven grand and a good pair of sunnies, into her backpack. She wasn't sure if the new device would even work after the skirmish.

"Hey, speedy," Nathalie said, entering the room, "did you see my cell phone? I couldn't find ... what are you doing?"

Alex continued to pack in haste.

"Hon, what's wrong?" She stepped up behind Alex, rubbing her shoulders.

Alex shrugged Nathalie's hands off, picking up the bags. "I'm going home," she said, shouldering the backpack and heading for the door.

"Why? Our flight to New York is in the morning. I switched the reserva—"

"Why did you set me up?" Alex blurted out, pivoting around, tears mixing with the anger in her voice. "Why?"

Nathalie stood motionless, her expression confused. "What do you mean? I didn't—"

"That guy, the one that just *happened* to be there to thump zNiNo, he's a cybercriminologist from New York. Here in Vegas. At an exchange that was set up just this afternoon."

"I don't understa—"

"His name is Alec. He stopped in the store a couple weeks ago."

Nathalie's face went pale as she slumped down on the end of the bed. "What?"

"Yeah, and *you* called him fifteen minutes before the meeting tonight." Alex's voice trembled, gaining volume as she tossed Nathalie's phone on the bed. "The same guy I saw *you* leave the casino with last night. The 'client' who was worried about his money."

Nathalie looked down at the phone, her recent call list displayed. She shook her head. "Alex … it's not what you think. He—"

"I *trusted* you. I confided in you about my hacking. I don't take anybody's money, so why would you turn me in? Do you know how devastated my parents would be if I were arrested?" Alex began breathing in gulps as the tears gushed down her face, her body visibly shaking. "Do … you?" She squeezed her eyes tight, head sagging, staccato sobs audible between gasps for air.

Nathalie rushed over, enveloping Alex with one arm while the other cradled her head, now buried in Nathalie's blouse. "It's OK, hon. I would never let that happen to you," she said, stroking Alex's hair.

Despite the accusations and tears, Alex wanted to believe Nathalie. She had turned her dormant little world into something exciting, not unlike her Tammaré adventures. *But for what purpose? Friendship, love, revenge, betrayal?* She was torn between going home, scuttling her equipment to protect herself, and returning to her safe and predictable life; or staying there in Nathalie's arms, intoxicated by the scent of her perfume that was none other than body chemistry itself, perhaps risking an unpleasant confrontation with Alec.

"Let's sit down and talk," Nathalie said, wiping off the damp smudges from Alex's face.

"No," Alex choked out, pulling away. "I need to go home." Alex started for the door, determined to get back to normalcy. Life had been a fast-moving train since Nathalie's arrival; it was time to jump off.

"Alex, wait," Nathalie pleaded, her voice cracking as Alex opened the door.

Alex paused but didn't bother to turn around. Her hand trembled on the door latch, her eyes shut tight, attempting to stem the stream of tears pouring out.

"Alec … is your brother."

The Hunt for Wolf_Eyes

Alec woke abruptly from his recurring dream to impatient barks a few inches from his head. It was already noon and Cassidy had been anxiously pacing for some time. "Sorry, boy," he said, yawning, the dream's closing credits rolling in his mind. This time he'd felt the presence of someone sitting alongside him while he spun like a top.

Despite fatigue, Alec failed to sleep much on the red-eye home from Las Vegas. Instead, he spent his time piecing together what the notes meant from the scrap piece of paper he found on the ground after the Wolf_Eyes and zNiNo drop turned ugly. Clear as day were his father's name and the initials "GIM" penned cursively on the legal paper, along with information about the Vegas Land Grab Fund, minimum buy information, even his great-grandfather's name.

He'd only recently learned about the bundled real-estate product when he walked in on his father pitching it at the office to some potential investors. It had been a boon for the firm, bringing in many new clients who wanted to cash in on the housing meltdown by way of a mutual fund of sorts, contributing to GIM's huge growth spurt over the past several years, taking their assets from a paltry $300 million to well over a billion, and steadily growing.

But why would a hacker who purportedly doesn't hack for personal profit be snooping around GIM, leaving behind Trojans coded in a mysterious language, and purchasing high-tech equipment? What would she stand to gain from it? Had she turned, gone bad? Was she personally affected by something GIM did?

Cassidy barked again, dancing by the front door. "OK, OK, boy," he said, throwing on some clothes.

"There you are," Thomas said, briskly approaching Alec, who held Cassidy's leash while the dog sniffed around the few dirt patches near his loft. "You weren't answering your phone and you said you'd be at work by ten. I got worried."

"Yes, sorry," Alec said, amused that Cassidy, who seemed on the verge of exploding in the loft, was now leisurely sniffing for the perfect spot to relieve himself. *Curiosity trumped urgency, apparently.* "I overslept. Long flight home." He remembered that he'd missed a morning class, too.

"Oh, OK ... cool shades. Makes you look like a Hollywood celebrity."

Alec continued to stare at Cassidy while taking note on how much better the sunglasses blocked the sun from his eyes and improved his vision than the other pair had. "Thanks. I picked them up in Vegas."

"Good trip?"

"Yes. I met some interesting people," he replied, deciding Cassidy needed some encouragement, pulling on the leash to go back inside. Instantly Cassidy's leg went up, adequately watering the tree. "We need to set up some surveillance on GIM's servers. The usual stuff."

"Really? Your dad's firm?"

"There's a credible threat, but we'll have to do it off-book for now. I know Henry won't approve man hours for it."

"Lips are sealed, Hollywood," Thomas said with a grin.

Alec shook his head at Thomas's latest nickname while Cassidy looked up, relieved, but now hungry.

Alex sat languid in the Las Vegas airport terminal, numbly staring at the departure board, its flickering rows displaying flights ready to depart to destinations near and far, her demeanor the portrait of a bad run in the casinos though brought on by very different circumstances. Nathalie conversed with airline personnel over at the check-in counter, requesting an upgrade on their tickets to first-class, where Alex would stand a better chance of sleeping on the long cross-country flight than in economy. She hadn't slept much the previous night.

"I don't have a brother," were Alex's first words after Nathalie dropped the improbable notion on her. She still couldn't believe it. *Is Nathalie trying to mess with me some more?* Nathalie's appealing mysteriousness was beginning to wane.

Alex contemplated the ticket in her hand to New York, still not convinced she wanted to continue with the trip, or deal with Frank Gordon and his investment scam. She glanced back at the departure board, searching for the next flight to the Bay Area, then closed her eyes, Nathalie's words hanging in the air: "Alec … is your brother."

Growing up, when Alex felt besieged by classmates and neighborhood kids, she'd taken to drawing on her mom's old art pads, sketching out scenes of an imaginary brother standing up for her. Later, as she took to computers, the virtual world gave her a sense of accomplishment and mastery, where she returned the favor in kind, protecting her virtual brother-in-arms from the vicissitudes in the future world of Tammaré.

"OK, we got the upgrade," Nathalie said, sitting down besides Alex. "I had a bunch of miles to use up," she continued, appearing cheery despite having consoled Alex through the night, replacing the old ticket in her lifeless hand with the first-class window seat. "You're going to love it." Nathalie brushed some hair back from Alex's expressionless face. "I'm so sorry, hon, that you found out about the adoption from me."

Alex didn't say anything. She simply stared out into the terminal, an unrecognizable abstraction of life, Nathalie's soothing touch sorting out the confusion, or perhaps adding to it. Alex digested the fact that not only did she have a brother, but she was also adopted. *Maggie and Phil aren't my real parents?*

The best Alex could recollect through the fog of the previous night's events and revelations was that Nathalie had met a guy during an Alcatraz tour a couple weeks back who had the same eye color as Alex. She struck up a conversation with him and the more she chatted with him, the more it convinced her that he was somehow related despite living in New York his whole life as an only child.

According to Nathalie, after meeting Alec she did some research, coming across a newspaper clipping about a two-car accident involving a family of four, a mother and father with their baby boy and girl twins in the little town of Sonoma, California. The parents didn't survive the accident. The news article didn't report what became of the twins, but it included a picture of the family taken days before the crash. Alex peered down at Nathalie's phone, displaying the article and adjoining photo, two proud parents holding twin babies, their beaming smiles a reflection of Alex's in happier times. She felt a visceral pain deep inside, empathizing with two people she didn't remember, holding her and her brother, whom she didn't know. *What would my life have been like had it not been for the accident?*

"Good morning, passengers," said the voice from behind the check-in counter that spread across the terminal. "This is the preboarding announcement for Flight 1703 to New York, LaGuardia. We are now inviting those passengers with small children—"

"Hon, that's us," Nathalie said, tapping Alex's arm. "You still up for the trip ... or do you want to head home? I'd understand if you wanted to go home. It's been a wild couple of days for you, and—"

"New York," Alex announced, snapping out of her funk, grabbing the backpack. "We need to see this through. The adoption thing doesn't change anything," she continued as they strode at a fast clip down the jet bridge onto the plane, finding their first-class seats. "If anything, it makes me more determined to right a wrong against people who took me in when everything I never knew was taken from me. The brother thing ... well, that too doesn't change anything, though it makes it more challenging since he's a cybercop living in New York. We'll just need to be more careful."

Alex didn't realize just how careful she needed to be. Nathalie hadn't told her that Alec was Frank Gordon's son. The life-altering adoption news, learning about her brother, and how Nathalie knew about it all precluded deeper examination of Alec's adopted family lineage.

Alec needed some perspective and fresh air. He called Henry at the task force to let him know he was going to take the day off. He filled him in on the details of the trip and conference, skipping the part that caused his right hand to require an ice pack every couple of hours. As a wide receiver in high school, Alec was accustomed to catching the football and pushing defenders away, not jabbing them with a right hook. A pugilist he wasn't.

He also mentioned a zNiNo sighting, suggesting a call to the feds would be wise. Henry agreed, then informed Alec he had another case for him to head up; a New York–based mortgage company, American Bank, with offices in West Virginia, had been experiencing unusual accounting issues related to security breaches. Alec welcomed the additional workload.

After hanging up with Henry, Alec noticed Cassidy's pleading-for-attention eyes staring back at him and shook his head. The dog knew how to lay on a guilt trip. He atoned for boarding Cassidy during the Vegas trip by hailing a dog-friendly cabbie up to Central Park, where Alec normally did his runs on those summer days when the oppressive East Coast mugginess abated.

The spring sun shined bright in the sky, trees sprouted white buds, young couples slowly pushed baby carriages across the Great Lawn, and Frisbees sailed through the air, chased and retrieved by eager dogs. Alec loved the place. Cassidy just enjoyed Alec's company, showing no interest in other dogs who felt the need to introduce themselves with their snouts.

Alec found a spot out on the grass to place the folding chair he'd toted along, near a mother and father introducing their twin children to the wonders of turtles in the nearby pond. A group of attractive college women passed by giggling and whispering and shooting furtive glances his way. They only reminded him of Nathalie.

"You want to meet Nathalie, Big Dog?" Alec said, scratching the belly of Cassidy, who let out a disapproving groan. He wasn't fond of sharing when Alec had the rare date over to the loft.

Alec pulled out his laptop, opening up a blank document to organize his thoughts on GIM and Wolf_Eyes.

Case Notes: The Hunt for Wolf_Eyes

- GIM servers are compromised in recent weeks, without any digital footprints left behind.
  - Trojan Horse is installed though intent unknown and comprised of unknown language
- Evidence in the form of a note suggests GIM is a target.
  - By Wolf_Eyes?
- Julius Archer (aka zNiNo) sells Wolf_Eyes (an unknown woman) a vCloud drive and specialized communication devices in Las Vegas
  - Does Wolf_Eyes live in Vegas where the purchase took place?
- Some IP-address tracking evidence suggests Wolf_Eyes operates out of Northern California
  - If so, then why Vegas?

I probably should've interrogated Julius more. Alec paused, flexing his hand, the soreness as fresh as the incident itself.

He continued to list out other germane facts—com-device purchase suggested more than one person involved—while listing out recent activity involving GIM: the *Insiders Business Review* article, its substantial growth in assets since the inclusion of the VLGF, and Frank's recent philanthropy award.

In Alec's preliminary profile on Wolf_Eyes, he summarized the plethora of computer-security breaches in the finance sector attributed to her, noting the lack of monetary loss reported in association with said hacks. Based on the note found, he described her handwriting as flowing and distinct, and her HRC activity suggested a witty, smart, and cautious woman.

Other than the note from the parking lot, I can't positively connect Wolf_Eyes to the GIM hacks, only that she has them in her sights. Something's up, I just don't know what yet. I need to talk to Dad, find out if there is something about the VLGF *worth provoking Wolf_Eyes.*

Cassidy rolled over to get a better angle of the sun on his thin coat when Alec's cell phone rang. "Hello, Thomas."

"Hey, Hollywood," Thomas said, "I've got the surveillance equipment gathered for you. Want me to bring it by your place or drop it off at your dad's office?"

"Thanks. Just leave it on my desk. I'll pick it up tonight," Alec said, looking up as the *tink* of a softball bursting off an aluminum bat pierced the din of the park from the diamond across the way. "And drop the Hollywood."

Alec jumped onto the HRC site to check for any buzz over the previous night's meet-up between zNiNo and Wolf_Eyes, but Hacker Nation showed no such drama, instead committed to plotting future digital chaos. He expected as much.

"Hi, Mom," Alex said with a cheery tone despite her weary state once she and Nathalie deplaned in New York, headed toward the yellow cab circle. Alex had slept only the last hour of the flight, the previous hours over the middle of the country spent configuring her new vCloud drive. Despite a scratch or two the drive functioned properly. She also tested the new communications devices, their size so small that when placed in the ear no one could tell they existed. She had Nathalie walk around the cabin as they secretly conversed with each other, Nathalie suggesting at one point she wanted to join the Mile High Club. Alex didn't understand, then blushed profusely when Nathalie explained the tradition. *In a bathroom? Seriously? That sounds weird.*

"Hi, sweetie. How is Las Vegas? Win your tuition for next year?" her mom said with a chuckle.

If she only knew. "Hey, Mom, I'm thinking of going to New York with Nathalie … Just for a couple days." After an emotionally restless night and fuzzy morning, she hadn't been in the right frame of mind to call them before leaving Vegas. She wanted to ask them if it was true about the adoption, if she had a brother, and, if she did, why hadn't he also been adopted by them? *Perhaps twins were too much to take on?* Instead, she decided *if* she was going to inquire, it would be in person, not over the phone. *They have their reasons for raising me as their own and maybe it should stay that way. I certainly don't love them any less for it.*

"Oh, hon, I don't know," her mom said. "It's been busy and you have your shifts to cover."

"Kara can cover my shifts," Alex replied, hopeful her mom wouldn't groan at the suggestion.

"Honey, the last time Kara covered your shift, she watered down the propane tank out back and poured a whole bag of chia seeds over it, thinking it would make it more beautiful." She sighed. "Honey, Kara's a sweet girl, but she's—"

"I know, Mom, but please, it's really important," Alex pleaded, wishing her dad had answered the phone. *This would already be a done deal.* "I met this guy in Vegas and he likes my work on the software I developed for the store, and wants me to come to New York to talk about selling it nationally." *Another white lie. How many do you tell before you start believing them yourself?*

"Really? That's exciting. Why sure, hon, go to New York. Do you need some money for airfare?"

"No, Mom, I'm good." She heaved a sigh of relief. "I'll call you when I know more about the meeting, and when I'll be back home. Love ya and tell Dad the same for me."

"Oh, speaking of your dad, he found Sundance chewing on a magazine in your bedroom the other day. Phil, what was that magazine called?" Alex could hear her dad's muffled response in the background. "*Insiders Business Review.* Your father wrestled it from him. He found an article about Frank Gordon and got worked up about it. Was that something you were reading, dear? He doesn't want you getting involved with him."

Alex turned toward Nathalie, who looked back at her. "What?" Nathalie whispered.

"My dad found the GIM article," Alex whispered back as a porter motioned and escorted the women toward the next available cab.

"Hey, Mom, I have to go. Tell Dad not to worry. I have an assignment for school that covers some financial stuff and the article fits into my paper. In New York, Nathalie and I *might* stop by their office to check up on them. Don't worry, I haven't turned into a spy." *Not yet anyway.* "Love ya."

Alex hung up, scooted into the cab, and scrunched her nose at the pungent smell left behind by the last fare. *Here I go again ... getting in over my head.* A reserved smile crossed her face.

Alec spent time with Sam installing the surveillance software on GIM's network, going over the details of its usage. They discussed the network's vulnerabilities and what needed to be done to shore up the multitude of ways hackers could get in, though even that might not be enough. Simple, easily surmised passwords, lax security settings on desktop computers, and social deception employed by hackers are often the weak and easy link into a network, something a small firm like GIM wouldn't be immune to.

Sam was a likable guy whose home-schooling tradition, sweaty palms, and colorful, untucked rugby shirts were endearing traits, though his information-technology aptitude left much to be desired, earning his computer-science degree online over the course of six years. Now twenty-seven years old, a little overweight, and meant for a junior system-administrator position, he found himself overseeing a network of computers responsible for hundreds of millions of dollars in an investment firm. His one true asset: being at Frank's beck and call.

Alec knew his dad had spent a pittance on the technology infrastructure for GIM since taking over, and less on someone to administer it. Unlike Jack Gordon, and his father before him, Frank spent money on appearances rather than on virtual behind-the-scenes necessities that mattered most, especially when it came to protecting financial assets. Part of the reason stemmed from a lack of appreciation for the real cyber threats that existed—out of sight, out of mind—and partly out of vanity.

Most of the software Alec implemented on the network was standard stuff, stealth tracking software, and file-protection traces that, if files were copied or downloaded, would return information on where they traveled to. The intent was not to prevent the intrusion or to let on that the system had monitored the breach, but to track it, trace it, and follow the trail to the person behind it. In this case, Alec knew even with plugging up all the known entry points, Wolf_Eyes had demonstrated enough skill to reenter, and that's what he counted on. *Shore up all the obvious holes, let her think the administrator had done his job, allow her to sneak in through some unknown hole, and watch what she does. It might take some time to track her down, if she's as good as she appears, but eventually I'll find her.*

Alec continued to wrestle with Wolf_Eyes's motive. *Why GIM? What about the VLGF was so appealing or unappealing?* For insight, he needed to speak with his father, a conversation Alec did not look forward to. For someone who commanded great respect and attention, Frank was prone to immense vagueness on complex matters. It rubbed against Alec's detail-oriented nature.

Alec sauntered into the GIM reception area, smiling at a newly arrived text message from Nathalie: "Will see you soon. In New York this week. XOXO."

"Hey, Alec," said Gina, GIM's resident flirt and a vital cog that had kept them running smoothly for the past seventeen years. Even at forty-eight and happily married, she never lost the charm of her youth. "Love the new shades. They certainly suit you."

"Thanks, Gina," he said, pulling them down over his eyes, tilting his head up and to the side while flashing her a big grin with hands on his hips. He couldn't remember a time in his life without her cheery personality.

"So who's the girl?"

Alec smiled. There was no fooling Gina. "Nathalie. I met her in San Francisco," he said before lowering his voice. "She's incredibly—"

"Alec, is that you?" Frank's voice bellowed from his office.

"Sexy," he mouthed to Gina with a wink, walking toward and into Frank's office. "Hi, Father. Do you have a few minutes?"

"Not really." Frank's focus didn't stray from his computer monitor. "I've got meetings all day and a phone conference with an Asian investment group who want in on the Vegas fund. I tell you, those—"

"That's what I want to talk to you about," Alec said, interrupting his father's forthcoming snide and potentially racist remark, "the Vegas Land Grab Fund. I need to understand it better as it might relate to the recent hacks."

"Why? What have you found out?" Frank asked, pausing from the margin-spread analysis he was working on. "What's with the stupid glasses on your head? You look like an idiot."

Alec ignored the comment. "There still is not enough evidence to open an official—"

"Enough evidence?!"

"But," Alec said, his hands motioning for Frank to relax, "there is reason to believe that the VLGF is of some interest to whoever is behind the latest hacks."

Frank rose from the desk, moving over to the window.

"I'm looking into it, but off the books, of course. Henry won't allocate—"

"Yeah, it's better that way," Frank said, turning back toward the desk. "Keep it in the family, between you and me. What do you need to know?"

Alec took a moment to phrase his next series of questions carefully so as not to intrude too much, too quickly, causing his father to clam up, offering his usual vague responses intended to give plausible information to chew on, but practically useless in the end. That he'd immediately captured his father's attention intrigued him, though he didn't know why. "Start with some background on it, and tell me how it's used as a financial tool."

Frank leaned back in his big leather chair, placed his hands behind his head, and stared out into the room as if ready to tell an epic tale. In one of the longest father-and-son discussions they'd had since Alec's decision to study cybercriminology, Frank explained the VLGF's structure and implementation. He had championed the unique financial product for GIM in order to bring in new investors who desired more than the real-estate ETFs currently available in the marketplace. The dire state of the housing market, well known throughout the country, was something even the least educated could understand and relate to.

Alec listened intently, took notes, and observed his father's body language, a habit he picked up from a course on the subject entitled "The Body Never Lies." Alec referenced the article that had appeared a few months earlier in *Insiders Business Review*, which suggested the numbers at GIM didn't add up. Frank riled immediately, ranting on about how the damn Learing Brothers firm had concocted the whole thing in an attempt to make him look bad and lure investors away. He flippantly suggested they were the ones behind the GIM hacks. Though Alec couldn't rule out another company resorting to such guerrilla tactics, he assured his father of its unlikeliness. Whistle-blowing was far more likely, but GIM's family-owned structure made that a stretch of the imagination.

"The damn SEC crawled through here and gave us a clean bill of health, for chrissakes," Frank sputtered out, grabbing the phone, obviously done with the discussion.

Alec stood up. "Has anybody lost money on the VLGF, enough to target GIM?"

"Are you suggesting that someone is seeking revenge for their losses?" his dad replied with an indignant tone. "There are no guarantees in investing."

"So, have there been some investors who have lost their proverbial shirt on it?"

"Their shirt? Of course not. Have there been some clients that haven't fared well? Probably. I don't have any numbers off the top of my head. Can't be many, though."

"Thanks, Father." Alec stood there and watched his dad jab buttons on the phone console as if perturbed, trying to understand the defensive behavior. "If it's possible, could you have Gina gather the names of those who have been negatively impacted? It might give me some leads to follow," he added, walking toward the door, Frank now talking on the phone, the list unlikely to reach Alec's hands. He knew the tight-lipped nature of the financial industry, and since he had shunned the family business, GIM's day-to-day activities remained proprietary, shrouded in doublespeak, far removed from him.

 # New York, New York

"OK, so what does this thing that almost got you killed do?" Nathalie asked Alex in their W Union Square hotel room a few hours after landing, handling the vCloud like a toy surprise she'd pulled out from a cereal box. "It's pretty small and—"

"Stop playing with that," Alex replied, snatching it from Nathalie before it endured any more abuse. "I wasn't almost killed." She snorted at the notion. Alex had been fortunate that airport security didn't take a closer look at the device when they passed through the TSA screening point in Vegas. It wasn't an imminent threat, but it appeared unusual enough to warrant further examination. She wisely slipped it under the laptop when she plopped it into the gray carrier, the vCloud's thin profile barely raised the laptop, avoiding attention. At worst it would've resembled a latch underneath.

"Do you know what Cloud computing is?" Alex said as she plugged the vCloud into her laptop while data obtained from the Scarab Trojan streamed from a computer in her bedroom back home.

"You're going to get all techie on me, aren't you?"

"It's pretty simple," Alex said, multitasking. "You probably use it already. Do you go to a website for your e-mail?"

"Yeah."

"That's Cloud computing in a nutshell."

"What do you mean?"

"Your computer doesn't have an e-mail program on it, and all your e-mails aren't there either. They are on another computer somewhere else in the world. Any program you use on the web or any information you store there is considered the Cloud," Alex said, taking a brief moment to air-quote "Cloud." "That way you can use any computer to access it. If it were all on your computer and you didn't have it with you … then you'd be out of luck."

"Why call it the *Cloud*?"

"Makes technology sound cute," Alex said with her usual wry smile. "Like *Apple* computers or *cookies*."

Part of Alex's plan to bring Frank Gordon to justice hinged on integrating with GIM's main servers and network. She knew at some point GIM would really lock down their network because of her previous hacks. She also knew that the Scarab Trojan would eventually be found, if it hadn't already, which would in all likelihood turn up the heat, perhaps get her newfound brother's cybercrime task force involved.

Alex set up the vCloud to mirror GIM's Ethernet operation, to record all the activity, so once connected, GIM employees would interact in the vCloud space while she controlled the real instance, leaving the servers unattended for her to do anything she needed, an idea she came up with after watching the *Ocean's Eleven* movie—where the crew set up a fake vault, fed the video feed of it to the security team, and then were allowed to roam freely in the real one. Alex took the concept to the virtual world.

"Wow, that's downright ingenious," Nathalie said. "How do you think up all this stuff?"

"I have a pretty good imagination, and I've had quite a bit of time in my life to think. Potent combination."

"What else have you thought about with all that time on your hands?" Nathalie asked, stripping her clothes off. With a flick of her foot she launched her bra from the floor toward Alex.

Alex stopped typing when the silk garment landed across her arm, peering up from the virtual Cloud to see Nathalie standing naked, hands on her hips. Alex had previously caught glimpses of Nathalie's bare form back home in her bedroom and at the B&B in Santa Cruz, but now she stood like a nude model posing for an art class, Alex gazing intently, her artistic mind rendering a Venus de Milo in the flesh. Alex couldn't deny her attraction to Nathalie—her mysterious outgoing nature, beauty, sex appeal— but Alex's timid nature continued to paralyze her when it came to exploring *life* outside the confines of Tammaré's virtual world.

"I said you're supposed to pose as an investor, Lady Herringbone, not a nude model," Alex mumbled several contemplative moments later, cheeks flushing, flicking the bra away, her attention back in the Cloud.

"Next time you should draw me on your art pads back home," Lady Herringbone said with a wink. "I'm going to jump in the shower to get the cab ride off me."

Alex glanced back at Nathalie, watching her saunter into the bathroom, recalling Doob's pickup line at the Surf Shack: *Your board need waxing?* She let out a little sigh right as Nathalie turned her head and flashed a *gotcha* grin. Alex's elbow slipped off the table, causing her arm to lurch, knocking the vCloud off its perch.

Frank got off the phone with Li Zhang, the head of Singapore's largest finance center. They'd met at Johnny's Steak House during the previous Gordon family dinner. Li had traveled to New York with a group of overseas investors searching for opportunities to invest in the US economy during the rebuilding phase after the downturn a few years back. Frank's ambition knew no bounds, and he immediately seized on the opportunity for GIM to bring in international clients and money.

Frank pitched his Vegas Land Grab Fund, citing the benefits of going through a firm like GIM rather than dealing directly with banks: it offloaded the burden of real-estate ownership on foreign soil and mitigated the risks associated with full ownership. "A mutual fund of toxic loans turned over into the hands of investment groups," as Frank was prone to summarize the financial product he'd devised.

Frank came across internationally uncultured to his foreign clientele, ignorant of their customs, lacking the social graces often necessary to negotiate with Pacific Rim business entities, his political incorrectness easily observed in VLGF's name itself, *Land Grab*, a contentious issue internationally—multinational companies scooping up large chunks of land cheaply in developing countries. But Frank had two things going for him: an affable charm, and a financial product unavailable elsewhere, his faux pas politely overlooked with two capable and opportunistic traits.

"Gina," Frank hollered as the business day wound down, "could you come in here for a moment?"

Gina entered his office as she had every time since Frank took over the firm, graciously smiling at his inability to embrace even the simplest technology: the intercom. It was too many buttons to push for such a simple *come hither* command. "What can I do for you, Frank?"

"I need you to put together a prospectus for Li Zhang on the VLGF. Send the usual template with a 3.25 percent origination fee added and forty-eight-hour expiration. Overnight it to him," he said, handing her the order sheet. "Also, put together a profile on Li and his firm."

"Of course," she replied, scribbling down some notes. "Breaking into the international market?"

"Yeah. About time, too. This firm needs to innovate and expand to new markets."

"Jack did well in his day."

"Sure, but nothing like this, creating new products, wealth, supporting the cultural arts—"

"Yes, Frank … you're making a name for yourself."

Frank raised an eyebrow, detecting a hint of appeasement to her tone.

"While you were on your conference call—"

"That'll be all, Gina."

"A Miss Nathalie Herringbone called to—"

"Never heard of her."

"She's in town visiting and requested a meeting with you regarding investing with—"

"Gina, tell her no. We don't deal with individual investors except by invite only. You know that. If she wants to invest, she'll need to work with a group, and we'll pitch our products to them. Now, if you'll—"

"She mentioned she represents several royal families in Europe," Gina said, turning to leave, "and sits on the board of directors for CAI here in New York."

Frank raised his head. "What's CAI?"

"Cultural Arts International. A new nonprofit organization promoting New York arts around the world," she replied on her way through the doorway.

Frank reclined in his chair with an ambitious grin. "Sure, set up an appointment with her as soon as possible."

"I didn't hear that, Frank," Gina said with a chuckle from her desk. "Use the intercom."

Frank pushed a couple of buttons on the phone console, auto-dialing a client by mistake. "Just set up an appointment with her for this week," Frank hollered.

Gina snickered, picking up the phone.

Frank patiently waited on hold in the after hours of the business day for Richard Janask. Since the conference call with the Singapore investment firm, Frank had been on and off the phone all evening, talking with his *big* clients, as he did at the end of every fiscal quarter.

As Frank waited, he went online to search for Cultural Arts International's website. The web results placed their link near the top of the list, which meant it was trending particularly high at the moment. "Promoting visibility and opportunity for New York artisans, exposing our artistic traditions, cultural vitality, and community well-being worldwide," read the mission statement underneath the eclectic graphic depicting art, music, and dance motifs splashed across the top of the page. It didn't have the wealth of information Frank had hoped for, but then he knew it was a new charity. *Probably still in the early developmental phase. Perfect. Something new I can sink my teeth into before someone else champions it.*

"Sorry, Frank, I needed to sign off on a few things," Richard said. "Now, what were you saying?"

"I asked about your dividend this quarter. How much of it do you want reinvested?"

"What's the figure?"

"One point two."

Richard let out a long elated whistle. "Nice. I don't know how you do it Frank, but you're the man."

"You're too kind, Richard," Frank said with feigned modesty in his voice. "Just a solid investing model to grab the low-hanging fruit. I'm surprised no one else out there follows the easy money. They all flock to the high-profile stocks that are as bloated as the housing bubble was."

"Whatever you're doing, keep it up," Richard said. "Go ahead and reinvest seventy-five percent. I have my eye on a summer place down in Palm Beach."

"Sounds great. I'll set up the wire transfer this week," Frank said, making an entry in the spreadsheet named "A-list." "Enjoy Florida. Say hi to Joann for me."

Frank may have been challenged when it came to using simple electronic gadgets around the office—intercom, electric stapler, paper shredder—but when it came to PowerPoint presentations and complex spreadsheet analysis he was a savant. The A-list spreadsheet tracked all his preferred clients, individual invite-only investors, the ones who garnered the most attention with their large investment stakes at GIM. The clients on this list had the most to gain and could give Frank the most for his labors. They often afforded him favorable perks throughout the community. *Win-win.*

Frank completed his A-list calls, then transferred nearly $8 million from his offshore account to a domestic one to cover their quarterly dividends.

Money, numbers, and bottom lines ran through Frank's veins like caffeine; managing the office's dimmer switch, a virus he couldn't shake.

CON THIS WAY

"Nathalie, can you hear me?" Alex whispered, the com device concealed in her ear as she turned the corner onto Barclay Street, glancing around to make sure she was alone, or as alone as one could be among eight million city dwellers. No response. She assumed for the moment Nathalie was in the elevator on her way up to GIM.

Sitting down on the empty bench butted up against the formidable stone-and-brick building where GIM was headquartered, Alex whipped out her netbook and portable IP scanner. While the system booted, she leaned back, craning her neck, searching for the building's top, but the old towering structure appeared to go on forever. Its earthy hues of thick stone slabs from various quarries near and far gave it a castle-like appearance. The deep chiseled engraving one could submerge their hand in subtly, but resolutely, pronounced its identity: Barclay Financial.

"Hi, Gina. My name is Nathalie Herringbone," her voice crackled in Alex's earpiece, the pronounced French accent catching her off guard. "I have a two p.m. appointment with Mr. Gordon."

"Yes, Miss Herringbone. Frank is in another meeting at the moment. Please have a seat."

A few quiet moments passed while Alex opened up various utilities on her laptop.

"You look familiar to me," Gina said. "Have we met before?"

Alex's hands froze over the keys. *Nathalie's cover is blown already? This doesn't bode well.*

"No, no, I don't believe so." Nathalie's voice sounded strained to Alex. "I spend most of my time on the West Coast."

"Really? I haven't spent any time out there. You look so familiar though ... If you will excuse me, I need to use the ladies' room."

Nathalie whispered to Alex a few moments later, "Hey, hon, you there?"

"Yeah. You sure you want to do this? What was I thinking, you posing as an investor?" Alex answered quickly, nervous about Nathalie's presence inside the lion's den as much as her own proximity to it, hacking out in the open.

"Take a deep breath. It's going to be fine."

Alex filled her lungs with a mixture of hot-dog steam and the scent of warm pretzel yeast, held it, then exhaled. "Does the receptionist know you?"

"We're fine. Stop worrying."

"Nice accent."

"*Merci, ma chérie.*"

Alex smiled as goose bumps formed. "What's it like in there?"

"A very regal feel to it ... like old money lives here."

"Any doors that look overly secured, like with a keypad?"

"Let me see ... not really. There are two conference rooms that are empty, the double doors leading into Frank's office, and an open door with a couple voices coming from it. That's all."

"Can you take a peek into the open room?"

"Yeah, hold on ... yep, two guys in there playing a video game. There are also quite a few computers with cables running along the wall."

"Bingo," Alex said, scanning the building for IP addresses, finding the one she initially used to drop Scarab through. "OK, got it. I don't see any added intrusion-detection software since my last hack. I can't believe they haven't done anything. Wait, they did remove Scarab. That's OK. We need to get the name of Frank's computer in his office so I know where to—"

"Sure, give me a call later today and we'll get the wire transfer set up for you," said the booming male voice that erupted in Alex's ear, causing her head to snap back as if someone might be standing in front of her. "You've made a great decision investing with us, Bernie. I'll talk to you later," the man's voice continued. "Ah, Miss Herringbone, sorry for the delay. Won't you please step into my office … Gina!"

"Gina took leave for the powder room. And you may call me Nathalie, Mr. Gordon."

"'Took leave for the powder room' … OK, Lady Herringbone," Alex said, snickering, disturbing the homeless man slumped on the nearby stoop.

"Of course, Nathalie," Frank said. "Please call me Frank. There you are, Gina. Hold all my calls."

Gina's delayed reply roused Alex's already nervous state. "Of course, Frank."

"Very impressive art collection you have. Is that a Kandinsky?" Nathalie said with an air of sophistication as Frank's office doors closed.

Alex rolled her eyes while Nathalie regurgitated material from the Fine Arts 101 course they'd met in.

"Why yes, it is. You know your abstract art. I picked it up last year in Prague. Have you been? It's splendid."

"No, no, I haven't. I'll be sure to make it my next excursion. I so do love to travel."

"Be sure to get as close to his desk as you can and set your purse down," Alex whispered, initializing the sync software she'd loaded on the burner phone Nathalie carried in her purse. "It needs to be within three or four feet of his—"

"Where did you get this beautiful antique French writing table?" Nathalie asked. "It's quite extraordinary."

Alex detected surprise in Nathalie's voice as the data transfer began. "You OK?" Alex asked, wondering why a table would pique her interest, though she knew Nathalie couldn't reply.

While Frank's phone synced with the hidden burner phone, Alex began obtrusively poking around GIM's network. *This should be obvious enough for Tweedledee and Tweedledum to notice.* She opened up files right on the desktop of the computer in the server room, where Sam and the intern were playing video games. *Hey, look at me, boys. Check this out. Take a time-out from Tammaré.*

Alex giggled at her playful hack, shunning, for a moment, the accepted notion that hackers did their snooping during the off hours of their target, reducing the likelihood of accidental discovery while roaming around the network. The road trip imposed certain risks for Alex to remain anonymous without her IP-address-cloaking equipment and software back in Palo Alto, but she didn't plan on staying on long. Just long enough.

Frank showed Nathalie around his office, dripping with art that represented no particular brand of taste or proclivity toward artist, period, or style. Instead it appeared like someone trying too hard to impress. In reality, Frank knew very little about the art world, or the paintings that hung on his office walls other than what his wife, June, had taught him. What Frank did know was that art meant access to a wealthy world, and buying pieces, though indiscriminately, gave him a superficial ticket into the gallery, and with his affinity for supporting the art and cultural charities throughout New York it served a convenient launch pad for making his name synonymous with philanthropy in that milieu.

Frank gave Nathalie the lowdown on GIM's financial tools that would safeguard and enrich her fortunes, and those of her clients, and the dividends his firm generated for preferred clients, omitting any mention about the VLGF. While Frank generally handpicked his preferred client list based on community reputation, social standing, and financial status, he willingly waived the usual standards with what Nathalie could bring him: philanthropy on a grand scale.

"What sort of asset base are we talking?" Frank asked, sizing up Nathalie, who appeared relaxed on the couch underneath a secondhand rendering of Delacroix's *Liberty Leading the People*. A perceptive judge of character, Frank knew when someone came from money or simply pretended they did. Nathalie came from money—European money, the international venture he yearned for. Her easy-on-the-eyes appearance caught Frank's attention as well, casual yet sophisticated attire, natural European beauty, and long red hair were in stark contrast to the high-maintenance, makeup-driven variety of New York City's nouveau riche.

"Conservatively, one hundred."

"Thousand," Frank muttered, more as a statement than a question, triggering calculations in his head, not the amount that interested him or worth his time other than for the VLGF side of the business.

"Million," she corrected without batting an eyelash, raising a hand to her ear to cover a high-pitched voice loudly echoing the amount.

Frank's brain stopped computing for a moment, grasping the new figure tossed into the formula. "One hundred million?"

"Is that a problem?"

"No, no," he sputtered, leaning forward in his chair, "not at all." He made a new entry and a few notes on the A-list spreadsheet. "I'll work up some numbers for you tonight and pass them along tomorrow."

"That would be most wonderful," Nathalie said, getting up from the couch and collecting her purse off the writing table. She paused to run her hand over the surface.

"I did have a question, if you don't mind, about the charity you head up," Frank said, moving toward Nathalie. "My secretary mentioned you sit on the board of Cultural Arts International."

Nathalie developed a wicked grin as she turned around. "Art is a lie that makes us realize the truth."

Frank paused halfway to where Nathalie stood, an arrested expression painted across his face.

"Picasso, 1923."

Frank let out a small uncomfortable chuckle before stepping up to Nathalie. "Of course."

Recovering from his momentary start, Frank expressed his desire to support the arts around New York, pointing out the numerous plaques sprinkled around the office honoring his charitable activities. "This is my most prized possession," he said, picking up the thick, glass-encased Philanthropist of the Year Award for New York he'd recently received.

"I'm impressed, Frank," Nathalie said, handling the heavy commemorative piece. "I had no idea you were so passionate about—"

"Mr. Gordon, Mr. Gordon!" Sam shouted, bursting through the office doors. "Sir, we've had another—" He stopped short when he spotted Nathalie.

"Sam … what are you doing?" Frank asked, restraining his anger. "I'm in a meeting, son."

"I'm … so sorry, sir," Sam stuttered, catching his breath after the short sprint from the server room, looking embarrassed, unsure if he should leave. "It's just … you said to immediately tell you if the hacker came back, and well … they're back."

"Right now?" Frank yelped, posturing awkwardly, searching for a way to mitigate the untimely news in front of the wealthy prospective client. "I'm sorry, Miss Herringbone, but we've had some intruders on our computers lately. Nothing to worry about, just some nosy ingrates—"

"Oh, not to worry, Frank," Nathalie interjected, masking more remarks coming through her ear bud. "It's simply the reality of doing business in the twenty-first century."

"Thanks for your understanding," Frank said humbly, though seething inside. "Sam, call Alec down at the CyberCrime Enforcement Agency and report it. Give him what he needs and let me know what he plans on doing about it," he said, further posturing to reduce any concerns Miss Herringbone might harbor toward GIM's network security.

Nathalie winced from the loud groan in her earpiece. "Shush," she hissed.

Frank turned his attention to Nathalie. "Excuse me?"

Nathalie let out a subtle sneeze. "My apologies, allergies. Might I suggest hiring a firm that specializes in closing any security holes your network may have?" she said, handing him a business card. "I've employed them and they're wonderful. Quick, efficient, and guaranteed to find all network vulnerabilities. Very affordable, too."

Frank read the card out loud, "'StealthWare Pen-Test Consultants'?"

"Short for penetration test. They act and think like hackers, looking for all manner of ways into your system, then write up a report along with recommendations to close them."

"Yeah, sir. I've heard about pen tests. They are pretty cool," Sam chimed in, looking hopeful for some help. "Kind of like Navy Seal exercises where commandos try to breach a secure ship and—"

"Fine, Sam, give them a call and set something up as soon as possible," Frank said, handing over the card. Frank had no interest in bringing an outside consultant in. After all, he'd hired Sam to administer and watch over the network, and Alec's education and task-force connection supposedly provided skilled resources in tracking down meddling hackers. But with a wealthy client in his mist, holding the key to philanthropy nirvana, he did what came naturally: put on airs.

A Tale of Two Kisses:

Kiss One

The crowd at Café Java Server & Apps was particularly boisterous when Alec dropped by after an evening class for his casual recon over root beer and scones. He stood outside where it was less noisy, bearing the cigarette smoke of those still a slave to the habit, under a light drizzle of rain while listening to new voice mails: one from Thomas, who offered his assistance with the new case Henry had assigned Alec, and the other from an out-of-breath, nearly frantic Sam. He'd hoped to hear Nathalie's voice.

"Alec, this is Sam. Hey, we had another hack just now, well, a few minutes ago. They weren't on for very long. I told your dad about it because he said to tell him immediately if it happened again. I interrupted a meeting he was in. He seemed a little mad. Anyway, he said to call you to report it and to find out what you plan on doing about it. I mean, he said that last part, not me. OK. Call me on my cell. Bye."

Alec returned Sam's call, inquiring about the hack. As he listened to Sam describe the breach's unusual nature—opening files in plain sight during business hours—he shook his head. *That doesn't make any sense. Certainly doesn't sound like the same person that's been in there the last couple of weeks. This hack seems juvenile by comparison, or perhaps they wanted to be seen. What hacker wants to be seen?*

"Did the IP tracer capture anything?" Alec asked, glancing inside the café, yearning for its warm, dry confines.

"Yeah, I wrote it down here somewhere. Where is it ... here," Sam exclaimed as a keyboard crashed to the floor. "Sorry 'bout that. It didn't have any hops and originated somewhere on Barclay Street in New York."

Alec took his hand off his forehead, staring blankly across the street. "Barclay Street?"

"Yeah, why?"

Alec shook his head again, less concerned about Sam's literal lack of street sense than where GIM's building resided. *They were down on the street outside the office?* "GIM is on Barclay Street, Sam."

"Oh, jeez, that's pretty close. Hey, Alec, your dad also wanted me to tell you—"

Alec waited for the rest of the sentence a few moments, then glanced at his cell phone: LOST CONNECTION. He didn't bother calling Sam back, uninterested in what his father *wanted* after a long day of classes.

"Hey, where is this place?" Nathalie asked, peering farther up the block as she strolled alongside Alex, a light mist coming down through the late-evening hours.

"It should be close, but I think it's on the other side of the street," Alex replied amidst the occasional horn honk, glancing down at her cell phone's GPS map tracker, then across four lanes of cabs and cars packed tightly together going nowhere. She had read on a local social-review website about a cool, hip hangout near their hotel called Café Java Server & Apps, interested in checking out the place with the clever tech play on words.

"I hope we find it soon because—" Nathalie started to say before Alex grabbed her by the arm, pulling them through the first door she found. "Hey!"

Alex couldn't believe her eyes. *Cybercop!* Outside Café Java Server & Apps stood Alec talking on his cell phone, leaned up against the building, staring in their direction.

"That cybercop, my brother, Alec is over there," she said, jabbing her finger on the tinted-glass doors they now stood behind, loud music thumping behind them.

"Think he saw us?"

"I don't know." Alex pressed her forehead against the window to get a clearer look.

"I doubt he'd recognize you in that cute outfit of yours."

"Let's go back to the hotel and order room service or something."

Nathalie turned around, checking out the ambience of the place they'd veered into. "I think we'll be safe here," she said with a broad grin.

"Why?"

"I doubt he'll be coming in here," she replied as the large woman with yellow spiked hair and studded dog collar around her neck stamped the Tulips Nightclub logo across the back of their hands. Despite the early hour the club had a large number of women in attendance. Though the dance floor appeared empty, the bar area brimmed with happy-hour-type activity, and the large, red circular couch upstairs shrouded in strobe lights hosted several female couples kissing and groping one another through untucked and partially unbuttoned clothing.

"We should probably go," Alex said, rubbing then smearing the club stamp across her knuckles.

"No, as long as we're here, we might as well hide out and have a drink," Nathalie said, sashaying over to one of the tall vacant tables for two near the dance floor. "Besides, we're all dressed up."

"No … I think it's safe to leave." Alex peeked back out the door to where Alec continued to linger. She turned back, losing Nathalie in the small crowd. Nathalie waved her hand and as Alex walked over to the table her gait stiffened, taking nervous glances at heads turned her way, their eyes fixed on her, devouring her, as if she were naked in a bad dream.

"I still have more work to do on the vCloud and the pen-test plan," she said, stepping up to the table, tugging down on the back of her skirt.

"Hon," Nathalie said as she grabbed then yanked Alex's arm, planting her on the barstool, "you need to have more fun if you're going to be a spy. It takes the edge off. Two dirty martinis," she ordered from the impassive waitress, who wore a see-through top and had purple streaks filtering through her long black hair and a pierced lower lip.

"I'm not … a spy," Alex said, averting her eyes from the braless waitress's perky breasts.

"Oh, come on. You spy on computers without anybody knowing it, gather secret information, right wrongs on your own outside the law, cover your tracks so no one finds you, make allies online, meet shady characters in dark parking lots to buy special gadgets … and turned a beautiful woman into an asset to go to New York and take part in a con … how are you not a spy?"

Alex had no immediate answer, partly because Nathalie left for the ladies' room, and partly because the argument was insightful if not compelling. *Not all hackers are spies, but are all spies essentially hackers … hacking personal information from a computer or individual, working toward a greater, selfless good?*

The drinks arrived quickly. Alex took a sip, shuddering when the punch of vodka jolted her senses. She surveyed the room, fidgeting under the stares drifting her way. The short skirt she'd bought earlier for their night on the town exposed her to wanting eyes. She crossed her legs, which only revealed more skin than she felt comfortable showing. In the time it took Nathalie to return, Alex received three phone numbers, numerous compliments on her eyes, and a peck on the cheek from an overly affectionate woman who called Amsterdam home, offering Alex some weed to share back at her place. Alex ditched the unsolicited invitations under the table when Nathalie returned.

"Someone's popular," Nathalie said, grinning. She dipped her finger into the martini glass, removing the ruby-red lipstick emblazoned across Alex's cheek.

Alex's face turned redder than the shade of removed affection. She didn't know what to say or how to respond, unsure if she liked women or just Nathalie, a discovery unlikely to occur at Tulips, where patrons had already embraced their preference. When Nathalie rose to order appetizers from the bar, Alex reached over, took hold of Nathalie's arm, drew her close, and planted a soft, parted-lips kiss on her surprised, moist lips that tasted like fresh strawberries.

"Well, hello there," Nathalie said several exploratory moments later. "And you say you're not a spy." Nathalie leaned in for another brief kiss before heading off.

Alex continued sipping on her martini, peering around the Sapphic landscape, giddy, a nervous but growing smile surfacing. She didn't receive another phone number in Nathalie's absence.

022 A TALE OF TWO KISSES:

KISS TWO

The next morning in the hotel room as Nathalie slept, Alex sat by the window with the shades partially drawn, finishing up the final preparations on the vCloud. Though her obvious hack on GIM during Nathalie's meeting with Frank Gordon the day before primarily acted to flush out the system administrator for an opportunity to pitch the pen test, it also served two other purposes: a final review of the network before deploying the virtual world GIM would unknowingly slip into, giving Alex unfettered rein over the entire network below; and confirming her suspicion that Frank's wire-transfer bank code was not on the network but rather stored on his phone, which she grabbed after they had cloned it during the meeting. It was a vital part of the plan.

Nathalie stirred under the sheets. "What are you doing, hon?" She yawned, lazily stretching.

"Getting things ready for the pen test this morning," Alex said, flipping Nathalie her phone. "You need to call Cyber Boy and get together with him today."

Nathalie sat up, pulling her knees against her naked chest. "Why?"

"You heard Frank yesterday. He's going to have Alec investigate. I can't have him there asking questions. Boy, does he ask a ton of questions," she said, recalling their interaction over the grill back home at the store.

"But wait. You're going *into* GIM? I thought you hacked in, performed some phantom tests, then did some upload thingy."

"Not this, remember? It has to be external to their system. I need to plug this baby into their main server. It would take me way too long to partition one of their servers, assuming they had enough free space, probably fifty or sixty gigabytes ..." She paused, catching Nathalie running a hand through her hair, staring blankly at the phone.

Alex realized through all the eye-opening revelations back in Vegas she hadn't inquired more on the nature of the relationship between Nathalie and Alec. *He's not a client, just some guy she met on a boat, right? Did they hit it off more than she let on? How often had they gotten together or spoke on the phone?* Alex had gotten caught upside down in the new version of her life, forgetting to dwell on the finer points that triggered the upheaval in the first place.

"Tell him you had some last-minute business in town," Alex said, preferring to leave some of Nathalie's dignity and mystery intact.

"Sure, hon," Nathalie replied, reaching for the phone, her cheery mood returning. "That's a good idea."

Alex puffed out her cheeks like a chipmunk as Nathalie passed by, headed for the bathroom, hoping to buoy her spirits about the tasks ahead. She perceived Nathalie as more ally than adversary now that she'd had time to think through the last forty-eight hours, or perhaps the kiss and slow dance at Tulips had turned her. She wasn't sure or even concerned at the moment. Sam, GIM's system administrator, called while they were at the nightclub to set up a pen-test meeting first thing in the morning.

It was time to pull the wool over Frank Gordon's ambitious eyes

Alex paced back and forth inside the elevator on its way up to GIM's office suite on the tenth floor inside Barclay Financial's building. She fidgeted with the vCloud, attempting to conceal it yet keep it at the ready for deployment once she found herself in position to do so. Her mind raced faster as the elevator rose past the seventh floor, the original plan back at the hotel—keep it in her sweatshirt pocket—abandoned, concerned it would fall out while leaning over stacks of computers as it nearly did twice on the cab ride over.

By the time the doors opened, she'd removed her sweatshirt, wrapped it around her waist, and tied it off in front, the vCloud tucked safely in her jeans pocket, the slight bulge hidden from view. Despite the quick makeover it did leave one thing exposed: the scar on her shoulder. Clean clothing options had dwindled since leaving home, necessitating Alex to borrow a tank top from Nathalie. *I guess this is where I start owning it.* The resemblance of her appearance to that of Alex Andra of Tammaré as reflected in the distorted image of the dulled gold elevator panels was not lost on her. *Welcome to reality, Miss Alex Andra.*

She cautiously entered the waiting area, surveying the suite's layout, recalling Nathalie's description.

"Hi, can I help you?" GIM's secretary, Gina, asked.

"Oh, hi, yeah, I'm Alex from StealthWare. I'm here for the ten a.m. pen test," she said, handing Gina a business card, knocking over the pen holder on the counter. "Sorry."

Alex bit down on her lower lip as she stood there, self-consciously patting her scarred shoulder while Gina glanced at the card, then back up at Alex for what felt like an eternity. Until yesterday she hadn't owned business cards, let alone passed one out.

"Remarkable," Gina said with a look of amazement. "You have the same eye color as—"

"Hi, Alex? Hi," Sam stammered, popping his head out from the server room, where he and Yuri were working. "We spoke on the phone about the pen test." He excitably shook Alex's hand, his chubby cheeks flushing, obviously gushing over the sight of an attractive *computer* girl.

"Sam, don't tear her arm off," Gina said, laughing. "You know about this … pen test?"

"Yeah, Mr. Gordon asked me to set it up."

Gina started to inquire about the pen test but the ringing phone cut her short. As Sam ushered Alex to the server room, she caught Gina staring at the shoulder scar with the same look of amazement displayed earlier about her eyes. *Yesterday she thought Nathalie looked familiar, and now she's taken a keen interest in me. Who is this woman?*

Entering the server room, Sam babbled on about the cool nature of pen tests, excited to see one in action. In reality, pen tests are performed without the knowledge of employees, to capture work life under normal everyday conditions, not heightened alert. Alex knew, for this purpose, the whole charade would be unnecessary. Neither Frank nor Sam would know if she'd followed protocol or not.

"Hey," Yuri said after Sam introduced him.

"Hey," Alex returned, taking stock of the disarray of computers, routers, and cables scattered throughout the cramped room. *Wow … this place blows.*

"So, what do you want to do first?" Sam asked, sneaking glances at Alex's tight tank top, smaller and snugger than she normally dared to wear, showing a hint of midriff.

"Well ..." Alex said, opening up her netbook, launching a utility that explored networks as they appeared from the outside world. By her count from the previous hacks, there were five holes. For the report, she planned on bringing them all to GIM's attention since the vCloud had a backdoor of its own. "See here," she continued, leaning over the netbook she'd placed on the bench in front of where Sam sat, his eyes with an unobstructed view of her modest cleavage, "a hacker can get in here, here, here"—she glanced at him, sensing his misplaced attention—"here, and here." Sam's innocent ogling amused Alex, forgoing the self-conscious reaction she often succumbed to under similar circumstances. She knew Sam's type: nerdy, lacked social skills around girls, yet desperately sought their affection. *He's harmless.*

Sam snapped his head toward the netbook. "So ... that many, huh?" he said, nodding as if digesting the information, Yuri laughing behind him.

"Script kiddies could crawl into this place," Alex added, Yuri chuckling now and nodding while Sam looked dumbfounded, her response designed to ascertain the intern's hacking experience. She didn't know for certain when they first met, but his intense interest in the homespun network utility and method she'd used, along with his recognition of the term "script kiddie" suggested as much. *This might be a little tougher to pull off with a hacker in the room.* Going forward, she'd need to improvise the deployment of the vCloud, but not so much as to tip her hand to the other hacker, who'd likely know what a true pen test entailed.

Alex surveyed the room, asking which server comprised the main terminal. Sam pointed to a black one atop three others in the corner on a rack next to the phone circuit board. Alex breathed a sigh of relief over the equipment's black casing, which would allow the vCloud to blend in better, and its inaccessibility—no one would easily stumble upon it.

"OK," Alex said, steadying herself for the moment of truth, "one of your vulnerabilities is that stack configuration. There's an open port that allows access to all three servers. It should be dedicated to only one." *Probably an upgrade at some point and no one ever turned the old computer off.*

"Really? We don't even use that one on the bottom anymore," Sam said, his attention on the netbook again.

"Yeah, that's a common problem."

"Told you," Yuri added.

Alex turned the computer box partially around, pretending to examine the cabling between the boxes as the guys argued the merits of shutting it down. She slyly lifted the vCloud out from her pocket, gliding the connecting stem into the main server's open socket until it snapped into place. She then unplugged the network cable from the retired computer, relocating it to the main server, bypassing the vulnerability.

"I've rerouted the cable from this server to the main one. Now that port is closed off," she said, powering down the old computer. Alex returned to her netbook, refreshing the network screen. Only four holes remained.

"Yay," Sam exclaimed.

What a goofball. Alex picked up her netbook, roamed the keys quickly and sent a software patch to Gina's computer, which plugged a hole on her system that Alex had purposely created during the previous hack. She needed an excuse for Gina to reboot her computer so the vCloud could seamlessly integrate without notice. "Could you ask Gina to reboot so the changes I made on her computer will take effect?"

"Sure," Yuri offered.

She didn't need to perform the same task on Frank's computer, since she could tell he wasn't in yet. Alex opened the vCloud dashboard and pressed the Initialization button. She had one minute to figure out how to distract Sam from the monitors in the room, when they would flutter, flash, and display cryptic startup messages for about fifteen seconds. At some point during this process she'd need to respond to one of the menu choices. Leaving the room was not an option, and Sam's fawning left him practically glued to her. *That's it!*

Alec opened the door, ecstatic to see Nathalie. They embraced like young, long-distant lovers while Cassidy gave Nathalie his usual once-over sniff and barked before groaning, then retreating to his oversized pillow.

"Yum, sweaty," Nathalie said once their impassioned kiss broke, running her hand across the sheen on his bare chest.

Alec simply grinned, enjoying her touch. "You're early." He'd just gotten off the exercise bike when Nathalie rang the buzzer.

"I wasn't that far away."

Alec took her hand, escorting her to the kitchen, where a spread of bagels, cream cheese, and assorted fruit filled the counter. "Help yourself. Coffee is over there and orange juice is in the fridge. There's plenty of pulp." Alec smiled, giving her another kiss before grabbing the towel off the bike's handlebars. "I'll be right back."

Nathalie helped herself to the continental breakfast, sitting down next to Cassidy, scratching his belly, taking in the simply decorated loft.

"You sure have a lot of information on Wolf_Eyes," Nathalie hollered while Alec changed in the bedroom, taking notice of the whiteboard that bore scribbled notes, timelines, and diagrams related to the mysterious female hacker. "Now I see why you were asking about her in Vegas."

"Did I mention Wolf_Eyes was a she?" Alec said upon returning, pouring himself a glass of juice.

Nathalie pointed toward one of the whiteboard notations, her mouth full of bagel, Cassidy unhappy she'd stopped petting him.

"Ah, yes. Wolf_Eyes is a female," Alec said, sitting down next to Nathalie, feeding her a fresh strawberry, enjoying the way her captivating eyes took him in. "I discovered that the hard way." He flexed his bruised right hand.

"Ouch! Honey, what happened? You get in a fight with her?" Nathalie mocked, giving his hand a kiss.

"Long story. Anyway, I saw her in Vegas, of all places. The night I caught the red-eye home."

Nathalie resumed eating her bagel, looking uneasy as Alec stood up, recounting the abridged story of Wolf_Eyes and zNiNo meeting in the dark parking lot. Then like a professor, he guided Nathalie through the trail of inscriptions on the whiteboard, bullet points profiling the hacker, including the note he found in Vegas that connected her to GIM, pondering what interest she might have with the firm, and the mysterious code found inside the Trojan Horse called Scarab they'd removed from the main server, which perplexed and concerned him.

"Does the cream cheese taste funny," Alec asked, pausing from his impromptu lecture when Nathalie winced at the mention of the note."

"Oh, no." She coughed a couple of times. "Didn't chew that last bite … enough."

Alec set down his breakfast dish, no longer interested in spending what little time Nathalie had to visit on his current obsession. Although she seemed a good sport for listening—his willingness to open up on matters he generally kept guarded felt liberating—he wanted to hold her, touch her, explore her, reconnect since their unforgettable time together in San Francisco.

Alec lifted Nathalie to her feet, wrapped her up in his arms, welcomed another deep kiss, and inched their way toward the bedroom, a trail of removed clothes scattered behind them.

As the initialization period wound down, Alex braced herself for something she'd never done before, at least intentionally: flirt.

"Hey, Sam, you played the latest Tammaré yet?"

"Yeah, it's great," he replied, his face lighting up. "You play?"

"Yeah. Ever done a quest with Alex Andra?" She undid her ponytail, hair falling across her shoulders, nervously eyeing the monitor moments away from switching over to the vCloud.

"No, but I'd like to. She's so …" Sam was saying before his face took on a stunned expression as Alex approached him, "hot-looking." He gulped.

"She is hot-looking, isn't she?" Alex cooed as best as she knew how, standing close to Sam, awkwardly leaning her chest into him, batting her wolf eyes, channeling as much lust in them as she could muster.

The screens throughout the room started blinking, momentarily distracting Sam from Alex's advances until she grabbed the back of his head, pulled his to hers, and unceremoniously planted her lips on his as he steadied himself against the nearby workbench. It reminded her of the kiss she shared with Billy back in high school: unplanned, awkward, minus the head bump. Sam squirmed, obviously unsure how to use his lips. His breath smelled of minestrone. Alex held him firmly against her body, her one open eye glancing over to the monitors as the startup process stalled, awaiting a response. Her finger quickly tapped the *A* key on the netbook in her free hand, the screen rushing through a series of commands just as the intern appeared at the door.

"Woo-hoo!" Yuri cheered. "Sam finally kissed a girl."

Alex held the kiss a few seconds longer until the monitors returned to normal, then released her hold on Sam's head. Out of breath, Sam stumbled backward into the office chair, his face beet-red, forehead perspiring, grin goofy. *That should blank his memory about the screen flutter.*

"We should do a quest sometime," Alex said, a bit flushed herself, closing the netbook and then shooting a wink his way. Alex strode toward the door, a surge of adrenaline rushing through her, slapping Yuri's butt when she passed by. "Keep those holes plugged, boys."

Occupied on the phone, Gina gestured Alex toward Frank's open office, giving Alex a long stare as if putting the pieces of an elaborate puzzle together. With the vCloud in place, she now needed to retrieve Frank's computer's name and connect a keystroke logger. With GIM aware of the recent hacks on their system, and the local cybercrime task force investigating, Alex couldn't afford to rely on another keystroke recorder in the form of a Trojan Horse as before—they'd find it and remove it. She needed to physically install a small, discreet device that simply looked like an extension to the cord already connecting the keyboard to the computer box.

Much to her relief, Frank had yet to arrive. She peered around the gaudy display of wall art that to her resembled a guy's college dorm room plastered with posters of rock-'n'-roll groups and sports heroes in action. *This place would give me nightmares.* She noticed the office had two desks, a large one centered in front of the window overlooking the city, and a small quaint one off near the couch. Alex walked over to the smaller one, recalling Nathalie's peculiar fascination with a French antique writing table during her meeting with Frank. *This must be it.* She stared at it closely, searching for any clues it might hold about Nathalie's past. *Did it remind her of something from childhood?* Alex admired the elegant cross-patterned wood inlay, running her fingers across the aged surface, but nothing out of the ordinary caught her attention.

"Morning, Gina." The baritone voice of Frank startled Alex. "Any messages from Miss Herringbone?"

Alex rushed over to the large desk, dropped to her knees, and scooted underneath.

"No, Frank, nothing from Miss Herringbone, but you have two other calls from—"

"Sir, Mr. Gordon, sir," Sam blurted out, emerging from the server room.

"What, Sam? Good lord, son, you're sweating more than usual."

"Oh, yeah, sorry, sir," Sam said, wiping his forehead while concealing a faint smile. "Hey, good news, the pen test is going really well. She's already closed up the system holes we had."

"She?" Frank sounded surprised. "Where is this savior?"

"She's checking out the system in your office," Gina said.

"What?" Frank yelped, lurching toward his office. "Is Alec here?"

"No, sir," Sam said, following Frank. "I lost phone service with him last night before I could tell him about—"

Frank speed-dialed Alec as he entered the office. "Where the hell are you? I need you here for the damn pen test," he said. "I don't want any excuses. Get in here now!"

Alec ran his hand through Nathalie's silky hair while she kissed his sore hand, their bodies spooning, her purrs soft. He had to add the nape of her neck to the growing list of things he adored about her: long, slender, graceful.

"You know," he said, his voice peaceful, caressing her shoulder, "when I hit the guy, I didn't know what came over me. It was like some instinct drove me to step in and protect someone I didn't even know. Someone who now might be the very person I'm attempting to track down. It's quite disturbing."

He divulged the sense of something missing in his life, the struggle with an emotional assailant who hid in the shadows of his mind, driving him to constantly search for answers in all facets of his life. A predisposition that compelled him to jump into fights that were not his to fight, stare at full moons looking for answers, and experience the recurring dream, its deep meaning not yet clear but its persistence urging him to keep digging. He often wondered if his parents held the key to these mysteries.

The ring of Alec's cell phone disturbed the peaceful lovers. "Where the hell are you?" the voice drummed out before Alec could even say hello. Alec sat up in bed when it sounded liked his father said "pen test," but before he could confirm it, Frank had demanded his presence immediately and hung up. *Pen test? That doesn't sound like something my father would know anything about.* Alec recalled Sam attempting to tell him one more thing the previous night before their cell connection dropped. *Did they hire someone to perform a pen test?*

"What's wrong, sweetie?" Nathalie asked, barely moving, her eyes sleepy.

"I'm not sure. Either my dad is having a seizure or something is going on down at the office that he wants me there for," he replied, kissing her one last time on the back of her neck.

Nathalie stirred, rolling over, eyes wide open. "You're going there now?" She glanced at the clock on the nightstand. It was barely half-past ten. "But I want to spend more time with you."

"I know. I'm very sorry," Alec said as he splashed water on his face, slapped on deodorant, and rapidly clothed himself. "Things have heated up on the GIM hacks and I told my father I would investigate. He said something about a pen test today."

"Pen test?" Nathalie said, her tone coy, glancing back at the clock.

"It's short for penetration test." Alec grabbed his keys, the jingle habitually brought Cassidy running. "People are hired to—"

"I'd say you passed the test," Nathalie said with a seductive smile, removing the sheets off her body. "But I think we should retest just to make sure."

Alec laughed. It pained him to leave, but two guiding principles were governing him at the moment: to figure out what was going on at GIM, and the self-imposed obligation to help out since his father had paid for college and supplemented the rent on the loft. Despite their strained relationship, Alec was proud of his father and didn't want anything to spoil his pursuits in life.

"You are so adorable," Alec said, kissing Nathalie. "Stay as long as you like. I'll call you later."

When Alec left the loft, Cassidy ran back into the bedroom, staring at Nathalie as if expecting an explanation.

"What? I tried keeping him here," she said, speed-dialing Alex's phone number as she chewed her nails.

Cassidy groaned, ambling back out to the living room.

Alex had just added the keystroke logger to the keyboard cable and plugged it back into the computer under the desk when Frank entered the room barking orders on the phone. She smacked her head as she sprang up. *Ow!* "I'm right here," she said, rubbing the painful spot as her vision exploded with stars.

"Hi," Frank said, stopping in his tracks, a confounded look on his face. "You're not what I expected." Frank slowly moved toward Alex, extending his hand to shake. "Find what you were looking for?"

Alex stepped out from behind the desk, accepting the handshake. "Yeah, men in suits don't blend in very well during a pen test," she said, steadying her nerves amidst the throbbing ache atop her head.

"I guess not. You sure do have those same crazy eyes as my son, though."

"Ah …" she said, puzzled by his comment, "you had an unassigned port on your router that could be exploited by a skilled hacker." She slipped her sweatshirt on, offsetting the sudden chill in the room, whipping out her netbook, showing Frank the same network images she'd demonstrated to Sam. After refreshing the screen the display showed the last vulnerability closed up from Frank's office.

"So this will stop the attacks from occurring?" he asked, stepping behind his desk, glancing at the monitor's dark screen.

"Yeah, as long as the security is maintained and all the latest patches are applied when they are released," she replied, glancing over at Sam, who blushed and sweated again.

"Yeah, sir … she showed me what to do."

"Good. That'll be all for now, Sam." Frank settled into his chair, peering down underneath the desk.

Alex nervously fiddled with the zipper on her backpack, watching Frank scan his desk. She'd purposely avoided turning the monitor on so everything would look as it had before she arrived.

"It wouldn't hurt to use tougher passwords," she said, hoping to distract him.

"Un-huh." he muttered, his focus still peering around the desk.

"This table looks cool."

Franked jumped out from his chair. "Why yes, it's a French antique writing table. It belonged to a financier in the building many years ago before he passed away. It's quite old, I hear." Frank waxed on about his love of antiques, pointing over to his liquor cabinet, coat rack, and reading chair he'd picked up at an estate sale in upstate New York.

Alex's phone buzzed in her back pocket. Without the ringer turned on she couldn't identify the caller. *Shouldn't be Nathalie … she's keeping Cyber Boy busy. Mom, Dad? It can wait.*

As Frank continued on about the artifacts and antiques in the office, Alex returned her attention to him, keenly aware of the time pressure to finish her task. She'd told Nathalie she needed a sixty-minute window once inside GIM at ten, just to be safe. It was nearly eleven. "That's cool. Hey, I have one more thing I need to check before I'm done," she said, pulling out the prefabricated report from her backpack. "I need you to log onto your computer so I can see the name assigned to it."

"Oh sure," he said, settling back into his chair. He flicked the monitor on and typed in his login credentials. "It's a bit slow these days. Should just take a minute."

"Frank, you have a call on line one … Li Zhang," Gina's voice crackled through the intercom.

"Thanks," he hollered toward the open office doors. "Damn thing confuses me to no end. Excuse me, I need to take this call." Frank took the call, pushing himself back from the desk, allowing Alex access to the keyboard and monitor.

Alex waited anxiously, her foot tapping out a distressed beat as the login process trudged along. *This thing is five years old. How do people live with old technology?* Her phone buzzed again. This time she grabbed it. *Nathalie! This can't be good.*

"Hey," Alex answered softly.

"You done?"

"Almost."

"You need to leave now."

"Why?"

"Alec is on his way to GIM."

"I thought—"

"I tried calling you earlier. He only lives a few minutes away."

"Crap," Alex said, sneaking a casual peek at Frank, who watched her while he spoke on the phone.

"Also, hon, there's something I should tell you—"

Alex hung up when Frank's computer displayed the desktop, the background image of Frank kissing his wife the night of the PAG. She moused her way to the Network icon, right-clicking it to view the particulars of Frank's machine. Simultaneously, she initiated the keystroke logger with a few keyboard commands conducted with her free hand out of view of Frank's watchful eyes. Alex closed the window, loaded the netbook into her backpack, and handed Frank the pen-test report. "I'll go over it with Sam," she whispered as she turned to leave.

"Hold on a moment," Frank said, taking a moment from his call. "I didn't catch your name."

"Oh, it's Alex."

"Alex, if you could stay around a little longer, I want you to meet my son."

"Sure … I'll hang out with Sam until he gets here," she said, unsure of Frank's objective, perhaps setting her up for a date, or to introduce his son as another computer guy. Alex had no intention of finding out. She'd been there long enough, and Cyber Boy's imminent arrival jeopardized the entire scheme. *What are the odds that Cyber Boy is Frank's son?* She shook her head and laughed to herself, though a little too heartily, the horrible and inconvenient possibility pushed to the recesses of her mind. *Vegas has better odds.*

As Alex neared Gina's desk, the elevator bell chimed as the illuminated light above the doors about to open glared at Alex. *Crap.* She gave Gina a grimaced look. "I'll be right back … nature calls," she said, rushing toward the bathrooms on the other side of the elevator, Gina's laughter fading behind her. She lifted the backpack high on her shoulder, masking her face, galloping past the parting elevator doors, picking up two voices discussing the Mets' prospects for the young baseball season. One voice she recognized as Alec's, the other she surmised was Frank's son.

She dashed into the bathroom, entering the first stall to hide in, her heart racing. *This is nuts. I can't stay in here, and I can't go back out there to meet Frank's son.* She quickly sent Sam a text message from the burner phone he'd called for the pen-test appointment. "Hey, Sam, Alex here. Late for another pen test. I'll call you later about the report … and our next quest."

Alex closed her eyes, pushed the sweatshirt sleeves up past her elbows, and took in then exhaled several deep breaths until the heavy thuds in her chest subsided so she could think. Once composed, she exited the stall and took a peek out from the bathroom door, where she spotted Alec flirting with Gina. *Hey, those are my sunnies! I have a brother for seventy-two hours and he's already taking my stuff.*

Frank's voice hollered out from his office, requesting Alec to step in. *I'd hate to have to work for this guy … always hollering.* Alex jumped when her cell phone beeped the arrival of a text message from Sam: "No problem. Nice meeting you!!!"

Alec disappeared into Frank's office, Sam scurrying in a few moments later when Frank summoned him. Alex peered around, straining as best she could to get a bead on Frank's son, the other voice she'd heard a few minutes earlier, but she couldn't locate him. *Probably went into his dad's office while I was in the stall.* She glanced over to the door across from the elevators that entered the stairwell. A moment later she rapidly descended the stairs down to the lobby, out onto the street, running, searching for the nearest subway station.

GIM's forecast looked cloudy.

CONNECTING THE DOTS

After a quick stop at GIM, Alec caught the 1 train up to Times Square, where he knew somebody he'd gone to high school with who now managed a high-end computer store. He needed information about the vCloud, its purpose, common application and, more important, potential for misuse. Sam and GIM's intern knew little about the newest technological gadget.

As a youngster, Alec preferred to stand while riding the subway, holding on to center poles and, eventually as his height allowed, overhead bars, even when seats were plenty. It was his way of imitating his grandfather, Jack, who rode along with young Alec and had told him about the time when the trains had loose straps tethered to the ceiling, earning those who used them the common nickname "Straphanger." He still enjoyed the physical experience, balancing with his legs while the train accelerated and decelerated from one station to the next, swaying with the twists and bumps of rough track connections in between. It also gave him a better view to hacker-watch.

Alec knew more about the New York subway system than most. In junior high, he and his childhood friend Johnny, spent one summer exploring the complex maze of over six hundred miles of track. They made a pact to ride every mile, spending their allowances on souvenirs from many of the four hundred stations scattered throughout most of the boroughs to commemorate the feat.

Hacking the subway system, beyond free fares and transfers, was probably the holy grail amongst recreational hackers. In part because no one had ever pulled it off, but mostly it appeared improbable to hack *and* get away with. Stealing the New York Stock Exchange building and fencing it held better odds. The MTA infrastructure was reputed to be so multidimensional that if someone got lucky enough to crack into one system they'd never be able to override all the necessary and vital programs within a period of time that would grant them access to, say, send a train in the wrong direction. It was locked down tighter than a pneumatic tube.

Alec's current route had an express train had he waited another twelve minutes, but the euphoria from his morning interlude with Nathalie left him unhurried. The extra twenty minutes on the local would give him time to come up with some proper plans to take her out on the town before she headed back to California, though it occurred to him that he didn't know where she hailed from, let alone where she lived.

Between the furtive over-the-shoulder glances of an older man who was hacking another passenger's smart phone—*free Wi-Fi isn't always free*—Alec read the pen tester's business card. He found it unusual, since no person's name appeared on it, only the company name, website address, and phone number. *StealthWare. That sounds familiar. Of course, that's the company that sells the spyware the task force uses. I thought they were out on the West Coast....*

The coincidence of StealthWare performing the pen test didn't intrigue Alec, but the thoroughness of the summary-and-recommendations report they left behind did. There were vulnerabilities he hadn't even known about. He knew the network was a sieve to the outside world, but he had no idea just how bad it was. Alec also knew it often took a former hacker to know how to fully exploit today's systems, to find often overlooked ways in, yet the report projected a college-educated style and tone to it. Most hard-core hackers rarely attended or finished college, or, if they did, rarely presented such a professional-looking exposé. As far as Alec knew, it had nothing to do with anything in particular. It simply fascinated him, the attention to detail.

Alec walked the several blocks from the Times Square station toward Octagonal Computer World, a stretch resembling long lines at an amusement park, intensely packed with a multinational flavor among the tall buildings flashing brilliant displays of advertisements. Alec wasn't a big fan of Times Square. In fact, it now reminded him of the Strip in Vegas: an overabundance of glitz.

"Panther Attack on three, break," Alec heard somewhere near the computer store's corner department. Instinctively, Alec broke like he had for three years at William Prep High, down the wide, carpeted aisle, hooking right, dodging startled customers like defensive backs, glancing over his shoulder, outstretching his hands to haul in the well-worn Nerf football, spiking it as soon as he crossed into Customer Service.

"The crowd goes wild for another Matterson-to-Gordon touchdown," Johnny cheered, both arms raised high above his crew cut.

"Man, those were some great times, I tell you," Alec said, walking up to his childhood friend and high school football teammate, giving him a heartfelt hug. "How are you doing? I heard about the injury."

"You know, I'm doing fine," Johnny said, rotating his throwing arm that would never again have the proper range of motion for him to play professional football, a track he'd been on since he first donned a helmet. "They say I will live a normal life." He winced at the thought.

Alec empathized with the disappointment his friend felt. For their last three years in high school, he and Johnny set state records for touchdown connections, their team compiling a daunting 30–4 record. Two of those losses were at the State Championships. Senior year they reversed their fortunes and walked away the best-ranked high school team in the country. Scholarships besieged the potent combination, but Alec had other plans; football was not one of them. Johnny signed with Ohio State University and led the team to three stellar seasons before incurring an awkward tackle while extending a late fourth-quarter play that twisted his arm between two players. It was not a pretty sight.

"I still say if you'd been on the field it would've been an easy six," Johnny said wistfully. "You always knew how to get open on broken plays, ever since we were kids."

"Yes, but Philip would've muffed the extra point," Alec replied, referring to one of their State Championship losses. Alec and Johnny shook their heads, now able to laugh at the painful memory.

Alec had great hands and Johnny exhibited a deadly accurate throwing arm, and the bond they'd formed as kids made for a nearly unbeatable connection when they entered high school. They knew each other's tendencies and moves without having to say a word. It was almost too easy. But Alec knew his size would be an issue, even in college football, and certainly at the professional level, so he forwent that route, setting his sights on academic matters instead. For Alec, teaming up with someone other than Johnny would not have been as fulfilling. His joy was the fun he shared with Johnny more than playing football or winning.

"What brings you to Midtown?" Johnny asked, taking Alec back to his office, away from the bustling field of commerce, settling his hulk of a body not yet detrained from years of conditioning into a chair a size too small.

"vCloud … ever hear of it?" Alec replied, checking out the black-and-white photos of memorable games from their past. "Is that Hannah? When are you two going to get married?" Alec turned back to his friend.

"That's on hold." Johnny sighed. "She needs time to think. She was pretty set on me going pro and all, you know."

"Ah, buddy, sorry to hear that."

"No matter. It'll all work out. Yeah, the vCloud, what do you want to know about it? It's not an official product yet."

"I watched a deal go down for one between a couple of elite hackers out in Vegas."

"Really? There have been a few prototypes put out by Vertox Solutions, but I haven't heard of them hitting the street yet. It's pretty new stuff, and not all that well received."

Though the concept of Cloud computing had been around for many years, it only recently evolved into the "next big thing" in the computing world as Johnny explained it. A new industry sprung from it as consumers and companies alike started storing their most prized data outside their private walls, with cheap space for rent in the Cloud and accessibility to it from any device, anywhere.

Tech insiders lauded vCloud as the next-generation external hard drive with Cloud computing configured on it. Instead of simply storing data on a portable hard drive, which merely allowed someone to add or retrieve information, vCloud consolidated management services, various business software, and other tasks normally reserved for traditional Web and database servers. A potent combination of storage and functional specifications in a small package.

On paper, it presented as more or less a theoretical exercise in what-if concocted by three MIT students. A startup company in the Boston area, Vertox Solutions, bought the technology from the graduate students in hopes of leveraging the idea. They packaged it for mid-sized companies, but no one bought it. It was a nifty idea, a cool tech gadget, but not worth investing in. In reality it had no practical use, except in the hands of a few creative hackers who figured out how to use it to create a mirror image of a computer or entire network, and then run it virtually, either remotely or onsite, while the original site remained hidden and under the hacker's control.

"Look at us discussing Cloud computing, technology, and hackers," Alec said after digesting the realm of the vCloud device and its potential for deceit. "Sure a long way from the days when we convinced the cheerleaders that rubbing our cups before the big game was good luck." He laughed hard like he only did with Johnny.

"After losing the State Championship game two years in a row it was a pretty easy sell. And it worked. Third time's the charm," Johnny said, laughing even louder. "Glory days indeed. Let's get a beer sometime and catch up. I hear your old man has a sweet skybox at Yankee Stadium now."

"Sure thing," Alec said, giving his adolescent partner in crime a slap on the back before leaving.

Alec made one more stop before heading home, getting off the subway near New York University. He strolled through Washington Square Park, where a handful of street performers atop unicycles rode around in circles, old and young alike played chess, and students rested on the steps around the large central fountain engaged in one technological gadget or another.

He hoped to meet with the linguistics professor he spoke to on the phone about the unusual language he found in the Scarab Trojan. Alec continued to search for a motive on Wolf_Eyes's interest in GIM despite the fact that his efforts to bait her into the network had been thwarted by the pen test his father ordered. With the doors theoretically closed she, or any other hacker for that matter, would be hard pressed to get in. Still, the hacker intrigued him, her motives, the vCloud purchase and its potential. *There has to be more to all of this.*

Professor Ian Brownstone, head of the Linguistic Anthropology Department, jumped up from his chair, greeting Alec promptly when he knocked on the door. "Alec Gordon, a pleasure to meet you," he said, shaking Alec's hand profusely, Brownstone's abundance of dark, curly hair jiggled in harmony. "Please have a seat."

Alec knew the quick acceptance of the meeting with the professor stemmed from the Gordon name more than from his current interest in linguistics. People, especially professors, clamored for Frank's attention in hopes of landing a generous donation to fund their programs, even if the program had nothing to do with the cultural arts.

"Thanks for meeting with me, Professor Brownstone," Alec said, taking a seat in the small but richly adorned office of ancient maps and framed posters with cryptic symbols on display.

"Please, call me Ian. What can I help you with today?"

Alec explained to Ian his current field of interest, the job he spent his spare time at, and the nature of his casework, in particular the mysterious code he had found, showing the professor a sample of it. Ian viewed it with antique rimmed spectacles for about two seconds.

"That's hieroglyphics, from ancient Egypt," the professor pronounced without hesitation. "As far as I know, it's rarely used anymore."

Alec stared at the sample printout for several moments, partially recalling a documentary he once watched about Egypt. "But ... isn't hieroglyphics a picture- or symbol-based language?"

"Quite. Very complex, too. It took thousands of years before anyone could decipher it."

"Could it be converted into a programming language for computers?"

Ian pondered the question for a few moments, concentration mapped across his face. "Theoretically, yes. It would take a gifted individual to translate it to something useful, but yes, it could be done. I would imagine it would be just as hard to decipher, too."

"Yes ... yes," Alec muttered. "Thank you very much, Professor. You've been most helpful."

"My pleasure, Alec. Be sure to tell your father congratulations on his philanthropy award for me. He's a remarkable man in this day and age."

"I will."

Alec wandered back through Washington Square Park, taking a seat near the fountain, where little kids attempted to fish out wishful pennies from the water. He considered the length to which someone would go to create a new programming language, and what purpose it might serve. *Sure, in the hands of a group of profiteering hackers it could be devastating. Even governments would want to get in on the act. So again, why would a vigilante hacker like Wolf_Eyes be connected to it, perhaps even have devised it, and plant it on GIM's servers?*

Alex and Nathalie regrouped back at the hotel once Alex had dashed away from GIM, got lost in the subway system, and found her way there. By the time Alex entered the room, Nathalie stood freshly showered in a towel, drying her hair. Still charged from her onsite exploits at GIM, Alex slapped Nathalie's butt as she passed by, then flopped down on the bed.

"Wow," Alex said with a sigh of relief, unwrapping a fully garnished hot dog she'd gotten from a street vendor while transferring stations. "That was a close one. And that subway system is hella confusing when you're in a hurry and don't know where you're going. A, B, 1, 2, express, local ... programming languages are easier to understand." She devoured the hot dog.

Nathalie grinned, wiggling her butt like she wanted another slap while Alex chewed with her mouth open for effect, wadded up the hot-dog wrapper, and launched it at Nathalie's moving terry-cloth target. *Bull's-eye!*

"Yeah, sorry about that. His ... Frank called," Nathalie stuttered, spilling some Champagne she'd ordered to celebrate the successful start of their campaign," while you were still there and demanded he come in right away." Nathalie handed Alex a glass of the bubbly. "Cheers. To the start of cleaning up this town."

"Cheers." Alex took a healthy sip, unaccustomed to the fizzy effect. She shook her head once it passed. "Never tasted Champagne before."

"What's next?"

"When do you meet with Frank again?"

"I have to call him to set something up."

"How do you know Alec won't be there?"

"I'll schedule it when he's in class."

Alex thought about the idea a moment while sipping the bubbly. "Still risky, though, if he comes by unannounced like today."

"He doesn't know my last name, so I could probably talk my way out of it."

"What *is* your last name?"

"You're such a spy ... don't even know my last name," Nathalie replied, setting her glass down, undoing her towel, and letting it drop to the floor. She ran her fingers through Alex's hair and pulled her close, letting their lips meld for several moments before parting, the bubbly tingling in their mouths. "Pierce is my last name," she whispered in Alex's ear, "and you're wearing my tank top."

The 4 train en route to Times Square, Central Park, and beyond lurched forward as Alex and Nathalie settled into their seats. The con was in motion, the GIM virtual world had been created, and now the waiting game began before the next step in the plan: get Frank to transfer money into the fake Cultural Arts International charity account. Alex wanted to get out of the hotel room, take Nathalie to the Metropolitan Museum of Art, where Alex first got her inspiration for HPL as a language to use for her surreptitious Ethernet ventures.

The train bustled with businessmen headed back to work after a long lunch, talking amongst themselves; students with backpacks over their shoulders and ear buds tuned out to music, staring at the floor; and elderly folk sitting tightly clutching personal belongings, watching one passenger or another who amused them. Alex sat with a glow on her face and a satisfied smile, unaffected by the tightly bunched crowd around her. She simply reclined, taking hold of Nathalie's hand.

Alex knew her connection with Nathalie flirted with complication, an undeniable bond, beyond simple attraction or sisters-in-arms. Without any relationship experience, no point of reference or idea what a relationship should look like, Alex refrained from defining what she and Nathalie had between them, instead simply enjoying the moments they shared. For all she knew, Nathalie represented the very thing Alex wanted for herself: an uninhibited and outgoing existence, the person she knew lurked deep inside, desperately seeking to escape Tammaré's virtual walls.

Once off the subway, Alex guided Nathalie the handful of blocks over to the Met, the largest art museum in the country, home to some two million works spread across just as many square feet. Established in 1870 by financiers, leading artists, and thinkers of the day its mission was to expose art and art education to the masses. Unless a person hurried by the hundreds of collections with no more than cursory interest, taking in the Met encompassed half a day for the first floor alone.

Back in high school when she and Billy Nordall spent a weekend in New York after their class trip to Washington, DC, Alex dragged him from exhibit to exhibit in the museum. She had been intent on viewing as much as she could until she stumbled across one of the Met's permanent collections: Ancient Egypt. She became enthralled in the maze of stone walls filled with hieroglyphs, the ancient Egyptian writing system with more than seven hundred symbols. While other visitors, even tech savants like Billy Nordall, saw random etchings in stone from a forgotten epoch, Alex unearthed a beautiful language she could harness into a secret coding language.

It was only a matter of time, as Alex saw it, when she would create her own programming language. While celebrating her tenth birthday at a local pizza parlor back home, she had stared intently at a large spool of paper with thousands of perforated marks scattered across it, spinning, playing melodies on the vintage player piano. Her illuminated eyes and imaginative smile said it all, recognizing a primitive decision-tree diagram in progress.

That day, years ago in the Met, standing in awe of the Egyptian language, from a culture that had built the world's largest pyramids, defying logic for the time and place, inspired Alex to create something that would confound the modern-day tech world.

"So this is where your HPL came from?" Nathalie asked with a sense of awe, scanning the walls of hieroglyphs. "And you program things with these symbols?"

"Yeah," Alex replied, reliving the moment of insight she'd had on the flight back home, doodling cryptic symbols with loosely translated equations on cocktail napkins she kept requesting from the flight attendant. By the time she landed she had the basis for a new language on nearly sixty airline napkins, including Billy's soda-stained one on which he drew out a rough schematic of a keyboard that would handle Alex's new language.

"And no one can figure it out?"

"As far as I know, no one has. It's pretty well disguised, so it's hard to detect on a system. It's not a virus so virus scanning software doesn't pick it up. And on the off chance it gets removed like it was at GIM ... good luck decrypting it," Alex said in her usual manic cadence.

"So ... it's impossible to trace back to you if they *do* find it?" Nathalie said quietly as they exited the hieroglyph maze.

"The code is, yeah," Alex replied, standing in front of the Great Pyramid of Giza display. "There is always the off chance, if I'm not careful, that a company can trace where the code was sent from, but I use some pretty sophisticated methods to mask my location."

Both women gazed up at the scaled-down replica of the largest and oldest pyramid in Egypt, one of the seven wonders of the Ancient World.

"Amazing stuff," Nathalie said.

Alex thought so too, but her mind drifted back to their miniature-golf outing, her inability to putt the golf ball into the hole on the pyramid's peak. She took many mulligans.

"Alex," Nathalie said, breaking the reminiscent mood, "there's something I think you should know ... about Alec."

Alex turned and eyeballed Nathalie, not sure she wanted to hear what that "something" was. "O-kaaay...."

"He knows that you, I mean you, Wolf_Eyes, are connected to the hacks at GIM."

Alex stared at Nathalie's grimacing face, processing the news, attempting to unravel how it could have happened. *All my hacks back home were clean, no trace. The thing with zNiNo wouldn't connect me even if Alec did figure out the meeting from the chat room. It's not possible unless Nathalie said something....*

"That night in Vegas, when you bought the Cloud thingy," Nathalie said, stepping closer to Alex, "from the other hacker."

Alex nodded.

"Well ... you borrowed my jacket—"

"And the notes you took at Earl's office fell out."

Crap! Alex shook her head. If she'd learned anything from her many Tammaré quests it was that nothing ever went according to plan. One had to adapt to the new situation and move on. It did no good to dwell on what couldn't be changed. She felt a pang of anxiety there at the Met, staring back up at the pyramid, wishing she were back home where she could think this out in the comfort of her bedroom, Sundance by her side.

"So he knows Wolf_Eyes is interested in GIM. Did he say if he knew why?" Alex switched into damage-control mode. "He doesn't know Wolf_Eyes is me, right?"

"No, hon, no he doesn't know it's you," she replied quickly. "He thinks he might've seen you, Alex, in Vegas at the blackjack tables, but I intercepted him before he could get a closer look. He also said he didn't get a good look at Wolf_Eyes during the zNiNo scuffle other than he knows you're a woman."

The faint hair on Alex's neck rose, flashbacks of Nathalie, Alec, the scuffle with zNiNo, and learning about her brother in Vegas all too fresh in her mind.

"If he sees you here in New York … he's very smart. I'm sure he'll put the pieces together quick enough."

OK, but I still have the element of surprise. He has nothing but a few hack attempts on GIM, which took nothing they know about, so they have no reason or trail to go after. As far as they're concerned, they've locked down their leaks with the pen test today.

"We're still good," Alex said, sorting through the twisted maze of events, disclosures, and scenarios like a neatly designed risk-management software program. "I, *we* just need to avoid running into him. If he's such a supersleuth then he'll connect the dots between you and me … then we're done."

Alex began walking briskly toward the exit. The relaxing afternoon of sightseeing turned to planning, scheming, and reviewing the likelihood of her brother running into them. "Any other *surprises* you'd like to lob my way?" Alex rhetorically joked.

"Speaking of last names," Nathalie replied, catching up to Alex's fast pace through the museum's main lobby, out the doors, and halfway down the numerous steps that served both as gateway into and out of the Met as well as unofficial lunchtime seating, "Alec is Alec Gordon, Frank Gordon's son."

Alex stopped abruptly, nearly knocked over by Nathalie. "You've *got* to be kidding me," she said, cringing emotionally over her denial of the nagging thought she'd pushed aside back at GIM.

Frank sat at his favorite table inside Johnny's Steak House's dimly lit lounge, Benny Goodman's sultry clarinet playing "You're a Heavenly Thing" through speakers in the back room by the empty parquet dance floor. His smile reflected the details of the wire-transfer receipt laid before him from Li Zhang in Singapore: $200 million, the international windfall Frank had been working toward.

"I'm so sorry I'm late, dear," June said as she arrived at the table, looking a bit harried. "There was a large crowd still lingering in the gallery at closing, and getting a cab was terrible. I didn't get a chance to stop by the dry cleaners, either." She plopped her modest Kooba handbag down onto the table and removed her whimsically colorful scarf, tossing it over the handbag, where it immediately slid off and onto the floor. "Oh …"

Frank had already risen before June finished her dramatic entrance, managing to give her a kiss and pick the scarf up off the floor. "Not to worry, my dear." Frank pulled out her chair and guided it under her once she settled into it. "Business picking up at the gallery? Did the NY Arts editor stop by?"

"No, that's next week … I think. The *Times* will be there for the grand opening, though." June took two quick sips of the mint julep that Frank had ordered for them when he arrived, the cocktail she drank on their first date when they met in Savannah, Georgia, one summer while Frank was on vacation. From that point on it became *their* drink. Other couples had *their* song; they had *their* drink.

As June expelled in one breath the laundry list of last-minute things she needed to do before the grand opening, Frank listened and smiled, taking her in much like he had on their second date when he presented her with a painting he'd bought for the occasion, a Jackson Pollock, though its authenticity had never been established. "I have some good news to share," he said once she paused for another sip, trying to conceal the childlike excitement that bubbled inside him as he placed a folder in front of her.

June set the cocktail down to collect her reading glasses. She opened the folder and leaned over, peering at the document inside that Frank had printed off from the Web that afternoon. The Helen Ward lyrics accompanying Benny's clarinet streamed through his mind like a gentle Savannah breeze as he watched a smile spread across her radiant face, which made him smile.

"Frank!" she screamed with delight. Nearby tables filled with patrons went silent as if witnessing a marriage proposal to someone's childhood sweetheart where they said yes. "CAI ... this is wonderful. Have you contributed yet?"

"I'll be making a sizable one tomorrow morning if you think it's a good idea. I met with one of the board members yesterday. We'll be the major backer on this one as it grows and expands."

"Oh, Frank ... yes, let's do it," she said, leaning over to give him a kiss that always warmed his heart. "I overheard someone mention it today at the gallery. It's quite the buzz on the Web—"

Frank and June looked up when they heard Jack's voice. "What did you do now, Frank? Hire a street performer for the office?" he said, chuckling as he stepped up to the table, his Scotch and soda nearly empty. "Hi, June Bug, my dear. Is he keeping you happy?" Jack gave her a kiss on the cheek.

"Very much so, Jack." She showed him the CAI mission statement.

"More art, eh?" he muttered. "Well, it's better than that wretched housing fund you're peddling." He finished off his drink and raised the glass to the bartender across the way, who nodded and started a fresh one. "Why you would sully the firm's reputation with toxic loans is beyond ... What's this?"

Before Frank could tuck away the Li Zhang wire-transfer receipt, Jack snatched it up and stared at it, old-school calculations computing in his mind. He shook his head and let the receipt drift back down in front of Frank. "This is going to ruin everything we've built, son." His head continued to shake slowly as if disappointment was now mixing with shame and regret over the former shadow of *his* father's legacy.

"It's a solid product, Dad. It's exceeded both your vision and Granddad's. I'm sure he would be proud of the direction I'm going."

Jack's drink arrived; his silence and stiff belt told Frank all he needed to know about his dad's opinion on the matter.

"What'd the doctor say, Jack?" June asked, hands folded on the table while her thumbs nervously rotated over each other.

"What about Gordon Galleries, son? It's not just the firm that's at stake with this VLGF now. June Bug's dream is on the line too. Do you really think the economy is out of the woods yet? We're in for another rough roller-coaster ride. The thing in '07 was just a warning shot. The next one is going to cripple this country. You need to play it safe."

"We'll be fine, Dad."

"Jack—"

"I'm fine, dear. Don't worry about me … I'm well preserved," he said smiling, tipping the tumbler over his lips again.

"Speaking of preserved, Jack," June said, taking a glance at Frank, then returning her gaze to Jack, "if you wouldn't mind refraining from your subtle comments about Alec's"—her voice lowered to a whisper—"adoption when he's around, we'd appreciate it. You were pretty overt at PAG the other night."

"Dad, you agreed. We all agreed—"

"He's going to figure it out sooner or later. He's very bright. What do you think he does for a living … tracks down people who cover their tracks. It's only a matter of time. You need to come clean."

"Frivolous nerds without a life is what he tracks down. He'll outgrow it eventually."

"He's searching for answers to questions he doesn't know are out there, and not just at work. He's not going to care one way or the other when you tell him. He'll understand. Can't you see that this *secret* drives him—"

"Jack," June said, placing her hand on his arm, "it's better this way." Her brown eyes had a pleading appeal to them that Frank knew always melted his dad. "Now, if you gentlemen will excuse me … play nice, now."

Frank and Jack watched her walk toward the ladies' room, though an outstretched arm halted her trip momentarily as she spoke with guests at another table.

"Dad, you know what this does to her, so please stop pushing for it."

"She shouldn't feel that way. No one is going to judge her because she can't have kids of her own."

"She hurts inside, Dad … please."

Jack sat there, nodding, agreeing like he always did when it came to the state of the family secret. "Sure, son." He emptied his drink and then rose. "Just be careful, Frank." He strolled up to the bar and took a seat next to a well-dressed man who gave Jack a hearty handshake and motioned the bartender for another round.

I know what I'm doing, Dad.

"Where's Jack?" June asked when she returned, though her glance over to the bar answered the question. "He means well."

"I know. Let's order some dinner before I head back to the office."

"First, let's dance."

 Sleight of Code

"Three, zero, zero, zero, zero, zero point zero, zero," Frank muttered, typing in the $300,000 he planned on wire-transferring to Richard Janask, one of GIM's preferred A-list clients. He set up another for Harry Donale for $670,000; Jerald Hansel, $550,000; George Larreld, $1,000,000; Kenneth Joilper, $825,000—all told roughly $7 million in dividend money paid out across twelve preferred clients. Clients that translated to heads of lobbyist firms, political campaign-fund managers, respected litigators, and high-ranking city officials, all of whom provided Frank Gordon with enviable perks in his quest to reign supreme among New York's power brokers.

The GIM offices sat quiet while Frank performed his quarter-end ritual. He'd let Sam go home early, content that the pen test performed earlier in the day had solved the company's hacking problem. He sipped his Scotch and soda between wire-transfer entries, watching the total queue up, particularly pleased with the day's events. Besides Li Zhang's investment, Nathalie Herringbone's had added $100 million to the pot, giving him a mountain of money to invest and philanthropize with. *This is going to be a banner year.*

Frank completed his entries and basic bookkeeping duties, submitting the transactions with the stroke of a single key. While the progress bar on the screen slowly crept along, Frank left Nathalie Herringbone a voice mail, requesting the routing number for the bank that the Cultural Arts International foundation used to manage their finances and accept donations; it was time to make a sizable contribution. He placed his next call to a friend who handled press releases and public relations. Frank wanted to promote his new charitable enterprise, cashing in on the storm of publicity he currently enjoyed after receiving the Philanthropist of the Year Award. *This will make that seem like child's play.*

"Tom, Frank here," he started off with his old Columbia University roommate.

"Hey, money man. How's the money tree shaking these days?"

"Can't complain. Got some international investors now."

"Impressive for a guy who couldn't balance his own checkbook back in college," Tom said, his horse laugh already grating on Frank's nerves.

"And look at me now," Frank replied. "And you're doing what?"

"The world needs people like me to put big egos like you on the map." Tom continued laughing, obviously enjoying the way he riled Frank.

"Money makes the world go 'round, my friend."

"Only if I spin it in the right direction."

Frank didn't care for Tom Patterson that much even back in college, where Tom poked fun at Frank's lofty view of life from the privileged seats the Gordons enjoyed. He still tolerated Tom because city officials and celebrities alike respected and listened to him, and because Tom combined a simple communications degree with an instinctual entrepreneurship, launching a meet-the-press-style company that organized press conferences and handled public-relations matters. Intimate access to such a public platform was worth the incessant digs Frank endured.

"I'd like to set up a press conference," Frank said, bailing on the futile banter.

"For what? International investing is hardly newsworthy on Wall Street, Frank."

"Of course not. No, I'm backing a new foundation here in New York … Cultural Arts International."

"Never heard of it."

"It's new, still in the planning stages, but it's going to promote the local arts internationally. This is going to be huge."

"OK, that is noteworthy," Tom said. "Hey, Frank, when did you become so interested in the arts? Back in college you didn't know the difference between Manet and mayonnaise."

"*I* grew up, Tom. Now, when can you set this up? I'd like it this week."

"Sure, Frank, let me check the schedule when I get into the office—"

Frank hung up the phone abruptly, perturbed at Tom's razzing. He took a final swig of Scotch and glanced at the monitor. The batch-transaction process had finished. He highlighted the entire selection of well-padded transfers, keyed in his unique bank authentication code, entered the password, and clicked the confirmation message that popped up. Roughly $7 million quickly disbursed.

The "Enter" command signal from Frank's keyboard traveled rapidly down the cord and was intercepted by the keystroke logger before it got to the physical computer under his desk. The logger shunted the request from the virtual cloud displayed on Frank's screen to GIM's real network underneath, triggering the "Requite" batch file. The packet of information paused momentarily while the script authored by Wolf_Eyes parsed its contents, identifying a list of twelve pending wire transfers totaling $7,020,300 from one account to a dozen accounts.

Requite.bat opened a prepared list of GIM investor accounts associated with the VLGF, sorted in ascending order from date of inception, then bubbled to the top an account named WCOF. The script created a new packet with lines of wire transfers from the sorted list of investor groups, each receiving a dollar amount commensurate to their initial investment stake until the $7,020,300 zeroed out. The new file contained thirty-two wire transfers with routing information, fully authenticated by Frank Gordon.

Once complete, Requite.bat released the original data packet and allowed it to continue to the virtual Cloud, bypassing the transfer command to the bank for processing, showing a successful transmission of funds on Frank's screen. The new data packet, however, zipped over fiber optic wires to the bank at nearly the speed of light, where it processed like any other wire transfer passing through its system.

Requite.bat had one last task to perform, creating a form document for each wire transfer recipient, which explained the disbursement and displayed Frank Gordon's signature, each attached to an automated e-mail sent to the account holder.

Once finished, Requite.bat sat dormant, patiently waiting the next opportunity to undo years of fraudulent investing.

Cassidy darted between the front door and Alec several times while he read the note Nathalie had left after their morning tryst. Both the note and the morning with her were too short for his taste: *"Wish you could've stayed in bed this morning. I miss your touch. Hope all is well at GIM. Talk to you soon. XOXO."*

Alec led Cassidy out to his favorite sniffing spot, listening to the typical evening sounds resonating around the neighborhood: horns honking from West Side Highway several blocks over, clanking pots on stoves through open windows above, and kids giggling, playing hopscotch between old cracks in the sidewalk. Alec collected his thoughts from an eventful day while Cassidy reacquainted himself with the dirt patch. *The hieroglyphic code is probably a red herring at this point. It doesn't matter what language she used, it has a purpose, or at least it did before Sam removed it. The vCloud … now, that is still a potential threat, but it needs to be connected to the main server at GIM in order for it to work. The pen test shored up the leaks … so what now? How does Wolf_Eyes get in to do whatever it is she has planned? The plan, what is her endgame here? It must have something to do with the Vegas Land Grab Fund. The* Insiders Business Review *article focused quite a bit on it.*

The aroma of homemade lasagna wafting down from his neighbor's kitchen stirred Alec's hunger pangs. He tugged on the leash, triggering Cassidy's reflexive leg hike.

Back in the loft, Alec boiled some water, tossed in noodles, and heated up spaghetti sauce as Cassidy crunched through a bowl of dry dog food. Alec fired up his laptop, checking e-mails, catching up with the day's sports scores and what class lectures he'd missed earlier that morning when Nathalie stopped by. *Time well spent.*

He navigated to the StealthWare website to double-check his hunch that they were the same group that not only distributed the spyware tool the task force used but also performed the pen test. He glanced at the business card Sam gave him. *Yes. Same logo. Hmmm … the support phone number on the website is West Coast—San Jose, in fact, but not the same number listed on the card. Interesting.*

Alec dialed the number from the business card while he perused the website, looking for a contact name but finding none. *Straight to voice mail. Generic automated greeting.* He left a brief message requesting a follow-up conversation and meeting with the person who had administered the pen test at GIM. He called the other number listed on the website, but the outgoing message suggested it was for the company hosting the website, not the person managing its contents. He hung up without leaving another message.

The pasta had reached al dente perfection. Alec grabbed a locally brewed root beer from the refrigerator, settled onto the couch, tuned in to the local sports station on the TV, and dug into a bowl of spaghetti. He glanced at Nathalie's Post-it note on the coffee table, reading it again, smiling at the little *x*'s and *o*'s before the baseball highlight of the day caught his eye. He turned up the volume.

"… extends above the wall and snags the ball before it leaves the yard. Oh my!" the sportscaster shouted, marveling over the defensive play. "He did the same thing in last night's game. I'm sure the odds makers in Vegas are—"

Alec stopped chewing, no longer impressed with the defensive star who would hopefully lead his beloved Mets to a World Series title. He turned his attention to the whiteboard filled with information and diagrams about Wolf_Eyes, including the note he found in the Vegas parking lot. The flowing cursive penmanship appeared strikingly familiar. He picked up Nathalie's note from the coffee table and placed it side-by-side with the one on the board, scanning them intently. His heart sank.

Nathalie AND Wolf_Eyes? His appetite diminished instantly.

025   ALTOCUMULUS

"Holy crap!" Alex blurted out, sitting on the hotel bed, staring at her laptop.

"What?" Nathalie asked, spilling her morning coffee as she hurried over.

"Frank wire transferred seven million dollars last night to his preferred client list," she replied, her hands a blur over the keyboard, verifying the observation and double-checking the effectiveness of her programming logic.

"So. Isn't that what we wanted him to do?"

"Yeah, no, not that much at one time. I didn't know he would do so many accounts at once," Alex said, shocked at the dollar amount.

"Is that a problem?" Nathalie walked away, showing little interest in Alex's panic.

"I guess not. He's going to freak out when he discovers all that money went to different investors."

"You set it up so it looks completely legit, right?"

"Yeah. I didn't think it would happen so fast, though … I mean thirty-two investor groups have been replenished, just like that," Alex said, gazing out the window at the New York cityscape that resembled an erratic day at the stock market.

"Does that mean—?" Nathalie started, her question interrupted by an incoming call on her cell phone while a text message arrived on Alex's.

"Yes … it … does," Alex muttered underneath her breath, reading the text message from her dad: "Hey, Doodle Bug, give me a call when you get this. Got some good news and one question." Alex looked back out the window, wondering how much she would have to explain. With so much happening in such a short period of time, she found herself not thinking everything all the way through, only the imminent details that mattered most at each step along the way.

Alex ignored Nathalie's phone conversation. Instead she navigated around the virtual cloud cast over GIM, ensuring everything continued to appear normal. At some point questions would arise around the office as Frank and his staff attempted to figure out why those transfers deviated from their intended paths. For the most part, Nathalie had explained, the banks would offer little or no help since they would simply check their nightly transfer logs and verify the wire transfers had executed properly with permission from Frank's authentication credentials. They most likely would suggest he'd made an accounting error or had a glitch in his accounting software. In essence, Frank would have no immediate recourse.

"That was Frank," Nathalie said, "requesting the routing number for the charity. I hope we're still good, because I gave it to him. He also wants me to attend a press conference early this afternoon to promote his involvement in it."

"Yeah, we're fine. I guess up until now it's all been a theoretical exercise in my head. But now it's actually happening … fast. Probably best."

"Why's that?"

"Since Alec is Frank's son, we really don't have much time before it all comes crashing down."

"At least your parents' savings has been returned."

"Yeah, but if Alec finds out I'm Wolf_Eyes, he'll know where to find me. And with all this money moving to unintended accounts, including one that my parents are connected to ..."

Nathalie stared at Alex spinning through all the potential scenarios that could make for a messy situation back home.

"Well, hey," Nathalie said, sitting down beside Alex, "if it goes bad, it goes bad. You'll just have to hack our way out of prison." She draped an arm around Alex, smiling. "Besides, everything is fine right now. We could always just go home."

Alex pondered the idea for several moments while Nathalie's fingers caressed her scar. *That is certainly an option, go home now. Mom and Dad have their money back, along with all the WCOF members. Alec doesn't know I'm Wolf_Eyes. Out of sight, out of mind. Mission accomplished?* "No, Frank will continue doing what he is doing: taking investors' money and giving it to his friends. He needs to go down. Once he deposits that money in the fake charity, we can expose him."

"What about your brother? He's doing his dad a favor by investigating the hacks. It's not an official task-force case. It might look like he's protecting GIM's interests by covering things up."

"You don't think he knows what his dad is up to?"

"No. He's like you, always searching for the truth. Of course, he does it the legal way," Nathalie said, chuckling afterward.

Alex sneered, pushing Nathalie away, still adjusting to the idea of Alec as her brother, and the fact he was Frank's son complicated matters. Alex's plan to expose Frank had passed the point of no return. Soon money would flow into the fake charity account, and despite Alec's decision not to follow in his dad's footsteps, employing unsanctioned task-force resources at GIM might look suspicious and implicate him nonetheless.

"You know, that press conference could be a good thing for us," Alex said, the wheels in her head spinning forward again.

"Why?"

"We'll make sure the reporter guy from *Insiders Business Review* is there," she said with a devious grin.

"Hey, Dad," Alex said, strolling through the hotel lobby before taking a seat by the water fountain, whose spray arced upward in spirals before splashing down. "What's up?"

"Doodle Bug, good to hear your voice. I haven't seen you in days. Everything going OK in New York?" Phil rattled off, his voice chipper, more than it had been in several months. "Any news on your software going national?"

"Not yet, Dad. It's looking good, though. I should know in a another day or two." Alex hated conveying such a vague message. He'd always leveled with her on difficult matters. "How's Kara doing at the store?"

"Oh, you know Kara, trying to make the world a more beautiful place, one wacky idea at a time," he said with muted laughter.

"Sorry about that," Alex replied, knowing Kara meant well even if her actions appeared chaotic. *I can certainly relate.*

"When do you think you'll be coming home?"

"Probably in a couple of days. Once I know about the software deal."

"OK, well, I have some good news that can't wait." Alex could hear the sound of the office door closing. "Trent Hudson stopped by the house this morning with a check from GIM." He paused a moment; the shuffling sound of paper filled the silence.

Alex considered how she should react to the preordained news.

"It's for the full amount we originally invested—"

"Really?" she squeaked out.

"Yeah, it didn't earn anything, but at least we got back what we put in. Trent said everybody from the WCOF that took part received checks too."

"That's awesome, Dad."

A long, uncomfortable silence followed as Alex picked at the scabs on her knee from the fall in Vegas, waiting for him to ask the big question.

"Alex … I know you were pretty upset about the whole GIM-WCOF meeting a couple weeks back … and I found the article on Frank Gordon in your room," Phil said softly.

Alex could picture him sitting at the makeshift desk in the store's tiny office with a hand cradling his chin.

"I know you're pretty sharp with computers and whatnot. Is this something that … I should worry about? Like the time when you and Billy hacked the memorabilia store downtown and had ten thousand Pogs delivered to the house?"

Her back to the fountain, overspray misting her, Alex watched the concierge give a young couple directions to the Statue of Liberty. She half smiled at her and Billy's first Bonnie and Clyde–style hack back in grade school at the age of eight, inspired by the price gouging the proprietor was engaging in for that year's hottest fad. They were never caught, but her dad knew, scolding her, preaching the virtues of not taking what didn't belong to her. He even took her computer away for a month. It was the last time Alex used her computer talents for personal gain.

"No, Dad, it's legit. Frank Gordon made that wire transfer on his own." She paused a moment. "The meeting and that article … they made me question certain things, like—"

"I taught you. I know," Phil said. "Just be careful of who or what you question. Not everybody likes it."

"I love you, Dad. I'll be home soon," Alex replied, oscillating between the glow of accomplishment and the apprehension of the complexities that lay ahead.

Alex listened to the voice mail that came in the previous night on the burner phone, a message from Alec Gordon inquiring about the pen test, requesting a follow-up call. *Yeah, right. I'm so glad I didn't print my real number on that card. Suicide.* Alex continued to grapple with how to protect or warn her twin brother about the events that were about to topple his adoptive father's empire. It had to be something that tipped him off without jeopardizing the plan.

Something he discovers on his own.

Frank leaned in closer, staring long and hard at his computer screen. *This doesn't make any sense.* He had strutted into the office that morning, chest puffed out more than usual, smile larger than life, with big international money infused into GIM and a new global charity to tout. He had called in a favor from his old college roommate, scheduling a press conference for 1:00 p.m. that day, in the grand lobby of the ballroom where the recent philanthropy awards were held. But by late morning, phone calls were pouring in from his preferred clients, all singing the same chorus: "Where's my money?" Again, Frank checked the wire-transfer status page from the night before. *It's right there, in black and white, all the transfers I made. They show they went through.*

"Good morning, Mr. Gordon," said the pleasant phone voice of the bank's executive branch manager. "How are you doing—"

"Sally," Frank interrupted, his fingers thumping loudly on the desk, "there's an issue with some quarter-end money transfers I made last night."

"I can take a look at that for you, Mr.—"

"I'm showing twelve transfers that went out successfully for seven million, but I'm getting calls today that they haven't shown up in their accounts."

"I see, let me bring up your account," Sally said, her cheery voice unwavering. "Yes, I see some transfers last night, but there were more than twelve—"

"What?"

"I show thirty-two money transfers for $7,020,300, Mr. Gordon. All around nine p.m. local—"

"That can't be. My screen only shows twelve. You must have made a mistake."

"No, sir, I'm quite sure. The screen here shows they all used your authenticated credentials. Did you make transfers last night with it?"

"Yes, but—"

"Then there must be something wrong with your accounting software, Mr. Gordon. Everything checks out here," she said, her tone courteous yet strict in manner, like that of a grade-school teacher dealing with a habitually complaining student.

"I need to cancel them," Frank demanded.

"I'm sorry, Mr. Gordon, but they have already been approved and processed. Unless you're telling me your personal wire-transfer ID was stolen and used without consent then I'm afraid they are considered valid transfers. You'll need to take it up with the clients who received the money, or the vendor who handles your accounting—"

"Now, you listen to me, bitch. I am a preferred customer with your—" Frank heard a click. "Hello?" Silence. *Dammit!* He slammed the phone down into the cradle, the loud plastic *crack* echoing throughout the office.

Gina came running in, her face frightened. "Frank, what's wrong?"

Frank seethed in silence, his nostrils flared, and the creases on his forehead deepened as he stared fiercely through incensed eyes at Gina, who appeared uncomfortable standing before him, wringing her hands.

"Is there an issue with the wire transfers I sent out this morning? I double-checked—"

"No, Gina," Frank said, audibly exhaling pent-up consternation, attempting to wrap his head around the situation. "Just a misunderstanding on my part. Your general account transfers were fine." He quickly rose and ushered Gina from the office, closed the doors, and slumped into his desk chair. *How in the hell did this happen?*

Frank logged into his account on the bank's website and confirmed what Sally had told him: thirty-two wire transfers of varying amounts to unfamiliar accounts, none to his preferred clients. He checked all the recipient account numbers, comparing them to his general client list. They were all clients of GIM, and all had taken part in the VLGF years earlier. He leaned back in the chair, his demeanor haunted, his mind stepping through the previous night's events—appetizer and drinks with a couple of Wall Street friends, dinner and celebration drink at Johnny's Steak House with his wife and Jack, then back to the office to make the wire transfers and enjoy a nightcap. *I left a voice mail for Nathalie and called Tom about the press conference.* Frank shook his head in disbelief. *What did I do last night? Seven mil out the window.*

GIM had two valid personnel authorized to make wire transfers, Gina and Frank, each with their own ID. Gina could only make transfers that Frank approved, and those covered the stock-fund portion of the business, client trades, dividend disbursements, and the like. Frank handled the rest of the transfers related to the VLGF, and the preferred-client dividend distributions every quarter. He played these cards close to the vest. This wasn't always the case, when his father, Jack, ran the business, when accountability and transparency played a stronger hand.

Frank called the accounting software support line, impatiently working his way through the myriad automated questions before reaching an actual person. The technician on the line conducted numerous tests on GIM's software configuration over the next hour, including test wire transfers, all of which checked out. After discussing the matter with Sam in the server room, Frank returned to his office convinced he'd made a gross error the previous night, perhaps not paying close enough attention to what he had been doing. He went about setting up another round of wire transfers, one for the CAI charity and twelve to his preferred client list. In order to cover the earlier unexpected payout he moved funds from the general holding account, where money from Singapore's investment and Nathalie Herringbone's contribution was stockpiled. *Just until next month when I can put it back.* He had several new VLGF clients coming on board.

Frank submitted the first transfer, to the charity, in the amount of $10.5 million, which appeared to go through successfully. He immediately called the bank, receiving confirmation it arrived in the account Frank had gotten from Miss Herringbone earlier in the morning. Hanging up, he sighed a breath of relief, commencing with the other wire transfers. They all went through the same processing steps, displaying a successful message when completed.

Frank checked his watch; the press conference an hour away. Time to go. He apologized to Gina on his way out, met Nathalie in the lobby, and drove away in the Town Car he'd summoned.

"Miss Herringbone, you look stunning in that dress," Frank said, his midmorning mood quickly altered, admiring Nathalie's black backless dress that flowed down her graceful body. "You exude class and sophistication."

"Thank you, Frank. Please, call me Nathalie," she said, handing him press notes about the charity.

"Excellent. The website is a tad sparse on details, so this will be good to have," he said, setting them on the seat alongside. "Please forgive me, I need to make a quick call."

"Of course, don't mind me," she replied, glancing down at her cell phone.

Frank called the bank, choosing to speak with a teller instead of Sally, attempting to confirm the twelve wire transfers he'd resubmitted. He was now getting calls to his personal cell phone instead of the office line about the missing quarter-end payouts. The bank teller placed Frank on hold twice, explaining the computers were running slow. He bided his time between glancing over the promo material Nathalie had given him, and her dress's plunging neckline. Frank couldn't believe the good fortune in meeting her, the right image, the right charitable organization, all here in New York. *Today is the day I've worked hard to achieve. Dad can't help but be proud of me now. I've done something he or Granddad never could: put GIM on the international map.*

Nathalie shifted around in her seat, looking concerned after a few text-message exchanges.

"Is everything OK, Nathalie?" Frank asked, still on hold with the bank.

"Oh, yes, my apologies," she replied, tucking the cell phone into her purse. "I'm just nervous about the press conference. It's my first one."

"Of course. There's nothing to worry about. I've done many of them. Just a bunch of wannabe writers working for news organizations. They'll ask a few basic questions and that'll be it."

"That doesn't sound so bad."

"I'll do most of the talking—" Frank heard a beep on his cell phone for an incoming call from Tom Patterson. *Dammit. I need to find out if those wire transfers went through.* Frank attempted to switch over to Tom's call without hanging up on the bank but disconnected from both parties. He dialed Tom back, Frank's jaw clenching tighter with every ring until Tom answered. "What?"

"Frank, we need to change the time and place of the press conference."

Frank started to bark his response but restrained himself in Nathalie's presence when her head swiveled in his direction. "... Why?"

"I just got a call from the guy at the *New York Times* telling me the mayor has called for an immediate press conference. He needs to cover it. I called a few of the other news outlets and they said the same thing."

Frank sighed. "Great …" He rubbed his forehead and leaned back, disappointed, though he understood city matters held greater importance than what he was promoting.

"If you want the same venue it'll have to be next week, I'm afraid."

"Hold on, Tom … Nathalie, how long are you in town?"

"I fly out tonight," she answered with a puzzled expression.

"Tom—"

"I heard. We could do it today at two in your suite if you'd like? The mayor's conference shouldn't last too long."

Frank contemplated the last-minute change. He hungered to broadcast the news, if for nothing else than to keep the momentum of celebrityhood going; he was still on a high. "Tom, that works for me. Set it up," Frank said, relaxing the tension in his jaw. "Driver, please return to GIM. Thank you. My sincerest apologies, Nathalie, but we'll need to hold the press conference at my office a little later than originally scheduled. I hope you don't mind."

Nathalie swallowed hard as a blanched look spread across her face. "Sure … that shouldn't be a problem."

"Today sure has been full of the unexpected, to say the least," Frank muttered, momentarily forgetting to call the bank back, instead going over in his mind what he needed to do to prep the office for a press conference. They hadn't held one there before. He called Gina, explaining the details while Nathalie pulled her cell phone from her purse, frantically sending out a text message.

Alec reviewed his text message to Nathalie a fourth time before sending it, playing wordsmith in hopes of concealing his concern she may somehow be connected to Wolf_Eyes and the mysterious plot against GIM. "Hey, sexy. Want to meet for dinner tonight?"

In the end, the projection of his fears onto the simple message showed a vulnerability that gnawed at him about the woman he was crazy for, and his uncertain knowledge about her. *Have I been duped?*

"Not today. Busy with meetings all day. Might be flying out tonight," her reply read.

"Give me a call before you leave, OK?"

"I'll try. Need to go."

Hmmm, not the usual XOXO at the end. Perhaps she's in a meeting right now. Alec turned his attention back to the handwriting of the two notes, viewing them with a magnifying glass and analyzing the slants, curves, and letter sizing, especially the common word between them: GIM. Alec didn't have special training in handwriting analysis, but his methodical approach in other aspects of his life gave him a starting point. *Certainly many similarities, especially the sweeping curve of the "G."*

Thirty minutes later, after meticulously analyzing the common letters, he was in no better position to conclusively say one way or the other. The distinct paper types, ball-point versus fine-point pens, and different spacing between the horizontal lines made it tough for his untrained eye. He hoped he wasn't blinded by matters of the heart.

Perched on a stool inside a bakery shop, Alex peered through the tinted, plate-glass window to where Nathalie was, across the street entering the black Town Car with Frank Gordon. *She looks great in that dress.*

Alex figured she needed fifteen minutes to enter the GIM offices and collect the vCloud from their server room, though the sentry of doormen and valet personnel out front appeared more intimidating than the day before when she had been an invited guest, *perhaps* necessitating more time. She'd already called Sam, who was all too happy to hear from her, letting him know she'd left something behind during the pen test and needed to retrieve it. *I sure hope I don't have to distract him again.* She shuddered at the thought.

She waited a few minutes before exiting the bakery while the Town Car slowly entered traffic, injecting its long black body into the parade of yellow cabs. The butterflies welled up again, her eyes darting around, scanning for any sign of her brother. Nathalie assured her he had classes throughout the late morning and afternoon, but with all the close calls of running into him, she didn't share Nathalie's optimism. *Twin thing?*

Alex approached the busy street corner as the traffic lights turned red. She became instantly confused when the sidewalk crowd swallowed her up after the cross-walk lights flashed green in all directions, halting traffic on all sides while pedestrians walked any which way through the intersection. *What the …?* She tucked in behind a group of businessmen toting briefcases crossing diagonally in the event a driver with a twitchy foot became impatient watching the pedestrian flash mob tie up the roadway.

Alex reached the opposite corner in one less junket than expected, passing through the heavy glass turnstile doors of Barclay Financial. The fifteen-minute window of opportunity had begun. Her focus narrowed as she pressed the Up arrow between the elevators. The doors behind her opened. She spun around and entered after a handful of people exited, firmly pressing the tenth-floor button. *Two … three … four … five* she counted to herself until the elevator slowed to take on additional passengers. Her cell phone chirped when the doors opened and a text message from Nathalie appeared. Alex's stomach churned as she read it: "Heading back to GIM. Press conference there."

The doors closed before Alex could stop the elevator from continuing. *Please stop before the tenth, please!* She watched each digital number increment without pause until they reached GIM's floor. *Crap!* The doors opened. The other passengers looked around as if waiting for someone to enter or exit. Alex stayed put in the corner, hopeful no one from GIM would pass by. *Close, close, close.*

Alex's fair cheeks flushed and the fine hair on the nape of her neck prickled until the doors closed. The elevator whisked her up to the eighteenth floor. She quickly exited. Her shallow breathing felt labored despite a lack of physical exertion, glancing at her phone for any new messages. There were none. *I can't risk taking the elevators down now. Stairs again? What about the lobby?* Alex walked over to the waiting area, sitting down across from a family of four, the two young kids well dressed and behaved for their ages. They watched Alex send off a text message to Nathalie: "Text me when in GIM. Stuck on 18."

Alex leaned back, smiled, and let out a deep breath, giving a little wave to the kids, whose fascination in her was evidenced by their giggling.

Back at GIM, Frank stopped by Gina's desk, finalizing plans for the forthcoming press conference. Gina casually slipped him a note while smiling at Nathalie, who stood off to the side fidgeting with her phone. Frank shook his head at the note that read: "Bank called. Eighteen wire transfers went through successfully." *No, no, no. Not eighteen, twelve dammit!*

He turned to Nathalie, his cheeks red, crushing the piece of paper with a forceful clench of the fist that startled Gina. "Why don't you make yourself comfortable in that conference room," he said, pointing to the glass-encased room in back, his voice strained yet congenial. "Gina can bring you some coffee or tea, if you'd like."

"Thank you, Frank," she responded. "I'm fine, Gina. I'll just move out of the way." Nathalie headed toward the room, both Frank and Gina admiring her graceful exit.

Frank then spoke with as much reserve as he could muster after enduring $14 million of misrouted funds to unintended clients. "Gina, I need you to go down to the bank and make these wire transfers." He pulled out the list he'd used for the second set of transfers before hopping into the Town Car.

"I can do them from—"

"No, no, there's a glitch with the software today, so these need to be made at the bank. Here's my authentication ID. Take the Town Car. It's parked out front. Please hurry back."

Frank rushed into his office, checked the bank's website, and confirmed his worst suspicions: the second set of payouts went awry; none of the accounts he had entered matched what actually paid out. He hurriedly moved additional funds from Singapore's account to cover the transfers he'd requested that Gina perform. *Another seven mil…At least they will get their money today.*

He wanted to point a finger at something or someone, but he had no idea what to make of the situation. He couldn't very well claim it had been stolen. Though he didn't check the second round of transfers, he suspected they, too, went to old clients invested in the VLGF. While the excess outlay of money stung Frank's bottom line, it did little to dent his cash reserve. Not knowing where else to turn, he called Alec. *Maybe we've been hacked again.*

After conversing with his son, Frank steadied his composure for the upcoming press conference. *Get it together, Frank. You need to look and act successful. This is your moment!*

Alec had just hopped on his bike, small backpack strapped to his shoulders, headed to the university for his midday study group session and afternoon classes. The cloudless sky left the sun unfiltered, rigorously testing the sunglasses he'd found in Vegas.

"Hello," Alec said, after activating his Bluetooth earpiece.

"Son, it's me," Frank said, his voice strained.

Alec pulled his bike up onto the sidewalk, stopping. *Son?* "Is everything OK, Dad?"

"I'm not sure." He sighed. "There seems ... I think there is ... the accounting software is having ... issues today."

Alec sat on his bike, staring up the street, unsure if they had a bad phone connection or if his dad was hard pressed to explain his dilemma. *Dad stumped? He's never at a loss for words, even when he's wrong.*

"Dad, I'm sorry. I don't think I heard all of that."

"Sorry, Alec," Frank said, clearing his throat. "Could you come by the office today? I want you to take a look at something on my computer. I see one thing, but it's doing something else."

The wheels in Alec's mind started spinning. *See one thing, doing another? Has Wolf_Eyes already deployed the vCloud? But how? When?*

"Sure, Father, I'll be right there," Alec said, running his bike back to the loft.

Alex took in the bustling office she hid out in, spotting a sign that read JP INVESTMENTS. *Another private investment firm? This city is full of them. JP, GIM ... why initials? So you don't know who is really taking your money?*

Her phone beeped, an alert from the vCloud. She quickly navigated to the phone app she'd hastily built to monitor any movement of money. It wasn't her usual elegant design, but it served the purpose. *Another $7 million transferred. Eighteen more forgotten clients reimbursed their investments. Take the $14 million, plus the $10.5 million deposited into the charity account....* Alex stared blankly at the small screen, unable to grasp the large sums of money exchanged so casually, like Monopoly money, unreal though symbolically immense.

She sat there half-pleased with the events she and Nathalie had set into motion—money moving in the right directions, press conference to open Frank up to scrutiny by the press and the public—and so far Cyber Boy had been held at bay. Her other half, however, was frightened and concerned at the magnitude of the whole affair. *Millions upon millions of dollars doled out while I'm hiding out in office buildings, running from my cybercop of a brother.* The weight of her actions began to slowly sink in.

"Hey," Alex answered halfway through the call's first ring.

"We're here in the office," Nathalie whispered. "Frank is *freaking out* about the wire transfers. He just heard about a second batch of them disappearing. I think he's sending Gina down to the bank to make them again. Tell me those aren't going—"

"Nathalie, relax," Alex said quickly. "Only the transfers he performs from his computer and with his authentication key code trigger the script. It's OK." Setting aside her own fears she added, "You look great in that dress, by the way."

Nathalie laughed. "Thanks, hon."

"Any sign of Alec?"

"No. Like I said, he has class right now. Are you sure you have to get the vCloud back?"

"Yep. That's how we expose him, by removing the curtain he's been standing behind," Alex explained. "Even if he somehow tripped up on his own, whatever agency confiscates the computers, they'll find the device."

"But won't that be a good thing?"

"Probably not. I'm sure Frank can afford a good lawyer, probably one from his A-list, and they'll get the charges dropped because some hacker tampered with the system."

"Yeah, you're right." Nathalie sighed. "Well, now's not a good time. What about tomorrow?"

Alex thought about it for a moment, then shook her head. "It needs to be today. With all that money moving around, the press conference, Alec knowing too much … I need to close the loop fast or we're doomed. You need to bail at the first sign of trouble, OK?"

"Don't worry about me, hon. Even if Alec shows up, I'm mysterious enough to keep him guessing," she said, snickering.

"Yes, you are, Miss Nathalie Herringbone-Pierce."

"And if that doesn't work, I'll tell him I'm not wearing any underwear."

Alex blushed despite the eight floors that separated them. "You're such a tease."

"What floor are you on again?"

"Eighteen. Some investment firm, JP Investments. Hey, before I forget, put your com device in."

Several moments passed by in silence. Alex checked her phone to see if the call had dropped. It hadn't.

"You still there?"

"I need to go. I hear somebody coming into the office. I'll call you when this thing is done."

Nathalie hung up before Alex could reply or remind her again to insert the com device. She couldn't help wondering whether Nathalie's long silence stemmed from the mention of JP Investments. Alex stepped up to the busy receptionist who was juggling half a dozen phone calls, searching for a business card. There were seven card holders touting the firm's initials. Between calls the lithe French woman asked Alex if she required any assistance.

"What's JP short for?" she asked, but the woman's heavy accent made it hard to understand, so Alex repeated the question, this time listening intently to the slurred words that strung together with little distinction. Turning toward the stairwell to head down to GIM, she nodded when she finally understood, another clue added to solving the mystery that was Nathalie.

Meet the Press

Alex cautiously descended the eight floors to GIM, hoping the press conference was under way, providing her an opportunity to sneak into the server room, say a quick hello to Sam, grab the vCloud, and be on her way. She partially opened the door from the stairwell, scanning the waiting area as best she could, listening for voices. Unfortunately, Nathalie hadn't turned on her com device. She could hear Frank speaking as if addressing an audience in the distance and Gina's chair sat empty, tucked under the reception desk.

Alex started to push through the door when the ding of the elevator caused her to jump back quickly, her heart pounding rapidly. A harried reporter rushed out, the gear flapping against his portly body. *Get a grip, girl.*

She opened the door again, assessing the situation one more time, steadying her nerves for the plunge back into the fray. She held her breath, ready to push through the door when she picked up the sound of hard-soled shoes ascending the stairs at a brisk pace behind her. She turned, peering down between the slates to the lower floors, straining to see how close they were, if they would exit to another floor before they reached her. *Who takes the stairs when there are elevators?*

She remained stationary, her grasp on the railing tight, going over her options when the individual came into view, first the flap of a trench coat, then her lost sunnies atop their head. *What are we, joined at the hip?*

She spun around, considering her two escape routes. Running up seemed viable until she heard a door from another floor open above. *Crap! The bathroom again.* She flung open the door and got one step out when the elevator doors parted again. Another late reporter ran out. Alex ducked into it, rapidly slapping buttons with the palm of her hand, leaning hard against the side wall as if plastered to it. *Close, close, close, close, close. Come on!*

The doors slowly slid toward each other much to her relief.

Ding!

Alex froze. Blood drained from her face. The doors retracted. A well-dressed couple stepped in, greeted her, then appeared perplexed at all the illuminated floor buttons. Alex could hear the sound of the stairwell door open and then close as she watched through the crack between the taller man and woman the back of her brother as he walked toward the lobby. *This doesn't bode well for Nathalie, no matter how mysterious she thinks she is.*

"Alec," called out the man masking Alex's position, extending his arm to halt the close of the elevator doors.

Alex's eyes bulged. She dropped to one knee, bumped the woman in front, and fiddled with a shoelace, letting her hair fall over her face.

"Jordan, how are you?" Alec asked.

"Great. You? Track down any hackers today?" Jordan chuckled.

"No, but the day is young."

"Are you OK?" the woman asked Alex.

Everybody turned their attention toward Alex as she ran her hand over the floor, face hidden from view. "Ah ... lost a contact lens."

The elevator doors lurched from their recessed panels. "I'll catch up with you later," Alec said as the doors sealed tight.

Alec sauntered into the offices at GIM after taking the stairs rather than the elevator. His morning spin workout had been preempted by the examination he performed on the similarly penned notes and the troublesome notion that he actually didn't know much about Nathalie. Biking to class offered a suitable substitute until his father called, trumping that physical effort as well. So the ten flights of stairs up to GIM offered one last opportunity, giving him that sense of physical exertion he enjoyed even if for a few brief moments.

"What's going on?" Alec asked Gina and Sam, who stood outside the room where the press conference had assembled, a dozen or so reporters and photographers seated near the podium Frank spoke from.

"Press conference for the new charity your father is backing," Gina said in a hushed manner, handing him the one-page press release she'd quickly prepared thirty minutes earlier.

Alec glanced over the basic information contained in the release, the organization's name unfamiliar to him, though his knowledge of the cultural-arts scene left much to be desired. *A $10.5 million contribution?* Alec's eyes glazed over, rereading the figure. *I had no idea about his generosity ... no wonder they celebrated him at PAG.* He turned his attention back to his father, gazing at him with newfound respect and admiration.

"I got a call from him a little while ago," Alec whispered, leaning close to Gina, "and he seemed, let's say, odd. Something about things not appearing as they should. Do you know what happened this morning?"

Gina shot him a startled look, eyes wide open. "I'm...not sure, Alec," she replied. "I heard him cursing on the phone with the bank earlier today, something about botched wire transfers. He slammed the phone down. I've never seen him so agitated." She took a peek in Frank's direction. "About forty-five minutes ago he told me to go to the bank and do the same transfers there in person. I think it happened twice. He mentioned a software glitch of some—"

Alec scratched his forehead, pondering the tangibles: *Had Wolf_Eyes already infiltrated GIM, planted the vCloud, and commenced with her plan? Did my reluctance to investigate early on allow this to happen? Would it be as simple as checking all the computers, looking for it? How much and what type of damage has been done so far?* The questions swirled around in his head, prompting him to take Sam aside as Frank introduced an elegantly dressed woman, who stood up, taking Frank's place behind the podium.

"Isn't she beautiful?" Gina said, quietly clapping.

Alec redirected his attention toward the woman while Sam politely excused himself to take a phone call.

"I swear I know her from somewhere but I can't place her," Gina went on.

Alec's mind went blank, thoughts of the vCloud momentarily drifting away. *Nathalie?* Through the crowd of hand-raising reporters and camera flashes he strained to make out the woman whose voice at first didn't project as prominently as Frank's. "Yes, she is," Alec said. "Who is she?"

"Nathalie Herringbone. She sits on the board of the charity. She's just so lovely and charming, the way she—"

Alec knew it was *his* Nathalie, the strawberry-blond hair, the crooked little smile she displayed when nervous, and despite the mysterious French accent, the sound of her soothing voice that captivated him. She could've waxed on about the Napoleonic War and he would've hung on her every word. "That's her," Alec said excitedly. "That's the woman I told you I met in San Francisco."

"The incredibly sexy one?"

"Yes!"

"You didn't know she was in town?" Gina asked, staring at him with a surprised look.

"I did, yes, but …" Alec knew how silly his behavior must've appeared. Sure, their time together since meeting had been limited, and perhaps such brevity dispensed with the particulars of their personal lives. *Surely she would've said something about meeting with my father. She knew Frank Gordon was my father. She said as much out on Alcatraz Island.*

The handwritten notes sprung back to mind, clouding his thoughts. *If it was her handwriting on both notes, and she is now connected to my father through this charity, then she's not what she appears to be. And with the unusual software activity today …*

Nathalie finished her statements on the charity and took a seat. The public-relations man added a few concluding remarks, wrapping up the press conference. A chorus of applause spilled out from the room.

Alex exited the elevator into the Barclay Financial main lobby that bustled with midday energy—a reporter dashing for the closing elevator behind her, men and women dressed for success, exchanging pleasantries and business cards, and a homeless man shuffling toward the bathrooms. With everybody she knew in New York City gathered in one small area upstairs she felt relatively at ease, though with all the scurrying and hiding she'd had to do in stairwells and elevators, she wondered if the building itself presented as much a hazard to her as its inhabitants did, perhaps sensing an imminent threat in her presence; she laughed at her Tammaré mindset.

Her thoughts on retrieving the vCloud returned. She called Sam from the burner phone, explaining her dilemma, running late and in a rush, if he could simply meet her in the lobby to save time, she'd be there in a few minutes. *He'd walk through fire for me, I suspect.* She instructed him on where to find the vCloud, telling him it was a high-tech testing tool when he inquired about it. At the sound of applause she could hear in the background, she wished Nathalie had put her com device in so they could communicate better.

"OK, got it," Sam said, apparently pleased with himself. "I'll bring it down in a minute. Mr. Gordon's son wants to talk to me."

Alex cringed. "OK … don't take too long. I'm in a hurry."

"Sure thing."

"Wait," Alex yelped. "I'd be embarrassed if you told anyone I left it behind, so could you keep it quiet from anybody there? It'll be our little secret."

"Oh sure, no problem. I did tell Gina you were coming by, but that's it."

"That's OK, thanks."

Gina's involvement didn't concern Alex, but Frank's and Alec's did. With everything going on today too many questions would be asked, and too many fingers might start pointing her way.

Alec had begun discussing with Sam the efforts for checking all the computers in the server room for unusual devices when he caught sight of his father escorting Nathalie from the conference room, motioning for him to come over. A reporter, who appeared to want additional information or quotes from Frank and Nathalie, had hung back after the others filed out of the office suite.

"Please, George, the press conference is over," Frank said curtly, avoiding eye contact. "If you have any further questions, you can call my PR guy, Tom—"

"Frank, I just have a couple of—"

"George, why don't you come with me," Gina insisted as she and Alec arrived. She quickly took George Orkan's arm and whisked him away.

Nathalie pulled Alec toward her, leaned in, and gave him a kiss. "Hey, honey."

"Well, aren't you full of surprises," Alec said, still perplexed yet drawn to the accent while his father appeared taken aback by their display of affection.

"You two know each other?"

"Yes, we met out in San Francisco," Alec said, unsure what else to say about it.

"You don't say," Frank muttered, distracted by the private conversation going on between Gina and George. "Excuse me, will you?"

"What's that all about?" Nathalie asked.

"That's George Orkan from *Insiders Business Review*. He wrote an inflammatory article on GIM a few months back," Alec said, watching Frank wave his arms at the reporter. "I'm surprised he was invited to the press conference ... especially here." He turned his attention back to Nathalie. "Board member of Cultural Arts International?"

"It was a last-minute thing with your dad. Until this morning I wasn't even sure it would happen," Nathalie said, speaking faster than usual. "I was going to say something yesterday but you left quickly."

Alec nodded, acknowledging that he had dominated the conversation about his casework before adjourning to the bedroom with her, and his dad did summon him quickly. "Of course, but a New York charity?"

"I'm originally from New York, sweetie," she said, sliding her arm through his, steering him away from the server room, where Sam was exiting. "We really need to spend more time together. I didn't realize your dad was so big into the cultural—"

Nathalie stopped short as she and Alec turned their heads toward the sound of George shouting something from the elevator at Frank, who stormed past them into his office, slamming the door behind him.

"Sam," Alec shouted as Sam slipped into the same elevator, the doors closing before he could reply.

"He'll be back shortly," Gina said. "He's dropping something off to the girl who did the pen test yesterday. Apparently, she 'forgot' something."

"She's here? Where?" Alec parted from Nathalie, moving to Gina's desk.

"In the lobby downstairs."

"Why there?" Alec asked, his intuition starting to percolate.

"I don't know. Probably for another kiss," Gina replied, smiling.

"Kiss?"

"Yeah, she kissed him in the server room yesterday."

"Sam finally kissed a girl," Alec said, momentarily amused.

"He's as much a man now as he'll ever be," Gina added, laughing. "I'm sorry, I'm just being funny," she said, her apology directed toward Nathalie.

Nathalie had her back to Gina and Alec, talking in hushed tones.

"Who are you talking to, Nathalie?" Alec asked, stepping up behind her.

"Just mumbling to myself," she responded, turning around, her purse flap open.

Alec's eyes narrowed, fixed on Nathalie's nervous smile. Her beautiful features began to fade in his mind, observing instead a woman he barely knew, showing up unexpectedly in Las Vegas and at his father's investment firm, talking to no one in particular, the handwritten notes too close a match for him to ignore any longer. He raised his hand, reaching for her face. She flinched. Holding still he waited until she relaxed, then brushed the hair back over her ear, and plucked the com device from it.

"Conversing with Wolf_Eyes, I presume?" he said in a flat tone. He reached into her open purse, pulling the cell phone out. "Gina, make sure she stays put."

"Alec, what's going on?"

"I'll explain later," he said, his voice trailing off as he dashed toward the stairwell, placing the com device in his ear, quickly descending two steps at a time.

Nathalie slumped into a chair, head hung down and buried in her hands, sobbing. Gina walked over and sat alongside her, placing an arm around Nathalie's shaking body, patting her on the back. "Here, dear," she said, handing her a tissue, "everything's going to be OK."

Subway or Bust

Part I

Alex waited patiently in the lobby, nervously watching building security escort the homeless man—who'd begun using the hand basin in the men's restroom to bathe himself—through the revolving doors to the street, where the uniformed men unceremoniously handed him over to two New York City cops parked out front. They quickly whisked him away.

She fiddled with the com device in her hand, rolling it between her fingers until she heard Sam call out, trundling toward her, his smile beaming. She could already smell the minestrone breath as he pulled the vCloud from his pocket.

"Here it is," he said, awkwardly placing the device in her hand.

"Thanks so much, Sam," she replied, stowing it in her jeans pocket. She studied his expectant chubby face, obviously forever changed after the "distraction" in the server room. She gave him a hug, kissing him on the cheek. "I'll see you online—"

"Sam!" barked the unmistakable voice Alex had heard right before her brother decked zNiNo in Vegas. He had just burst through the stairwell door across the way into the lobby.

"Gotta go," Alex blurted out, bolting to the revolving door, timed perfectly to catch an empty slot that guided her out onto the congested sidewalk.

"Did you give anything to her?" Alec shouted to Sam, rushing by him, not able to catch the revolving doors as efficiently.

Sam looked confused, swiveling his head back and forth between the one twin chasing the other. "Yeah, some sort of—" was all Sam spit out before Alec worked himself through the doors.

The all-walk signs were counting down, three, two, one, when Alex approached the intersection that had befuddled her earlier. This time she didn't hesitate, running diagonally across, her ponytail bouncing rhythmically with every foot strike. She glanced over her shoulder as Alec exited the building, sprinting after her. *He won't make the light.*

As best she could, Alex dodged the slower-moving pedestrians going in each direction, serpentining, bumping the occasional arm or shoulder that strayed from its proper course, their startled reactions a blur of confusion followed by a growing wave of irritation left in her wake as she haphazardly navigated the sea of New Yorkers.

She patted her jean pocket, ensuring the vCloud was secure. The com device still in the palm of her hand, she placed it in an ear. *Nathalie, please be on.* "Nathalie, you there?" Alex could hear heavy breathing, along with ambient noise. "Nathalie?"

"Let me introduce myself, Wolf_Eyes," the voice said, filling her head with conflicting memories. "My name is Alec. We need to talk."

Alex glanced back. Cybercop had crossed the street, running fast, her sunnies focused squarely on her. *Crap! What happened to Nathalie?*

"I want my sunglasses back!" Alex shouted. She tossed the com device out into the street, hung a sharp left, and sideswiped a man waiting in line for a hot pretzel. "Sorry!"

She dashed into the street, spotting an unimpeded path between parked cars and intolerant oncoming traffic. That got her to the next block, where she had to dart in between double-parked cars, avoiding a collision with a messenger bike bearing down on her. *Whoa!* Glancing back she eyed Alec rounding the corner, still in hot pursuit, his pace noticeably faster than hers. Another crosswalk light favored her escape, but she knew her luck wouldn't last long. She needed to start thinking about where she was heading.

Disoriented by the sudden onset of the chase, Alex didn't know where she was in relation to the subway station she'd planned on taking back to the hotel, scanning the area, searching for something familiar, a street name, store sign, building … *Nothing.*

The next corner light changed before she got very far into the crosswalk, stopping abruptly, her breathing suspended, frightened by the taxicab's blaring horn, the cabby's coarse accent yelling out the window, ready to make her a hood ornament. She jumped back, spun around, catching the stares of those standing in line ready to load onto the city bus. *Bus?* Peering up the sidewalk, she spotted Alec barreling toward her and closing fast. She bolted across the street with the other green light, leaping over the large grate shrouded in steam that extended out from the curb.

I'm not going to be able to outrun him. Alex tried to suppress the twinge of panic slowly seeping in, lost in a city she didn't know, chased for something she had that would undoubtedly land her in jail, and worried about Nathalie's fate. She wanted to stop for a brief moment, check her phone—which had the route to the hotel mapped out, and a transit app with station locations, departure times—but the gap between her and Alec made it too risky.

Pulling her cell phone out, she attempted to read the GPS information on the run, but her hand moved erratically, making proper viewing impossible. She pocketed the phone after she swerved around a dog walker handling three inquisitive animals, bumping another man carrying a bag of groceries that spilled to the ground. "I'm so sorry," she sputtered out, grabbing a head of lettuce as it rolled along the dirty sidewalk, tossing it back, then sprinting away as fast as possible, ignoring the man yelling vehemently in another language.

Halfway down the next block, she caught sight of a street bazaar taking place between the buildings, and hurriedly changed directions toward it. Reaching for all the money in her back pocket, she pulled out several twenty-dollar bills. Her legs ached, her lungs burned, and she needed a break, as much for her body as for figuring out where she needed to go.

In the thick of the bazaar she ran by a display stand of baseball hats, quickly stopped, grabbed the first one her hand reached, and tossed a bill at the young Asian woman engrossed in a conversation on her cell phone.

Running again, she tucked her ponytail inside the Mets cap before covering her head. A few seconds later a table with colorful shawls stacked neatly on top caught her eye. Slapping the rest of the money down, she nabbed one of the items off the table without slowing, swinging it over her shoulders and backpack, making the first left she could once free of the bazaar. Pulling up out of sight, she stopped, out of breath, adrenaline coursing through her veins. Tying the Tahitian-themed shawl in front with trembling hands, she carefully peeked around the brick building back toward the bazaar. No one was trailing her.

Alex pulled her cell phone out, inspecting the GPS map that loaded slowly. She moved her phone around, attempting to improve the signal, now barely perceptible. Glancing back at the bazaar she spotted Alec marching through, his head scanning each aisle that he passed. *What is he, a bloodhound? Give it a rest, buddy. It's just a few million dollars and a life behind bars for dear old Dad.*

Heavy breathing in check and a good disguise in place buoyed her spirits on escaping. The only thing missing: a stronger cell signal.

Back running again, down a less-crowded street, still nothing looked familiar. She ducked into a small ethnic market that smelled of cloves and ginger. The voice of a foreign DJ squawked from a portable radio behind the checkout counter. She shoved the door closed, rattling the nearby window, shyly smiling at the attendant.

"Subway?" Alex asked.

The expressionless elderly woman dressed in drab clothing, playing a card game by herself, uttered something Alex didn't understand.

Striding down an aisle filled with packaged food items labeled with symbols she'd never seen before, Alex found a slightly stronger signal than before, but the map display crawled along, showing only partial segments from where she had already been. *Come on!*

The front door opened, jolting her to attention, but it was only a man with his little boy, conversing with the woman at the counter, speaking in high-pitched tones, the words unrecognizable.

Should I text Nathalie? Would she be able to reply? "Are you OK? Got the vCloud. Heading back to the hotel," Alex typed, then sent.

The door opened again, the man and boy were leaving. As the door closed, she spied Alec on the sidewalk out front, staring at something in the palm of his hand. She leaned against the corner post, partially hidden, keeping an eye on which way he would go next. Her phone beeped. *Nathalie.*

"You still want your sunglasses? Let's talk. The streets of New York are no place for a lone wolf to run around in." *He's got Nathalie's cell phone. This isn't good, AT ALL!*

Cut off completely from Nathalie, Alex's stomach churned, and a lump formed in her throat, growing lightheaded amongst the tall grocery shelves crumbling down in her mind. *The whole charity con was my idea. I got her into this. We could've stopped after Frank made the wire transfers, before going to the press conference. Now what's going to happen to her?* She stood there half keeping tabs on Alec, who was scanning the street in all directions, and half wanting to call her dad—but what would she say? —ready to cry. Hopelessness set in.

Alex's reaction to the virtually imperceptible ripple of her shawl bordered on terrifying and she nearly jumped out of her skin, her heart stuttering, when the drably dressed woman from the front counter barely touched it. A broad smile cracked her aging face as she fondled the material. The woman motioned Alex with a frail hand to follow, through the stockroom, out the back door into the alley. Alex stayed close, unsure where she was being led. The woman pointed toward an adjoining alley, to a sign that read SUBWAY and stuck a MetroCard in Alex's trembling hand. Glancing at the pass, then the woman, Alex didn't know what to say, even if she had known the language the woman spoke. Alex removed her shawl, wrapped it around the woman's bony shoulders, and adjusted the overlapping layers. The woman hugged herself, the brightly-colored garment not nearly as radiant as the warm, luminous smile that filled her wrinkled face, perhaps the most beautiful gift ever bestowed upon her.

Alex gave the woman a hug before dashing off in the direction of the subway sign, steeling herself as she entered and worked her way down the alley, her senses instantly assaulted by grimy, discarded clothing, broken bottles, and rotting trash; where tall buildings not much more than a car's width apart blocked the sun, casting a dark shadow on an otherwise sunny afternoon; and scraggly cats darted out from behind Dumpsters, stopping to nonchalantly lick their paws, pretending to pay Alex no attention as she hurried on by.

She reached the alley's end, peering around the corner in all directions, searching for her sunnies on a determined cybersleuth. Once she descended the stairs into the depths of the subway station she'd be all but trapped, little chance to escape. The coast looked clear. She glanced at the transit app on her cell phone. It didn't matter which train she got on as long as Alec wasn't on it. *Next train, two minutes.* She scanned the area again, then bolted towards the subway stairs, disappearing below the city.

The slow-moving crowd impeded her hurried pace, weaving through as best she could in the enclosed stairwell's noisy confines. She reached a flat open level fed by several staircases from different street entrances; the underground maze still perplexed her. According to the signs overhead she needed to descend one more level to the platform, where the screech of steel brakes against steel wheels announced the train's arrival. *One more minute.*

She pushed through a couple who couldn't locate their subway passes, sliding her card through the turnstile to begin another hindered descent among people who didn't share her sense of urgency. Blocked, she simply had to wait it out down the last twenty steps until she heard shouting from the level above. She turned to see Alec helping a man up from the ground before hollering for others to move aside. Alex focused forward, the platform now fifteen steps away, the muffled sounds of a recorded announcement echoing off the concrete walls below. Behind her, Alec bore through the tightly packed crowd fast.

She hopped up on the metal hand railing, her butt crashing down hard on it, then steadied herself and pushed off, sliding down until she went airborne at the bottom. Landing on her feet, she sprinted with everything her fatigued legs had left, the Mets cap started to lift, the train doors began to close, and platform onlookers gasped. Those on the train not otherwise engaged watched in fascinated will-she-make-it silence.

"Alex, don't do it," her brother shouted, his descent complete, running, though too far from the train to make it himself. Alex didn't flinch at the sound of her name that he now knew after the ill-fated text message to Nathalie. She was determined to get on the train, her only salvation.

The piercing sound of a policeman's whistle, the roar of a train on another track whooshing in, and her brother's plea, all receded to the background, Alex's sights set keenly on the ever narrowing gap of the sliding doors, the rest of the platform a kaleidoscope of immateriality.

Contorting her slim frame sideways, she held her breath, closed her eyes, and wedged through, the doors pinching the flap of her jacket, spinning her around to face the door window, the Mets cap drifting to the floor. She'd made it but could no longer conceal her true identity from Alec.

She stood transfixed, heart pounding, staring at her brother through the window, reading the bewildered look on his face, like he'd seen a figment of his imagination.

The train accelerated, separating them once again.

NATHALIE

"You're JP's daughter?" Gina said, immensely relieved. The alluring woman's familiarity had eluded her since the day she'd walked into GIM for a meeting with Frank. "Nathalie, right?"

Nathalie nodded, eyes red and puffy, using the tissue Gina had given her to clear her vision. "Yes," she said weakly, brushing tear-matted hair from her face.

"Do you remember me? I used to—"

"I do," Nathalie said, blowing her nose. "You worked for Papa. You taught me how to use the ten-key calculator when I was six. I remember." A faint smile crossed her face at the memory.

Gina rubbed Nathalie's shoulder, empathizing with Nathalie's tragic loss. "I'm so sorry about your father. He was a good man, admired by many."

Nathalie nodded some more, staring aimlessly, her demeanor showing the harsh reality of his plunging death years earlier.

"You know, Frank is too much like that Wall Street sociopath who swindled your father's investment assets," Gina said. "As soon he took over the firm from Jack ..." She shook her head. "I saw a change that was all too familiar ... and just as frightening."

The women sat in silence, with only Nathalie's occasional sniffle and Frank's muted voice behind closed doors filling the void. Gina had told Sam to go home for the day when he returned from the main lobby asking why Alec was chasing Alex. Gina didn't have a good answer, though she had her suspicions.

"Do you think it'll work?" Gina asked.

Nathalie turned to Gina, her despondent face lacked an understanding of the question. Gina tilted her head, directing Nathalie's attention to the closed doors of Frank's office. Nathalie's eyes wandered to the office, then darted quickly back to Gina, opening wide. She blew her nose again, nodding. "It has to," her raspy voice replied.

Gina contemplated the day's events, along with her misgivings over Frank's financial dealings. The present-day culture at the firm no longer reflected the ideals she'd signed on for during Jack Gordon's tenure.

"I can see why Alec likes you so much," Gina said, rising to her feet. Despite Nathalie's current vulnerable state, Gina could see in the woman's eyes a deep, caring soul, recalling the little girl who spent her Sundays helping her father at the office, learning the trade, and leaving humorous doodles on Gina's desk. "You know Alec is adopted?"

Nathalie nodded.

"And Alex is his …" she added, recalling the same eye color and matching scar of the pen-test girl.

Nathalie nodded again.

"You know, Miss Herringbone," Gina said, "I need to use the powder room. If you wouldn't mind staying put until I return, I'd be most obliged." Gina winked before walking away.

When Gina returned, only Frank's muffled voice in the background disturbed the peacefulness of the empty reception area. Gina sat down at her desk, reached for her purse, and pulled out some lip gloss to reapply it. Her compact vanity mirror reflected a satisfied smile spread across a cherubic face.

Subway or Bust

Part II

Dazed, Alec stepped back from the train departing the station, his chase of Wolf_Eyes seemingly in vain, though now he had a name to go along with the hacker alias: Alex. He recalled her face from the market in Palo Alto, and the blackjack table in Vegas. He'd crossed paths with her so many times in recent weeks without knowing her as Wolf_Eyes. All that paled in comparison, however, to the astonishment of the mirror-like reflection he witnessed through the train-door window. Strip away the long hair and her feminine features, and there stood an uncanny resemblance; the eye color, nose shape, jaw line, cheekbones, the scar he observed in Vegas … all spelled sibling. *That's not possible … I'm an only child.*

"Is everything OK, son?" asked the on-duty officer.

Alec snapped to. "Yes, Officer, I'm fine." He glanced at the hanging signage, getting his bearing on which station he'd stormed into, and where Wolf_Eyes's next stop would be. *She'll probably get off at the first stop and disappear into the city.* She'd gotten on the 2 train headed uptown whose first stop would be Park Place, just a minute or two from the Fulton station Alec stood in. He shook his head in defeat and nearly cursed under his breath when he noticed an MTA service-change flier on the nearby pillar informing commuters that due to construction the 2 train northbound would skip the next two stops. *It's turned into an express!* It would be a while before the next stop at Fourteenth Street, a lucky break.

Alec sprinted up the now-less-crowded staircase, surfacing to the street, his mind on how best to reach the next destination. Traffic was thick, negating the value of even the most veteran cab driver, and running again would be futile. The sound of a bell caught his attention, a bike messenger dismounting with package in hand disappeared into a store. Alec reacted quickly, grabbed the bike, hopped on, and veered out into the throng of cars and commercial vehicles, accelerating through the intersection's yellow, then red light. Not since he and Johnny Matterson absconded as kids with a bushel of freshly picked apples from the neighbor's tree had Alec taken something that didn't belong to him.

Years of riding the subway imbued Alec with a vast knowledge of the routes throughout the city. Express trains, while faster than others, didn't always rumble along at a constant speed. At this time of the day empty trains coming into service for the commuter hour would slow the speed of others as they merged onto the tracks. Unexpected delays could result in periodic slowdowns to prevent trains from stacking up at stations. Toss in the current route Wolf_Eyes had jumped on, which would make a quick hard left and then a hard right turn halfway to the next stop, and Alec stood a slim chance of heading her off when it arrived by going crosstown.

Alec sling-shotted around a line of cars waiting for the light to change, steering the single-speed bike around the corner in front of them, narrowly missing a pedestrian standing too far out in the street. His spin-bike conditioning at the loft catapulted him dangerously through traffic, screaming through busy intersections, weaving from one lane to the next, taking whatever lane had available space to maneuver, flashing by vehicles reduced to a crawl, hanging lefts then rights at intersections when the traffic appeared favorable, rapidly etching out a diagonal route across town compared to the train's indirect path.

Alec glanced at his watch. *This is going to be close.* He activated his Bluetooth ear device, calling Thomas. Unless it was an extreme emergency, Alec knew he'd never get the police or the Metropolitan Transit Authority to hold the train up for inspection. His best bet: commandeer as many available officers in the area to watch for Wolf_Eyes when the passengers disembarked.

"Thomas," Alec shouted, winded from the intense pace he was exerting. "I need you to call metro … and any available officer at or near the Fourteenth Street and Seventh Avenue station … have them on the northbound platform."

"Sure, boss," Thomas replied. "What's going on?"

"Wolf_Eyes," Alec gasped. "I found Wolf_Eyes."

"What? The mythical hacker?"

"Yes. Marshal the resources quickly … there's only three minutes before … the train should arrive."

"OK. What description should I tell them to—"

"Whoa!" Alec's heart skipped a beat when a car pulled out in front of him, causing him to lock his rear brake, an elongated track of rubber laid out behind him as he skidded to within inches of the oblivious driver's bumper

"What?"

"Nothing … tell them to look for a female version of me." Adrenaline spiked, he regained his speed quickly, passing the cell-phone-talking driver who nearly ended the pursuit painfully.

"Say that again?"

"Have them look for someone who could be my twin sis—" His reply was cut short when another woeful driver merged into his lane, thumping the pedal, Alec's warning shout too late. The frightened driver swerved away after the sound of grinding metal pierced the car's rolled-up windows. Alec's rapid cadence stuttered and pitched him forward onto the handlebars, his pugilist hand thrust hard against it, the painful yell muffled by gridlock. The Bluetooth tumbled to the ground while the front tire wobbled violently, tossing his torso back and forth as he strained for control to avoid meeting the pavement with an agonizing thud.

He lifted his feet off the constant spinning, fixed-gear pedals, grabbed the handle on the back of a delivery truck to his left, and steadied himself, gritting his teeth at the throbbing pain emanating from his right hand.

More determined than ever, feet firmly planted back on the pedals, he stood up from the saddle with clenched teeth, pumping harder to catch the next yellow light that stood between him and the subway station he desperately needed to reach before Wolf_Eyes vanished with the vCloud, possibly forever. The light switched to red as Alec entered the intersection, his mind committed, catching the lurch to his left and right four lanes of heavy traffic in his peripheral. Horns honked, voices screamed obscenities, and a motorcycle jetted across his bow before he swerved through a startled group of tourists crossing in front, a blast of dispersed exhaust from a delivery truck trailing him as the bike's rear wheel cleared the last white crosswalk line.

Alec jumped the bike up onto the sidewalk, pulled hard on the rear brake, skidding it through bewildered pedestrians before hopping off, the carbon frame sliding on its side then crashing into a newsstand. Alec raced for the subway entrance and hugged the railing, taking two and three steps at a time as the arrival of Wolf_Eyes's train below filled the tunnel with a burst of displaced air that violently whipped loose trash around.

On the platform he spotted several city cops and uniformed MTA employees who appeared more attentive than usual. *Thomas came through!* Racing alongside the train as it slowed, Alec picked the car Wolf_Eyes had entered at the last station. He stopped where it did, peering inside as the doors parted, passengers brushing by him. She wasn't there.

Jumping up on a bench, he scanned the crowd, but still saw no sign of her, or anyone leaving more quickly than usual. Out of desperation, he ran along the platform once more, poking his head into a couple open doors. *Nothing.*

The doors closed, the train continued on.

Alec shook his head. *How did I miss her? Was she disguised? Was she hiding on the train?* He looked over at a city cop standing several feet away and raised his hands in a questioning manner. The officer shook his head.

Dammit!

Alec stood there, face red from the blood coursing through his body, right hand aching, legs exhausted from the intense ride, his mind slowly coming to the realization that he'd let his dad down. Duped by a beautiful woman, outsmarted by a notorious hacker. It was not a proud moment for him. *Sure, Dad hired unqualified computer personnel, even college interns who were known hackers, rashly ordered a pen test often performed by ex-hackers, kept an antiquated network … set himself up for something like this to happen … still no excuse for what I could've done to prevent it.*

He didn't know what damage had been inflicted, but the fact that Wolf_Eyes had reclaimed the vCloud meant that whatever the plan, it was complete; that much he knew. At least he had Nathalie back at GIM. *Perhaps I can get some answers from her.* His emotions were mixed about how that encounter would go. He was too exhausted and discouraged to consider it just yet.

"Excuse me, mister," a teenage boy's crackly voice turned him around. "Are you Alec?" The gangly kid, whose Mets cap sat askew on his head, stood nearly as tall as Alec despite many fewer years.

"Yes."

"Here, this is for you." The kid handed him a thick piece of paper folded several times, containing a solid object inside. "The lady said to give it to someone with sunglasses on his head named Alec. Said you'd have the same-colored eyes as her, and be running around the platform at this station."

Alec stared in disbelief at the concealed item, then the kid. "Where is she?"

"I think she got off at the last stop," he replied, glancing back at his teenage friends, who had hollered his name, impatiently waiting for his return.

"Last stop? But it was supposed to skip from Fulton to here."

"Yeah, I know. It was crazy. Everybody was confused, people getting off, then back on, but it went local and stopped at Christopher Street. Anyway, I got to go, mister," the kid said, lumbering off toward his cohorts.

Alec unfolded the neatly folded legal paper, revealing a small device. *The vCloud!* A message was scrawled across the paper: *Follow your hunch. We are not all that different, you and I.* He sized up the device in his hand and then turned the paper over, where he found another note scribbled: *One more thing … I want my sunnies back!*

Alex flopped down on the subway bench, her legs less shaky, her heart rate returning to normal, staring at the Mets cap in her hand. Passengers resumed their self-absorbed activities except for a trio of snickering teenage boys shooting admiring glances her way as the train disappeared into the dark tunnel outside the station.

She glanced around, checking out what train she had daringly jumped into, unsure of its destination, though it hardly mattered. The chase was over; she could relax, get off at the next stop and regroup. The signage along the ceiling displayed the train's route, but its current direction—uptown, downtown, somewhere— escaped her. Leaning back she closed her eyes, letting the jostle of the train melt away the tension in her body, content on resting until the next stop.

Alex's body jerked when someone passing by bumped her foot, jarring her from a few dozing moments. She rearranged herself in the seat, noticing the bright illumination of a station flash by, the crowd on the platform a blur of business suits, hoodies, and skirts. Overhead, the conductor's voice crackled something through the speakers, but Alex couldn't make out the garbled message. She sat upright, confused. *Did I miss it?* None of the other passengers appeared inconvenienced. She stared at the route sign again, but couldn't figure out why it hadn't stop.

"Construction," said the old bearded man seated across from her, whose hands rested on a walking cane. "We're skipping this and the next stop." He gestured toward the front of the train as if it were within viewing distance. "Don't worry, Dear, you can get off at the next stop and take the southbound train back to the station you need."

The old man continued on about some past story of his life involving the subway, but Alex had already moved onto more pressing matters, checking the route sign yet again. *Eight minutes until the next stop.* Her mind processed the impact of the skipped stops, if any. She didn't think Alec could command the agency in charge of the subway system to stop a train for something as benign as a hacker on the run. *Unless he is faster than a speeding train he won't get to the next stop in time, will he? Taxicab?* She shook that off, as well as the bus option, as having the capability to outdo the subway.

As the train careened along and a southbound train streaked by frighteningly close several yards away, Alex pulled out her cell phone, reviewing her current route. Noticing the train had already made a left turn and would soon make a right one, she took a different view of the city, as if on a grid, recognizing the slim chance a savvy, determined New Yorker could traverse the city from where she got on to where the train would stop next simply by cutting across instead of following the train's route. *A shortcut ... would that even be possible?*

Despite Alex's reservations about the possibility, she couldn't ignore her brother's tenacious spirit and uncanny ability to be places she least expected him. *Besides, he thinks I've robbed his father's firm. He's motivated.* She grabbed the netbook from her backpack, connected to the free Wi-Fi hotspot on the train, and immediately entered the HCR. The only way for her to ensure an unlikely meeting with Alec at the next stop would be to get off before then, and that meant hacking in and taking control of the New York subway system. *It's never been done.*

She scrolled through the list of hackers currently online, searching for one in particular, the one person who'd theoretically postulated it could be done: zNiNo. Despite their less-than-friendly business encounter in Vegas, and her brother roughing him up, she had paid him in full. *Hopefully he'll forgive and forget, especially if he can get credit for the hack of all hacks.*

"zNiNo, interested in rolling 10000 hack?" Alex typed, glancing at her watch, its Tammaré minute hand unforgiving in its movement, a mere seven minutes until hurtling through the last possible station before the next regular stop. Several painful seconds passed by without a response. *Guess not.*

Alex knew hacking the subway system exceeded her expertise. Her domain lay in banks and financial entities. While servers and networks followed similar protocols and structure, each industry often employed its own brand of protection and architecture specific to its needs. It would take her weeks to plan such an attempt, not minutes.

"Wolf_Eyes, we meet again. vCloud treating you well?" zNiNo's message read.

Alex could picture him blowing smoke rings in some secret room somewhere in the world. "Too well. On the run. Up for it?"

"Not possible. Too many moving parts to do remotely. Need 2 peeps, 1 on, 1 off."

"I'm on. U in? 6 minutes!" It wasn't the most secure method of communicating, but with time of the essence it would have to suffice. *Besides, this will go down faster than anyone could possibly respond. And zNiNo certainly is not averse to bluntly making things happen. He'll just move on to another city.*

"Bold move. Worthy of my admiration. I'm in. Hold on."

Deep down, Alex felt guys like zNiNo were more bravado than tough. It was easy to sit behind a keyboard, be something other than yourself. That part she recognized in herself.

Several minutes blurred by as Alex and zNiNo exchanged pertinent information—IP addresses, account logins, passwords, server names, backdoors around firewalls—each running commands and scripts from their respective wireless devices. Anybody from Hacker Nation online witnessing the live chat-cast between the two elite hackers would probably later brag they were there the day the New York City subway got hacked.

Alex waited for zNiNo to run a final script, planting a Trojan on the main MTA server downtown, which would allow her to hack the train she was on. The crucial component, her situated on the train, allowed them the rare opportunity to time a hack that otherwise would not be possible. If zNiNo couldn't get the Trojan in place, there was no altering the train's pre-programmed list of stops, other than putting a gun to the conductor's head.

While zNiNo worked his magic, Alex pulled out the vCloud uncomfortably wedged in her jean pocket. Staring at it, she reflected on the remarkable job it had performed—keeping GIM in the clouds while she ran around underneath its blanket, shunting money Frank intended for one set of accounts to others, setting up a hidden account to store money earmarked for the fake charity, Nathalie's supposed investment deposit nothing more than doctored accounting records.

The power of the ruse and trail of deception nestled in the palm of her hand.

She decided the best way for her brother to learn the truth about his adoptive father was down the path of self-discovery. *He won't believe it any other way. Nathalie said he's been studying me.*

He must know something's amiss if I'm snooping around GIM, moving that much money around.

Less than a minute remained before the train would rush by the last-chance station and the probable moment of reckoning with Alec when zNiNo's message came through; the Trojan was in place. She motioned to the tall, freckled teenage kid who with his friends had curiously monitored her every move since her dive into the train car. She offered him her new Mets cap, which he gladly accepted, then tore a sheet of paper from his notepad, scribbling a message across it before folding it several times with the vCloud tucked neatly inside. She started to pass it to the kid, telling him who to give it to at the next stop, when she flashed a sportive smile, adding a note to the other side.

Per zNiNo's instructions, she needed to find the train's IP address from a list that randomly changed every time they passed a station. She navigated to the train's virtual server, scanning the addresses, looking for one that had been static longer than the rest. There were two to choose from. She selected the first one, glancing around to see if anything would happen. Nothing. She moved to the second choice, initiating it. Several seconds passed, her hopes fading when her body shifted in the seat, the netbook slid off her lap, and attentive passengers shot confused looks at one another. Those standing grabbed center poles to steady themselves as the train stopped prematurely.

Alex grabbed her netbook and stuffed it into her backpack, shooting a thankful smile to the messenger kid before bolting out the doors and up the stairs. She didn't want to be around if anybody started asking questions.

Nathalie's Curtain Con

George Orkan was a no-nonsense reporter hired by *Insiders Business Review* magazine for his ability to leave no stone unturned when it came to investigating the major players on Wall Street. His short, sturdy build, balding head, and hard staring eyes that rarely blinked personified his approach.

The publication had only been in circulation for a year, instantly making a huge splash around the financial community, though not always a favorable one. Its mission wasn't merely to report what trade magazines already drizzled out, or simply applaud those who enjoyed extended rides atop the Wall Street bull. It aspired to reveal the inner workings of the industry responsible for trillions of dollars in assets so discerning investors and money managers could better understand the risks they took on or advised others to take. In many ways it was an attempt to go where the SEC could not or dared not go in policing an industry it was mandated to oversee.

The article George had written a few months back on GIM, "Too Bulky? Gordon Investments Rise to the Top," ruffled only one feather, that of Frank Gordon, and was ultimately dismissed after the SEC reported their investigation revealed nothing to substantiate the "rumors," as they put it. George didn't take the SEC report personally, largely in part because he knew it often took several crusades to topple a crooked empire, and in part because his source, while genuine, had limited access. He could only report on what facts he knew or could confirm elsewhere. His instincts told him something didn't ring true at GIM, not since Frank took over, a man whose evasive nature when probed on investment details surrounding the VLGF was particularly telling.

After exchanging heated words with Frank at the press conference's conclusion and taking a walk outside to simmer down, George waited in the main lobby of Barclay Financial, hoping to catch Nathalie Herringbone on her way out for a few follow-up questions about the CAI organization. His invite to the press conference surprised him, especially at GIM's headquarters. He certainly wasn't on the short list of reporters informed of noteworthy GIM events, even less so for a philanthropic one. But he received two calls that suggested he attend, one from his source and the other from an anonymous caller. The latter intrigued him the most.

George spotted Nathalie stepping out from the elevator, appearing as divine as anyone he'd interviewed in his fourteen years of journalism. She gracefully strode toward the exit, sunglasses already donned.

"Excuse me, Miss Herringbone," George said, moving alongside her. "Would it be possible to ask a few more questions about your charity?" George tempered his normal what-do-you-have-to-say-about approach with her after Frank had rudely forced him from the GIM offices. He didn't want her to spurn him so quickly.

"Hi. George, right?"

"That's right," he replied, flattered she knew his name, extending his hand to shake. "Do you mind if I ask some follow-up questions?"

"No, I don't mind. Let's go around the corner to the coffee shop," she said, heading toward the exit. "This place makes me nervous."

George followed Nathalie outside, surprised by her comment.

He bought them each a cup of coffee, taking a table near the street-facing window, chatting about the New York arts scene, of which George felt she knew surprisingly little. When pressed to name some of the more notable artists in New York City, she offered a few names he wasn't familiar with. He didn't consider himself art literate in the least, but thirty minutes on the Internet had prepped him enough to attend the press conference and that token effort exceeded what Nathalie appeared to know.

"Tell me a little bit about your charity, beyond what was presented during the press conference, such as what inspired you to start it." George pulled out his pen and notepad.

Nathalie fidgeted in her chair, taking quick sips of coffee, her sunglasses shading her eyes. "Well, good question," she said, deliberating over which brand of sugar packet to use. "I really don't remember. It was something Frank approached me about."

"Really? Frank approached you to start the charity?"

"I probably shouldn't talk about it. Frank wouldn't approve," Nathalie replied, removing her sunglasses.

George jotted a few notes down, preparing his next question, when he noticed her red eyes, indicative of a recent outburst of emotion. "Are you OK, Miss Herringbone?"

"Oh, I'm fine. Just an emotional afternoon. You know Frank, Mr. Ambition, go, go, go."

George leaned back in his chair, his stare confused. This was not the same woman who spoke with poise upstairs a short while earlier. Even her French accent appeared to have faded.

"I noticed on the website that the charity didn't list its status as 501 c 3. Do you happen to know the EIN for the charity?"

"Well … I'm not really sure about that," she said, rummaging through her purse. "He set up the website and told me he was going to take care of the tax-exempt stuff." She pulled out a piece of paper containing bank account and routing numbers, and handed it to George. "He gave me this. Is that what you're looking for? He said he was going to use it as a holding account until he could … do something. I'm sorry, I really don't know much about this."

George sat dumbfounded, staring at the paper, then at Nathalie. *No wonder Frank didn't want me talking to her. She's clueless. A beautiful, clueless spokesperson.* "And the ten and a half million he spoke of today, has that been donated?"

"I believe so. He called me this morning to confirm it."

"Why did he approach you about this?"

Nathalie explained that she'd made an appointment with Frank to discuss investing in the VLGF. He took the appointment, confiding in her that the investment was for chumps. Instead, he had a better proposition, where he promised to double her investment if she'd act as the spokesperson for a charity he'd spearheaded.

"You know, I really need to go, George," she said, standing up, quickly gathering her stuff. "Thank you very much for the coffee."

"Nathalie, I'd liked to—"

"Give Alec Gordon a call. He would be more helpful to you."

Frank's son? The suggestion surprised George. *He's not in the business, as far I as I can tell. What would he know?* By the time George pondered Nathalie's suggestion, she'd vanished. He made a few notes before calling the bank where the routing numbers led to. Again his gut urged him to question Frank's financial operation. This time he hoped to uncover a more incriminating story if he could find one.

Back to the Drawing Board

Alec caught the next subway train headed back to GIM. Exhausted and deflated he took a seat rather than stand. The sore hand from the right hook he landed in Vegas was tender again from smashing into the bike handlebars, though it was the least of his pains.

He stared at nothing in particular, the entire scene replaying in his head, trying to make sense of it all now that *he* had the vCloud. *What was the whole chase about in the first place if she simply handed it over to me? Follow my hunch? What hunch?* He shook his head, flopped it against the back of the seat, and closed his eyes, squeezing the vCloud tightly for the brief journey back to his destination.

The office was quiet when he exited the elevator on GIM's floor, in sharp contrast to how he'd left it an hour earlier. Gina apparently gone for the day, he poked his head into the server room, but only the dull buzz of fans cooling the equipment filled the emptiness, leaving his dad's muffled voice behind the closed doors to his office the last remnants of a roller-coaster day of eye-opening revelations.

Despite the dread of confronting Nathalie face-to-face after their disarming encounter earlier, he needed answers, but she too had vanished. Part of him felt relieved, unsure which side of the fence he'd choose when gazing into those eyes that melted him and hearing the soothing voice that hypnotized him. He cringed at the frightful reaction she'd had when he raised his hand to retrieve the com device. He wished he could apologize. With her cell phone in his hand, her true identity a mystery, and place of residence unknown, he knew she was gone forever.

Standing comatose, staring at the pile of wadded-up, tear-soaked tissues on the magazine table, he half wanted to go home, collapse on the couch, and let the day finish out without any further drama, but whatever plan the two women had hatched was for all intents and purposes complete and he needed to assess the damage for his dad's sake.

He gently knocked on Frank's office door, letting himself in. Alec nodded hello to his dad, who conversed on the phone, and took a seat on the couch as his cell phone beeped, alerting him to a new text message from a number he didn't recognize. *Nathalie?* He knew that was unlikely. Wolf_Eyes, or Alex, seemed just as unlikely. He'd follow up later.

"Sure, Ken, we'll talk some more tomorrow," Frank said, hanging up the phone. "Alec, you look like a mess. I searched for you after the press conference."

"I'm fine. I had to dash out for a quick meeting. It took longer than expected," Alec replied, the aches from the run and bike-sprint across town spreading through his legs and back. He sat up on the couch, searching for a more comfortable position. "On the phone this morning, you mentioned some odd occurrences."

Frank reclined a few moments, staring off into the office as if searching for the right words to express the situation. "It's not there now," he said. "What I saw this morning is gone, so I think we're back to normal."

Alec knew why, or at least it made sense. The vCloud rested benignly in his pocket, no longer doing what it had been designed to do. Still attempting to put Wolf_Eyes's subway note into context, he delayed revealing the events of the chase and the discovery of Nathalie's connection to Wolf_Eyes. If he wanted to follow his "hunch," he'd need to know more about GIM's operations, and his dad would likely clam up if he believed things had returned to normal.

"So nothing was disturbed after whatever glitch you may or may not have noticed this morning?"

Frank didn't reply immediately. Alec could tell his father was formulating the right choice of words to manage the interrogation. "Some things were moved around, but nothing that can't be accounted for."

"'Accounted for' … as in accounting issues?"

His dad sat silent.

"Was there any money—?"

"No, Alec. I said it was moved around."

"Look, Frank," Alec blurted out, jumping to his feet, fed up with and tired of the figurative and literal runaround he'd endured all day, "you wanted me to investigate the computer hacks. Well, I have, and every time I turn around you've sabotaged my efforts. First the vague Vegas Land Grab Fund discussion, then the pen test—"

Frank appeared taken aback by Alec's use of his proper name. "Son, please, sit down," he said, gesturing with his hands. Alec sat down, more for the fact his father had referred to him as "son" for the second time that day. "Thank you for helping out, but I took care of the problem with the pen test. We're fine."

Alec smirked. "Really? You don't think it's odd that the day after you had the problem 'taken care of' there's a glitch, which mysteriously moved money around? Let me ask you, how many times has this glitch occurred before?"

Frank's eyes drifted downward, his face a study of timelines, projections, and fear. "You don't think the girl who did the pen test—"

"Yes, Father ... I do. In fact, I'd almost guarantee it."

Frank searched for the business card Nathalie Herringbone had given him. "I must've given Sam the—"

"Do you actually believe someone who just hacked and robbed you would leave a trail leading back to them? I took the card from Sam. It's a dead end."

Frank slouched in his chair, his face getting whiter by the second. Alec watched his dad mentally connect the dots.

"So you think Nathalie ... and the charity were a scam?"

"That I don't know," Alec said, unsure of the entire plot himself, though it seemed probable. But as he watched his dad's demeanor run the gamut of emotions one might experience after being conned, Alec circled back to his question mark on Wolf_Eyes's motive: why would she suddenly start profiteering from her unauthorized technological exploits. It was no longer a simple matter of hacking into financial firms, which she was reputed to favor. Now it involved a con artist in the likes of Nathalie, or whatever her name was, and daring onsite heroics. This displayed a whole new level of subterfuge usually beyond the scope of hackers. They preferred doing their work remotely, not getting caught up in schemes that included wild chases through metropolitan streets and daring escapes on subways.

"We should probably call"—Alec groaned as he stood back up, his leg muscles already dealing with the lactic-acid burn from the intense ride on the messenger bike—"the authorities." He halted his inquiry on the matter as Frank showed signs of going into his turtle shell, as Alec referred to it, whenever he cut too close to the bone on something his dad didn't want to share. If illegitimate activities *were* going on at GIM, the best way to rouse Frank would be to suggest someone from the outside step in to handle the situation. *Perhaps he'll open up then.*

Alec reached the door before Frank snapped out of his intense deliberation. "Alec, wait."

He paused at what sounded like a plea to him.

"Let's figure things out before contacting the authorities."

Alec half smiled, hobbling back to the chair alongside Frank's desk. *Now we're getting somewhere.* "Tell me what happened today so I can piece this thing together. The hacker I suspect in this matter has certain tendencies and I might be able to track her down," he said, omitting the fact that with some effort he could find where she lived out in California. After all, he'd recognized her from the market that served up that memorable lunch.

Frank showed Alec the two sets of wire transfers he'd set up the previous night and earlier that day, but his recount of the experience lacked the detail Alec desired, so he continued to grill his father on the subject. *He really should run for office someday.*

Eventually Alec learned of the details for the $14 million errantly routed. Toss in the third set of transfers Frank had Gina perform down at the bank, as well the $10.5 million to the charity, and Alec sat dumbfounded, wondering why his father was neither on the verge of a fit of rage nor on the phone with the authorities. It all felt a little too matter-of-fact for Alec. *Easy come, easy go?*

"These random accounts you mentioned," Alec started, attempting to understand why Wolf_Eyes chose them, since the second wire-transfer batch didn't repeat the same pattern, "did you notice anything they might have in common with one another?"

"Not particularly, other than they were older accounts. Why?" Frank replied, getting that where-is-this-going look in his eyes that Alec had seen before.

"Were they associated with the VLGF, for instance?"

Frank bristled, retorting, "I'd have to look into that."

That was the last straw. Alec took a deep breath in and let it out slowly. He'd had enough of his father's vague responses. He got up, this time to leave in earnest. "So it doesn't bother you that fourteen million dollars just walked out the door to unintended accounts, or another ten and a half million ended up possibly going to a fake—?"

"I'll call Miss Herringbone tomorrow to straighten it all out. I'm sure it's just a misunderstanding."

"And the wire transfers? Another misunderstanding?" Alec said sarcastically as he neared the door. *And good luck calling* Miss Herringbone ... *I have her phone.*

"Why would you understand?" Frank blurted out. "You don't have Gordon blood in—"

What? Alec paused at the door, sizing up his dad's inexplicably cavalier behavior and strange parting remark. Perhaps he should've told him about Nathalie's connection to Wolf_Eyes, or even simply about Wolf_Eyes, but his dad hadn't been forthcoming on pertinent matters, so he kept it under his cap for the time being. *It's your money.*

His cell phone beeped the arrival of another text message as he caught the elevator down. It reminded him of the other one that had come in earlier. He glanced down at the two messages, both from the same number: "Meet me at Café Java Server & Apps. We need to talk. It's important," read the first one. The second: "Please come. Life is not what it seems."

Alec shook his head after rereading the texts. *Nathalie? Wolf_Eyes?* He knew it wasn't a number he'd called before. Nathalie no longer had a phone as far as he knew, and Wolf_Eyes's burner phone used for the pen test was a different number.

Curiosity trumped his strong desire to go home, heading, instead, for his favorite hacker café.

Alex Andra in the
Real World

Alex quickly checked out from the hotel once she'd gathered her belongings. She grabbed Nathalie's stuff as well, unsure of her status, though it seemed unlikely she'd come back to the hotel. Now that Alec had names, faces, and, more troublesome, Nathalie's cell phone, staying at the hotel was too risky.

She caught a cab to the airport, grabbing a last-minute evening fare back to California. Leaving Nathalie behind made Alex ill at ease, putting her on the verge of tears several times, but under the circumstances it was the most prudent move. They had never discussed the worst-case scenario, what to do should they become separated or caught. It never occurred to them things would go down the way they did. Alex knew she couldn't help Nathalie by getting caught herself. Returning home would allow her to sort things out, even undo some of the fake charity transactions if that would help Nathalie's situation.

Legally, Alex didn't know what that situation looked like, hers or theirs. It all came down to what Frank Gordon would likely do when he found out about the ruse. *Would he call the authorities? Write off the lost money, sweeping it under the rug? On paper, no money had been stolen, just returned to its rightful owners with a little nudging.* All the charity-related items—account, website, wire-transfer donation—had been *legitimately* set up and executed by Frank. There were too many unknowns for Alex to consider.

She slept the entire six-hour flight after quietly crying herself to sleep, clutching the small airline pillow against her chest, waking when the airplane's wheels touched down in San Jose. A subtle form of relief spread over her.

With her backpack squarely on and a duffel bag swung over each shoulder, Alex resembled a student returning home from a summer-long trek through Europe in desperate need of a hot shower and a good meal. She shuffled through the terminal out past the security checkpoint, where friends and family awaited loved ones and airport greeters held handmade signs with arriving passenger names scrawled across them. As she approached the wall of people with their expectant eyes a placard caught her attention: ALEX ANDRA.

Alex stopped, staring at the professionally dressed man, a limo driver's cap atop his head, announcing her Tammaré avatar's moniker. She turned her head side to side a few times, waiting for either someone to head over there to claim their ride, or for men in uniform to escort her to some holding room. Neither scenario occurred. She contemplated moving on, ignoring the situation altogether, but curiosity got the better of her.

"Hi, I'm Alex Andra."

"Very well, Miss Andra," said the polite man, folding the sign and tucking it inside his jacket. "Here, let me take those bags for you." Before Alex could tell him it wasn't necessary, he'd hoisted both duffel bags off her. "Right this way, please."

"Where are we going?" she asked, following the tall man who walked with long, efficient strides, navigating around a large group of travelers who appeared lost.

"Your home in Palo Alto. I have the address in the Town Car."

Alex slowed to a stop, taking sidelong glances. Getting into a car with a stranger didn't seem like a good idea after the day she'd had, no matter how official his appearance. "Excuse me, but who are you and who sent you?" she said, her initial curiosity waning.

"My apologies. I don't do this often," the man said, retracing his steps back to her. "My name is Brandon. Lady Herringbone called ahead to ensure you would get home safely." He smiled, handing her an envelope from his jacket.

She stared at the man, taking the envelope from him, apprehension seeping in as she opened it to read the note inside. "Glad my Little Grommet made it back to Cali. Don't worry about me … I told you I was mysterious. XOXO." *Nathalie made it out of GIM!* Alex let out a burst of laughter that melted her guilt, worry, and worst fears.

Sitting in the Town Car, Alex reset her watch to midnight Pacific Standard Time as the new day began. She peered out the window, readjusting to the wider roadways, familiar skyline, lower humidity, and Nathalie not by her side; that emptiness moderately tempered by the knowledge that she was safe. Without a phone to call, Alex's only ability to contact Nathalie would be at her condo, but recollection of the directions to it were lost somewhere in the ride on the back of the Ducati. Even with Nathalie's last name in hand she feared she'd never see her again.

033   The Whistle Stop

Alec entered Café Java Server & Apps unsure who had texted him. He scanned the full house, but no one beckoned him over to a table. He ordered a Guinness at the counter, keeping a lookout, when he spotted Gina sitting by herself. With his mysterious texter a no-show he wandered over, hoping to learn what had happened to Nathalie.

"Gina," he said, sitting down gingerly.

"Are you OK?" she asked, staring at the discoloration spreading across his hand.

"I'll be fine. I'm glad I ran into you," he said, taking a much-deserved swig from his glass stein. "What happened to Nathalie, or whatever her name is?"

Gina sat there quiet, her hands folded on the table.

"Gina?" Alec studied her face. It lacked the bubbly exterior he'd adored all his life. He took note of the absence of drink or food on the table, instead a copy of *Insiders Business Review*, the issue that ran the accusatory article about Frank and GIM. He rubbed his chin, sizing up the implications. *It was Gina who texted me.* "You're the whistleblower." He let out a palpable sigh.

Gina nodded. "I'm very sorry, Alec," she said, her face a portrait of someone looking for forgiveness after betraying another. "Your father ... it's not what I signed up—"

"And Nathalie," Alec said, taking a gulp of beer, "how did she factor into all of this?"

"I don't know, really. She showed up looking to invest with GIM. Frank wanted her because of the international money and charity connections she had. Next thing I know there's the pen test, then wire-transfer issues—"

"Where is she now?"

Gina's demeanor hadn't deviated from its somber state since Alec's arrival, a study of contrition in matters cutting to the heart of him and his family. "I don't know."

Alec closed his eyes. The image of Nathalie leaned up against him by the San Francisco Bay filled the darkness. It wasn't so much that Gina had let her go that pained him as much as his hopes for another chance to talk to her. He had to let the image go.

"What do you think is going on with my dad?" Alec asked, leaning back with the stein in his good hand, ready to hear another tale, adding to an already-epic day of tales.

Gina laid out for Alec her observation of the influx of investor money, where only certain clients appeared to reap the benefits of quarterly dividends despite the fact these "special" clients didn't have a position or stake in the VLGF. At first she didn't give it much thought, since Frank took care of the wire transfers himself. After a while she overheard his conversations on the phone with clients—he wasn't treating all his clients the same way. In fact, he rarely placed or took calls from ordinary investors, and often had consultants handle their needs as required. Her access to GIM's books and records dwindled when Frank took over full-time for Jack, further creating suspicion he might be hiding something.

"My husband and I wanted to invest in the Vegas Land Grab Fund when he added it to the firm's portfolio, because he made it sound so good, but he told us no," Gina said.

"Did he say why?"

"He wouldn't take on individual investors for it," she replied, sitting several moments in silence afterward. "Anyway, between that, his use of a different bank every year to perform the annual audit, and inflated dividends on some accounts, I felt something wasn't right, so I contacted George Orkan to see if he could dig a little deeper. There were just too many irregularities to ignore after working with your grandfather for so many years.... I didn't want to be a part of a Madoff-type scheme."

Alec nodded, partly in agreement and partly because the beer was numbing his unfathomable day away. He certainly never imagined days like today, or the encounter with zNiNo in Vegas, when he enrolled in cybercriminology.

Gina handed him the list of transfers she'd made in person at the bank earlier in the day. "Here's a list of the clients who receive generous dividends every quarter. Until today, I was never allowed to see them. Perhaps you can use it."

Alec polished off the rest of the beer, took the list from Gina, then slowly rose to his feet. He wasn't upset with her, but he also couldn't bring himself to let her off the hook, either. At least, not yet. Her concerns over his dad's business dealings dovetailed with what he'd learned earlier back at the office. Since the moment he connected Wolf_Eyes to GIM, the haunting question had always been *why?* Now, it was starting to look like he had a working motive: restitution, though the $10.5 million siphoned off for the charity constituted fraud if it turned up fake, as he suspected it would. It all seemed like an immense amount of work and planning to pull off, yet his observations and chance encounters painted a less-than-thought-out strategy. Perhaps the vCloud would shed some light on the matter. *It'll have to wait until tomorrow.*

Alec moved away from the table, slowly heading for the exit. Gina immediately followed.

"Let me drive you home, Alec."

"No, I'll take the subway … thanks."

"Please, I insist."

Alec stood outside a few moments, gazing into the evening sky, the full moon a couple of days away, before relenting. Silence filled the ride to the loft, the image of his female doppelgänger indelibly etched in his mind. He recalled their surreal handshake in California weeks earlier, the familial quality it held.

"Here you go."

Alec stared up at the dark loft window, Cassidy's curious white eyes peering back at him. "Thanks."

"Alec," she said before he had a chance to open the door, "there's something you should know. It might not be my place to say, but I've watched you grow up trying to please your dad, and I've always kept my peace about the way he treats you. I think it's time you knew the truth."

Alec wasn't sure he could take too much more *truth* for the day. The truth was, the truth confused him. Nonetheless, he sobered up enough to hear what she had to say.

"You know the accident you were in as a child?"

Alec stared back, apprehensively nodding.

"Well … you were in an accident but … the front passengers didn't survive."

Alec went numb, waiting for Gina to confirm what he was thinking, putting his father's "you don't have Gordon blood in you" comment into perspective. Even his grandfather, Jack, had made similarly veiled remarks over the years when he'd been drinking. *I'm adopted!*

Alec stared out the window, the afternoon's events flashing before his eyes. Gina didn't need to continue. "And Alex, the girl I chased today, is my … sister?"

"Twin sister," Gina replied, placing her hand on his limp arm.

 # What Lies Beneath

The loud metallic crash of the city sanitation truck emptying the heavy Dumpster outside Alec's front window interrupted his restless slumber, the recurring dream assimilating the image of his twin sister sliding away from him on the subway platform. Lying there, Cassidy licking his bruised hand, Alec connected the presence alongside him in previous dreams as his sister, Alex, spinning around and around together in a car; the bright-orange light illuminating their view, the fiery explosion that killed their biological parents. After years wondering what was amiss in his life, he'd uncovered the answer: he had a sister. And if that weren't enough of a discovery, a sister on the opposite side of the law from him. At once everything made sense, and then nothing made sense. He covered his face with both hands, shaking his head.

Alec slowly gathered himself, first checking his cell phone for any new fires that might've sprouted at GIM. There were none. He checked Nathalie's cell phone, but it too showed no recent activity, the inevitable lull in the aftermath of the chaotic events. He took a tour of her phone, checking contacts, e-mails, texts, surprised by its emptiness, revealing nothing more than that her first name appeared to actually be Nathalie. Redialing the number that had sent the phone a text during the chase resulted in an out-of-service message. He figured Alex would disconnect her phone, severing all communication ties. He might not be able to track her down directly, but he knew where to find her adoptive parents.

He explored Nathalie's photo library, finding a few miscellaneous pictures of Santa Cruz, Las Vegas, New York, and one that caught his eye, a grainy newspaper clipping about a car accident that had killed two people, leaving two children parentless twenty years ago, corroborating Gina's story. Taking a closer look he found a picture of the family of four, the proud parents holding their twin son and daughter days before the tragedy. He stared at the baby picture of him for several minutes. *It always seemed odd that my parents didn't have pictures of me before the age of two.*

He worked his way through a bowl of cereal while the vCloud booted up on his computer, then ran integrity diagnostics on it, checking to see if anything had been deleted, tampered with, or wiped clean. The integrity check showed no such containment activity on her part. That didn't surprise him, given the amount of time Wolf_Eyes had possession of it between Sam retrieving it for her and handing it off to the messenger kid. Between running to and hacking the subway system, she wouldn't have had much time to do anything with the vCloud data. It now served as a definitive archeological dig on all matters related to Wolf_Eyes and GIM, the truth about her plan and his father's business dealings. *If only it would be that simple.*

Let's see what's going on here. Alec launched the one and only executable file listed in the directory, immediately opening a dashboard that rivaled something a world-class software manufacturer might design for Fortune one-hundred companies. It was feature-rich. He scanned the many icon choices—GIM client account lists, preferred-client lists, VLGF assets, wire transfers, charity accounts, and many others. Alec ventured into the wire-transfers section, the smoking gun from the day prior.

Sure enough, there on the screen were details of the two sets of wire transfers gone awry. Alec reviewed the intended list, comparing it to the list Gina had given him the night before. *Identical.* He glanced over the fifty accounts the money actually ended up in, not sure what to make of them yet. The page allowed him to drill down into the account details, which revealed what his father alluded to: they were older accounts, some going back five years or so. The other pattern he observed supported his own initial premise: all recipients had invested in the VLGF. He quickly checked the primary list, noting that none of them were connected to the VLGF but rather were heavily invested in GIM's main holding-account investments. *Well, that supports Gina's observations.*

Alec was curious about how the wire transfers were shunted in different directions. Under the Cloud layer where GIM had been suspended for twenty-four hours, Alec isolated the real inner workings of Wolf_Eyes's plan. Fortunately, the scripts and programs that lurked underneath weren't coded in hieroglyphics like Scarab had been, and they lacked encryption or additional protection. *Not surprising, I suppose. Between the time she purchased the vCloud and deployed it, little time existed to add extra precautions. Besides, she obviously planned on retrieving it.*

Alec marveled at the cleverness of the vCloud setup, the programming logic, and the overall thoroughness he unraveled over the course of the morning and into the afternoon, proud for a moment of his sister's creative and skillful handling of complex tasks in such a short period of time, despite their fraudulent agenda. *If my sister is going to be a hacker, then it's nice to know she's a good one. A worthy adversary.*

Admiration aside, Alec struggled to understand the *why* of it all. As far as he could tell, the preferred-client list reaped quarterly benefits, while those in the VLGF investment did not, but that didn't constitute any wrongdoing on GIM's part. *Different asset classes, different payouts.* The other thing that kept him from suspecting his dad of any wrongdoing stemmed from the fact that all the VLGF investment accounts received a 10 percent dividend after one year, though it appeared to be the only money they ever received. That is, until Wolf_Eyes got involved.

Alec pored over the vCloud in detail, piecing together GIM's business affairs. His father would crucify him if he knew what information he was now privy to, but such knowledge furnished him with the only conclusive measure for deciding the right party from the wrong party or, as his gut gnawed, how gray things likely were.

Nearly fifteen hours had elapsed between the time Alex laid her head on the pillow after the chauffeur had dropped her off and when she felt Sundance licking her face. Piled around her were various articles of clothing and small objects Sundance had bestowed upon her throughout the long, restful slumber.

"Who's the good boy?" Alex's raspy voice cooed, playing tug-of-war with his latest offering.

It was late afternoon on the West Coast, though her body wrestled with which time zone to respect. Once she rolled out of bed, she immediately went about wiping her computer and server hard drives of any and all GIM-related data, including the code base that supported the Scarab Trojan. If law enforcement came knocking on her door, they'd have no cyber evidence to link her to the commotion in New York.

Alex searched the bedroom for her cell phone a few minutes before she remembered she'd chucked it, and the burner phone, into one of the waterways in New York, the name of which escaped her. The act was a rash attempt to sever as many ties with her brother as she could, at least the cybercriminologist side of him. Her desperate text message to Nathalie's phone during the chase revealed Alec possessed it, and ultimately a traceable phone number back to her. Ditching it and disconnecting the number sounded like a good idea at the time, though now, with a clearer head, she realized it may have been a moot exercise. *He could probably get a warrant and locate the number's billing address.*

Alex found a note from her mom welcoming her home when she wandered into the kitchen for some food. She couldn't remember the last thing she had eaten, or when. Watching Sundance lick himself clean in the living room, Alex methodically worked her way through a large bowl of organic based cereal as if restoring some semblance of order in her life. She was back home but she didn't necessarily feel safely removed from her actions in New York. *Nathalie appears to be safe, which means they can't ask her any questions about me. Alec will track me down through the store, since he saw me there. But when? It'll take him a couple of days to sift through the vCloud data. But what does he have on me? What can come back on me? He has the vCloud and only circumstantial evidence can connect it back to me, right? No money was stolen. What can GIM really report? What would they be willing to report? That's the key question. Not much I can do now except wait it out and see what he comes after me for.*

Alex had no better clarity on her predicament as a wave of unrest fell over her on having handed the vCloud over to Alec, but after stowing the cereal bowl in the dishwasher she knew what she needed to do for now: take a hot shower to wash off the long trip home, and buy a new cell phone.

By midafternoon, Alec needed a break to clear his head. He took Cassidy for a cab ride up to the Conservatory Garden on the east side of Central Park, strolling around until they'd reached the quaint water fountain. Sitting in near solitude, he let Cassidy off the leash, turning an uncharacteristic blind eye to the city's dog leash law, then stared at the water spraying upward from the fountain's center pipe that fanned out before it cascaded downward like a folded umbrella and rippled the water underneath, where tiny bubbles floated outward. The gentle, consistent movement relaxed him while Cassidy sniffed symmetrically pruned hedges.

Alec's cell phone brought him out of the trancelike state he'd slipped into. "Hello, Henry," he answered, clapping his one good hand on his pant leg, getting Cassidy's wandering attention.

"Hey, Speed Racer," Henry chuckled. "Thomas told me to add the Speed Racer."

Alec had to laugh. *Thomas is all right.* "Yes, it was quite a scene."

"I take it you didn't catch her?"

"No, sir. My apologies."

"You don't need to apologize to me, son. You are the first person to report a Wolf_Eyes sighting. It proves she's real. That's impressive stuff."

Alec smiled, explaining his zNiNo and Wolf_Eyes sighting in Vegas in more detail than before.

"Son, you're either the luckiest son of a bitch on the planet or they're relatives of yours."

Alec laughed under his breath. He knew calling Thomas during the chase would get back to Henry, but it was the only option at the time. He gave Henry the lowdown on the evidence he'd obtained in Vegas demonstrating GIM as a target, and the path it led him down, culminating in the chase through Manhattan.

"The thing I'm having trouble wrapping my head around is how my father doesn't seem rattled about the money, like if you or I lost a twenty-dollar bill. Granted, the coffers are flowing, but still …" Alec said, his voice trailing off, dazed by the immense amount of money he found sitting in GIM's various on- and offshore accounts.

"And you say the vast majority of the money flows in from the Vegas Land Grab Fund?"

"Yes." Alec could hear Henry get out of his chair and walk around the office. He said it helped him think better, despite the limp.

"Ever hear of crowd-funding?"

"No."

"It's a way for certain activities or projects, even campaigns, to get their whatever funded by the public, those who want to support it as a group."

"OK."

"Let's say I'm in a band and I can't get a record deal. I set up a website, promote myself, and get people to fund my recording time in exchange for, say, a free copy of the CD if, as a group, they hit some preestablished amount. Start-up companies are beginning to use the concept to finance their R&D efforts instead of getting into bed with venture capitalists."

"So, they are basically donating money to some cause?"

"They're claiming a stake in the success of whatever they've pooled their money towards. They get something for it, like the CD from my band or a free concert in their home," Henry said, chuckling.

"Groups are funding the VLGF at GIM?"

"It's conjecture, mind you. You mentioned your father only works with groups on this investment product, kicks back ten percent after one year, and is always bringing in new clients. So unless he owns all of Nevada or is constantly buying bulk lots of homes, he's probably trading on the same security, over and over again. Let's face it; real estate is not bouncing back in leaps and bounds, especially out in the desert."

Alec's mind started extrapolating the flow of money with the timelines since VLGF's inception at GIM, the rise in charitable donations and campaign contributions that followed. If all that the VLGF investors got back was a 10 percent dividend from their initial investment, it might keep them at bay for years, leaving 90 percent of the money to use for other purposes, like passing on to preferred clients. *That might explain why Dad wasn't so eager to go after the misrouted money ... it's constantly flowing in.*

Henry explained that the JOBS Act—Jumpstart Our Business Startups—essentially opened the door to this type of fund-raising, extending to the public the ability to stake equity claims on everything from new tech widgets to investment securities. "The SEC hasn't even set out guidelines for it yet," Henry added.

"Thanks, Henry. That helps quite a bit. I'll talk to you later."

Alec now knew what he needed to look for on the vCloud in order to resolve his misgivings about GIM's business affairs.

035 Adoptive Confrontation

On Alex's way to Maggie's Organic Market, cleansed and new cell phone in hand, the startling matter she'd set aside for several days came screaming back when she pulled into the parking lot: *I'm adopted.* For the first time since the disclosure, she was about to face them, the two people she'd called Mom and Dad her whole life. She hadn't spent any time deciding whether to ask them about it or not. What with all that went on in New York it didn't seem important; there were larger issues at stake.

"Alex!" her mom screamed with joy when the small bell jingled.

"Hey, Mom."

"You look great, honey," Maggie said, giving her a big hug. "I love that tank top you're wearing. Did you do something with your hair?" She took Alex in as if she'd been gone for an entire summer.

"No, Mom, nothing with the hair," she responded with a smile.

Alex chatted with her mom about parts of the trip that didn't involve her and Nathalie's questionable activities, reading Maggie's face as if a long lost chapter had been discovered.

"Well, your dad will be excited to see you," Maggie said as customers began to queue up at the checkout stand. "He's back in the office. I'm glad you're home, sweetie."

"Me too, Mom." *Me too.*

Alex knew she walked a fine line with her parents, the line between her recent exploits and what she told them, a position she didn't enjoy very much. After all they had provided her with over the years, this was not how she wanted their relationship defined, especially now.

"Doodle Bug!" Phil shouted, jumping up from his chair to give her a hug, lifting her feet off the floor. "I'm so glad you're back. You look great. Did you do something with your hair?"

"No, Dad." She laughed, enjoying the way his long arms wrapped tightly around her, hugging him back just as hard.

"Oh, my bad manners," Phil said, setting her down. "This is Harris." He gestured toward the man standing behind him. "He's also a member of the WCOF community."

"Hi, Alex," Harris said, shaking her hand. "It's been a while. You were just a little girl the last time I saw you. Look at you now, all grown-up and beautiful-looking, just like your mother."

Alex blushed at the ever-charming Harris, whom she did remember from childhood for his ability to make her laugh uncontrollably. "Thanks, it has been a while."

"Well, I'll let you two catch up," Harris said, heading toward the door as Phil picked up the ringing phone.

"Here," Harris whispered to Alex, handing her a business card. "If you need *anything* give my brother a call. He's the top defense attorney in the country. We're all very grateful." He gave her a wink as he left.

Alex quickly tucked the card away before her dad hung up the phone. She knew the elephant in the room would be the *how* of the whole WCOF reimbursement. He nearly said as much when they last spoke the day after the vCloud went live.

"How's the store been, Dad?"

"Oh, it's good. Tell me about the software meeting. Is it something they're interested in?" Phil said, sitting down after clearing off the only other chair in the office for Alex.

"No, I don't think it's going to work out. After they took a closer look at it, they didn't seem that interested. I did leave them a copy in case they wanted to pursue it further," Alex replied, searching her dad's eyes, hoping he'd understand and leave things at that.

"That's too bad," he said. "Their loss, right?"

Alex smiled and nodded.

"Oh, I almost forgot, I need to cover for your mom." He stood and grabbed his work apron. "She's going to a dinner party."

"Let me cover for Mom, and you guys go together."

"You sure?" he asked with a surprised look.

"Yeah, go. You two haven't been out in a while."

"Here … use my apron."

Alex took a look at his well-worn apron with the day's toils on it and smiled. "I'll grab a new one in back."

"Hey, Alex," her dad said as she reached the door. "Welcome home. We're very proud of you."

Alex smiled, all but cementing her inclination to leave their adoption secret just that: secret.

Phil escorted Maggie out the front door as if he had Cinderella on his arm, each giving Alex big thank-you smiles. She watched her parents ham it up, dancing like long-lost hippies from the '60s, before getting into the car and driving off.

The closing hours at the store were particularly busy. Alex greeted customers and chatted with them, portraying her mom's steadfast cheer and charm while Kara bagged their groceries and drew smiley faces on the paper bags. Those who had shopped there for years commented on how much she'd grown since the last time they'd seen her. One little boy buying some candy, who didn't have quite enough money to cover the sale, told her she had cool eyes after she let his shortage slide.

The warm Palo Alto evening reminded her how good it felt to be back home, wrapped in a clean store apron that acted as comfort wear, and each time the front door's bell jingled she'd glance up, hopeful Nathalie would appear, but she never did.

As an avid New York Mets fan for as long as he could remember, Alec felt out of place strolling through the new Yankee Stadium, but that hardly tarnished the satisfaction he got from the sight of the pristine green grass and meticulous white chalk lines that defined fair and foul play on the baseball field. *If only life could be so easily marked.* His grandfather, Jack, had taken him to numerous games every season, from the moment he was tall enough to push through the turnstiles at the ballpark.

Now that Frank had become one of New York's familiar names, it afforded him the opportunity to buy a luxury suite at America's most celebrated ballpark of success. Hosting preferred clients, and future preferred clients, to a Yankees home game offered one of the hotter tickets in town when baseball season was in full-swing. The game itself didn't interest Frank, but a Yankee skybox did, just the ticket to partake in something *very* New York.

Alec knew that most New Yorkers were either passionate Mets fans or dedicated Yankee fans; no middle ground or overlapping area existed. Relationships often fizzle out when opposing alliances are revealed. Alec rooted for the Mets, despite their abysmal history, mostly out of his disdain for the Yankees penchant to buy guns-for-hire—rather than cultivating teams—than for anything else. Reaching for the checkbook didn't make a team in his book, but rather demonstrated a business transaction. The fact they wore pinstripes simply perpetuated the notion. His father, on the other hand, identified with success, and the Yanks sold the perception.

When Alec reached the luxury seats, he spotted his father chatting with a tall man sporting a Boston Red Sox cap on his head. *I'm surprised they let him in up here.* Frank wouldn't necessarily be expecting Alec at the game, but an invitation was always extended. He needed to ask some questions to quell his concerns about GIM's investing model, and the ballpark was where his dad could be found.

He ordered up a stadium hot dog and drink, taking a seat near the railing as the lineups echoed over the public-address system. A few bites into the steamed concession item reminded Alec how much better-tasting the links had been out in California. The stadium teemed with Yankee faithfuls as the setting sun cast shadows on large sections of the outfield. This was the first time Alec had watched a game from the luxurious seats. He preferred sitting out in the crowd, connected to the game in a way that cushy seats, catered food, and TV monitors couldn't provide.

"Alec," Frank said, walking up as a local celebrity tossed out the honorary first pitch. "One of these days that'll be me."

"That would be something." *Hopefully, he won't bounce it to the plate.*

"What brings you out to the game? Finally come to the realization the Mets are losers?" He chuckled.

"There's more to the game than big paychecks."

"You've been saying that for years. But the fact remains people want winners, not whiners. Money is the only way to ensure it."

"Certainly helps, but it's not the only way," Alec replied, launching into his patented list of seasons where the mighty Yankee payroll succumbed to lesser bankrolled teams who played with more guts than panache. Frank failed to respond as Alec anticipated, allowing him to switch gears. "Were you able to reach Nathalie Herringbone?"

Frank took in the first couple pitches of the game. "No."

"I didn't think you would. I'm sure she's long gone … I have uncovered a possible motive for the hacks on GIM and the subsequent redirected wire transfers."

"Like I said yesterday, everything is back to normal."

"How do you know it won't happen again? The pen test could've created additional vulnerabilities."

"I hired the consultant who set up our network a few years back to clean things up. We'll be OK."

"Forgive me, but I'm at a loss on how you can treat so much money going to wrong accounts and fake charities as if it were nothing."

"Alec, it's the cost of doing business. You said it yourself. I haven't spent enough on the network. Now I am."

"That's good to hear."

Father and son quietly sipped on their respective drinks as the Yankees took care of the visiting team one, two, three to start the first inning.

"On the motive, not that you are worried, but it appears they were paying back accounts who had invested in the Vegas Land Grab Fund from years ago," Alec started back in, attempting to stage a discussion where his father might reveal deeper insight for the breaches in the first place.

"I know."

"Any thoughts as to why?"

Frank shifted in his chair as if seeking a better view of the batter at the plate for his honorary team. "Alec, I'd say whoever was behind the hacks probably had an ax to grind and paid themselves back. I'm not interested in chasing this thing. It'll cost me more money to litigate than it's worth. Besides, the publicity for GIM getting hacked *and* conned would be bad for business."

"I understand, but there's a trail of evidence that doesn't paint a flattering picture of the business dealings at GIM," Alec said, impatient with his father's insistence on skirting around the whole affair.

Frank directed his attention at Alec, appearing to hold his breath, eyes narrowed and focused.

"In the wrong hands, it might stir up stronger accusations by the likes of *Insiders Business*—"

"What evidence?"

Alec spoke in hushed tones, explaining in vague terms the essence of what the vCloud had captured during its twenty-four hours of activity, and briefly how he came by it, omitting details about the chase. Alec knew he had crossed the line, lying to exact the truth from his father, a trade-off Alec accepted for the lie his adoptive parents had perpetuated his whole life.

"If you have it, then what's the issue?"

"She could've made a copy. She could use it against you in the future."

Frank watched a Yankee player who'd gotten a free pass to first base get thrown out stealing second, the crowd moaning its disapproval at the call. "Ill-gotten evidence. The case would be tossed out. GIM was hacked. Clients received money. End of story."

He assumed Frank had consulted with an attorney based on the response, probably anticipating blowback from the whole affair. Alec knew he needed to push his dad further into a corner in order for him to open up about the investment oddities he'd observed on the vCloud. "True, but I'm not suggesting legal action would be her play."

"Blackmail?" Frank snorted a little too loudly.

"Possibly, or simply turning more evidence over to the reporter George Orkan. He might be able to publish another scathing article. The more noise reporters make, the more investors get nervous these—"

Frank tried to interject a comment, but Alec didn't pause, his tone more determined, painting a picture of the crowd-funding concept Henry had educated him on, which Alec corroborated from the audit trail on the vCloud. It finally made sense, running into Nathalie and Wolf_Eyes in Vegas. They were there checking firsthand the Vegas property that GIM supposedly owned. They would've found a disproportionate amount of investment assets compared to actual property owned and raised capital. In essence, they uncovered the scam Frank devised and peddled, then hatched a plan of their own to do something about it.

"I read a study several years ago," Frank said after Alec had presented his theory. "They took all the wealth in a town and redistributed it equally among all its residents. Within thirty days, the money was back in the hands where it first started. The poor were poor again and the rich were rich again." He paused as the inning ended and the Yankees trotted back out onto the field. "Alec, money is something you either know how to manage or you don't. I simply funnel it from those who lack fiscal responsibility to those who understand its power. I put the money into the hands of those who can do something worthwhile, important, and meaningful with it—lobbyists, policymakers, campaign funds, the arts that inspire—rather than have it spent on consumer products that are outdated six months after they're purchased. Half the time folks do things they don't understand simply because someone else told them to do it. I turn their investments into something truly worthwhile to invest in, even if they don't fully realize it."

"Are you kidding me? What about *their* choice on how to spend *their* money?" Alec said, barely able to hear the boos from the crowd as the Yankees' third baseman muffed a routine grounder.

"Choice is an illusion, Alec," Frank said matter-of-factly. "Choice is a function of habit, and habits are created by the marketing geniuses on Madison Avenue. People don't think about what they buy, they simply buy what they are told to, based on the needs and desires they are informed a product will fulfill in them. Their choices are merely a reaction to satisfy a craving they didn't even know they had. The average person spends their money on needless consumer crap, year in year out: HD TVs, cars, the latest electronic gadgets, designer clothes, etcetera. More, more, more.

It's never-ending. And for what? So they can say they have it all? They end up in debt by living well above their means. With me, I give them hope, a chance to make money. They know investments are risky. I don't ask them to invest more than they can afford to lose. I kick back ten percent after a year and they can write off the rest on their income tax. They'll always earn more money. That's what they're good for in this country. You need to open your eyes, son."

Alec stared in disbelief at Frank, the swollen hand throbbing as his blood boiled, wondering how anyone, especially someone whom he'd called *Father* his whole life, could say such things. Alec stood up, contempt spilling from his eyes. He'd had enough of his father's convoluted mores concerning the fiscally challenged public, unsettled by the twisted nature of its legality.

"You're right. I do need to open my eyes. And I have. You can stop calling me *son*, not that you ever do. I know I'm adopted," he said, storming away, furious that for years he looked up to Frank, admired him, futilely striving to impress him, only to hear him spout off self-serving philosophical bullshit.

Striding toward the exit, Alec could hear Frank's fading question regarding who had informed him about the adoption. He ignored it. *It's irrelevant.* What concerned Alec now was what to do. *Does anybody in the family know about this? Probably not. It would devastate them if this got out. Would anybody even believe me if I went public? Probably not. Everything is circumstantial, and a good lawyer would question the information if they knew a hacker was involved.*

The one aspect of cybercriminology that had inspired Alec to pursue it centered on bringing to justice those who wreaked havoc on people's lives with their computer hacking exploits. That motivated him to track down Wolf_Eyes; her cyber meddling certainly threatened Frank and Jack's legacy at GIM, and June's dream and legacy at Gordon Galleries. Another part of Alec, the part that left him yearning for something he could never put a finger on, happened to be the very person leveling this threat against the only family he knew. His thoughts drifted to Nathalie. Despite her involvement with Wolf_Eyes, he knew she'd be the one person who could help him sort things out.

He wanted to reach out, but she had faded away. He was spinning again, only this time it wasn't a dream.

036   Is Blood Thicker Than Water?

Alex sat partially attentive in the front row during her last afternoon class, wondering why she had bothered going, her body functioning on a different time zone and her mind lost in myriad thoughts unrelated to the lecture topic. After opening the store that morning, she ventured back home before class, rummaging through an old dusty box she'd pulled down from a shelf in the garage that held family photos, heirlooms, and documents from yesteryear, finding a few baby pictures of herself she'd never seen before, including two from a sealed envelope she opened, showing her and Alec seated together on a linoleum kitchen floor with openmouthed smiles, smearing Jell-O on each other's face. She could almost hear their shared squeals of laughter.

She sifted through folders containing various items, ranging from Phil's dissertation on organic growing methods to Woodstock memorabilia, including pictures of Phil and Maggie covered in mud, kissing. Alex smiled, running her finger over the old, glossy, black-and-white Polaroids. After witnessing the fruits of her wireless capers in her father's eyes, she had no intention of letting on that she knew about her adoptive state. The question still lingered, however, about why they hadn't adopted Alec, but it wasn't enough to bring her to burst their bubble.

Nearly to the bottom of the box with little to show for her efforts, she discovered a medical file with her name on it. Opening it she found her birth certificate, and her real parents' names. Reading it brought the weight of the reality home. *It's really true.* She sat there, staring at it, unmoved over a document that conveyed an alternate history, instead simply accepting it as a new fact of life.

Still, curiosity and the need for closure urged her to go online, locating the hospital where the family had been taken after the car accident. She hacked the hospital's admission-records system, and after sorting through dozens of personnel who were employed back then, and had worked that night, she found one nurse who still worked there, and who happened to be on shift that very evening. With a newfound thirst for *real* adventure, Alex decided on another quest, north, by car this time, just her and Sundance, leaving behind her laptop and the virtual world of Tammaré.

Alec awakened from a deep sleep as the captain of the coast-to-coast flight announced they'd begun their descent into San Jose International Airport. For a brief moment Alec stared at the air-phone molded neatly into the patterned fabric of the headrest before him, his dazed expression induced by the cumulative fatigue over the past several days. He stretched as best he could from the window seat before someone tapped his shoulder during mid-yawn. He glanced over to a young girl with black curly hair and freckled cheeks who was traveling with her mother.

"Mister, you dropped this," the girl said, handing him the vCloud. "I kept it safe for you while you were sleeping."

"Thank you," Alec said, giving it a long stare.

"What is it, some kind of magic key?" she asked with wide-eyed wonderment, clearly fascinated with Alec, and had obviously watched over him during his slumber, ensuring he received the complimentary peanuts when they were handed out.

Alec smiled, taken by the little girl's protective and inquisitive nature. "Yes, it is."

"Well, I hope it lets you into wherever you wish to go," she said, exuding wishful thoughts from her beaming smile. "My name is Lucy, and me and my mom are going to see my brother, who's living with my dad on account of they are divorced."

Alec listened to Lucy talk about her younger brother, how he always took her things when they were together, and while watching a movie the way he would fart under the blanket they shared, then smother her with it, but she loved him anyway. By the time they landed and taxied to the gate Lucy had given Alec the lowdown on how she would spend her time in California during the week-long vacation, and had introduced him to her mother, informing him she said she thought he was cute, at which point the mother turned red from embarrassment.

Bidding Lucy and her mom farewell in the terminal, Alec headed toward the rental cars, grinning over the abridged version of what having a sister might've been like growing up, something he now knew had been tugging at him all these years. In Johnny Matterson he'd developed a semblance of a brother, but it had a different quality to it, one that approached camaraderie more than it did a sibling bond.

On the shuttle ride to the rental-car lot, Alec checked his phone for messages—six from his father, one from his mother, one from Karen Mickles at the San Jose Technology Task Force, one from Gina, and one from an unknown number. He knew what his father had likely said in his, so he chose to ignore them for the time being. His mother's message conveyed an apology of sorts but more a reassurance that they loved him. Karen simply was returning the call he'd made to her before his flight departed. He'd called requesting support on bringing Wolf_Eyes in. Gina's message was blank, which Alec surmised had he answered it when it initially rang would've been a heads-up about the next call.

"Alec, this is George Orkan from *Insiders Business Review* magazine," the message started. "We haven't had a chance to talk before, but I have a couple sources who suggested I speak with you. It concerns the charity your father recently contributed to. If you'd like to chat, give me a call."

A couple sources? Who else besides Gina? He mentioned the new charity. Nathalie, too? The charity aspect of the plot continued to elude Alec, lacking comprehension. *Did Nathalie solicit Wolf_Eyes to hack GIM so they could also con Frank out of several million dollars? Whose bank account did it go to? Nathalie's? Alex's? Did they spilt it?*

Alec's initial dive into the vCloud had focused on the wire transfers, the unusual business pattern he uncovered and later confronted his dad about, but the charity angle dangled out there for exploration. He assumed the women had absconded with it, which compelled him to pursue his only lead, Wolf_Eyes, despite his father's intention to let the matter go entirely. He'd started down this road to unravel the mystery of Wolf_Eyes, and her genetic connection didn't sway his pursuit. Her intentions to right Frank Gordon's maladjusted fiscal views may have been noble, but vigilante hacking was not the proper way to handle things, in his view.

Once on the road he returned George's call. *I might as well see what he has to say. Could shed some light on things.*

"George here."

"Hello, this is Alec Gordon. I'm returning your call."

"Oh, yes, Alec. I didn't expect to hear from you."

"I didn't expect to be calling, but it's been an unusual week. What can I do for you?"

"Like I said, I have a couple sources who—"

"Gina and Nathalie. Yes, I know."

"So I'm focusing my attention on the nature of the charity."

"OK."

"I've done some digging and it doesn't appear to be legit. It's not registered with the state of New York as a nonprofit, and there are a few other irregularities."

"OK," Alec said, not surprised to hear George's investigative notes. *It's a scam; what would you expect?* "George, I'm not involved with GIM in any capacity, so I'm not privy to what goes on there. I'm afraid I can't offer you any help." He had no interest in providing George with what he knew. If George had an angle on the dubious nature of GIM's investing model, he would have to prove it some other way, not from additional insider information. Alec may have been furious with Frank's ethical bent, but he wasn't going to turn him over based on illegally obtained evidence. He hoped to protect his granddad's reputation, and his mom's gallery from the embarrassment of it all. *I won't be the reason they are publicly exposed.*

"I understand. I only called because the two sources urged me to. The thing is … the charity website host told me it was set up and paid for by Frank. I've also traced the money trail from GIM to the bank that handles the charity's donations and … it circles back to a new personal account Frank set up. He essentially transferred the money to himself."

Alec stared out the windshield, reacting to flashes of brake lights and left-hand turn signals as the lane he navigated began merging with the next one over, assimilating George's comments. *Dad set up the site? The money never left GIM?*

"I'm sure I don't have to tell you, Alec, how this looks. It could be very damaging considering the vast amount of money he donates every—"

"Yes, yes, I get it," Alec blurted out, disconnecting from the call, his mind grasping what Nathalie and Wolf_Eyes had ultimately done. *They* did*n't steal the money.* The deeper implication, Frank's lack of interest in pursuing the matter, left him wide open to a scathing investigation, which would easily put him behind bars, especially if they dug deeper and discovered the securities-recycling model he perpetuated. The one thing that could exonerate his father from a precipitous fall from grace was the vCloud. It had the proof of Herringbone's con and Wolf_Eyes's virtual wizardry.

With it as a legal defense, Frank would be spared. Without it, he'd be defenseless.

Alex and Sundance crossed the Golden Gate Bridge as the sun slowly sank into the watery horizon and the full moon began its celestial journey, Alex's freshly washed old Toyota Corolla winding its way north on Highway 101 towards the city of Sonoma, bisecting rolling hillsides of expansive vineyards and pastoral lands dotted with grazing cattle coated with black-and-white markings. Through an online-news-service search, Alex eventually discovered where her biological parents had been laid to rest. After a stop at the hospital, she planned on paying her respects.

The long, picturesque corridor leading into the quaint town rolled along two lanes of asphalt, nestled between thousand-foot, tree-lined peaks, connecting dozens of world-renowned wineries. It was the same route where an intoxicated wine taster crossed the center divider and collided with the car Alex, her brother, and their parents were traveling in, sending them spinning around and around, the car bursting into flames before coming to a stop on the side of the road.

Driving along the main street, Alex recalled fond memories of the town square filled with artists selling their paintings and sketches. It had been a trip she and her adoptive mother frequently made before Maggie quit drawing to spend more time working at the grocery store with Phil. The evening drive had turned night when Alex pulled up to the hospital. Walking toward the entrance she hoped something might jar loose a long-forgotten memory, the sound of sirens, crashing metal, frantic voices, but as she stepped inside, nothing came forth.

"May I help you?" said the nurse standing behind the admitting window, a Rubenesque woman holding a stack of clipboards in one hand while a finger on the other hand briskly punched numbers on the phone console, the receiver cradled between her chin and shoulder pressed to an ear.

"Ah … is Jill working tonight?" Alex asked, the hospital's sterile smell starting to make her queasy. "Jill Stew—"

"I need to talk to Doctor Sorenson now!" the nurse barked, startling Alex, who turned toward the doorway where the nurse was pointing. "She's down at the ICU station tonight."

Alex slowly walked down the hallway toward the ICU, her nose scrunching with every new scent that crossed her path, bringing with them hazy memories that made her skin tingle as she caught the blank stares of those in hospital beds from semi-lit rooms.

"I'm taking my break, Janette," said a woman as she stepped out from behind a counter, nearly running over Alex, knocking the folder out of her hand. "I'm so sorry, dear. Are you all right?"

"Yeah," Alex said, picking the folder up off the floor. "I'm looking for Jill."

"Well, that would be me. What can I do for you?"

"Ah," Alex started, suddenly unsure what she wanted to ask or say, staring at the fortysomething woman wearing colorful scrubs. "I was wondering … I'm doing an article on a car accident that occurred twenty years ago with a family of four where the parents died," she said, pulling out the scanned newspaper clipping of the event, a slight tremor in her hand as she passed it to the nurse.

Jill put on her reading glasses that hung from her neck, taking a long look at the article and accompanying picture. "Yes, I remember that accident," she said, reviewing it. "Such a tragedy. The twins survived, but ended up being adopted by different families." The nurse handed the article back to Alex. "And why are you writing an—" She paused, removing her glasses, staring at Alex. A wide smile filled her face. "You're baby Alexandra, aren't you? I'd recognize that adorable face and those beautiful eyes anywhere."

Alex smiled back, nodding like one does when they've been recognized yet have no idea who the other person is.

"Oh, you were so young, I'm sure you don't remember me. I was on shift the night when they brought the family in."

"Yeah, I don't remember even being in the accident."

"Of course not. I'm so glad to see you. You're not really here to write an article, now, are you?"

"No, not really," Alex said sheepishly. She explained her recent discovery of the adoption and her twin brother. Her biggest question: why were they separated?

Jill glanced back at the ICU counter before motioning for Alex to follow, leading her toward the nurses' break room, where she began telling Alex in a low voice about the circumstances that night twenty years earlier, which led to the twins going separate ways days after their second birthday. There had been quite a bit of confusion about what to do initially because the twins were so young and had no other family to take guardianship. A few days after the accident a married couple on vacation from New York happened to be visiting an old friend who worked at the hospital. The twins were doing well by then and the couple inquired about adopting. Apparently the woman was not able to bear children. The husband wanted only the boy, so after much discussion with hospital administration and Social Services it was decided they could adopt the male twin.

A day later Phil and Maggie were in Sonoma out on the town square, enjoying a weekend art festival. Jill was out there as well and recognized Maggie from the Oregon commune where they once stayed. After some catching-up, the Smyths mentioned their desire to adopt. Jill immediately took them to the hospital, where they fell instantly in love with baby Alexandra.

Tears streamed down Alex's cheeks, passing over a smile as she listened to Jill's story, picturing in her mind her adoptive parents' reaction, the same affection she'd felt every day since.

"Do my parents know about Alec?" she asked, drying her cheeks.

"I don't think so. The hospital administrators let it slide due to the unusual circumstances surrounding the whole affair. I know the couple who adopted Alec were pretty adamant about severing all ties. They even sweetened the deal with a generous donation to the children's foundation here at the hospital."

Alex bristled and let out a snort, shaking her head. "Frank Gordon."

"You know, I wouldn't have recalled the name unless someone said it, but yes, I believe it was. Do you know him?"

"We've crossed paths, more or less," Alex replied. She thanked Jill for the trip down memory lane, for helping her understand the divergent paths that ensued.

Back in the parking lot, Alex sat in the car, running a hand through Sundance's thick coat where her tears intermittently trickled, pondering the vastly different roads she and Alec had traveled.

Alec pulled into Maggie's Organic Market's parking lot, the only link he had to Wolf_Eyes. If he had not seen her face on the subway platform, there would've been no straightforward path back to her, other than a lengthy interstate turf war between communications companies for a warrant on her cell-phone records.

He worked on what he would likely say in an attempt to locate her if she wasn't already in the store. Despite his personal research, utilizing task force resources to obtain further information on Wolf_Eyes's real identity, the lack of a warrant or charges filed eroded any legal leg he had to stand on. His out-of-state status further undermined his position to demand too much. He dialed Karen Mickles again but she had left the office, no longer taking calls so late in the day.

Still undecided, Alec stalled for more time by listening to his father's voice mails. After what George Orkan had said, they might be interesting. Instead, they played out as he'd expected, starting with a demand to know who'd informed him about the adoption, to yes he was adopted but they raised him like their own, to it would be best if he brought the hard evidence to the firm's attorney for safekeeping, to backpedaling on the finer points concerning his investing philosophies. *Nothing noteworthy.*

Alec had put things off long enough. It was time to go in.

"Well, hello again," Maggie said, as gracious as Alec remembered from his last visit. "Back for some more sausage links?"

"Hi … Maggie," Alec said, stumbling the delivery when he caught himself about to refer to her as Mrs. Smyth. "You know, they do stick with you, don't they?" Alec hadn't thought about food since earlier that morning. As if on cue, his stomach growled.

"I'm so glad you came back, and all the way from New York no less. We don't have the grill going today but it will only take a few minutes to fire it up," she said, picking up the phone.

"Oh, really, you don't need to go to all that trouble. I can—"

"Nonsense. It's no trouble, hon," she said, "Phil, honey, could you grill up a couple of today's links? We have a special customer all the way from New York … thanks."

Alec wasn't sure how to react to the special attention paid him. "That's very kind of you, but really—"

"Say no more. You know, I didn't get your name the last time."

"Alec Gordon," he said, extending his hand to shake, tensing as soon as the words left his mouth.

"You wouldn't by chance be related to a Frank Gordon in New York, would you?"

"Oh, no, ma'am … different family."

"Well, that's good. I hear he's not a very respectable businessman. You certainly don't look anything like him. I meant to tell you last time that your eyes are very unusual. I've only ever seen them once before. Our daughter, Alex, has them too. You two could almost be twins. I wish she were here, but she worked earlier today. How long are you in town for?"

"I'm not sure how long. I'm here on business."

"Well, then, next time. She just got back from New York the other day herself. Someone there is interested in the software she developed for the store. She was even in the newspaper for it." Maggie led Alec over to the wall to show him the clippings.

While Maggie spoke of her daughter's precocious accomplishments, Alec glanced around the large bulletin board that displayed pictures of the Smyth family at the beach and backyard barbecues, newspaper clippings honoring the store's commitment to the community, and candid pictures of Alex making funny, contorted faces at the camera. One item pinned next to the Better Business Bureau certificate caught his eye.

"What's this?" Alec asked, pointing to the Worshipful Company of Organic Food plaque, the acronym for which reminded him of the first account that had received the initial misrouted wire transfer.

"Oh, that's the WCOF we belong to," Maggie said. "It's a pretty large group now. I'd say about a hundred and twenty members. We lobby for better food-labeling practices, among other things."

Alec stared at it, recalling a snide remark his father had made about a bunch of protesting, organic hippies out in California. *This was probably them. They'd invested in the Vegas Land Grab Fund. No wonder Alex made them the first replenished account. She was protecting not only her family but the community at large.*

"Here you go, hot off the grill," Phil said, striding into the store from the patio and handing the plate to Alec, his voice excited despite the late hour.

"Thank you," Alec said, taking in the jovial man whose face, while aged, exuded a youthful energy.

"Phil, this is Alec. Alec, my husband," Maggie said. "Honey, look at his eyes." She moved closer to Phil, wrapping an arm around his waist.

Phil leaned forward, peering into Alec's eyes. "Wow, that's amazing. They're just like Doodle Bug's … I mean Alex's. She's our daughter."

"Do you know where she is?" Maggie asked Phil.

"I got a text from her. She took Sundance for a drive to Sonoma for the evening."

"You see how I rate?" Maggie winked, laughing and playfully elbowing Phil's ribs. "Such a Daddy's girl."

Phil grinned, nodding.

"She hasn't been up there in a long while. I wonder why tonight," Maggie said.

Phil shrugged, staring at Alec as if amazed by something besides the eye color.

"Sundance?" Alec asked.

"Her dog," Maggie replied.

"Funny, I have a dog named Cassidy."

"Butch Cassidy and the Sundance Kid." Phil chuckled.

"Like two peas in a pod, I tell you," Maggie added. "We should let him eat. Here, hon, follow me and you can sit in our little side kitchen. All the fixin's are there too. Grab something to drink on the way."

"Thank you, sir," Alec said to Phil. "It was nice meeting you."

"My pleasure, son. Enjoy," Phil said, his face filled with curiosity, watching Alec follow Maggie down the drink aisle.

By the time Alec had garnished the sausage links in their buns, he was famished, wasting little time in devouring them. They were as good as he'd remembered. On the table lay a copy of the local weekly newspaper, its headlines announcing the return of WCOF's $4.5 million investment from GIM. He scanned the short article, learning that until recently the investment had been deemed all but lost. The WCOF spokesperson was quoted as saying, "Though the reason for its return is not fully understood, it brings us great relief."

He leaned back in the chair sipping his drink, taking in the little kitchen area normally reserved for store employees. Among the laminated employment-regulatory postings were more pictures of Alex at various stages in her life. He walked over, taking long looks at them, imagining what it might've been like to have been there, alongside her, perhaps giving her a noogie as she posed for the picture. *That's why her face would've been goofy for the camera.*

"Here you go," Phil said, entering the kitchen, handing Alec a small cup of ice cream. "A little chocolate is always good after those spicy links."

"Thank you," Alec replied, spoiled by all the attention. He spooned out a bite, surprised by the taste. "Wow, this is quite good."

"A friend of ours makes a homemade batch once a month for us."

Alec eagerly spooned a few more bites while viewing colorful childlike sketches. "Were these drawn by your daughter?"

"Yeah," Phil replied, taking a closer look. "As a youngster she used to draw all the time because she got teased about her eyes and scar. She'd pretend she had an imaginary brother and he'd beat up—"

Alec choked on a spoonful of ice cream, letting out a couple hearty coughs to clear things up.

"You OK?"

"Yes, just too quick with … the scoops." He let out another cough to compose himself, though he could barely take his mind off the "imaginary brother" comment. *For nearly twenty years we've both been unknowingly searching for the same thing.* "They teased her because of her eyes?"

"Oh, sure. 'Wolf Eyes,' they called her. It was mean, but they were just kids. Didn't you ever get teased about yours?"

Wolf_Eyes … yes, of course … Alec smiled to himself. "No, not once. Women love them."

Phil gave a knowing grin. "Anyway, she probably went up to Sonoma tonight because that's where Maggie used to take her during the art fairs on the town square. She seemed to like it."

Alec had a different idea as to why she had ventured there.

He couldn't thank Maggie and Phil enough for their hospitality, though something told him it reflected their genuine nature: hardworking, unassuming parents who loved their daughter very much. Envy had never been part of Alec's character. Until that moment. The pang rising from deep inside.

Alec returned to the 101, heading north, toward the city of Sonoma, the weight of two families' lives heavy on his mind, the cloudy resolution sitting on the passenger seat. Crossing the Golden Gate Bridge he glanced above the railing, sneaking a peek at the full moon looming over the Bay, its bright spotlight exposing the dark rock of Alcatraz.

The nugget he'd been searching for in full moons since childhood finally revealed itself.

037 Noble Beginnings—

California

"What's your name?" asked the young nurse in the colorful paisley scrubs, walking up to the little girl with strawberry-blond hair who stood on a chair peering through the window into the ICU at Drake General Hospital in Sonoma, California.

"Nathalie," she said, looking up with big blue eyes at the nurse.

"That's a beautiful name, Nathalie."

"Why are they in there?" Nathalie asked with a sense of concern, pointing to two toddlers, just two years in age, lying asleep on side-by-side beds with various wires and tubes attached.

"They were in a car accident, and we're making them better," the nurse answered, her voice reassuring. She squatted down to Nathalie's eye level, wrapping an arm around her.

"Are they going to be OK?"

"Yes, they are."

"Where are their mommy and daddy?" five-year-old Nathalie asked.

The nurse stayed quiet a few moments as Nathalie watched the fraternal twins, her delicate face a portrait of wonderment and curiosity at the little boy stirring, his head raised momentarily, peering in her direction. Nathalie turned to the nurse, awaiting an answer.

"They've gone to heaven," the nurse said softly. "Do you know what heaven is?"

Little Nathalie nodded. "My gram-mommy is in heaven too."

The nurse squeezed the girl's shoulder, who returned her attention to the twins with sadness in her eyes, and pressed a hand against the thick glass window.

"Who is going to take care of them?"

"Another other mommy and daddy are going to adopt them so they can have a home again."

Nathalie considered the notion of having a new mom and dad. She loved her parents, and couldn't imagine loving different ones. "What if they don't like them?"

The nurse remained quiet a few moments before answering. "How about you become their guardian angel … so they *will* like them?"

"What's a gar … de … angel?"

"Someone who watches over people to make sure they are safe and happy," the nurse said. "Whenever you think of them, they will be happy with their new mommy and daddy."

Nathalie returned her gaze to the twins, thought about it a moment, smiled, and nodded in acceptance of the lifetime duty, giving the nurse a big hug. Nathalie jumped down from the chair, running off down the corridor, shouting, "Papa, Papa, guess what I am …"

Alex sat cross-legged on the dewy manicured grass, staring at the unassuming side-by-side gravestones, a soft whisper of wind blowing through the oak trees above. The full moon arced high in the sky while leafy shadows danced quietly across the moonlit ground, just as they had nearly twenty years ago when her biological parents were laid to rest on the knoll overlooking the Sonoma Valley below. A tear worked its way down her cheek as Sundance laid his head in her lap.

She could hear the footsteps of heavy shoes steadily marching up behind her, something jingling with each stride; handcuffs or keys, she couldn't tell. Alex didn't bother turning around. It no longer mattered. *I've been hiding long enough. Whatever happens next, good or bad, I'm happy, no regrets.*

"Alexandra Murphy Smyth," the stern voice called out, intruding on her moment of mourning and causing Sundance to raise and tilt his head with a dumbfounded expression, "aka Wolf Eyes?"

Alex hadn't heard her middle name said aloud in years, its origin now apparent: her real parents' last name. She closed her eyes.

"Alex?" the voice said.

"Are you here to arrest me?" she asked, less concerned about the answer than in ending the prolonged suspense.

A long silence followed while the city lights shimmered below, before Sundance interrupted the tension with a couple of restless whimpers and a deep groan that trailed off. The footsteps resumed their march toward her. Alex stared at the gravesite resigned to her fate.

"No," her fraternal twin brother, Alec, said. He sat down beside her, handed the vCloud over, and gave Sundance a pat on the head. "I'm here to meet my sister and to pay respects to our parents."

Alex glanced at the drive, then over to her brother, staring into the eyes of her genetic likeness. In that moment she discovered the inherent beauty of their shared trait, the subtle variations in pigmentation that made them unique. She had never viewed them objectively, only through the uneasy stares and odd remarks she'd heard all too often growing up.

Alec put his arm around her, drawing his sister against him, their scarred shoulders reuniting for the first time since the accident that forged them, the last time they were bonded as siblings.

"That's good," she said, leaning her head against him. "I'd hate to have to kick your ass."

"I don't think so, Wolf Eyes."

"Hey, Cyber Sherlock, I had you chasing your tail."

"I saved your butt in Vegas."

"I could've handled him. You owe me a pair of sunnies."

"Finders keepers. Did you really kiss Sam? It's all he talks about."

"Crap."

"Nice hack on the subway, by the way."

"I can't believe you beat it to the next stop."

"I am older than you."

"Yeah, like by two minutes."

"Still."

"Whatever."

The Ducati motorbike roared to life back where the twins' cars were parked, breaking the moment of their long-overdue reunion. Alex and Alec looked at each other, flashed a knowing smile, and then turned in its direction, watching the bike disappear over the hillside, into the darkness.

ACKNOWLEDGMENTS

I want to thank the following family members and friends who took the time to read the early, and considerably less polished, drafts of this novel, and provided me with invaluable feedback as well as encouragement to see it through the indie-publishing gauntlet: Ceej Rust, Casey Strange, Liz Bernstein, Lorinda Miller, Lily Ruane, and Brigitte Ironside.

Also, to Mark Spencer, who provided the vital content edit and helped shape the story, pointing out certain plausibility and coherency concerns, making the story that much stronger. And last but not least, Rachelle Mandik, who not only handled the important copyediting aspect but, as a New Yorker, provided me with deeper insight into the scenes that take place throughout Manhattan and Queens.

www.ingramcontent.com/pod-product-compliance
Lightning Source LLC
Chambersburg PA
CBHW031128120726
47905CB00006B/1604